Dekarta Arameri's ...
I could ...

"For my heir, Granddaughter. I intend to name you to that position today."

The silence turned to stone as hard as my grandfather's chair.

It came to me that some response was expected.

"You already have heirs," I said.

"Not as diplomatic as she could be," Viraine said in a dry tone.

Dekarta ignored this. "It is true, there are two other candidates," he said to me. "My niece and nephew, Scimina and Relad. Your cousins, once removed."

I had heard of them, of course; everyone had. Rumor constantly made one or the other heir, though no one knew for certain which. *Both* was something that had not occurred to me.

"If I may suggest, Grandfather," I said carefully, though it was impossible to be careful in this conversation, "I would make two heirs too many."

"Indeed," he said. "But just enough for an interesting competition, I think."

"I don't understand, Grandfather."

He lifted his hand in a gesture that would have been graceful, once. Now his hand shook badly. "It is very simple. I have named three heirs. One of you will actually manage to succeed me. The other two will doubtless kill each other or be killed by the victor. As for which lives, and which die—" He shrugged. "That is for you to decide."

By N. K. Jemisin

The Hundred Thousand Kingdoms

The Hundred Thousand Kingdoms

Book One of the Inheritance Trilogy

N. K. Jemisin

orbit

www.orbitbooks.net

Orbit
Hachette Book Group
1290 Avenue of the Americas, New York, NY 10104
www.HachetteBookGroup.com

First Edition: February 2010

Orbit is an imprint of Hachette Book Group, Inc. The Orbit name
and logo are trademarks of Little, Brown Book Group Limited.

Library of Congress Cataloging-in-Publication Data

Jemisin, N. K.
    The hundred thousand kingdoms / N.K. Jemisin.
    p. cm.
    ISBN 978-0-316-04391-5
    1. Gods—Fiction. I. Title.
    PS3610.E46H86 2010
    813'.6—dc22
                        2009002075

        10 9 8 7

Printed in the United States of America

1

Grandfather

I AM NOT AS I ONCE WAS. They have done this to me, broken me open and torn out my heart. I do not know who I am anymore.

I must try to remember.

* * *

My people tell stories of the night I was born. They say my mother crossed her legs in the middle of labor and fought with all her strength not to release me into the world. I was born anyhow, of course; nature cannot be denied. Yet it does not surprise me that she tried.

* * *

My mother was an heiress of the Arameri. There was a ball for the lesser nobility—the sort of thing that happens once a decade as a backhanded sop to their self-esteem. My father dared ask my mother to dance; she deigned to consent. I have often wondered what he said and did that night to make her fall in love with him so powerfully, for she eventually abdicated her position to be with him. It is the stuff of great tales, yes? Very romantic. In the tales, such a couple lives happily ever after. The tales do not say what happens when the most powerful family in the world is offended in the process.

* * *

But I forget myself. Who was I, again? Ah, yes.

My name is Yeine. In my people's way I am Yeine dau she Kinneth tai wer Somem kanna Darre, which means that I am the daughter of Kinneth, and that my tribe within the Darre people is called Somem. Tribes mean little to us these days, though before the Gods' War they were more important.

I am nineteen years old. I also am, or was, the chieftain of my people, called *ennu*. In the Arameri way, which is the way of the Amn race from whom they originated, I am the Baroness Yeine Darr.

One month after my mother died, I received a message from my grandfather Dekarta Arameri, inviting me to visit the family seat. Because one does not refuse an invitation from the Arameri, I set forth. It took the better part of three months to travel from the High North continent to Senm, across the Repentance Sea. Despite Darr's relative poverty, I traveled in style the whole way, first by palanquin and ocean vessel, and finally by chauffeured horse-coach. This was not my choice. The Darre Warriors' Council, which rather desperately hoped that I might restore us to the Arameri's good graces, thought that this extravagance would help. It is well known that Amn respect displays of wealth.

Thus arrayed, I arrived at my destination on the cusp of the winter solstice. And as the driver stopped the coach on a hill outside the city, ostensibly to water the horses but more likely because he was a local and liked to watch foreigners gawk, I got my first glimpse of the Hundred Thousand Kingdoms' heart.

There is a rose that is famous in High North. (This is not a digression.) It is called the altarskirt rose. Not only do its petals unfold in a radiance of pearled white, but frequently it grows an incomplete secondary flower about the base of its stem. In its most prized form, the altarskirt grows a layer of overlarge petals that drape the ground. The two bloom in tandem, seedbearing head and skirt, glory above and below.

This was the city called Sky. On the ground, sprawling over a small mountain or an oversize hill: a circle of high walls, mounting tiers of buildings, all resplendent in white, per Arameri decree. Above the city, smaller but brighter, the pearl of its tiers occasionally obscured by scuds of cloud, was the palace—also called Sky, and perhaps more deserving of the name. I knew the column was there, the impossibly thin column that supported such a massive structure, but from that distance I couldn't see it. Palace floated above city, linked in spirit, both so unearthly in their beauty that I held my breath at the sight.

The altarskirt rose is priceless because of the difficulty of producing it. The most famous lines are heavily inbred; it originated as a deformity that some savvy breeder deemed useful. The primary flower's scent, sweet to us, is apparently repugnant to insects; these roses must be pollinated by hand. The secondary flower saps nutrients crucial for the plant's fertility. Seeds are rare, and for every one that grows into a perfect altarskirt, ten others become plants that must be destroyed for their hideousness.

* * *

At the gates of Sky (the palace) I was turned away, though not for the reasons I'd expected. My grandfather was not present, it seemed. He had left instructions in the event of my arrival.

Sky is the Arameri's home; business is never done there. This is because, officially, they do not rule the world. The Nobles' Consortium does, with the benevolent assistance of the Order of Itempas. The Consortium meets in the Salon, a huge, stately building—white-walled, of course—that sits among a cluster of official buildings at the foot of the palace. It is very impressive, and would be more so if it did not sit squarely in Sky's elegant shadow.

I went inside and announced myself to the Consortium staff, whereupon they all looked very surprised, though politely so. One of them—a very junior aide, I gathered—was dispatched to escort me to the central chamber, where the day's session was well under way.

As a lesser noble, I had always been welcome to attend a Consortium gathering, but there had never seemed any point. Besides the expense and months of travel time required to attend, Darr was simply too small, poor, and ill-favored to have any clout, even without my mother's abdication adding to our collective stain. Most of High North is regarded as a backwater, and only the largest nations there have enough prestige or money to make their voices heard among our noble peers. So I was not surprised to find that the seat reserved for me on the Consortium floor—in a shadowed area, behind a pillar—was currently occupied by an excess delegate from one of the Senm-continent nations. It would be terribly rude, the aide stammered anxiously, to dislodge this man, who was elderly and had bad knees. Perhaps I would not mind standing? Since I had just spent many long hours cramped in a carriage, I was happy to agree.

So the aide positioned me at the side of the Consortium floor, where I actually had a good view of the goings-on. The Consortium chamber was magnificently apportioned, with white marble and rich, dark wood that had probably come from Darr's forests in better days. The nobles—three hundred or so in total—sat in comfortable chairs on the chamber's floor or along elevated tiers above. Aides, pages, and scribes occupied the periphery with me, ready to fetch documents or run errands as needed. At the head of the chamber, the Consortium Overseer stood atop an elaborate podium, pointing to members as they indicated a desire to speak. Apparently there was a dispute over water rights in a desert somewhere; five countries were involved. None of the conversation's participants spoke out of turn; no tempers were lost; there were no snide comments or veiled insults. It was all very orderly and polite, despite the size of the gathering and the fact that most of those present were accustomed to speaking however they pleased among their own people.

One reason for this extraordinary good behavior stood on a plinth behind the Overseer's podium: a life-size statue of the Skyfather in one of His most famous poses, the Appeal to Mortal Reason. Hard to speak out of turn under that stern gaze. But more repressive, I suspected, was the stern gaze of the man who sat behind the Overseer in an elevated box. I could not see him well from where I stood, but he was elderly, richly dressed, and flanked by a younger blond man and a dark-haired woman, as well as a handful of retainers.

It did not take much to guess this man's identity, though he wore no crown, had no visible guards, and neither he nor anyone in his entourage spoke throughout the meeting.

"Hello, Grandfather," I murmured to myself, and smiled at him across the chamber, though I knew he could not see me. The pages and scribes gave me the oddest looks for the rest of the afternoon.

*   *   *

I knelt before my grandfather with my head bowed, hearing titters of laughter.

No, wait.

*   *   *

There were three gods once.

Only three, I mean. Now there are dozens, perhaps hundreds. They breed like rabbits. But once there were only three, most powerful and glorious of all: the god of day, the god of night, and the goddess of twilight and dawn. Or light and darkness and the shades between. Or order, chaos, and balance. None of that is important because one of them died, the other might as well have, and the last is the only one who matters anymore.

The Arameri get their power from this remaining god. He is called the Skyfather, Bright Itempas, and the ancestors of the Arameri were His most devoted priests. He rewarded them by giving them a weapon so mighty that no army could stand against it. They used this weapon—weapons, really—to make themselves rulers of the world.

That's better. Now.

*   *   *

I knelt before my grandfather with my head bowed and my knife laid on the floor.

We were in Sky, having transferred there following the Consortium session, via the magic of the Vertical Gate. Immediately

6

upon arrival I had been summoned to my grandfather's audience chamber, which felt much like a throne room. The chamber was roughly circular because circles are sacred to Itempas. The vaulted ceiling made the members of the court look taller—unnecessarily, since Amn are a tall people compared to my own. Tall and pale and endlessly poised, like statues of human beings rather than real flesh and blood.

"Most high Lord Arameri," I said. "I am honored to be in your presence."

I had heard titters of laughter when I entered the room. Now they sounded again, muffled by hands and kerchiefs and fans. I was reminded of bird flocks roosting in a forest canopy.

Before me sat Dekarta Arameri, uncrowned king of the world. He was old; perhaps the oldest man I have ever seen, though Amn usually live longer than my people, so this was not surprising. His thin hair had gone completely white, and he was so gaunt and stooped that the elevated stone chair on which he sat—it was never called a throne—seemed to swallow him whole.

"Granddaughter," he said, and the titters stopped. The silence was heavy enough to hold in my hand. He was head of the Arameri family, and his word was law. No one had expected him to acknowledge me as kin, least of all myself.

"Stand," he said. "Let me have a look at you."

I did, reclaiming my knife since no one had taken it. There was more silence. I am not very interesting to look at. It might have been different if I had gotten the traits of my two peoples in a better combination—Amn height with Darre curves, perhaps, or thick straight Darre hair colored Amn-pale. I have

7

Amn eyes: faded green in color, more unnerving than pretty. Otherwise, I am short and flat and brown as forestwood, and my hair is a curled mess. Because I find it unmanageable otherwise, I wear it short. I am sometimes mistaken for a boy.

As the silence wore on, I saw Dekarta frown. There was an odd sort of marking on his forehead, I noticed: a perfect circle of black, as if someone had dipped a coin in ink and pressed it to his flesh. On either side of this was a thick chevron, bracketing the circle.

"You look nothing like her," he said at last. "But I suppose that is just as well. Viraine?"

This last was directed at a man who stood among the courtiers closest to the throne. For an instant I thought he was another elder, then I realized my error: though his hair was stark white, he was only somewhere in his fourth decade. He, too, bore a forehead mark, though his was less elaborate than Dekarta's: just the black circle.

"She's not hopeless," he said, folding his arms. "Nothing to be done about her looks; I doubt even makeup will help. But put her in civilized attire and she can convey…nobility, at least." His eyes narrowed, taking me apart by degrees. My best Darren clothing, a long vest of white civvetfur and calf-length leggings, earned me a sigh. (I had gotten the odd look for this outfit at the Salon, but I hadn't realized it was *that* bad.) He examined my face so long that I wondered if I should show my teeth.

Instead he smiled, showing his. "Her mother has trained her. Look how she shows no fear or resentment, even now."

"She will do, then," said Dekarta.

"Do for what, Grandfather?" I asked. The weight in the room

grew heavier, expectant, though he had already named me granddaughter. There was a certain risk involved in my daring to address him the same familiar way, of course—powerful men are touchy over odd things. But my mother had indeed trained me well, and I knew it was worth the risk to establish myself in the court's eyes.

Dekarta Arameri's face did not change; I could not read it. "For my heir, Granddaughter. I intend to name you to that position today."

The silence turned to stone as hard as my grandfather's chair.

I thought he might be joking, but no one laughed. That was what made me believe him at last: the utter shock and horror on the faces of the courtiers as they stared at their lord. Except the one called Viraine. He watched me.

It came to me that some response was expected.

"You already have heirs," I said.

"Not as diplomatic as she could be," Viraine said in a dry tone.

Dekarta ignored this. "It is true, there are two other candidates," he said to me. "My niece and nephew, Scimina and Relad. Your cousins, once removed."

I had heard of them, of course; everyone had. Rumor constantly made one or the other heir, though no one knew for certain which. *Both* was something that had not occurred to me.

"If I may suggest, Grandfather," I said carefully, though it was impossible to be careful in this conversation, "I would make two heirs too many."

It was the eyes that made Dekarta seem so old, I would realize

9

much later. I had no idea what color they had originally been; age had bleached and filmed them to near-white. There were lifetimes in those eyes, none of them happy.

"Indeed," he said. "But just enough for an interesting competition, I think."

"I don't understand, Grandfather."

He lifted his hand in a gesture that would have been graceful, once. Now his hand shook badly. "It is very simple. I have named three heirs. One of you will actually manage to succeed me. The other two will doubtless kill each other or be killed by the victor. As for which lives, and which die—" He shrugged. "That is for you to decide."

My mother had taught me never to show fear, but emotions will not be stilled so easily. I began to sweat. I have been the target of an assassination attempt only once in my life—the benefit of being heir to such a tiny, impoverished nation. No one wanted my job. But now there would be two others who did. Lord Relad and Lady Scimina were wealthy and powerful beyond my wildest dreams. They had spent their whole lives striving against each other toward the goal of ruling the world. And here came I, unknown, with no resources and few friends, into the fray.

"There will be no decision," I said. To my credit, my voice did not shake. "And no contest. They will kill me at once and turn their attention back to each other."

"That is possible," said my grandfather.

I could think of nothing to say that would save me. He was insane; that was obvious. Why else turn rulership of the world into a contest prize? If he died tomorrow, Relad and Scimina would rip the earth asunder between them. The killing might not end for decades. And for all he knew, I was an idiot. If by some impossible chance I managed to gain the throne, I could plunge the Hundred Thousand Kingdoms into a spiral of mismanagement and suffering. He had to know that.

One cannot argue with madness. But sometimes, with luck and the Skyfather's blessing, one can understand it. "Why?"

He nodded as if he had expected my question. "Your mother deprived me of an heir when she left our family. You will pay her debt."

"She is four months in the grave," I snapped. "Do you honestly want revenge against a dead woman?"

"This has nothing to do with revenge, Granddaughter. It is a matter of duty." He made a gesture with his left hand, and another courtier detached himself from the throng. Unlike the first man—indeed, unlike most of the courtiers whose faces I could see—the mark on this man's forehead was a downturned half-moon, like an exaggerated frown. He knelt before the dais that held Dekarta's chair, his waist-length red braid falling over one shoulder to curl on the floor.

"I cannot hope that your mother has taught you duty," Dekarta said to me over this man's back. "She abandoned hers to dally with her sweet-tongued savage. I allowed this—an indulgence I have often regretted. So I will assuage that regret by bringing you back into the fold, Granddaughter. Whether you live or die is irrelevant. You are Arameri, and like all of us, you will serve."

Then he waved to the red-haired man. "Prepare her as best you can."

There was nothing more. The red-haired man rose and came to me, murmuring that I should follow him. I did. Thus ended my first meeting with my grandfather, and thus began my first day as an Arameri. It was not the worst of the days to come.

2

The Other Sky

THE CAPITAL OF MY LAND is called Arrebaia. It is a place of ancient stone, its walls overgrown by vines and guarded by beasts that do not exist. We have forgotten when it was founded, but it has been the capital for at least two thousand years. People there walk slowly and speak softly out of respect for the generations that have trodden those streets before, or perhaps just because they do not feel like being loud.

Sky—the city, I mean—is only five hundred years old, built when some disaster befell the previous Arameri seat. This makes it an adolescent as cities go—and a rude, uncouth one at that. As my carriage rode through the city's center, other carriages went past in a clatter of wheels and horseshoes. People covered every sidewalk, bumping and milling and bustling, not talking. They all seemed in a hurry. The air was thick with familiar smells like horses and stagnant water amid indefinable scents, some acrid and some sickly sweet. There was nothing green in sight.

*   *   *

What was I—?

Oh, yes. The gods.

Not the gods that remain in the heavens, who are loyal to Bright Itempas. There are others who were not loyal. Perhaps I should not call them gods, since no one worships them anymore. (How does one define "god"?) There must be a better name for what they are. Prisoners of war? Slaves? What did I call them before—weapons?

Weapons. Yes.

They are said to be somewhere in Sky, four of them, trapped in tangible vessels and kept under lock and key and magic chain. Perhaps they sleep in crystal cases and are awakened on occasion to be polished and oiled. Perhaps they are shown off to honored guests.

But sometimes, sometimes, their masters call them forth. And then there are strange new plagues. Occasionally the population of an entire city will vanish overnight. Once, jagged, steaming pits appeared where there had been mountains.

It is not safe to hate the Arameri. Instead we hate their weapons, because weapons do not care.

*   *   *

My courtier companion was T'vril, who introduced himself as the palace steward. The name told me at least part of his heritage at once, but he went on to explain: he was a halfbreed like me, part Amn and part Ken. The Ken inhabit an island far to the east; they are famous for their seacraft. His strange red-colored hair came from them.

"Dekarta's beloved wife, the Lady Ygreth, died tragically

young more than forty years ago," T'vril explained. He spoke briskly as we walked through Sky's white halls, not sounding particularly broken up about the tragedy of the dead lady. "Kinneth was just a child at the time, but it was already clear she would grow up to be a more-than-suitable heir, so I suppose Dekarta felt no pressing need to remarry. When Kinneth, er, left the family fold, he turned to the children of his late brother. There were four of them originally; Relad and Scimina were the youngest. Twins—runs in the family. Alas, their elder sister met with an unfortunate accident, or so the official story goes."

I just listened. It was a useful, if appalling, education about my new kin, which was probably why T'vril had decided to tell me. He had also informed me of my new title, duties, and privileges, at least in brief. I was Yeine Arameri now, no longer Yeine Darr. I would have new lands to oversee and wealth beyond imagining. I would be expected to attend Consortium sessions regularly and sit in the Arameri private box when I did so. I would be permitted to dwell permanently in Sky in the welcoming bosom of my maternal relatives, and I would never see my homeland again.

It was hard not to dwell on that last bit, as T'vril continued.

"Their elder brother was my father—also dead, thanks to his own efforts. He was fond of young women. Very young women." He made a face, though I had the sense he'd told the story often enough that it didn't really trouble him. "Unfortunately for him, my mother was just old enough to get with child. Dekarta executed him when her family took exception." He sighed and shrugged. "We highbloods can get away with a great many things, but... well, there are rules. We were the ones to establish a worldwide age of consent, after all. To ignore our own laws would be an offense to the Skyfather."

I wanted to ask why that mattered when Bright Itempas didn't seem to care what else the Arameri did, but I held my tongue. There had been a note of dry irony in T'vril's voice in any case; no comment was necessary.

With a brisk efficiency that would have made my no-nonsense grandmother jealous, T'vril had me measured for new clothing, scheduled for a visit to a stylist, and assigned quarters all in the span of an hour. Then came a brief tour, during which T'vril chattered endlessly as we walked through corridors lined with white mica or mother-of-pearl or whatever shining stuff the palace was made of.

I stopped listening to him at about this point. If I had paid attention, I probably could have gleaned valuable information about important players in the palace hierarchy, power struggles, juicy rumors, and more. But my mind was still in shock, trying to absorb too many new things at once. He was the least important of them, so I shut him out.

He must have noticed, though he didn't seem to mind. Finally we reached my new apartment. Floor-to-ceiling windows ran along one wall, which afforded me a stunning view of the city and countryside below—far, far below. I stared, my mouth hanging open in a way that would have earned me a scold from my mother, had she still been alive. We were so high that I couldn't even make out people on the streets below.

T'vril said something then that I simply did not digest, so he said it again. This time I looked at him. "This," he said, pointing to his forehead. The half-moon mark.

"What?"

He repeated himself a third time, showing no sign of the exasperation he should have felt. "We must see Viraine, so that he can apply the blood sigil to your brow. He should be free from court duty by now. Then you can rest for the evening."

"Why?"

He stared at me for a moment. "Your mother did not tell you?"

"Tell me what?"

"Of the Enefadeh."

"The Enewhat?"

The look that crossed T'vril's face was somewhere between pity and dismay. "Lady Kinneth didn't prepare you for this at all, did she?" Before I could think of a response to that, he moved on. "The Enefadeh are the reason we wear the blood sigils, Lady Yeine. No one may pass the night in Sky without one. It isn't safe."

I pulled my thoughts away from the strangeness of my new title. "Why isn't it safe, Lord T'vril?"

He winced. "Just T'vril, please. Lord Dekarta has decreed that you are to receive a fullblood mark. You are of the Central Family. I am a mere halfblood."

I could not tell if I had missed important information, or if something had been left unsaid. Probably several somethings. "T'vril. You must realize nothing you're saying makes any sense to me."

"Perhaps not." He ran a hand over his hair; this was the first sign of discomfort he'd shown. "But an explanation would take too long. There's less than an hour 'til sunset."

17

I supposed that this, too, was one of those rules the Arameri insisted on being sticklers for, though I could not imagine why. "All right, but..." I frowned. "What of my coachman? He's waiting for me in the forecourt."

"Waiting?"

"I didn't think I'd be staying."

T'vril's jaw flexed, containing whatever honest reply he might have made. Instead he said, "I'll have someone send him away and give him a bonus for his trouble. He won't be needed; we have plenty of servants here."

I had seen them throughout our tour—silent, efficient figures bustling about Sky's halls, clad all in white. An impractical color for people whose job it was to clean, I thought, but I didn't run the place.

"That coachman traveled across this continent with me," I said. I was irked and trying not to show it. "He's tired and his horses are, too. Can he not be given a room for the night? Give him one of those marks and then let him leave in the morning. That's only courteous."

"Only Arameri may wear the blood sigil, my lady. It's permanent."

"Only—" Understanding leapt in my head. "The servants here are *family*?"

The look he threw me was not bitter, though perhaps it should have been. He had given me the clues already, after all: his roaming father, his own status as the steward. A high-ranking servant, but still a servant. He was as Arameri as I, but his parents had not been married; strict Itempans frowned on illegitimacy. And his father had never been Dekarta's favorite.

As if reading my thoughts, T'vril said, "As Lord Dekarta said, Lady Yeine—all descendants of Shahar Arameri must serve. One way or another."

There were so many untold tales in his words. How many of our relatives had been forced to leave their homelands, and whatever future they might have had, to come here and mop floors or peel vegetables? How many had been born here and never left? What happened to those who tried to escape?

Would I become one of them, like T'vril?

No. T'vril was unimportant, no threat to those who stood to inherit the family's power. I would not be so lucky.

He touched my hand with what I hoped was compassion. "It's not far."

*　　*　　*

On its upper levels, Sky seemed to have windows everywhere. Some corridors even had ceilings of clear glass or crystal, though the view was only of the sky and the palace's many rounded spires. The sun had not yet set—its lower curve had only touched the horizon in the past few minutes—but T'vril set a more brisk pace than before. I paid closer attention to the servants as we walked, seeking the small commonalities of our shared lineage. There were a few: many sets of green eyes, a certain structure of the face (which I lacked completely, having taken after my father). A certain cynicism, though that might have been my imagination. Beyond that, they were all as disparate as T'vril and I, though most seemed to be Amn or some Senmite race. And each of them bore a forehead marking; I had noticed that before but dismissed it as some local fashion. A few had triangles or diamond shapes, but most wore a simple black bar.

I did not like the way they looked at me, eyes flicking near and then away.

"Lady Yeine." T'vril stopped a few paces ahead, noticing that I had fallen behind. He had inherited the long legs of his Amn heritage. I had not, and it had been a very trying day. "Please, we have little time."

"All right, all right," I said, too tired to be strictly polite anymore. But he did not resume walking, and after a moment I saw that he had gone stiff, staring down the corridor in the direction we were to go.

A man stood above us.

I call him a man, in retrospect, because that is what he seemed at the time. He stood on a balcony overlooking our corridor, framed perfectly by the ceiling's arch. I gathered he had been traveling along a perpendicular corridor up there; his body still faced that direction, frozen in midpace. Only his head had turned toward us. By some trick of the shadows, I could not see his face, yet I felt the weight of his eyes.

He put a hand on the balcony railing with slow, palpable deliberation.

"What is it, Naha?" said a woman's voice, echoing faintly along the corridor. A moment later she appeared. Unlike the man, she was clearly visible to me: a reedy Amn beauty of sable hair, patrician features, and regal grace. I recognized her by that hair as the woman who'd sat beside Dekarta at the Salon. She wore the kind of dress that only an Amn woman could do justice to—a long straight tube the color of deep, bloody garnets.

"What do you see?" she asked, looking at me although her words were for the man. She lifted her hands, twirling something in her fingers, and I saw then that she held a delicate silver chain. It dangled from her hand and curved back up; I realized that the chain was connected to the man.

"Aunt," T'vril said, pitching his voice with a care that let me know at once who she was. The lady Scimina—my cousin and rival heir. "You look lovely this evening."

"Thank you, T'vril," she replied, though her eyes never left my face. "And who is this?"

There was the faintest pause. By the taut look on T'vril's face, I gathered he was trying to think of a safe answer. Some quirk of my own nature—in my land, only weak women allowed men to protect them—made me step forward and incline my head. "My name is Yeine Darr."

Her smile said that she'd already guessed it. There could not have been many Darre in the palace. "Ah, yes. Someone spoke of you after Uncle's audience today. Kinneth's daughter, are you?"

"I am." In Darr, I would have drawn a knife at the malice in her sweet, falsely polite tone. But this was Sky, blessed palace of Bright Itempas, the lord of order and peace. Such things were not done here. I looked to T'vril for an introduction.

"The lady Scimina Arameri," he said. He did not swallow or fidget, to his credit, but I saw how his eyes flicked back and forth between my cousin and the motionless man. I waited for T'vril to introduce the man, but he did not.

"Ah, yes." I did not try to mimic Scimina's tone. My mother had tried, on multiple occasions, to teach me how to sound friendly when I did not feel friendly, but I was too Darre for that. "Greetings, Cousin."

"If you'll excuse us," T'vril said to Scimina almost the instant

I closed my mouth, "I'm showing Lady Yeine around the palace—"

The man beside Scimina chose that moment to catch his breath in a shuddering gasp. His hair, long and black and thick enough to make any Darre man jealous, fell forward to obscure his face; his hand on the railing tightened.

"A moment, T'vril." Scimina examined the man thoughtfully, then lifted her hand as if to cup his cheek under the curtain of hair. There was a click, and she pulled away a delicate, cleverly jointed silver collar.

"I'm sorry, Aunt," T'vril said, and now he was no longer bothering to hide his fear; he caught my hand in his own, tight. "Viraine's expecting us, you know how he hates—"

"You will wait," Scimina said, cold in an instant. "Or I may forget that you have made yourself so useful, T'vril. A good little servant…" She glanced at the black-haired man and smiled indulgently. "So many good servants here in Sky. Don't you think, Nahadoth?"

Nahadoth was the black-haired man's name, then. Something about the name stirred a feeling of recognition in me, but I could not recall where I'd heard it before.

"Don't do this," T'vril said. "Scimina."

"She has no mark," Scimina replied. "You know the rules."

"This has nothing to do with the rules and you know it!" T'vril said with some heat. But she ignored him.

I felt it then. I think I had felt it since the man's gasp—a shiver of the atmosphere. A vase rattled nearby. There was no visible cause for this, but somehow I knew: somewhere, on an unseen plane, a part of reality was shifting aside. Making room for something new.

The black-haired man lifted his head to look at me. He was smiling. I could see his face now, and his mad, mad eyes, and I suddenly knew who he was. *What* he was.

"Listen to me." T'vril, his voice tight in my ear. I could not look away from the black-haired creature's eyes. "You must get to Viraine. Only a fullblood can command him off now, and Viraine is the only one— Oh, for demons' sake, look at me!"

He moved into my line of sight, blocking my view of those eyes. I could hear a soft murmur, Scimina speaking in a low voice. It sounded like she was giving instructions, which made a peculiar parallel with T'vril in front of me doing the same. I barely heard them both. I felt so cold.

"Viraine's study is two levels above us. There are lifting chambers at every third corridor juncture; look for an alcove between vases of flowers. Just—just get to one of those, and then think *up*. The door will be straight ahead. While there's still light in the sky you have a chance. Go. Run!"

He pushed me, and I stumbled off. Behind me rose an inhuman howl, like the voices of a hundred wolves and a hundred jaguars and a hundred winter winds, all of them hungry for my flesh. Then there was silence, and that was most frightening of all.

I ran. I ran. I ran.

3

Darkness

SHOULD I PAUSE TO EXPLAIN? It is poor storytelling. But I must remember everything, remember and remember and remember, to keep a tight grip on it. So many bits of myself have escaped already.

So.

There were once three gods. The one who matters killed one of the ones who didn't and cast the other into a hellish prison. The walls of this prison were blood and bone; the barred windows were eyes; the punishments included sleep and pain and hunger and all the other incessant demands of mortal flesh. Then this creature, trapped in his tangible vessel, was given to the Arameri for safekeeping, along with three of his godly children. After the horror of incarnation, what difference could mere slavery make?

As a little girl, I learned from the priests of Bright Itempas that this fallen god was pure evil. In the time of the Three, his followers had been a dark, savage cult devoted to violent midnight revels, worshipping madness as a sacrament. If that one had won the war between the gods, the priests intoned direly, mortalkind would probably no longer exist.

"So be good," the priests would add, "or the Nightlord will get you."

*   *   *

I ran from the Nightlord through halls of light. Some property of the stuff that made up Sky's substance made it glow with its own soft, white luminescence now that the sun had set. Twenty paces behind me charged the god of darkness and chaos. On the one occasion that I risked a glance back, I saw the gentle glow of the hallway fade into a throat of blackness so deep looking that way hurt the eye. I did not look back again.

I could not go straight. All that had saved me thus far was my head start, and the fact that the monster behind me seemed incapable of moving faster than a mortal's pace. Perhaps the god retained a human form somewhere within all that dark; even so, his legs were longer than mine.

So I turned at nearly every juncture, slamming into walls to brake my speed and give me something to push against as I sprinted away. I say this as if the wall slamming was deliberate on my part; it was not. If I had been able to reason through my abject terror, I might have retained a general sense of which direction I was going in. As it was, I was already hopelessly lost.

Fortunately, where reason failed, blind panic served well enough.

Spying one of the alcoves that T'vril had described, I flung myself into it, pressing against the back wall. He had told me to think *up*, which would activate the lifting spell and propel me to the next level of the palace. Instead I thought *AWAY AWAY AWAY*, not realizing the magic would oblige that, too.

25

When the coach had brought me from the Salon to Sky-the-palace, I'd had the curtains closed. The coachman had simply driven us to a particular spot and stopped; my skin had prickled; a moment later the coachman opened the door to reveal we were there. It had not occurred to me that the magic had pulled me through half a mile of solid matter in the blink of an eye.

Now it happened again. The little alcove, which had been growing dim as the Nightlord closed in, suddenly seemed to stretch, its entrance moving impossibly farther away while I remained still. There was an inbreath of tension, and then I shot forward as if from a sling. Walls flew at my face; I screamed and flung my arms over my eyes even as they passed through me. And then everything stopped.

I lowered my arms slowly. Before I could muster my wits enough to wonder whether this was the same alcove or another just like it, a child thrust his face through the opening, looked around, and spied me.

"Come on," he said. "Hurry up. It won't take him long to find us."

*   *   *

The Arameri magic had brought me to a vast open chamber within the body of Sky. Dumb, I looked around at the cold, featureless space as we hurried through it.

"The arena," said the boy ahead of me. "Some of the highbloods fancy themselves warriors. This way."

I glanced back toward the alcove, wondering if there was some way to block it off so the Nightlord couldn't follow.

"No, that won't work," said the boy, following my gaze. "But the palace itself inhibits his power on a night like this. He can hunt you using only his senses." (*As opposed to what else?* I wondered.) "On a moonless night you'd be in trouble, but tonight he's just a man."

"That was not a man," I said. My voice sounded high and shaky in my own ears.

"If that were true, you wouldn't be running for your life right now." And apparently I wasn't running fast enough. The boy caught my hand and pulled me along faster. He glanced back at me, and I caught a glimpse of a high-cheekboned, pointed face that would one day be handsome.

"Where are you taking me?" My ability to reason was returning, though slowly. "To Viraine?"

He uttered a derisive snort. We left the arena and passed into more of the mazelike white halls. "Don't be foolish. We're going to hide."

"But that man—" Nahadoth. Now I remembered where I'd heard the name. *Never whisper it in the dark*, read the children's tales, *unless you want him to answer.*

"Oh, so now he's a man? We just have to keep ahead of him and everything will be fine." The boy ran around a corner, more nimble than me; I stumbled to keep up. He darted his eyes around the corridor, looking for something. "Don't worry. I get away from him all the time."

This did not sound wise. "I w-want to go to Viraine." I tried to say it with authority, but I was still too frightened, and winded now besides.

The boy responded by stopping, but not because of me. "Here!" he said, and put his hand against one of the pearlescent walls. *"Atadie!"*

The wall opened.

It was like watching ripples in water. The pearly stuff moved away from his hand in steady waves, forming an opening—a hole—a door. Beyond the wall lay an oddly shaped, narrow chamber, not so much a room as a *space between*. When the door was big enough for us both, the boy pulled me inside.

"What is this?" I asked.

"Dead space in the body of the palace. All these curving corridors and round rooms. There's another half a palace in between that no one uses—except me." The boy turned to me and flashed an up-to-no-good grin. "We can rest for a little while."

I was beginning to catch my breath, and with it came a weakness that I recognized as the aftermath of adrenaline. The wall had rippled shut behind me, becoming as solid as before. I leaned back against it gingerly at first, then gratefully. And then I examined my rescuer.

He wasn't much smaller than me, maybe nine years old, with the spindly look of a fast grower. Not Amn, not with skin as dark as mine and sharpfold eyes like those of the Tema people. They were a murky, tired green, those eyes—like my own, and my mother's. Maybe his father had been another wandering Arameri.

He was examining me as well. After a moment, his grin widened. "I'm Sieh."

Two syllables. "Sieh Arameri?"

"Just Sieh." With a child's boneless grace, he stretched his arms above his head. "You don't look like much."

I was too tired to take offense. "I've found it useful," I replied, "to be underestimated."

"Yes. Always good strategy, that." Lightning-quick, he straightened and grew serious. "He'll find us if we don't keep moving. *En!*"

I jumped, startled by his shout. But Sieh was looking up. A moment later, a child's yellow kickball fell into his hands.

Puzzled, I looked up. The dead space went up several floors, a featureless triangular shaft; I saw no openings from which the ball could have come. There was certainly no one hovering above who could have thrown the ball to him.

I looked at the boy and suffered a sudden, chilling suspicion.

Sieh laughed at my face and put the ball on the floor. Then he sat on it, cross-legged. The ball held perfectly still beneath him until he was comfortable, and then it rose into the air. It stopped when he was a few feet above the ground and hovered. Then the boy who was not a boy reached out to me.

"I won't hurt you," he said. "I'm helping you, aren't I?"

I just looked at his hand, pressing myself back against the wall.

"I could have led you in a circle, you know. Right back to him."

There was that. After a moment, I took his hand. His grip left no question; this was not a child's strength.

"Just a little ways," he said. Then, dangling me like a snared rabbit, he floated us both up through the shaft.

*   *   *

There is another thing I remember from my childhood. A song, and it went...How did it go? Ah, yes. "*Trickster, trickster / Stole*

29

the sun for a prank. / Will you really ride it? / Where will you hide it? / Down by the riverbank . . ."

It was not *our* sun, mind you.

*   *   *

Sieh opened two ceilings and another wall before finally setting me down in a dead space that was as big as Grandfather Dekarta's audience chamber. But it was not the size of this space that made my mouth gape.

More spheres floated in this room, dozens of them. They were fantastically varied—of all shapes and sizes and colors—turning slowly and drifting through the air. They seemed to be nothing more than a child's toys, until I looked closely at one and saw clouds swirling over its surface.

Sieh hovered near as I wandered among his toys, his expression somewhere between anxiety and pride. The yellow ball had taken up position near the center of the room; all the other balls revolved around it.

"They're pretty, aren't they?" he asked me, while I stared at a tiny red marble. A great cloud mass—a storm?—devoured the nearer hemisphere. I tore my eyes from it to look at Sieh. He bounced on his toes, impatient for my answer. "It's a good collection."

Trickster, trickster, stole the sun for a prank. And apparently because it was pretty. The Three had borne many children before their falling-out. Sieh was immeasurably old, another of the Arameri's deadly weapons, and yet I could not bring myself to dash the shy hope I saw in his eyes.

"They're all beautiful," I agreed. It was true.

He beamed and took my hand again—not pulling me anywhere, just feeling companionable. "I think the others will like you," he said. "Even Naha, when he calms down. It's been a long time since we had a mortal of our own to talk to."

His words were gibberish strung together without meaning. Others? Naha? Calm?

He laughed at me again. "I especially like your face. You don't show much emotion—is that a Darre thing, or your mother's training?—but when you do, all the world can read it."

My mother had warned me of the same thing long ago. "Sieh—" I had a thousand questions and couldn't decide where to begin. One of the balls, a plain green one with bright white poles, went past us, tumbling end over end. I didn't register it as an anomaly until Sieh saw it and stiffened. That was when my own instincts belatedly sent a warning.

I turned to find that Nahadoth stood behind us.

In the instant that my mind and body froze, he could have had me. He was only a few paces away. But he did not move or speak, and so we stared at each other. Face like the moon, pale and somehow wavering. I could get the gist of his features, but none of it stuck in my mind beyond an impression of astonishing beauty. His long, long hair wafted around him like black smoke, its tendrils curling and moving of their own volition. His cloak—or perhaps that was hair, too—shifted as if in an unfelt wind. I could not recall him wearing a cloak before, on the balcony.

The madness still lurked in his face, but it was a quieter madness now, not the rabid-animal savagery of before. Something else—I could not bring myself to call it humanity—stirred underneath the gleam.

Sieh stepped forward, careful not to move in front of me. "Are you with us yet, Naha?"

Nahadoth did not answer, did not even seem to see Sieh. Sieh's toys, I noticed with the fragment of my mind that wasn't frozen, went wild when they came near him. Their slow, graceful orbits changed: some drifted in a different direction, some froze in place, some sped up. One split in half and fell broken to the floor as I watched. He took a step forward, sending more of the colored balls spinning out of control.

That one step was enough to jar me out of my paralysis. I stumbled back and would have fled screaming if I'd known how to make the walls open.

"Don't run!" Sieh's voice snapped at me like a whip. I froze.

Nahadoth stepped forward again, close enough that I could see a minute shiver pass through him. His hands flexed. He opened his mouth; struggled a moment; spoke. "P-predictable, Sieh." His voice was deep, but shockingly human. I had expected a bestial growl.

Sieh hunched, a sulky little boy again. "Didn't think you'd catch up that fast." He cocked his head, studying Nahadoth's face, and spoke slowly, as if to a simpleton. "You are here, aren't you?"

"I can *see* it," whispered the Nightlord. His eyes were fixed on my face.

To my surprise, Sieh nodded as if he knew what such ravings meant. "I wasn't expecting that, either," he said softly. "But perhaps you remember now—we need this one. Do you remember?" Sieh stepped forward, reaching for his hand.

I did not see that hand move. I was watching Nahadoth's face. All I saw was the flash of blind, murderous rage that crossed his features, and then one of his hands was 'round Sieh's throat. Sieh had no chance to cry out before he was lifted off the ground, gagging and kicking.

For a breath I was too shocked to react.

Then I got angry.

I *burned* with anger—and madness, too, which is the only possible explanation for what I did then. I drew my knife and cried, "Leave him alone!"

As well a rabbit threaten a wolf. But to my utter shock, the Nightlord looked at me. He did not lower Sieh, but he blinked. Just that quickly, the madness left him, replaced by a look of astonishment and dawning wonder. It was the look of a man who has just discovered treasure beneath a pile of offal. But he was still choking the life out of Sieh.

"Let him go!" I crouched, shifting my stance the way my Darren grandmother had taught me. My hands shook—not with fear, but with that mad, wild, righteous fury. Sieh was a *child.* "Stop it!"

Nahadoth smiled.

I lunged. The knife went into his chest, going deep before lodging in bone with such a sudden impact that my hand was jarred free of the hilt. There was an instant in which I braced myself against his chest, trying to push away. I marveled that he was solid, warm, flesh and blood despite the power writhing about him. I marveled even more when his free hand wrapped around my wrist like a vise. So fast, despite the knife in his heart.

With the strength in that hand, he could have crushed my

wrist. Instead he held me in place. His blood coated my hand, hotter than my rage. I looked up; his eyes were warm, gentle, desperate. *Human.*

"I have waited so long for you," the god breathed. Then he kissed me.

Then he fell.

4

Magician

W<small>HEN THE</small> N<small>IGHTLORD</small> <small>SAGGED</small> to the ground, dropping Sieh in the process, I nearly fell with them. I had no idea why I was still alive. The tales of the Arameri's weapons are full of them slaughtering whole armies. There are no stories of crazed barbarian girls fighting back.

Sieh, to my great relief, immediately pushed himself up on his elbows. He seemed fine, though his eyes went very round at the sight of Nahadoth's motionless form. "Look what you did!"

"I…" I was shaking, almost too hard to talk. "I didn't mean… He was killing you. I couldn't"—I swallowed hard—"let him."

"Nahadoth would not have killed Sieh," said a new voice behind me. My nerves did not like this. I jumped and grabbed for the knife that was no longer tucked into my back-sheath. A woman resolved out of the silent drift of Sieh's toys. The first thing I noticed was that she was huge, like the great sea ships of the Ken. She was built like one of those ships, too, broad and powerful and astonishingly graceful; none of it was fat. I could not guess her race, because no woman of any race I knew was that damned big.

She knelt to help Sieh up. Sieh was shaking, too, though with excitement. "Did you see what she did?" he asked the newcomer. He pointed at Nahadoth; he was grinning.

"Yes, I saw." Setting Sieh on his feet, the woman turned to regard me for a moment. Kneeling, she was taller than Sieh standing. Her clothing was simple—gray tunic and pants, a gray kerchief covering her hair. Maybe it was her *grayness* after the unrelenting black of the Nightlord, but there was something about her that seemed fundamentally gentle to me.

"There is no greater warrior than a mother protecting her child," the woman said. "But Sieh is far less fragile than you, Lady Yeine."

I nodded slowly, not allowing myself to feel foolish. Logic had not been part of what I'd done.

Sieh came over and took my hand. "Thank you anyway," he said shyly. The purpled, ugly handprint around his throat was fading even as I watched.

We all looked over at Nahadoth. He sat on his knees as he had fallen, the knife still hilt-deep in his chest, his head slumped. With a soft sigh, the gray woman went to him and pulled the knife out. I had felt it lodge in bone, but she made the withdrawal look easy. She examined it, shook her head, then offered it to me hilt first.

I made myself take it, getting more god's blood on my hand. I thought that she held the blade more firmly than necessary because my hand was shaking so badly. But as I got a better grip on the hilt, the woman's fingers trailed down the blade.

When I had the knife again, I realized that not only was it clean of blood, but it was a different shape—curved now—and finely honed.

"That suits you better," said the woman, giving a solemn nod at my stare. Unthinking, I put the knife into its sheath at the small of my back, though it should no longer have fit. It did; the sheath had changed, too.

"So, Zhakka, you like her." Sieh leaned against me, wrapping his arms around my waist and resting his head on my breast. Immortal or not, there was such innocence in the way he did it that I did not push him away. I put my arm around him without thinking, and he uttered a deep, contented sigh.

"Yes," said the woman without prevarication. She leaned forward, peering into Nahadoth's face. "Father?"

I did not jump, not with Sieh leaning against me, but he felt me stiffen. "Shhh," he said, rubbing my back. That touch was not quite childlike enough to be truly soothing. A moment later, Nahadoth stirred.

"You're back," said Sieh, straightening with a bright smile. I took that opportunity to step away from Nahadoth. Sieh caught my hand quickly, all earnestness. "It's all right, Yeine. He's different now. You're safe."

"She will not believe you," said Nahadoth. He sounded like a man waking from a deep sleep. "She will not trust us now."

"It isn't your fault." Sieh sounded unhappy. "We just need to explain, and she'll understand."

Nahadoth looked at me, which made me jump again, though it seemed the madness was indeed gone. Nor did I see that other look—when he'd held my hand in his heartblood and whispered soft, longing words. And that kiss...no. I had imagined it. That was clear, as the Nightlord who sat before me now was detached, regal even on his knees, and contemptuous. I was reminded painfully of Dekarta.

"Will you understand?" he asked me.

I could not help taking another step back in answer. Nahadoth shook his head and rose, nodding gracefully to the woman Sieh had called Zhakka. Though Zhakka towered over Nahadoth, there was no question which was the superior and which the subordinate.

"We have no time for this," Nahadoth said. "Viraine will be looking for her. Mark her and be done with it." Zhakka nodded and came toward me. I stepped back a third time, unnerved by the intent in her eyes.

Sieh let go of me and stood between us, a flea confronting a dog. He barely came up to Zhakka's waist. "This isn't the way we were supposed to do it. We agreed to try and win her over."

"That isn't possible now," said Nahadoth.

"What's to stop her from telling Viraine about this, then?" Sieh put his hands on his hips. Zhakka had stopped, waiting patiently for the dispute to be resolved. I felt forgotten and supremely unimportant—as I probably should, given that I stood in the presence of three gods. The term *former* gods just didn't seem to fit.

Nahadoth's face showed something less than a smile. He glanced at me. "Tell Viraine and we'll kill you." His gaze returned to Sieh. "Satisfied?"

I must have been tired. After so many threats that evening, I didn't even flinch.

Sieh frowned and shook his head, but he stepped out of Zhakka's path. "This wasn't what we'd planned," he said with a hint of petulance.

"Plans change," said Zhakka. Then she stood before me.

"What are you going to do?" I asked. Somehow, despite her size, she did not frighten me near as much as Nahadoth.

"I will mark your brow with a sigil," she said. "One that cannot be seen. It will interfere with the sigil Viraine intends to put on you. You will look like one of them, but in truth you'll be free."

"Are they..." All the sigil-marked Arameri? Was that who she meant? "...not free?"

"No more than we, for all they think otherwise," said Nahadoth. There was, for just that moment, a hint of the softness in him that I'd seen before. Then he turned away. "Hurry up."

Zhakka nodded, and touched my forehead with the tip of a finger. Her fists were the size of dinner plates; her finger seemed to sear like a brand when it touched me. I cried out and tried to slap her finger away, but she lifted her hand before I could. She was done.

Sieh, his sulk forgotten, peered at the spot and nodded sagely. "That will do."

"Take her to Viraine, then," said Zhakka. She inclined her head to me in courteous farewell, then turned away to join Nahadoth.

Sieh took my hand. I was so confused and shaken that I did not fight when he led me toward the nearest of the dead space's walls. But I did glance back over my shoulder once, to watch the Nightlord walk away.

*   *   *

My mother was the most beautiful woman in the world. I say that not because I am her daughter, and not because she was tall and graceful, with hair like clouded sunlight. I say it because she was strong. Perhaps it is my Darre heritage, but strength has always been the marker of beauty in my eyes.

My people were not kind to her. No one said it in front of my father, but I heard the murmurs when we walked through Arrebaia sometimes. *Amn whore. Bone-white bitch.* They would spit on the ground after she passed, to wash the streets of her Arameri taint. Through all this she maintained her dignity and was never less than polite to people who were anything but. My father, in one of the few clear memories of him that I have, said this made her better than them.

I am not sure why I remember this now, but I am certain it is somehow important.

*   *   *

Sieh made me run after we left the dead space, so that I would be out of breath when we arrived at Viraine's workshop.

Viraine opened the door after Sieh's third impatient knock, looking irritated. The white-haired man from Dekarta's audience, who had judged me "not hopeless."

"Sieh? What in demons—ah." He looked at me and raised his eyebrows. "Yes, I'd rather thought T'vril was taking too long. The sun went down nearly an hour ago."

"Scimina sicced Naha on her," said Sieh. Then he looked up at me. "But the game was to end if you made it here, right? You're safe now."

This was my explanation, then. "That was what T'vril said."

I glanced back down the hall as if I was still afraid. It was not difficult to pretend.

"Scimina would have given him specific parameters," Viraine said, which I suppose was meant to reassure me. "She knows what he's like in that state. Come in, Lady Yeine."

He stepped aside, and I entered the chamber. Even if I hadn't been bone tired I would have stopped there, for I stood in a room like nothing I had ever seen. It was long and oval-shaped, and there were floor-to-ceiling windows down both of the longer walls. Twin rows of workbenches had been placed along either side of the room; I saw books, flasks, and incomprehensible contraptions on each. Along the far wall were cages, some containing rabbits and birds. In the center of the chamber was a huge white orb set on a low plinth. It was as tall as me and completely opaque.

"Over here," Viraine said, heading toward one of the workbenches. Two stools sat in front of it. He chose one of them and patted the other for me. I followed him, but then hesitated.

"I'm afraid you have the advantage of me, sir."

He looked surprised, then smiled and gave me an informal, not-quite-mocking half bow. "Ah, yes, manners. I am Viraine, the palace scrivener. Also a relative of yours in some way or another—too distant and convoluted to determine, though Lord Dekarta has seen fit to welcome me into the Central Family." He tapped the black circle on his forehead.

Scriveners: Amn scholars who made a study of the gods' written language. This scrivener did not look like the cold-eyed ascetics I'd imagined. He was younger, for one—perhaps a few years younger than my mother had been. Certainly not old enough for such stark white hair. Perhaps he was like T'vril and I, part Amn of a more exotic variety.

"A pleasure," I said. "Though I cannot help but wonder why the palace needs a scrivener. Why study the gods' power when you have actual gods right here?"

He looked pleased by my question; perhaps few people asked him about his work. "Well, for one thing, they can't do everything or be everywhere. There are hundreds of people in this palace using small magics on an everyday basis. If we had to stop and call an Enefadeh every time we needed something, very little would get done. The lift, for example, that carried you to this level of the palace. The air—this far above the ground, it would ordinarily be thin and cold, hard to breathe. Magic keeps the palace comfortable."

I sat down carefully on one of the stools, eyeing the bench beside me. The items there were laid out neatly: various fine paintbrushes, a dish of ink, and a small block of polished stone, incised on its face with a strange, complicated character of spikes and curlicues. The character was so fundamentally alien, so jarring to the eye, that I could not look at it long. The urge to look away was part of what it was, because it was gods' language; a sigil.

Viraine sat opposite me while Sieh, unbidden, claimed a seat across the bench and rested his chin on his folded arms.

"For another thing," Viraine continued, "there are certain magics that even the Enefadeh cannot perform. Gods are peculiar beings, incredibly powerful within their sphere of influence, so to speak, but limited beyond that. Nahadoth is powerless by day. Sieh cannot be quiet and well-behaved unless he's up to something." He eyed Sieh, who gave us both an innocent smile. "In many ways, we mortals are more . . . versatile, for lack of a better term. More *complete*. For example, none of them can create or extend life. The simple act of having children—something any unlucky barmaid or careless soldier can do—is a power that has been lost to the gods for millennia."

From the corner of my eye, I saw Sieh's smile fade.

"*Extend* life?" I had heard rumors about what some scriveners did with their powers—terrible, foul rumors. It occurred to me suddenly that my grandfather was very, very old.

Viraine nodded, his eyes twinkling at the disapproval in my tone. "It is the great quest of our profession. Someday we might even achieve immortality . . ." He read the horror in my face and smiled. "Though that goal is not without controversy."

My grandmother had always said the Amn were unnatural people. I looked away. "T'vril said you were going to mark me."

He grinned, openly amused now. Laughing at the prudish savage. "Mmm-hmm."

"What does this mark do?"

"Keeps the Enefadeh from killing you, among other things. You've seen what they can be like."

I licked my lips. "Ah. Yes. I . . . didn't know they were . . ." I gestured vaguely, unsure how to say what I meant without offending Sieh.

"Running around loose?" Sieh asked brightly. There was a wicked look in his eye; he was enjoying my discomfiture.

I winced. "Yes."

"Mortal form is their prison," Viraine said, ignoring Sieh. "And every soul in Sky, their jailer. They are bound by Bright

Itempas to serve the descendants of Shahar Arameri, His great-est priestess. But since Shahar's descendants now number in the thousands..." He gestured toward the windows, as if the whole world was one clan. Or perhaps he simply meant Sky, the only world that mattered to him. "Our ancestors chose to impose a more orderly structure on the situation. The mark confirms for the Enefadeh that you're Arameri; without it they will not obey you. It also specifies your rank within the family. How close you are to the main line of descent, I mean, which in turn dictates how much power you have to command them."

He picked up a brush, though he did not dip it in the ink; instead he reached up to my face, pushing my hair back from my forehead. My heart clenched as he examined me. Clearly Viraine was some sort of expert; could he truly not see Zhakka's mark? For an instant I thought he had, because his eyes flicked down to hold mine for half a breath. But apparently the gods had done their work well, because after a moment Viraine let my hair go and began to stir the ink.

"T'vril said the mark was permanent," I said, mostly to quell my nervousness. The black liquid looked like simple writing ink, though the sigil-marked block was clearly no ordinary inkstone.

"Unless Dekarta orders it removed, yes. Like a tattoo, though painless. You'll get used to it."

I was not fond of a permanent mark, though I knew better than to protest. To distract myself I asked, "Why do you call them Enefadeh?"

The look that crossed Viraine's face was fleeting, but I recog-nized it by instinct: calculation. I had just revealed some stun-ning bit of ignorance to him, and he meant to use it.

Casually, Viraine jabbed a thumb at Sieh, who was surreptitiously eyeing the items on Viraine's worktable. "It's what they call themselves. We just find the label convenient."

"Why not—"

"We don't call them gods." Viraine smiled faintly. "That would be an offense to the Skyfather, our only true god, and those of the Skyfather's children who stayed loyal. But we can't call them slaves, either. After all, we outlawed slavery centuries ago."

This was the sort of thing that made people hate the Arameri—truly hate them, not just resent their power or their willingness to use it. They found so many ways to lie about the things they did. It mocked the suffering of their victims.

"Why not just call them what they are?" I asked. "Weapons."

Sieh glanced at me, his gaze too neutral to be a child's in that instant.

Viraine winced delicately. "Spoken like a true barbarian," he said, and though he smiled, that did nothing to alleviate the insult. "The thing you must understand, Lady Yeine, is that like our ancestress Shahar, we Arameri are first and foremost the servants of Itempas Skyfather. It is in His name that we have imposed the age of the Bright upon the world. Peace, order, enlightenment." He spread his hands. "Itempas's servants do not use, or need, weapons. Tools, though..."

I had heard enough. I had no idea of his rank relative to mine, but I was tired and confused and far from home, and if barbarians' manners would serve better to get me through this day, then so be it.

"Does 'Enefadeh' mean 'tool,' then?" I demanded. "Or is it just 'slave' in another tongue?"

"It means 'we who remember Enefa,'" said Sieh. He had propped his chin on his fist. The items on Viraine's workbench looked the same, but I was certain he had done something to them. "She was the one murdered by Itempas long ago. We went to war with Him to avenge her."

Enefa. The priests never said her name. "The Betrayer," I murmured without thought.

"She betrayed no one," Sieh snapped.

Viraine's glance at Sieh was heavy-lidded and unreadable. "True. A whore's business can hardly be termed a betrayal, can it?"

Sieh hissed. For an eyeblink there was something inhuman about his face—something sharp and feral—and then he was a boy again, sliding off the stool and trembling with fury. For a moment I half-expected him to poke out his tongue, but the hatred in his eyes was too old for that.

"I will laugh when you're dead," he said softly. The small hairs along my skin prickled, for his voice was a grown man's now, tenor malevolence. "I will claim your heart as a toy and kick it for a hundred years. And when I am finally free, I will hunt down all your descendants and make their children just like me."

With that, he vanished. I blinked. Viraine sighed.

"And that, Lady Yeine, is why we use the blood sigils," he said. "Silly as that threat was, he meant every word of it. The sigil prevents him from carrying it out, yet even that protection is limited. A higher-ranking Arameri's order, or stupidity on your part, could leave you vulnerable."

I frowned, remembering the moment when T'vril had urged

me to get to Viraine. *Only a fullblood can command him off now.* And T'vril was a—what had he called it?—a halfblood.

"Stupidity on my part?" I asked.

Viraine gave me a hard look. "They must respond to any imperative statement you make, Lady. Consider how many such statements we make carelessly, or figuratively, with no thought given to other interpretations." When I frowned in thought, he rolled his eyes. "The common folk are fond of saying 'To the hells with you!' Ever said it yourself, in a moment of anger?" At my slow nod, he leaned closer. "The subject of the phrase is implied, of course; we usually mean 'You should go.' But the phrase could also be understood as 'I want to go, and you will take me.'"

He paused to see if I understood. I did. At my shudder, he nodded and sat back.

"Just don't talk to them unless you have to," he said. "Now. Shall we—" He reached for the ink dish and cursed as it toppled the instant his fingers touched it; Sieh had somehow lodged a brush underneath. The ink splattered across the tabletop like

like

and then Viraine touched my hand. "Lady Yeine? Are you all right?"

*   *   *

That was how it happened, yes. The first time.

*   *   *

I blinked. "What?"

He smiled, all condescending kindness again. "Been a hard day, has it? Well, this won't take long." He'd cleaned up the ink spill; there was enough left in the dish that apparently he could continue. "If you could hold your hair back for me..."

47

I didn't move. "Why did Grandfather Dekarta do this, Scrivener Viraine? Why did he bring me here?"

He raised his eyebrows, as if surprised that I would even ask. "I'm not privy to his thoughts. I have no idea."

"Is he senile?"

He groaned. "You really are a savage. No, he isn't senile."

"Then why?"

"I just told you—"

"If he wanted to kill me, he could have simply had me executed. Trump up an excuse, if he even bothered. Or he could have done what he did to my mother. An assassin in the night, poison in my sleep."

I had finally surprised him. He grew very still, his eyes meeting mine and then flicking away. "I would not confront Dekarta with the evidence, if I were you."

At least he hadn't tried to deny it.

"I hardly needed evidence. A healthy woman in her forties doesn't die in her sleep. But I had her body searched by the physician. There was a mark, a small puncture, on her forehead. On the—" I trailed off for a moment, suddenly understanding something I'd never questioned in my life. "On the scar she had, right here." I touched my own forehead, where my Arameri sigil would be.

Viraine faced me full-on now, quiet and serious. "If an Arameri assassin left a mark that could be seen—and if you expected to see it—then, Lady Yeine, you understand more of Dekarta's intentions than any of us. Why do *you* think he brought you here?"

I shook my head slowly. All along the journey to Sky, I'd

suspected. Dekarta was angry at my mother, hated my father. There could be no good reason for his invitation. In the back of my mind I'd expected to be executed at best, perhaps tortured first, maybe on the steps of the Salon. My grandmother had been afraid for me. If there'd been any hope of escape, I think she would have urged me to run. But one does not run from the Arameri.

And a Darre woman does not run from revenge.

"This mark," I said at last. "It will help me survive this place?"

"Yes. The Enefadeh won't be able to hurt you unless you do something stupid. As for Scimina, Relad, and other dangers..." He shrugged. "Well. Magic can only do so much."

I closed my eyes and traced my mother's face against my memory for the ten thousandth time. She had died with tears on her cheeks, perhaps knowing what I would face.

"Then let's begin," I said.

5

Chaos

THAT NIGHT AS I SLEPT, I dreamt of him.

*   *   *

It is an ugly, stormcloud-choked night.

Above the clouds, the sky is lightening with the approach of dawn. Below the clouds, this has made absolutely no difference in the battlefield's illumination. A thousand torches burning amid a hundred thousand soldiers are more than enough light. The capital, too, is a gentle radiance nearby.

(It is not the Sky that I know. This city sprawls across a floodplain rather than over a hill, and the palace is embedded at its heart, not hovering overhead. I am not me.)

"A respectable force," says Zhakka, beside me. Zhakkarn, I know now, goddess of battle and bloodshed. In place of her usual headscarf is a helm that fits her head almost as closely. She wears shining silver armor, its surface a glory of engraved sigils and incomprehensible designs that glow red as if hot. There is a message written in the gods' words there. Memories I should not possess tease me with its meaning, though in the end they fail.

"Yes," I say, and my voice is male, though high-pitched and nasal. I know myself to be Arameri. I feel myself to be powerful. I am the family head. "I would have been offended if they had come with even one soldier less."

"Then since you are not offended, perhaps you can parley with them," says a woman beside me. She is sternly beautiful: her hair is the color of bronze, and a pair of enormous wings feathered in gold, silver, and platinum are folded on her back. Kurue, called Wise.

I feel arrogance. "Parley? They're not worth the time."

(I do not think I like this other me.)

"What then?"

I turn to look at the ones behind me. Sieh sits cross-legged on his floating yellow ball. He has propped his chin on his fist; he is bored. Beyond Sieh lurks a smoking, pent presence. I had not noticed this one move behind me. He watches me as if he has been imagining my death.

I make myself smile, unwilling to reveal how he unnerves me. "Well, Nahadoth? How long has it been since you had any fun?"

I have surprised him. It gratifies me to realize that I can. An eagerness fills his face that is chilling to behold, but I have given no command, and so he waits.

The others are surprised, too, less pleasantly. Sieh straightens and glares at me. "Are you out of your mind?"

Kurue is more diplomatic. "That is unnecessary, Lord Haker. Zhakkarn or even I can take care of this army."

"Or me," says Sieh, stung.

I look at Nahadoth and consider how the stories will go when word spreads that I unleashed the Nightlord on those who dared to challenge me. He is the most powerful of my weapons, yet I have never witnessed any significant display of his capabilities. I am curious.

"Nahadoth," I say. His stillness and the power I have over him are thrilling, but I know to keep my head. I have heard the stories, passed down from previous family heads. It is important to give just the right instructions. He thinks in loopholes.

"Go onto the battlefield and dispose of this army. Do not allow them to advance on this position, or Sky. Do not allow survivors to escape." I almost forget but quickly add, "And do not kill me in the process."

"Is that all?" he asks.

"Yes."

He smiles. "As you wish."

"You're a fool," says Kurue, abandoning politeness. The other me ignores her.

"Keep him safe," says Nahadoth to his children. He is still smiling as he walks onto the battlefield.

The enemy are so numerous that I cannot see the end of them. As Nahadoth walks toward their front line he seems tiny. Helpless. Human. I can hear, echoing across the flat expanse of the plain, some among their soldiers laughing. The commanders at the center of the line are silent. They know what he is.

Nahadoth holds his hands out from his sides, and a great curved sword appears in each. He runs at the line, a black streak, and pierces it like an arrow. Shields split; armor and swords shatter; body parts fly. The enemy dies by the dozen. I clap and laugh. "What a marvelous show!"

Around me, the other Enefadeh are tense and afraid.

Nahadoth cuts a swath through the army until he reaches its general center. No one can stand against him. When he finally stops, having carved a circle of death 'round himself, the enemy soldiers are falling over themselves trying to get away. I cannot see him well from here, even though the black smoke of his aura seems to have flared higher in the intervening minutes.

"The sun comes," says Zhakkarn.

"Not soon enough," says Kurue.

At the center of the army, there is a sound. No, not a sound, a vibration. Like a pulse, except that it shakes the whole earth.

And then a black star blazes to life at the army's heart. I can think of no other words to describe it. It is a sphere of darkness so concentrated that it glows, so heavy with power that the earth groans and sags beneath it. A pit forms, radiating deep cracks. The enemy fall inward. I cannot hear their screams because the black star sucks in the sound. It sucks in their bodies. It sucks in everything.

The earth shakes so violently that I fall to my hands and knees. There is a hollow, rushing roar all around me. I look up to see that the very air is visible as it flies past, sucked down into the pit and the ravening horror that Nahadoth has become. Kurue and the others are around me, murmuring in their tongue to command the winds and whatever other terrible forces their father has unleashed. Because of that we are safe, enclosed in a bubble of calm, but nothing else is. Above us, the very clouds have bent, funneling down into the star. The enemy army is gone. All that remains is the land we stand on, and the continent around it, and the planet beneath that.

I finally realize my error: with his children protecting me, Nahadoth is free to devour it all.

It takes all my will to overcome my own choking fear. "S-stop!" I shout. "Nahadoth, stop!" The words are lost in the howling wind. He is bound by magic even more powerful than himself to obey my commands, but only if he can hear me. Perhaps he intended to drown me out—or perhaps he is simply lost in the glory of his own power, reveling in the chaos that is his nature.

The pit beneath him erupts as he strikes molten rock. A tendril of fiery lava rises and swirls about the blackness before it, too, is swallowed. Tornado above, volcano below, and at the heart of it, the black star, growing ever larger.

It is, in a terrible way, the most beautiful thing I have ever seen.

At the end, we are saved by the Skyfather. The torn clouds reveal a light-streaked sky, and in the instant that I feel the stones beneath my hands shiver, ready to fly away, the sun peeks above the horizon.

The black star vanishes.

Something—charred, pitiful, not enough of a human form to be called a body—hovers in the star's place for a moment, then falls toward the lava below. Sieh curses and streaks off on his yellow ball, breaking the bubble, but the bubble is no longer necessary. The air is hot and thin around me; it is hard to breathe. Already I can see storm-clouds forming in the distance and rushing this way to fill the void.

The nearby capital . . . oh. Oh, no.

I see the broken shells of a few buildings. The rest has been devoured. Part of the land has fallen into the churning red pit; the palace was on that land.

My wife. My son.

Zhakkarn looks at me. She is too much the soldier to show her contempt, though I know she feels it. Kurue helps me to my feet, and her face, too, is blank as she faces me. You have done this, her eyes say.

I will think it over and over as I mourn.

"Sieh has him," says Zhakkarn. "It will take him years to recover."

"He had no business calling on that kind of power," Kurue snaps. "Not in human flesh."

"It doesn't matter," I say, and for once I am right.

The earth has not stopped shaking. Nahadoth has broken something deep within it. This was once beautiful country, the perfect seat for the capital of a global empire. Now it is ruined.

"Take me away," I whisper.

"Where?" asks Zhakkarn. My home is gone.

I almost say anywhere, *but I am not a complete fool. These beings are not as volatile as Nahadoth, not as hateful, but neither are they my friends. One colossal folly for the day is enough.*

"To Senm," I say. "The Amn homeland. We will rebuild there."

So they carry me away. Behind me, over the next few days, the continent breaks apart and sinks into the sea.

6

Alliances

YEINE." MY MOTHER, murdered by jealousy, grasps my hand.
I hold the hilt of a dagger that has been thrust into my own
breast. Blood hotter than rage coats my hand; she leans close to
kiss me. "You're dead."

You lie, Amn whore, bone-white bitch. I will see all your
lying kind swallowed into the darkest depths of
   myself

*   *   *

There was another Consortium session the next morning.
Apparently this was the body's peak season, in which they
met every day for several weeks trying to resolve fiscal business
before a lengthy winter break. T'vril arrived early that morning
to wake me for the occasion, which took some doing. When
I got up, my feet ached dully, as did the bruises I'd sustained
running from Nahadoth the night before. I'd slept like death,
exhausted emotionally and physically.

"Dekarta attends nearly all the sessions, when his health per-
mits," T'vril explained, while I dressed in the next room. The

tailor had worked an overnight miracle, delivering me an entire rack of garments deemed appropriate for a woman of my station. He was very good; instead of simply hemming the long Amn styles, he'd given me a selection of skirts and dresses that complemented my shorter frame. They were still far more decorative and less practical than I was used to, not to mention constricting in all the oddest places. I felt ridiculous. But it would not do for an Arameri heir to look like a savage—even if she was one—so I asked T'vril to convey my thanks for the tailor's efforts.

Between the foreign garments and the stark black circle on my forehead, I barely recognized myself in the mirror.

"Relad and Scimina aren't required to attend—and they often don't," T'vril said. He'd come in to give me a shrewd once-over as I stood in the mirror; by his pleased nod, I evidently met with his approval. "But everyone knows them, while you're an unknown quantity. Dekarta asks that you attend today in particular, so that all can see his newest heir."

Which meant that I had no choice. I sighed and nodded. "I doubt most of the nobles will be pleased," I said. "I was too minor to be worth their time before this whole mess. I imagine they'll resent having to be nice to me now."

"You're probably right," T'vril said, airily unconcerned. He crossed the room to my windows, gazing out at the view while I fussed with my unruly hair in a mirror. This was just nerves on my part; my hair never looked any better.

"Dekarta doesn't waste his time with politics," T'vril continued. "He considers the Central Family above such things. So naturally, any nobles with a cause tend to approach Relad or Scimina. And now you."

Lovely. I sighed, turning to him. "I don't suppose there's any chance I might be disowned if I get myself involved in a scandal or two? Maybe then I could be banished to some backwater land up north."

"More likely you'd end up like my father," he said, shrugging. "That's the usual way the family deals with embarassments."

"Oh." For a moment I felt uneasy for reminding him of tragedy, but then I realized he didn't care.

"In any case, Dekarta seems determined to have you here. I imagine that if you cause enough trouble, he'll simply have you trussed up and delivered to the succession ceremony at the appropriate time. Though for all I know, that's how the ceremony usually goes."

That surprised me. "You don't know?"

"About the ceremony?" T'vril shook his head. "Only members of the Central Family are allowed to witness that. There hasn't been one for forty years, anyhow—not since Dekarta's ascension."

"I see." I put aside this information to consider later. "All right, then. At the Salon, are there any nobles I should beware of?" He threw me a wry look, and I amended myself. "Any *in particular?*"

"You'll learn that before I will," he said. "I imagine both your allies and your enemies will introduce themselves rather quickly. In fact, I suspect *everything* will happen rather quickly, now. So, are you ready?"

I was not. And I wanted badly to ask him about his last comment. Things would happen even more quickly than they had been? Was that possible?

But my questions would have to wait for later. "I'm ready."

So T'vril led me out of the apartment and through the white corridors. My apartment, like that of most fullbloods, was on the topmost floor of Sky's main bulk, though I understood there were apartments and chambers within the spires as well. There was another, smaller Vertical Gate on this level, intended solely for fullblood use. Unlike the Gate in Sky's forecourt, T'vril explained, this Gate had more than one terminus; it apparently went to a number of offices in the city below. That way the fullbloods could conduct family business without getting rained or snowed upon—or without being seen in public, if they so wished.

No one else was about. "Has my grandfather already gone down?" I asked, stopping on the edge of the Gate. Like the main Gate and the palace lifts, it consisted of black tiles set into the floor in a mosaic that formed a gods' sigil. This one resembled nothing so much as a huge spiderwebbed crack in the floor: an uncomfortably suggestive similarity that made me look away more quickly than usual.

"Probably," T'vril said. "He likes to be early. Now, Lady Yeine, remember: at the Consortium you must not speak. The Arameri merely advise the nobles, and only Dekarta has the right to address them. He doesn't do it often. Don't even speak to him while you're there. Your task is simply to observe and be observed."

"And…introduced?"

"Formally? No, that will happen later. But they'll notice you, never fear. Dekarta won't need to say a word."

And with that, he nodded, and I stepped onto the mosaic.

One blurring, terrifying transition later, I found myself in a lovely marble room, standing atop a mosaic of inlaid blackwood. Three Consortium aides—not so junior this time, or so surprised—stood waiting to greet and escort me. I followed them through a shadowed corridor and up a carpeted ramp to find myself in the Arameri private box.

Dekarta sat in his customary place; he did not turn as I arrived. Scimina sat on his right side. She glanced around and smiled at me. I managed not to stop and glare, though it took a powerful effort on my part. But I was very aware of the gathering nobles, who milled around the Salon floor as they waited for the Overseer to begin the session. I saw more than a few glances directed toward the private box; they were watching.

So I inclined my head to Scimina in greeting, though I could not bring myself to return her smile.

Two chairs stood unoccupied at Dekarta's left. Assuming the nearer seat was for my yet-unseen cousin Relad, I moved to take the farther of the two. Then I caught Dekarta's hand movement; he did not look at me, but he beckoned me closer. So I took the nearer seat instead—just in time, as the Overseer called the meeting to order.

This time I paid more attention to what was going on. The meeting proceeded by region, beginning with the Senmite nations. Each region had its representative—nobles appointed by the Consortium to speak for themselves and their neighboring lands. The fairness of this representation varied widely, however, and I could not make heads or tails of how it was organized. The city of Sky had its own representative, for example, yet all the High North continent had only two. The latter did not surprise me—High North had never been highly regarded—but the former did, because no other single city had its own speaker. Sky wasn't *that* important.

But then, as the session went on, I saw that I'd misunderstood. As I paid close attention to the edicts that Sky's representative put forth and supported, I realized that he spoke not just on behalf of Sky the city, but Sky the palace as well. Understandable, then, if unfair; Dekarta already commanded the entire world. The Consortium existed only to do the ugly, messy work of world governance, with which the Arameri couldn't be bothered. Everyone knew that. What was the point in being overrepresented on a governing body that was little more than a puppet show to begin with?

But perhaps that was just the way of power: no such thing as too much.

I found the High North representatives more interesting. I had never met either of them, though I recalled hearing complaints about them from the Darre Warriors' Council. The first, Wohi Ubm—I think the latter name was a title of some sort—came from the largest nation on the continent, a sleepy agrarian land called Rue, which had been one of Darr's strongest allies before my parents' marriage. Since then any correspondence that we sent her got returned unopened; she certainly didn't speak for my people. I noticed her glancing at me now and again as the session went on, and looking extremely uncomfortable as she did so. Had I been a more petty woman, I would have found her unease amusing.

The other High Norther was Ras Onchi, a venerable elder who spoke for the easterly kingdoms and the nearer islands. She didn't say much, being well past the usual age of retirement and, as rumor had it, a bit senile—but she was one of the few nobles on the floor who stared directly at me, for nearly the whole session. Her people were relatives of my own, with similar customs, and so I stared back as a show of respect, which seemed to please her. She nodded once, minutely, in a moment when Dekarta's head was turned away. I didn't dare nod back with so many eyes watching every move I made, but I was intrigued by the gesture all the same.

And then the session was over, as the Overseer rang the chime that closed the day's business. I tried not to exhale in relief, because the whole thing had lasted four hours. I was hungry, in dire need of the ladies' room, and restless to be up and moving about. Still, I followed Dekarta's and Scimina's lead and rose only when they rose, walking out with the same unhurried pace, nodding politely when a whole phalanx of aides descended upon us in escort.

"Uncle," said Scimina, as we walked back to the mosaic chamber, "perhaps Cousin Yeine would like to be shown around the Salon? She can't have seen much of it before."

As if anything would induce me to agree, after that patronizing suggestion. "No, thank you," I said, forcing a smile. "Though I would like to know where the ladies' room is."

"Oh—right this way, Lady Yeine," said one of the aides, stepping aside and gesturing for me to lead the way.

I paused, noting that Dekarta continued onward with no indication that he'd heard either me or Scimina. So that was how things went. I inclined my head to Scimina, who'd also stopped. "No need to wait on my account."

"As you like," she said, and turned gracefully to follow Dekarta.

I followed the aide down the longest hallway in the city, or so it felt, because now that I'd stood my bladder had become most insistent about being emptied. When we at last reached the small chamber—the door was marked *Private* in Senmite, and I took it to mean "for the highest-ranking Salon guests only"—it took all my willpower not to rush undignified into the very large, roomlike stall.

My business completed, I was beginning the complicated process of reassembling my Amn underclothes when I heard the outer chamber door open. *Scimina*, I thought, and stifled both annoyance and a hint of trepidation.

Yet when I emerged from the stall, I was surprised to see Ras Onchi beside the sinks, obviously waiting for me.

For a moment I considered letting my confusion show, then decided against it. I inclined my head instead and said in Nirva—the common tongue of the north long before the Arameri had imposed Senmite on the world—"Good afternoon to you, Auntie."

She smiled, flashing a mouth that was nearly toothless. Her voice lacked for nothing, though, when she spoke. "And to you," she said in the same language, "though I'm no auntie of yours. You're Arameri, and I am nothing."

I flinched before I could stop myself. What does one say to something like that? What did Arameri say? I didn't want to know. To break the awkwardness, I moved past her and began to wash my hands.

She watched me in the mirror. "You don't look much like your mother."

I frowned up at her. What was she about? "So I've been told."

"We were ordered not to speak to her, or your people," she said quietly. "Wohi and I, and Wohi's predecessor. The words came from the Consortium Overseer, but the sentiment?" She smiled. "Who knows? I just thought you might want to know."

This was rapidly beginning to feel like an entirely different conversation. I rinsed my hands, picked up a towel, and turned to her. "Have you got something to say to me, Old Aunt?"

Ras shrugged and turned to head for the door. As she turned, a necklace that she wore caught the light. It had an odd sort of pendant: like a tiny gold treenut or cherrystone. I hadn't noticed it before because it was half-hidden on a chain that dipped below her neckline. A link of chain had caught on her clothing, though, pulling the pendant up into view. I found myself staring at it rather than her.

"I have nothing to tell you that you don't already know," she said, as she walked away. "If you're Arameri, that is."

I scowled after her. "And if I'm not?"

She paused at the door and turned back to me, giving me a very shrewd look. Unthinkingly I straightened, so that she would think better of me. Such was her presence.

"If you're not Arameri," she said after a moment, "then we'll speak again." With that, she left.

I went back to Sky alone, feeling more out of place than ever.

*　　*　　*

I had been given three nations to oversee, as T'vril reminded me that afternoon, when he came to continue my hurried education in Arameri life.

Each of the three lands was bigger than my Darr. Each also had its own perfectly competent rulers, which meant that I had very little to do with regard to their management. They paid me a regular stipend for the privilege of my oversight, which they probably resented deeply, and which instantly made me wealthier than I'd ever been.

I was given another magic thing, a silvery orb that would, on command, show me the face of any person I requested. If I tapped the orb a certain way, they would see my face, hovering in the air like some sort of decapitated spirit. I had been the recipient of such messages before—it was how I'd gotten the invitation from Grandfather Dekarta—and I found them unnerving. Still, this would allow me to communicate with my lands' rulers whenever I wished.

"I'd like to arrange a meeting with my lord cousin Relad as soon as possible," I said after T'vril finished showing me how to use the orb. "I don't know if he'll be any friendlier than Scimina, but I take heart in the fact that he hasn't tried to kill me yet."

"Wait," T'vril muttered.

Not promising. Still, I had a half-formed strategy in my head, and I wanted to pursue it. The problem was that I did not know the rules of this Arameri game of inheritance. How did one "win" when Dekarta himself would not choose? Relad knew the answer to that question, but would he share it with me? Especially when I had nothing to offer in return?

"Tender the invitation anyhow, please," I said. "In the meantime, it might be wise for me to meet with others in the palace who are influential. Who would you suggest?"

T'vril considered for a moment, then spread his hands. "You've already met everyone here who matters, except Relad."

I stared at him. "That can't be true."

He smiled without humor. "Sky is both very large and very small, Lady Yeine. There are other fullbloods, yes, but most of them waste their hours indulging all sorts of whims." He kept his face neutral, and I remembered the silver chain and collar Scimina had put on Nahadoth. Her perversity did not surprise me, for I had heard rumors of far worse within Sky's walls. What astounded me was that she dared play such games with that monster.

"The few fullbloods, halfbloods, and quarters who bother to do any legitimate work are often away from the palace," T'vril continued, "overseeing the family's business interests. Most of them have no hope of winning Dekarta's favor; he made that clear when he named his brother's children potential heirs rather than any of them. The ones who stay are the courtiers— pedants and sycophants for the most part, with impressive-sounding titles and no real power. Dekarta despises them, so you'd do better to avoid them altogether. Beyond that there are only servants."

I glanced at him. "Some servants can be useful to know."

He smiled unselfconsciously. "As I said, Lady Yeine—you've already met everyone who matters. Though I'm happy to arrange meetings for you with anyone you like."

I stretched, still stiff after the long hours of sitting at the Salon. As I did so, one of my bruises twinged, reminding me that I had more than earthly problems to worry about.

"Thank you for saving my life," I said.

T'vril chuckled with a hint of irony, though he looked pleased. "Well, as you suggested...it could be useful to have influence in certain quarters."

I inclined my head to acknowledge the debt. "If I have the power to help you in any way, please ask."

"As you like, Lady Yeine."

"Yeine."

He hesitated. "Cousin," he said instead, and smiled at me over his shoulder as he left my apartment. He really was a superb diplomat. I supposed that was a necessity for someone in his position.

I went from the sitting room into my bedroom and stopped.

"I thought he'd never leave," said Sieh, grinning from the middle of my bed.

I took a deep breath, slowly. "Good afternoon, Lord Sieh."

He pouted, flopping forward onto his belly and regarding me from his folded arms. "You're not happy to see me."

"I'm wondering what I've done to deserve such attention from a god of games and tricks."

"I'm not a god, remember?" He scowled. "Just a weapon. That word was more fitting than you know, Yeine, and how it burns these Arameri to hear it. No wonder they call you a barbarian."

I sat in the reading chair beside the bed. "My mother often told me I was too blunt," I said. "Why are you here?"

"Do I need a reason? Maybe I just like being around you."

"I would be honored if that were true," I said.

He laughed, high and carefree. "It *is* true, Yeine, whether you believe me or not." He got up then and began jumping on the bed. I wondered fleetingly whether anyone had ever tried to spank him.

"But?" I was sure there was a *but*.

He stopped after his third jump and glanced at me over his shoulder, his grin sly. "But it's not the only reason I came. The others sent me."

"For what reason?"

He hopped down from the bed and came over to my chair, putting his hands on my knees and leaning over me. He was still grinning, but again there was that indefinable something in his smile that was not childlike. Not at all.

"Relad isn't going to ally with you."

My stomach clenched in unease. Had he been in here all along, listening to my conversation with T'vril? Or was my strategy for survival just so painfully obvious? "You know this?"

He shrugged. "Why would he? You're useless to him. He has his hands full dealing with Scimina and can't afford distractions. The time—of the succession, I mean—is too close."

I had suspected that as well. That was almost surely why they'd brought me here. It was probably why the family kept a scrivener in-house, to ensure that Dekarta didn't die off schedule. It might even have been the reason for my mother's murder after twenty years of freedom. Dekarta didn't have much time left to tie up loose ends.

Abruptly Sieh climbed into the chair with me, straddling my lap, knees on either side of my hips. I flinched in surprise, and again when he flopped against me, resting his head on my shoulder.

"What are you—?"

"Please, Yeine," he whispered. I felt his hands fist in the cloth of my jacket, at my sides. The gesture was so much that of a child seeking comfort that I could not help it; the stiffness went out of me. He sighed and snuggled closer, reveling in my tacit welcome. "Just let me do this a moment."

So I sat still, wondering many things.

I thought he had fallen asleep when he finally spoke. "Kurue—my sister, Kurue, our leader inasmuch as we have one—invites you to meet."

"Why?"

"You seek allies."

I pushed at him; he sat back on my knees. "What are you saying? Are you offering yourselves?"

"Maybe." The sly look was back. "You have to meet with us to find out."

I narrowed my eyes in what I hoped was an intimidating look. "Why? As you said, I'm useless. What would you gain from allying with me?"

"You have something very important," he said, serious now. "Something we could force you to give us—but we don't want to do that. We are not Arameri. You have proven yourself worthy of respect, and so we will *ask* you to give that something to us willingly."

I did not ask what they wanted. It was their bargaining chip; they would tell me if I met with them. I was rabidly curious, though—and excited, because he was right. The Enefadeh would make powerful, knowledgeable allies, even hobbled as they were. But I dared not reveal my eagerness. Sieh was nowhere near as childish, or as neutral, as he pretended to be.

"I will consider your request for a meeting," I said in my most dignified voice. "Please convey to the Lady Kurue that I will give you a response in no more than three days."

Sieh laughed and jumped off me, returning to the bed. He curled up in the middle of it and grinned at me. "Kurue's going to *hate* you. She thought you'd jump at the chance, and here you are keeping her waiting!"

"An alliance made in fear or haste will not last," I said. "I need a better understanding of my position before I do anything that will strengthen or weaken it. The Enefadeh must realize that."

"I do," he said, "but Kurue is wise and I'm not. She does what's smart. I do what's fun." He shrugged, then yawned. "Can I sleep here, sometimes, with you?"

I opened my mouth, then caught myself. He played innocent so well that I'd almost said yes automatically.

"I'm not sure that would be proper," I said at last. "You are very much older than me, and yet clearly underage. It would be a scandal, either way."

His eyebrows flew up almost into his hairline. Then he burst out laughing, rolling onto his back and holding his middle. He laughed for a long time. Eventually, a bit annoyed, I got up and went to the door to summon a servant and order lunch. I ordered two meals out of politeness, though I had no idea what, or whether, gods ate.

When I turned, Sieh had finally stopped laughing. He sat on the edge of the bed, watching me, thoughtful.

"I could be older," he said softly. "If you'd rather have me older, I mean. I don't have to be a child."

I stared at him and did not know whether to feel pity, nausea, or both at once.

"I want you to be what you are," I said.

His expression grew solemn. "That isn't possible. Not while I'm in this prison." He touched his chest.

"Do—" I did not want to call them my family. "Do others ask you to be older?"

He smiled. It was, most horribly, very much a child's smile. "Younger, usually."

Nausea won. I put a hand to my mouth and turned away. Never mind what Ras Onchi thought. I would never call myself Arameri, never.

He sighed and came over, wrapping arms around me from behind and resting his head on my shoulder. I did not understand his constant need to touch me. I didn't mind, but it made me wonder who he cuddled when I was not around. I wondered what price they demanded of him in exchange.

"I was ancient when your kind first began to speak and use fire, Yeine. These petty torments are nothing to me."

"That's beside the point," I said. "You're still..." I groped for words. *Human* might be taken as an insult.

He shook his head. "Only Enefa's death hurts me, and that was no mortal's doing."

In that moment there was a deep, basso shudder throughout the palace. My skin prickled; in the bathroom something rattled for an instant, then went still.

"Sunset," Sieh said. He sounded pleased as he straightened and went to one of my windows. The western sky was layered clouds, spectrum-painted. "My father returns."

Where had he gone? I wondered, though I was distracted by another thought. The monster of my nightmares, the beast who had hunted me through walls, was *father* to Sieh.

"He tried to kill you yesterday," I said.

Sieh shook his head dismissively, then clapped his hands, making me jump. "*En. Naiasouwamehikach.*"

It was gibberish, spoken in a singsong lilt, and for an instant while the sound lingered, my perception changed. I became aware of the faint echoes of each syllable from the room's walls, overlapping and blending. I noticed the way the air felt as the sounds rippled through it. Along my floor into the walls. Through the walls to the support column that held up Sky. Down that column to the earth.

And the sound was carried along as the earth rolled over like a sleepy child, as we hurtled around the sun through the cycle of seasons and the stars around us did a graceful cartwheel turn—

I blinked, momentarily surprised to find myself still in the room. But then I understood. The earliest decades of the scrivening art's history were littered with its founders' deaths, until they'd restricted themselves to the written form of the language. It amazed me now that they'd even tried. A tongue whose meaning depended upon not only syntax and pronunciation and tone, but also one's position in the universe at any given moment—how could they even have imagined mastering that? It was beyond any mortal.

Sieh's yellow ball appeared out of nowhere and bounced into his hands. "Go and see, then find me," he commanded, and threw the ball away. It bounced against a nearby wall, then vanished.

"I'll deliver your message to Kurue," he said, heading toward the wall beside my bed. "Consider our offer, Yeine, but do it quickly, will you? Time passes so swiftly with your kind. Dekarta will be dead before you know it."

He spoke to the wall and it opened before him, revealing another narrow dead space. The last thing I saw was his grin as it closed behind him.

7

Love

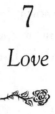

Hᴏᴡ sᴛʀᴀɴɢᴇ. I have only now realized that this whole affair was nothing more than one family squabble pitted against another.

*   *   *

From my window in Sky, it seemed as though I could see the whole of the Hundred Thousand Kingdoms. That was a fallacy, I knew; scriveners have proven that the world is round. Yet it was easy to imagine. So many winking lights, like stars on the ground.

My people were audacious builders once. We carved our cities into mountainsides and positioned our temples to make a calendar of the stars—but we could never have built anything like Sky. Nor could the Amn, of course, not without the aid of their captive gods, but this is not the main reason Sky is deeply, profoundly wrong in Darre eyes. It is blasphemy to separate oneself from the earth and look down on it like a god. It is more than blasphemy; it is dangerous. We can never be gods, after all—but we can become something less than human with frightening ease.

Still... I could not help drinking in the view. It is important to appreciate beauty, even when it is evil.

I was very tired. I had been in Sky for little more than a day, and so much of my life had changed. In Darr, I was effectively dead. I had left no heirs, and now the council would appoint some other young woman, of some other lineage, as *ennu*. My grandmother would be so disappointed—and yet this was nothing more than what she had feared all along. I was not dead, but I had become Arameri, and that was just as bad.

As an Arameri, I was expected to show no favoritism to my birthland and consider the needs of all nations equally. I had not done so, of course. As soon as T'vril and Sieh were gone, I had contacted each of my assigned nations and suggested—knowing full well that a suggestion from an Arameri heir is not a suggestion—that they consider resuming trade with Darr. It had not been an official trade embargo, the lean years since my mother's defection from the Arameri. We could have protested an embargo to the Consortium, or found ways to circumvent it. Instead, every nation that hoped to curry favor with our rulers simply chose to ignore Darr's existence. Contracts were broken, financial obligations abandoned, lawsuits dismissed; even smugglers avoided us. We became pariah.

So the least I could do with my newfound, unwanted Arameri power was to accomplish part of my purpose in coming here.

As for the rest of my purpose... well. The walls of Sky were hollow, its corridors a maze. This left many places wherein the secrets of my mother's death could hide.

I would hunt them down, every one.

*   *   *

I had slept well my first night in Sky. Worn out by shock and running for my life, I didn't even remember lying down.

On the second night, sleep stubbornly refused to come. I lay in the too-big, too-soft bed of my quarters, staring up at the glowing ceiling and walls that made my room bright as day. Sky embodied the Bright; the Arameri allowed no darkness here. But how did the other members of my illustrious family get any sleep?

After what felt like hours of tossing, I finally managed a sort of half doze, but my mind never settled. In the silence I was free to think of all that had happened in the past days, and to wonder about my family and friends back in Darr, and to worry whether I had a hope in the Maelstrom of surviving this place.

Presently, however, it came to me that I was being watched.

My grandmother had trained me well; I came fully awake. But though I mastered the urge to open my eyes or otherwise react, a deep voice said, "You are awake."

So I opened my eyes and sat up, and had to suppress an entirely different urge when I saw the Nightlord standing not ten paces away.

It would do no good to run. So I said, "Good evening, Lord Nahadoth." I was proud that my voice did not quaver.

He inclined his head to me, then just stood there smoldering and looking ominous at the foot of my bed. Realizing that a god's sense of time was probably very different from a mortal's, I prompted, "To what do I owe the honor of this visit?"

"I wanted to see you," he said.

"Why?"

To this he did not answer. But he moved at last, turning and pacing over to the windows, his back to me. He was harder to see there, with the night view as a backdrop. His cloak? hair?—the nimbus of dark that constantly shifted 'round him—tended to blend with the black starry sky.

This was neither the violent monster that had hunted me nor the coldly superior being who had threatened to kill me afterward. I could not read him, but there was a softness to him now that I had glimpsed only for an instant before. When he had held my hand, and bled on me, and honored me with a kiss.

I wanted to ask him about that, but too many things about the memory disturbed me. So instead I asked, "Why did you try to kill me, yesterday?"

"I wouldn't have killed you. Scimina commanded me to leave you alive."

That was curious, and even more disturbing. "Why?"

"I assume because she didn't want you dead."

I was dangerously close to growing annoyed. "What would you have done to me, then, if not kill me?"

"Hurt you."

This time I was glad he was so opaque.

I swallowed. "As you hurt Sieh?"

There was a pause, and he turned to me. The moon, half-full, shone through the window above him. His face had the same faint, pale glow. He said nothing, but abruptly I understood: he did not remember hurting Sieh.

"So you truly are different," I said. I wrapped my arms around myself. The room had grown chilly, and I wore only a thin shirt and pantlets for sleep. "Sieh said something to that effect, and T'vril, too. 'While there's still light in the sky...'"

"By day I am human," said the Nightlord. "At night I am . . . something closer to my true self." He spread his hands. "Sunset and dawn are when the transition takes place."

"And you become . . . that." I carefully did not say *monster.*

"The mortal mind, imbued with a god's power and knowledge for even a few moments, rarely reacts well."

"And yet Scimina can command you through this madness?"

He nodded. "Itempas's compulsion overrides all." He paused then, and his eyes abruptly became very clear to me—cold and hard, black as the sky. "If you don't want me here, command me to leave."

*   *   *

Consider: An immensely powerful being is yours to command. He must obey your every whim. Wouldn't the temptation to diminish him, to humble him and make yourself feel powerful by doing so, be almost irresistible?

I think it would be.

Yes, it definitely would be.

*   *   *

"I would rather know why you've come in the first place," I said. "But I won't force you to explain."

"Why not?" There was something dangerous in his voice. Why was he angry? Because I had power over him and chose not to use it? Was he worried that I would?

The answer to his question came to my mind at once: *because it would be wrong.* I hesitated to say that, however. The answer wasn't even correct—he had entered my room unbidden, a breach of manners in any land. If he had been human, I wouldn't have hesitated to order him out.

No; not human. If he had been *free*.

But he was not free. Viraine had explained further the evening before, during the painting of my sigil. My commands to the Enefadeh had to be simple and precise. I was to avoid metaphors or colloquialisms, and above all *think* about whatever I told them to do, lest I trigger unintended consequences. If I said something like, "Nahadoth, get out," he would be free to leave not only my room, but the palace entire. Skyfather knew what he'd get up to then, and only Dekarta could summon him back. Or if I said, "Nahadoth, be silent," he would be rendered mute until I or some other fullblooded Arameri rescinded the order.

And if I were ever so careless as to say, "Nahadoth, do as you please," he would kill me. Because killing Arameri pleased him. It had happened before, many times over the centuries, according to Viraine. (A service, he called it, as stupider Arameri were usually eliminated before they could breed or embarrass the family further.)

"I won't command you because I'm considering the alliance proposed by your Lady Kurue," I said at last. "An alliance should be based on mutual respect."

"Respect is irrelevant," he said. "I am your slave."

I could not help wincing at the word. "I'm a captive here, too."

"A captive whose every command I must obey. Forgive me if I feel little sympathy."

I did not like the guilt his words triggered in me. Perhaps that was why my temper slipped, before I could think to rein it in. "You are a god," I snapped. "You're a deadly beast on a leash who has already turned on me once. I may have power over you, but I would be a fool to think that makes me safe. Far wiser to offer you courtesy, *ask* for what I want, and hope for your cooperation in return."

"Ask. And then command."

"Ask, and if you say no, accept that answer. That, too, is part of respect."

He fell silent for a long while. In that silence I replayed my words in my head, praying I had left him no opening to exploit.

"You cannot sleep," he said.

I blinked in confusion, then realized it was a question. "No. The bed...the light."

Nahadoth nodded. Abruptly the walls went dim, their light fading until shadows shrouded the room, and the only illumination came from the moon and stars and the lights of the city. The Nightlord was a darker shadow etched against the windows. He had put out the unlight of his face as well.

"You have offered me courtesy," he said. "I offer cooperation in return."

I could not help swallowing, remembering my dream of the black star. If it was true—it had felt true, but who could say with dreams?—then Nahadoth was more than capable of destroying the world, even diminished as he was. Yet it was his simple gesture of putting out the lights that filled me with awe. Tired as I was, I suppose that mattered more to me than the whole of the world.

"Thank you," I managed at last. "And—" There was no subtle way to say it. "Will you leave now? Please?"

He was a silhouette. "All that happens in darkness, I see," he said. "Every whisper, every sigh, I hear. Even if I leave, some part of me will remain. That cannot be helped."

Only later would his words disturb me. For now, I was just grateful. "It will be enough," I said. "Thank you."

He inclined his head, then vanished—not all at once, as Sieh had done, but fading over the space of several breaths. Even after I could no longer see him, I felt his presence, but eventually that faded, too. I felt, properly or not, alone.

I climbed back into bed and was asleep in a span of minutes.

* * *

There is a tale of the Nightlord that the priests allow.

Once long ago, before the war between the gods, the Nightlord descended to earth, seeking entertainment. He found a lady in a tower—the wife of some ruler, shut away and lonely. It was not difficult for him to seduce her. Some while later, the woman gave birth to a child. It was not her husband's. It was not human. It was the first of the great demons, and after it and others like it were born, the gods realized they had made a terrible mistake. So they hunted their own offspring, slaying them down to the tiniest infant. The woman, who had been turned out by her husband and was now deprived of her child as well, froze to death alone in a snowy forest.

My grandmother told me a different version of the tale. After the demon-children were hunted down, the Nightlord found the woman again and begged her forgiveness for what he'd done. In atonement he built her another tower and gave her riches so that she might live in comfort, and he visited her ever afterward to see that she was all right. But she never forgave him, and eventually she killed herself for grief.

The priests' lesson: beware the Nightlord, for his pleasure is a mortal's doom. My grandmother's lesson: beware love, especially with the wrong man.

8

Cousin

THE NEXT MORNING, a servant arrived to help me dress and groom myself. Ridiculous. Still, it seemed appropriate to at least try to behave like an Arameri, so I bit my tongue while she fussed about me. She did my buttons and shifted my clothing minutely as if that would somehow make me look more elegant, then brushed my short hair and helped me put on makeup. The last I did actually need help with, as Darre women do not wear cosmetics. I could not help feeling some consternation as she turned the mirror to show me all in paint. It didn't look bad. Just...strange.

I must have frowned too much, because the servant grew anxious and began rummaging in the large bag she'd brought with her. "I have just the thing," she said, and lifted out something that I thought at first was a party masque. It certainly looked like one, with a wire eyeframe attached to a satin-wrapped rod. But the masque itself was peculiar, seeming to consist only of a pair of bright blue feathery objects like the eyes of a peacock's tail.

Then they blinked. I started, looked closer, and saw that they were not feathers at all.

"All the highblood ladies use these," said the servant eagerly. "They're very fashionable right now. Watch." She lifted the frame to her face so that the blue eyes superimposed her own rather pretty gray ones. She blinked, lowered the frame—and suddenly her eyes were bright blue, surrounded by long, exotically thick black lashes. I stared, then saw that the eyes in the frame were now gray, staring blankly and fringed with the servant's own very ordinary lashes. Then she put the frame back to her face, and her eyes were her own again.

"You see?" She held the rod out to me. Now I could see the tiny black sigils, barely visible, etched along its length. "Blue would look lovely with that dress."

I recoiled, and it took me another few seconds to speak through my revulsion. "Wh-whose eyes were they?"

"What?"

"The eyes, the eyes. Where did they come from?"

The servant stared at me as if I'd asked where the moon had come from. "I don't know, my lady," she said after a flustered pause. "I could inquire, if you like."

"No," I said, very softly. "There's no need."

I thanked the servant for her assistance, praised her skill, and let her know I would have no further need of a dressing servant for the remainder of my stay in Sky.

*   *   *

Another servant arrived shortly afterward with word from T'vril: as expected, Relad had declined my request for a meeting. As it was a rest day, there was no Consortium meeting, so I ordered breakfast and a copy of the latest financial reports on my assigned nations.

As I studied the reports over raw fish and poached fruit—I did not dislike Amn food, but they never seemed to know what to cook and what to leave alone—Viraine dropped by. To see how I was doing, he said, but I had not forgotten my earlier sense that he wanted something of me. I felt that more strongly than ever as he paced about my room.

"Interesting to see you taking such an active interest in governance," he said, as I set aside a sheaf of papers. "Most Arameri don't bother even with basic economics."

"I rule—ruled—a poor nation," I said, draping a cloth over the remains of my breakfast. "I've never had that luxury."

"Ah, yes. But you've taken steps to remedy that poverty, haven't you? I heard Dekarta commenting on it this morning. You ordered your assigned kingdoms to resume trade with Darr."

I paused in the midst of drinking my tea. "He's watching what I do?"

"He watches all his heirs, Lady Yeine. Very little else entertains him these days."

I thought of the magic orb I'd been given, through which I had contacted my nations the night before. I wondered how difficult it would be to create an orb that would not alert the person being observed.

"Have you secrets to hide already?" Viraine raised his eyebrows at my silence, amused. "Visitors in the night, secret trysts, conspiracies afoot?"

I have never possessed the innate talent for lying. Fortunately, when my mother realized this, she taught me alternative tactics. "That would seem to be the order of business here," I said. "Though I haven't tried to kill anyone yet. I haven't turned the future of our civilization into a contest for my amusement."

"If those small things trouble you, Lady, you won't last long here," Viraine said. He moved to sit in a chair across from me, steepling his fingers. "Would you like some advice? From someone who was once a newcomer here himself?"

"I welcome your counsel, Scrivener Viraine."

"Don't get involved with the Enefadeh."

I considered whether to stare at him or feign ignorance and ask what he meant. I chose to stare.

"Sieh seems to have taken a liking to you," he said. "He does that sometimes, like a child. And like a child, he's affectionate; he amuses and exasperates; he's very easy to love. Don't."

"I'm aware that he's not truly a child."

"Are you aware that he's killed as many people over the years as Nahadoth?"

I could not help flinching. Viraine smiled.

"He *is* a child, mind you—not in age, but in nature. He acts on impulse. He has a child's creativity...a child's cruelty. And he is Nahadoth's, blood and soul. Just think about that, Lady. The Nightlord, living embodiment of all that we who serve the Bright fear and despise. Sieh is his firstborn son."

I did think about it. But strangely, the image that came most clearly to mind was Sieh's utter contentment when I'd put an arm around him that first night. Later I would understand that I had already begun to love Sieh, possibly in that very moment.

Some part of me agreed with Viraine: to love such a creature was beyond foolish, edging into suicidal. Yet I did.

Viraine saw me shudder. With perfect solicitousness he came over and touched my shoulder. "You aren't entirely surrounded by enemies," he said gently, and so discomfited was I that for a moment I actually took comfort from his words. "T'vril seems to like you, too—though that isn't surprising, given his history. And you have me, Yeine. I was your mother's friend before she left Sky; I can be yours as well."

If he had not spoken those last words, I might have indeed considered him a friend.

"Thank you, Scrivener Viraine," I said. For once, thank the gods, my Darre nature did not assert itself. I tried to sound sincere. Tried not to show my instant dislike and suspicion. Judging by his pleased look, I succeeded.

He left, and I sat silent in his wake for a long time, thinking.

*　　*　　*

It would occur to me shortly thereafter that Viraine had warned me off only Sieh, not Nahadoth.

*　　*　　*

I needed to know more about my mother.

Viraine had said he was her friend. Everything I knew of my mother said this was a lie. Viraine's strange mix of solicitousness and nonchalance, his callous help and false comfort—no. My mother had always valued people who were straightforward in their dealings with others. I could not imagine her being friendly toward, much less close to, someone like Viraine.

But I had no idea where to begin learning more about my mother. The obvious source for information was Dekarta, though I had no desire to ask him for the intimate details of my mother's past in front of the entire Salon. A private meeting, though...yes. That would suffice.

Not yet, though. Not until I understood better why he had brought me to Sky in the first place.

That left other members of the Central Family, some of whom were more than old enough to have remembered the days when my mother was heir. But T'vril's warning lingered in my mind; any of the Central Family who truly had been friends to my mother were off doing family business, no doubt to keep themselves apart and safe from the viper pit that was life in Sky. No one who remained would speak honestly to me. They were Dekarta's people—or Scimina's, or Relad's.

Ah, but there was an idea. Relad.

He had refused my request for a meeting. Protocol dictated that I not try again—but protocol was a guideline, not an absolute, and among family protocol took whatever form its members permitted. Perhaps a man used to dealing with someone like Scimina would value a direct approach. I went in search of T'vril.

I found him in a spacious, neat little office on one of the palace's lower levels. The walls glowed down here, even though it was a bright day outside. This was because the lower levels of the palace were underneath the broadest part of its bulk and cast into perpetual shadow as a result. I could not help noticing that I saw only servants on these levels, most of them wearing the blood sigil that looked like a simple black bar. Distant relatives, I knew now, thanks to Viraine's explanations. Six generations or more removed from the Central Family.

T'vril was giving instructions to a group of his staff when I arrived. I stopped just beyond the open door, listening idly but not interrupting or making my presence known, as he told a young woman, "No. There won't be another warning. When the signal comes, you'll have one chance. If you're still near the shaft when it comes..." He said nothing more.

The grim silence that fell in the wake of his words was what finally caught my attention. This sounded like more than the usual instructions to clean rooms or deliver food more quickly. I stepped closer to the doorway to listen, and that was when one of T'vril's people spotted me. He must have made some sort of signal to T'vril, because T'vril immediately looked my way. He stared at me for half a breath, then told his people, "Thank you; that's all."

I stood aside to let the servants disperse through the doorway, which they did with a brisk efficiency and lack of chatter that I found unsurprising. T'vril had struck me as the type to run a tight ship. When the room was clear, T'vril bowed me inside and shut the door behind us in deference to my rank.

"How may I help you, Cousin?" he asked.

I wanted to ask him about the shaft, whatever that was, and the signal, whatever that was, and why his staff looked as though he had just announced an execution. It was obvious, though, that he preferred not to speak of it. His movements were ever so slightly forced as he beckoned me to a seat in front of his desk and offered me wine. I saw his hand tremble as he poured it, until he noticed me watching and set the carafe down.

He had saved my life; for that I owed him courtesy. So I said only, "Where do you think Lord Relad might be about now?"

He opened his mouth to reply, then paused, frowning. I saw

him consider attempting to dissuade me, then decide against it. He closed his mouth, then said, "The solarium, most likely. He spends most of his idle time there."

T'vril had shown me this the day before, during my tour of the palace. Sky's uppermost levels culminated in a number of platforms and airy spires, most of which contained the apartments and entertainments of the fullbloods. The solarium was one of the entertainments: a vast glass-ceilinged chamber of tropical plants, artfully made couches and grottoes, and pools for bathing or...other things. T'vril had not led me far inside during our tour, but I'd caught a glimpse of movement through the fronds and heard a cry of unmistakable ardor. I had not pressed T'vril for a further look, but now it seemed I would have no choice.

"Thank you," I said, and rose.

"Wait," he said, and went behind his desk. He rummaged through the drawers for a moment, then straightened, holding a small, beautifully painted ceramic flask. He handed this to me.

"See if that helps," he said. "He could buy himself bucketsful if he wanted, but he likes being bribed."

I pocketed the flask and memorized the information. Yet the whole exchange raised a new question. "T'vril, why are you helping me?"

"I wish I knew," he replied, sounding abruptly weary. "It's clearly bad for me; that flask cost me a month's wages. I was saving it for whenever I needed a favor from Relad."

I was wealthy now. I made a mental note to order three of the flasks sent to T'vril in compensation. "Then why?"

He looked at me for a long moment, perhaps trying to decide

the answer for himself. Finally he sighed. "Because I don't like what they're doing to you. Because you're like me. I honestly don't know."

Like him. An outsider? He had been raised here, had as much connection to the Central Family as me, but he would never be a true Arameri in Dekarta's eyes. Or did he mean that I was the only other decent, honorable soul in the whole place? If that was true.

"Did you know my mother?" I asked.

He looked surprised. "Lady Kinneth? I was a child when she left to be with your father. I can't say I remember her well."

"What do you remember?"

He leaned against the edge of his desk, folding his arms and thinking. In the Skystuff light his braided hair shone like copper rope, a color that would have seemed unnatural to me only a short time before. Now I lived among the Arameri and consorted with gods. My standards had changed.

"She was beautiful," he said. "Well, the Central Family are all beautiful; what nature doesn't give them, magic can. But it was more than that with her." He frowned to himself. "She always seemed a little sad to me, somehow. I never saw her smile."

I remembered my mother's smile. She had done it more often while my father was alive, but sometimes she had smiled for me, too. I swallowed against a knot in my throat, and coughed to cover it. "I imagine she was kind to you. She always liked children."

"No." T'vril's expression was sober. He had probably noticed my momentary lapse, but thankfully he was too much the diplomat to mention it. "She was polite, certainly, but I was only a halfblood, being raised by servants. It would have been strange if she'd shown kindness, or even interest, toward any of us."

I frowned before I could stop myself. In Darr, my mother had seen to it that all the children of our servants got gifts for their birthing days and light-dedication ceremonies. During the hot, thick Darr summers, she had allowed the servants to take their rest hours in our garden, where it was cooler. She'd treated our steward like a member of the family.

"I was a child," T'vril said again. "If you want a better recollection, you should speak to the older servants."

"Is there anyone you'd recommend?"

"Any of them will speak to you. As for which one might remember your mother best—that I can't say." He shrugged.

Not quite what I'd hoped for, but it was something I'd have to look into later. "Thank you again, T'vril," I said, and went in search of Relad.

*   *   *

In a child's eyes, a mother is a goddess. She can be glorious or terrible, benevolent or filled with wrath, but she commands love either way. I am convinced that this is the greatest power in the universe.

My mother—

No. Not yet.

*   *   *

In the solarium the air was warm and humid and fragrant with flowering trees. Above the trees rose one of Sky's spires—the centralmost and tallest one, whose entrance must have been somewhere amid the winding paths. Unlike the rest of the spires, this one quickly tapered to a point only a few feet in diameter, too narrow to house apartments or chambers of any great size. Perhaps it was purely decorative.

If I kept my eyes half-lidded, I could ignore the spire and almost imagine I was in Darr. The trees were wrong—too tall and thin, too far apart. In my land the forests were thick and wet and dark as mysteries, full of tangled vines and small hidden creatures. Still, the sounds and smells were similar enough to assuage my homesickness. I stayed there until the sound of nearby voices pushed my imagination away.

Pushed *sharply*; one of the voices was Scimina's.

I could not hear her words, but she was very close. Somewhere in one of the alcoves ahead, concealed behind a copse of brush and trees. The white-pebbled path beneath my feet ran in that direction and probably branched toward it in some way that would make my approach obvious to anyone there.

To the infinite hells with obviousness, I decided.

My father had been a great huntsman before his death. He'd taught me to roll my feet in a forest, so as to minimize the crackle of leaf litter. And I knew to stay low, because it is human nature to react to movement at eye level, while that which is higher or lower often goes unnoticed. If this had been a Darren forest, I would have climbed the nearest tree, but I could not easily climb these skinny, bare-trunked things. Low it was.

When I got close—just barely close enough to hear, but any closer and I risked being seen—I hunkered down at the foot of a tree to listen.

"Come, Brother, it's not too much, is it?" Scimina's voice, warm and cajoling. I could not help shivering at the sound of it, both in remembered fear and anger. She had set *a god* on me, like a trained attack dog, for her own amusement. It had been a long time since I'd hated anyone so fiercely.

"Anything you want is too much," said a new voice—male, tenor, with a petulant edge. Relad? "Go away and let me think."

"You know these darkling races, Brother. They have no patience, no higher reason. Always angry over things that happened generations ago…" I lost the rest of her words. I could hear occasional footsteps, which meant that she was pacing, toward me and away. When she moved away, it was hard to hear her. "Just have your people sign the supply agreement. It's nothing but profit for them and for you."

"That, sweet Sister, is a lie. You would never offer me anything solely for my benefit." A weary sigh, a mutter I didn't catch, and then: "Go *away*, I said. My head hurts."

"I'm sure it does, given your indulgences." Scimina's voice had changed. It was still cultured, still light and pleasant, but the warmth had left it now that Relad clearly meant to refuse her. I marveled that such a subtle change could make her sound so different. "Very well; I'll come back when you're feeling better. —By the way. Have you met our new cousin?"

I held my breath.

"Come here," Relad said. I knew at once he was speaking to someone else, perhaps a servant; I couldn't imagine him using that peremptory tone with Scimina. "No. I hear you tried to kill her, though. Was that wise?"

"I was only playing. I couldn't resist; she's such a serious little thing. Do you know, she honestly believes she's a contender for Uncle's position?"

I stiffened. So, apparently, did Relad, because Scimina added, "Ah. You didn't realize?"

"You don't know for sure. The old man loved Kinneth. And the girl is nothing to us."

"You really should read more of our family history, Brother. The pattern…" And she paced away. Infuriating. But I did not dare creep closer, because only a thin layer of branches and leaves separated me from them. This close, they would hear me breathing if they listened hard enough. All I had to count on was their absorption in the conversation.

There were a few more comments exchanged between them, most of which I missed. Then Scimina sighed. "Well, you must do as you see fit, Brother, and I shall do the same, as always."

"Good luck." Was this quiet wish sincere or sarcastic? I guessed the latter, but there was something in it that hinted at the former. I could not tell without seeing him.

"And to you, Brother." I heard the click of her heels along the path stones, rapidly fading.

I sat where I was against the tree for a long while, waiting for my nerves to settle before I attempted to leave. My thoughts, too, though that took longer, as they whirled in the aftermath of what I'd heard. *She honestly believes she's a contender.* Did that mean I wasn't? Relad apparently believed I was, but even he wondered, as I did: why had Dekarta brought me to Sky?

Something to ponder for later. First things first. Rising, I began to make my careful way back through the brush—but before I could, the branches parted not five feet away, and a man stumbled through. Blond, tall, well-dressed, with a fullblood mark: Relad. I froze, but it was too late; I was standing in plain sight, caught in midcreep. But to my utter amazement, he didn't see me. He walked over to a tree, unfastened his pants, and began voiding his bladder with much sighing and groaning.

I stared at him, unsure what to be more disgusted by: his choice to urinate in a public place, where others would smell his reek for days; his utter obliviousness; or my own carelessness.

Still, I had not been caught yet. I could have ducked back down, hidden myself behind a tree, and probably gone unnoticed. But perhaps an opportunity had presented itself. Surely a brother of Scimina would appreciate boldness from his newest rival.

So I waited until he finished and fastened his clothing. He turned to go, and probably still wouldn't have seen me if I hadn't chosen that moment to clear my throat.

Relad started and turned, blinking blearily at me for a full three breaths before either of us spoke.

"Cousin," I said at last.

He let out a long sigh that was hard to interpret. Was he angry? Resigned? Both, perhaps. "I see. So you were listening."

"Yes."

"Is this what they teach you in that jungle of yours?"

"Among other things. I thought I might stick to what I know best, Cousin, since no one has seen fit to tell me the proper way Arameri do things. I was actually hoping you might help me with that."

"Help you—" He started to laugh, then shook his head. "Come on, then. You might be a barbarian, but I want to sit down like a civilized man."

This was promising. Already Relad seemed saner than his sister, though that wasn't difficult. Relieved, I followed him through the brush into the clearing. It was a lovely little spot, so meticulously landscaped that it looked natural, except in its impossible perfection. A large boulder, contoured in exactly the right ways to serve as a lounging chair, dominated one side of the space. Relad, none too steady on his feet to begin with, slumped into this with a heavy sigh.

Across from the seat was a bathing pool, too small to hold more than two people comfortably. A young woman sat here: beautiful, nude, with a black bar on her forehead. A servant, then. She met my eyes and then looked away, elegantly expressionless. Another young woman—clothed in a diaphanous gown so sheer she might as well have been nude—crouched near Relad's lounge, holding a cup and flask on a tray. I made no wonder that he'd had to relieve himself, seeing this; the flask was not small, and it was nearly empty. Amazing he could still walk straight.

There was nowhere for me to sit, so I clasped my hands behind my back and stood in polite silence.

"All right, then," Relad said. He picked up an empty glass and peered at it, as if checking for cleanliness. It had obviously been used. "What in every demon's unknown name do you want?"

"As I said, Cousin: help."

"Why would I possibly help you?"

"We could perhaps help each other," I replied. "I have no interest in becoming heir after Grandfather. But I would be more than willing to support another candidate, under the right circumstances."

Relad picked up the flask to pour a glass, but his hand wavered so badly that he spilled a third of it. Such waste. I had to fight the urge to take it from him and pour properly.

"You're useless to me," he said at last. "You'd only get in my way—or worse, leave me vulnerable to her." Neither of us needed clarification on who he meant by *her*.

"She came here to meet with you about something completely different," I said. "Do you think it's a coincidence she mentioned me in the process? It seems to me that a woman does not discuss one rival with another—unless she hopes to play them against each other. Perhaps she perceives us both as threats."

"Threats?" He laughed, then tossed back the glass of whatever-it-was. He couldn't have tasted it that fast. "Gods, you're as stupid as you are ugly. And the old man honestly thinks you're a match for her? Unbelievable."

Heat flashed through me, but I had heard far worse in my life; I kept my temper. "I'm not interested in matching her." I said it with more edge than I would have preferred, but I doubted he cared. "All I want is to get out of this godsforsaken place alive."

The look he threw me made me feel ill. It wasn't cynical, or even derisive, just horrifyingly matter-of-fact. *You'll never get out*, that look said, in his flat eyes and weary smile. *You have no chance.*

But instead of voicing this aloud, Relad spoke with a gentleness that unnerved me more than his scorn. "I can't help you, Cousin. But I will offer one piece of advice, if you're willing to listen."

"I would welcome it, Cousin."

"My sister's favorite weapon is love. If you love anyone, anything, beware. That's where she'll attack."

I frowned in confusion. I'd had no important lovers in Darr, produced no children. My parents were already dead. I loved my grandmother, of course, and my uncles and cousins and few friends, but I could not see how—

Ah. It was plain as day, once I thought about it. Darr itself. It was not one of Scimina's territories, but she was Arameri; nothing was beyond her reach. I would have to find some means of protecting my people.

Relad shook his head as if reading my mind. "You can't protect the things you love, Cousin—not forever. Not completely. Your only real defense is not to love in the first place."

I frowned. "That's impossible." How could any human being live like that?

He smiled, and it made me shiver. "Well. Good luck, then."

He beckoned to the women. Both of them rose from their places and came over to his couch, awaiting his next command. That was when I noticed: both were tall, patrician, beautiful in that flat, angular Amn way, and sable-haired. They did not look much like Scimina, but the similarity was undeniable.

Relad gazed at them with such bitterness that for a moment, I felt pity. I wondered whom he had loved and lost. And I wondered when I had decided that Relad was as useless to me as I was to him. Better to struggle alone than rely on this empty shell of a man.

"Thank you, Cousin," I replied, and inclined my head. Then I left him to his fantasies.

On my way back to my room, I stopped at T'vril's office and returned the ceramic flask. T'vril put it away without a word.

9

Memories

‑‑‑‑‑‑🌹‑

THERE IS A SICKNESS CALLED the Walking Death. The disease causes tremors, terrible fever, unconsciousness, and in its final stages a peculiar kind of manic behavior. The victim is compelled to rise from the sickbed and walk—walk anywhere, even back and forth in the confines of a room. Walk, while the fever grows so great that the victim's skin cracks and bleeds; walk while the brain dies. And then walk a little more.

There have been many outbreaks of the Walking Death over the centuries. When the disease first appeared, thousands died because no one understood how it spread. The walking, you see. Unimpeded, the infected always walk to wherever healthy people can be found. They shed their blood and die there, and thus the sickness is passed on. Now we are wise. Now we build a wall around any place the Death has touched, and we close our hearts to the cries of the healthy trapped within. If they are still alive a few weeks later, we let them out. Survival is not unheard of. We are not cruel.

It escapes no one's notice that the Death afflicts only the

laboring classes. Priests, nobles, scholars, wealthy merchants… it is more than that they have guards and the resources to quarantine themselves in their citadels and temples. In the early years there were no quarantines, and they still did not die. Unless they rose recently from the lower classes themselves, the wealthy and powerful are immune.

Of course such a plague is nothing natural.

When the Death came to Darr a little while before I was born, no one expected my father to catch it. We were minor nobility, but still nobility. But my paternal grandfather had been a commoner as Darre reckon it—a handsome hunter who caught my grandmother's eye. That was enough for the disease, apparently.

Still… my father survived.

I will remember later why this is relevant.

*   *   *

That night as I readied myself for bed, I came out of the bath to find Sieh eating my dinner and reading one of the books I'd brought from Darr. The dinner I did not mind. The book was another matter.

"I like this," Sieh said, throwing me a vague wave by way of greeting. He never lifted his eyes from the book. "I've never read Darre poetry. It's strange—from talking with you I'd thought all Darre were straightforward. But this: every line is full of misdirection. Whoever wrote this thinks in circles."

I sat down on the bed to brush my hair. "It's considered courteous to ask before invading others' privacy."

He didn't put the book down, though he did close it. "I've

offended you." There was a contemplative look on his face. "How did I do that?"

"The poet was my father."

His face registered surprise. "He's a fine poet. Why does it bother you to have others read his work?"

"Because it's mine." He had been dead a decade—a hunting accident, such a typically male way to die—and still it hurt to think of him. I lowered the brush, looking down at the dark curls caught in the bristles. Amn curls, like my Amn eyes. I wondered, sometimes, whether my father had thought me ugly, as so many Darre did. If he had, would it have been because of my Amn features—or because I did not look *more* Amn, like my mother?

Sieh gazed at me for a long moment. "I meant no offense." And he got up and replaced the book on my small shelf.

I felt something in me relax, though I resumed brushing to cover it. "I'm surprised you care," I said. "Mortals die all the time. You must grow tired of dancing around our grief."

Sieh smiled. "My mother is dead, too."

The Betrayer, who betrayed no one. I had never thought of her as someone's mother.

"Besides, you tried to kill Nahadoth for me. That earns you a little extra consideration." He shifted to sit on my vanity table, his rump shoving aside my few toiletries; the extra consideration apparently did not extend that far. "So what is it you want?"

I started. He grinned.

"You were glad to see me until you saw what I was reading."

"Oh."

"Well?"

"I wondered…" Abruptly I felt foolish. How many problems did I have right now? Why was I obsessing over the dead?

Sieh drew up and folded his legs, and waited. I sighed.

"I wondered if you could tell me what you know of…of my mother."

"Not Dekarta, or Scimina, or Relad? Or even *my* peculiar family?" He cocked his head, and his pupils doubled in size in the span of a breath. I stared, momentarily distracted by this. "Interesting. What brings this on?"

"I met Relad today." I groped for words to explain further.

"Quite a pair, aren't they? Him and Scimina. The stories I could tell you about their little war…"

"I don't want to know about that." My voice was too sharp as I said it. I hadn't meant to let him see how much the meeting with Relad had troubled me. I had expected another Scimina, but the drunken, bitter reality was worse. Would I become another Relad if I did not escape Sky soon?

Sieh fell silent, probably reading every thought on my face. So it did not entirely surprise me when a look of calculation came into his eyes, and he gave me a lazy, wicked smile.

"I'll tell you what I can," he said. "But what will you give me in return?"

"What do you want?"

His smile faded, his expression changing to one of utter seriousness. "I said it before. Let me sleep with you."

I stared at him. He shook his head quickly.

"Not as a man does with a woman." He actually looked revolted by the notion. "I'm a child, remember?"

"You aren't a child."

"As gods go, I am. Nahadoth was born before time even existed; he makes me and all my siblings combined look like infants." He shifted again, wrapping arms around his knees. He looked terribly young, and terribly vulnerable. Still, I was not a fool.

"Why?"

He uttered a soft sigh. "I just like you, Yeine. Does there have to be a reason for everything?"

"I'm beginning to think so, with you."

He scowled. "Well, there isn't. I told you; I do what I like, whatever feels good, as children do. There's no logic to it. Accept that or not, as you please." Then he put his chin on one knee and looked away, doing as perfect a sulk as I'd ever seen.

I sighed, and tried to consider whether saying yes to him would somehow make me susceptible to Enefadeh trickery or some Arameri plot. But at last it came to me: none of that mattered.

"I suppose I should be flattered," I said, and sighed.

Instantly Sieh brightened and bounded over to my bed, pulling back the bedcovers and patting my side of the mattress. "Can I brush your hair?"

I could not help laughing. "You are a very, very strange person."

"Immortality gets very, very boring. You'd be surprised at how interesting the small mundanities of life can seem after a few millennia."

I came to the bed and sat down, offering him the brush. He all but purred as he took hold of it, but I held on.

He grinned. "I have a feeling I'm about to have my own bargain thrown back in my face."

"No. But it only seems wise, when bargaining with a trickster, to demand that he hold up his end of the deal first."

He laughed, letting go of the brush to slap his leg. "You're *so* much fun. I like you better than all the other Arameri."

I did not like that he considered me Arameri. But... "Better than my mother?" I asked.

He sobered, then settled against me, leaning on my back. "I liked her well enough. She didn't often command us. Only when she had to; other than that she left us alone. The smart ones tend to do that, exceptions like Scimina notwithstanding. No sense getting to know your weapons on a close personal basis."

I did not like hearing such a casual dismissal of my mother's motives, either. "Perhaps she did it on principle. So many of the Arameri abuse their power over you. It isn't right."

He lifted his head from my shoulder and looked at me for a moment, amused. Then he lay back down. "I suppose it could have been that."

"But you don't think so."

"Do you want truth, Yeine? Or comfort? No, I don't think it was principle that made her leave us alone. I think Kinneth simply had other things on her mind. You could see that in her eyes. A drive."

I frowned, remembering. There had been a driven look to her, yes; a grim, unyielding sort of resolve. There had been flickers of other things, too, especially when she'd thought herself unobserved. Covetousness. Regret.

I imagined her thoughts when, sometimes, she had turned that look on me. *I will make you my instrument, my tool, to strike back at them*, perhaps, though she would have known far better than me how slim my chances were. Or perhaps, *At last, here is my chance to shape a world, even if it is only that of a child.* And now that I had seen what Sky and the Arameri were like, a new possibility came to me. *I will raise you sane.*

But if she had also worn that look during her days in Sky, long before my birth, then it had nothing whatsoever to do with me.

"There was no contest in her case, was there?" I asked. "I thought she was the sole heir."

"No contest. There was never any question Kinneth would be the next head of the clan. Not until the day she announced her abdication." Sieh shrugged. "Even after that, for a time, Dekarta expected her to change her mind. But then something changed, and you could taste the difference in the air. It was summer that day, but Dekarta's rage was ice on metal."

"That day?"

Sieh did not answer for a moment. Abruptly I knew, with an instinct that I neither understood nor questioned, that he was going to lie. Or, at least, withhold some part of the truth.

But that was fine. He was a trickster, and a god, and when all was said and done I was a member of the family that had kept him in bondage for centuries. I could not expect complete trust from him. I would take what I could get.

"The day she came to the palace," Sieh said. He spoke more slowly than usual, palpably considering each word. "A year or so after she married your father. Dekarta ordered the halls empty when she arrived. So that she could save face, you see; even then he looked out for her. He met her alone for the same reason, so no one knows what was said between them. But we all knew what he expected."

"That she was coming back." Fortunately she had not, or I might never have been born.

But why *had* she come, then?

I needed to find that out, next.

I offered Sieh the brush. He took it, sat up on his knees, and very gently began working on my hair.

* * *

Sieh slept in a sprawl, taking over much of the very large bed. I had expected him to cuddle close, but he seemed content merely to have some part of his body in contact with me—a leg and a hand this time, tossed over my own leg and belly respectively. I did not mind the sprawl, nor the faint snoring. I did, once again, mind the daylight-bright walls.

Despite that, I dozed off anyhow. I must have been tired. Sometime later I half-woke and opened my eyes, bleary, to see that the room had gone dark. Since dark rooms at night were normal to me, I thought nothing of it and drifted off again. But in the morning I would recall something—a taste in the air, as Sieh had termed it. That taste was something I had little experience with, yet I knew it the way an infant knows love, or an animal knows fear. Jealousy, even between father and son, is a fact of nature.

That morning I turned over and found Sieh awake, his green eyes dark with regret. Wordlessly he rose, smiled at me, and vanished. I knew that he would never sleep with me again.

10

Family

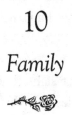

Aᴛᴛᴇʀ Sɪᴇʜ ʟᴇꜰᴛ I ʀᴏꜱᴇ ᴇᴀʀʟʏ, intent upon finding T'vril
before the day's visit to the Salon. Despite his reassurance that
I'd already met everyone who mattered, that had been in refer-
ence to the contest of heirs. In the matter of my mother, I hoped
someone might know more about the night of her abdication.

But I turned left where I should have turned right, and didn't
take the lift far enough down, and instead of T'vril's office I
found myself at the palace entrance, facing the forecourt where
my life's most unpleasant saga had begun.

And Dekarta was there.

*   *   *

When I was five or six, I learned about the world from my Itempan tutors. "There is the universe, ruled by the gods," they told
me. "Bright Itempas is chief among these. And there is the
world, where the Noble Consortium rules with the guidance of
the Arameri family. Dekarta, the Lord Arameri, is chief among
them."

I had said to my mother, later, that this Lord Arameri must be a very great man.

"He is," she'd said, and that was the end of the conversation.

It was not the words that had stuck in my mind, but the way she said them.

*   *   *

Sky's forecourt is the first sight that visitors see, so it is calculated to impress. Besides the Vertical Gate and the palace entrance—a cavernous tunnel of concentric arches, around which stands the intimidating bulk of Sky itself—there is also the Garden of the Hundred Thousand, and the Pier. Of course nothing docks at this Pier, as it juts out from the forecourt over a half-mile drop. It has a thin, elegant railing, about waist-high. This railing would do nothing to stop a person intent on suicide, but I suppose it provides some reassurance to everyone else.

Dekarta stood with Viraine and several others at the foot of the Pier. The group was some ways off, and they had not yet seen me. I would have turned at once and headed back into the palace if I hadn't recognized one of the figures with Dekarta and Viraine. Zhakkarn, the warrior goddess.

That made me pause. The other people present were Dekarta's courtiers; I remembered some of them vaguely from my first day. Another man, not nearly as well-dressed as the rest, stood a few paces onto the Pier, as if gazing at the view—but he was shivering. I could see that even from where I stood.

Dekarta said something, and Zhakkarn lifted a hand and conjured a gleaming silver pike. Pointing this at the man, she took three steps forward. The pike's tip hovered, rock-steady despite the wind, a few inches from the man's back.

The man took a step forward, then looked back. Wind whipped his hair in a wispy cloud about his head; he looked Amn, or of some sister race. I recognized his manner, though, and his wild, defiant eyes. A heretic, flouter of the Bright. Once there had been entire armies like him, but now there were only a few left, hiding in isolated pockets and worshipping their fallen gods in secret. This one must have been careless.

"You cannot keep them chained forever," the man said. The wind carried his words toward me and away, teasing my ears. The protective magic that kept the air warm and calm within Sky apparently did not operate on the Pier. "Not even the Sky-father is infallible!"

Dekarta said nothing to this, though he leaned forward and murmured something to Zhakkarn. The man on the Pier stiffened. "No! You can't! You can't!" He turned and tried to move past Zhakkarn and the jutting pike, his eyes fixed on Dekarta.

Zhakkarn merely moved the pike's tip, and the man impaled himself.

I cried out, putting my hands to my mouth. The palace entrance amplified the sound; Dekarta and Viraine both glanced back at me. But then came a sound that dwarfed my cry, as the man began to scream.

It went through me like Zhakkarn's pike. Hunched around the pike and clutching its shaft, the man's body shivered even harder than before. Belatedly I realized that some other force besides his cry shook him, as his chest began to glow red-hot around the pike's tip. Smoke rose from his sleeves, his collar, his mouth and nose. His eyes were the worst of it, because he was aware. He knew what was happening to him, knew it and despaired, and that, too, was part of his suffering.

I fled. Skyfather help me, but I could not bear it; I ran back into the palace and ducked around a corner. Even that did not help, for I could still hear him screaming, screaming, *screaming* as he burned from the inside out, on and on until I thought I would go mad and hear nothing more for the rest of my life.

Thank all the gods, even Nahadoth, that it eventually ended.

I don't know how long I crouched there with my hands over my ears. After a time I became aware that I was no longer alone, and I lifted my head. Dekarta, leaning heavily on a dark polished cane whose wood might have come from Darr's forests, stood watching me, Viraine beside him. The other courtiers had dispersed down the corridor. Zhakkarn was nowhere to be seen.

"Well," said Dekarta, his voice thick with derision, "we see the truth of it now. It is her father's cowardice that flows strongest in her, not Arameri courage."

That replaced my shock with fury. I leapt up from my crouch.

"The Darre were famous warriors once," said Viraine, before I could speak and damn myself. Unlike Dekarta, his expression was neutral. "But centuries under the Skyfather's peaceful rule have civilized even the most savage races, my lord, and we cannot blame her for that. I doubt she has ever seen a man killed."

"The members of this family must be stronger," said Dekarta. "It is the price we pay for our power. We cannot be like the darkling races, who gave up their gods to save their necks. We must be like that man, misguided though he was." He pointed back toward the Pier, or wherever the dead heretic's corpse was now. "Like Shahar. We must be willing to die—and kill—for our

Lord Itempas." He smiled; my skin crawled. "Perhaps I should have you deal with the next one, Granddaughter."

I was too upset, too angry, to even try to control the hatred in my face. "What strength does it take to kill an unarmed man? To order *someone else* to kill him? And like that—" I shook my head. The scream still rang in my ears. "That was cruelty, not justice!"

"Was it?" To my surprise, Dekarta actually looked thoughtful. "This world belongs to the Skyfather. That is indisputable. That man was caught distributing forbidden books, books which denied this reality. And every one of those books' readers—every good citizen who saw this blasphemy and failed to denounce it—has now joined in his delusion. They are all criminals in our midst, intent on stealing not gold, not even lives, but *hearts*. Minds. Sanity and peace." Dekarta sighed. "True justice would be to wipe out that entire nation; cauterize the taint before it spreads. Instead, I've merely ordered the deaths of everyone in his faction, and their spouses and children. Only those who are beyond redemption."

I stared at Dekarta, too horrified for words. Now I knew why the man had turned back to impale himself. Now I knew where Zhakkarn had gone.

"Lord Dekarta did give him a choice," Viraine added. "Jumping would have been the easier death. The winds usually spin them into the palace's support column, so nothing hits the ground. It's . . . quick."

"You . . ." I wanted to put my hands over my ears again. "You call yourselves servants of Itempas? You're rabid beasts. Demons!"

Dekarta shook his head. "I am a fool to keep looking for anything of her in you." He turned away then and began moving down the hall, slow even with the cane. Viraine fell in beside him, ready to assist if Dekarta stumbled. He looked back at me once; Dekarta did not.

I pushed myself away from the wall. "My mother lived truer to the Bright than you ever could!"

Dekarta stopped, and for a heartbeat I felt fear, realizing I had gone too far. But he did not turn back.

"That is true," Dekarta said, his voice very soft. "Your mother wouldn't have shown any mercy at all."

He moved on. I leaned back against the wall and did not stop trembling for a long time.

* * *

I skipped the Salon that day. I couldn't have sat there beside Dekarta, pretending indifference, while my mind still rang with the heretic's screams. I was not Arameri and would never be Arameri, so where was the point in my acting like them? And for the time being, I had other concerns.

I walked into T'vril's office as he was filling out paperwork. Before he could rise to greet me, I put a hand on his desk. "My mother's belongings. Where are they?"

He closed his mouth, then opened it again to speak. "Her apartment is in Spire Seven."

It was my turn to pause. "Her apartment is intact?"

"Dekarta ordered it kept that way when she left. After it became clear that she would not return..." He spread his hands. "My predecessor valued his life too much to suggest that the apartment be emptied. So do I."

He added then, diplomatic as ever, "I'll have someone show you the way."

*　　*　　*

My mother's quarters.

The servant had left me alone on my unspoken order. With the door closed, a stillness fell. Ovals of sunlight layered the floor. The curtains were heavy and had not stirred at my entrance. T'vril's people had kept the apartment clean, so not even dust motes danced in the light. If I held my breath I could almost believe I stood within a portrait, not a place in the here and now.

I took a step forward. This was the reception room. Bureau, couch, table for tea or work. A few personal touches here and there—paintings on the wall, sculpture on small shelves, a beautifully carved altar in the Senmite style. All very elegant.

None of it felt like her.

I went through the apartment. Bathchamber on the left. Bigger than mine, but my mother had always loved bathing. I remembered sitting in bubbles with her, giggling as she piled her hair on top of her head and made silly faces—

No. None of that, or I would soon be useless.

The bedchamber. The bed was a huge oval twice the size of mine, white, deep with pillows. Dressers, a vanity, a hearth and mantel—decorative, since there was no need for fire in Sky. Another table. Here, too, were personal touches: bottles carefully arranged on the vanity to put my mother's favorites at the front. Several potted plants, huge and verdant after so many years. Portraits on the walls.

These caught my eye. I went to the mantel for a better look at the largest of them, a framed rendering of a handsome blonde Amn woman. She was richly dressed, with a bearing that spoke of an upbringing far more refined than mine, but something about her expression intrigued me. Her smile was only the barest curve of lips, and although she faced the viewer, her eyes were vague rather than focused. Daydreaming? Or troubled? The artist had been a master to capture that.

The resemblance between her and my mother was striking. My grandmother, then, Dekarta's tragically dead wife. No wonder she looked troubled, marrying into this family.

I turned to take in the whole room. "What were you in this place, Mother?" I whispered aloud. My voice did not break the stillness. Here within the closed, frozen moment of the room, I was merely an observer. "Were you the mother I remember, or were you an Arameri?"

This had nothing to do with her death. It was just something I had to know.

I began to search the apartment. It went slowly because I could not bring myself to ransack the place. Not only would I offend the servants by doing so, but I felt that it would somehow disrespect my mother. She had always liked things neat.

Thus the sun had set by the time I finally found a small chest in the headboard cabinet of her bed. I hadn't even realized the headboard had a cabinet until I rested my hand on its edge and felt the seam. A hiding space? The chest was open, stuffed with a bouquet of folded and rolled papers. I was already reaching for it when my eyes caught a glimpse of my father's handwriting on one of the scrolls.

My hands shook as I lifted the chest from the cabinet. It left a clean square amid the thick layer of dust on the cabinet's inside;

apparently the servants hadn't cleaned within. Perhaps they, like me, hadn't realized the headboard opened. Blowing dust off the topmost layer of papers, I picked up the first folded sheet.

A love letter, from my father to my mother.

I pulled out each paper, examining and arranging them in order by date. They were all love letters, from him to her and a few from her to him, spanning a year or so in my parents' lives. Swallowing hard and steeling myself, I began to read.

An hour later I stopped, and lay down on the bed, and wept myself to sleep.

When I awakened, the room was dark.

*   *   *

And I was not afraid. A bad sign.

*   *   *

"You should not wander the palace alone," said the Nightlord.

I sat up. He sat beside me on the bed, gazing at the window. The moon was high and bright through a smear of cloud; I must have slept for hours. I rubbed my face and said, greatly daring, "I would like to think we have an understanding, Lord Nahadoth."

My reward was his smile, though he still did not turn to me. "Respect. Yes. But there are more dangers in Sky than me."

"Some things are worth the risk." I looked at the bed. The pile of letters lay there, along with other small items I'd taken from the chest: a sachet of dried flowers; a lock of straight black hair that must have been my father's; a curl of paper that held several crossed-out lines of poetry in my mother's hand; and a tiny silver pendant on a thin leather cord. The treasures of a woman in love. I picked up the pendant and tried again, unsuccessfully, to determine what it was. It looked like a rough, flattened lump, oblong with pointed ends. Familiar, somehow.

"A fruitstone," said Nahadoth. He watched me now, sidelong.

Yes, it did look like that—apricot, perhaps, or gingko. I remembered then where I'd seen something similar: in gold, around Ras Onchi's neck. "Why...?"

"The fruit dies, but within lies the spark of new life. Enefa had power over life and death."

I frowned in confusion. Perhaps the silver fruitstone was Enefa's symbol, like Itempas's white-jade ring. But why would my mother possess a symbol of Enefa? Or rather—why would my father have given it to her?

"She was the strongest of us," Nahadoth murmured. He was gazing out at the night sky again, though it was clear his thoughts were somewhere else entirely. "If Itempas hadn't used poison, He could never have slain her outright. But she trusted Him. Loved Him."

He lowered his eyes, smiling gently, ruefully, to himself. "Then again, so did I."

I nearly dropped the pendant.

*　　*　　*

Here is what the priests taught me:

Once upon a time there were three great gods. Bright Itempas, Lord of Day, was the one destined by fate or the Maelstrom or some unfathomable design to rule. All was well until Enefa, His upstart sister, decided that she wanted to rule in Bright Itempas's place. She convinced their brother Nahadoth to assist her, and together with some of their godling children they attempted a coup. Itempas, mightier than both His siblings combined, defeated them soundly. He slew Enefa, punished Nahadoth and the rebels, and established an even greater peace—for without His dark brother and wild sister to appease, He was free to bring true light and order to all creation.

But—

*   *   *

"P-poison?"

Nahadoth sighed. Behind him his hair shifted restlessly, like curtains wafting in a night breeze. "We created the weapon ourselves in our dalliances with humans, though we did not realize this for some time."

The Nightlord descended to earth, seeking entertainment— "The demons," I whispered.

"Humans made that word an epithet. The demons were as beautiful and perfect as our godborn children—but mortal. Put into our bodies, their blood taught our flesh how to die. It was the only poison that could harm us."

But the Nightlord's lover never forgave him— "You hunted them down."

"We feared they would mingle with mortals, passing on the taint to their descendants, until the entire human race became lethal to us. But Itempas kept one alive, in hiding."

To murder one's own children...I shuddered. So the priests' story was true. And yet I could sense the shame in Nahadoth, the lingering pain. That meant my grandmother's version of the story was true, too.

"So Lord Itempas used this...poison to subdue Enefa when she attacked Him."

"She did not attack Him."

Queasiness. The world was tilting in my head. "Then…
why…?"

He lowered his gaze. His hair fell forward to obscure his face,
and I was thrown back in time three nights to our first meeting.
The smile that curved his lips now was not mad, but held such
bitterness that it might as well have been.

"They quarreled," he said, "over me."

*   *   *

For half an instant, something changed in me. I looked at
Nahadoth and did not see him as the powerful, unpredictable,
deadly entity that he was.

I wanted him. To entice him. To control him. I saw myself
naked on green grass, my arms and legs wrapped around
Nahadoth as he shuddered upon me, trapped and helpless in
the pleasure of my flesh. Mine. I saw myself caress his midnight
hair, and look up to meet my own eyes, and smile in smug, possessive satisfaction.

I rejected that image, that feeling, almost as soon as it came
to my mind. But it was another warning.

*   *   *

"The Maelstrom that begat us was slow," Nahadoth said. If he
sensed my sudden unease, he gave no sign. "I was born first, then
Itempas. For uncountable eternities He and I were alone in the
universe—first enemies, then beloved. He liked it that way."

I tried not to think of the priests' tales. Tried not to wonder
if Nahadoth was lying, too—though there was a feel of truth to
his words that rang within me on an almost instinctive level.
The Three were more than siblings; they were forces of nature,

opposed yet inextricably linked. I, an only child and a mortal who had never had a beloved of her own, could not begin to understand their relationship. Yet I felt compelled to try.

"When Enefa came along...Lord Itempas saw her as an interloper?"

"Yes. Even though before her we felt our incompleteness. We were made to be Three, not two. Itempas resented that, as well."

Then Nahadoth glanced at me sidelong. In the shadow of my body, for just an instant, the uncertain shift of his face resolved into a singular perfection of lines and features that made my breath catch. I had never seen anything so beautiful. At once I understood why Itempas had killed Enefa to have him.

"Does it amuse you to hear that we can be just as selfish and prideful as humankind?" There was an edge to Nahadoth's voice now. I barely noticed it. I could not look away from his face. "We made you in our image, remember. All our flaws are yours."

"No," I said. "A-all that surprises me are...the lies I've been told."

"I would have expected the Darre to do a better job of preserving the truth." He leaned closer, slow, subtle. Something predatory was in his eyes—and I, entranced, was easy prey. "Not every race of humankind worships Itempas by choice, after all. I would have thought their *ennu* at least would know the old ways."

I would have thought so, too. I clenched my hand around the silver fruitstone, feeling light-headed. I knew that once my people had been heretics. That was why the Amn called races like mine *darkling*: we had accepted the Bright only to save ourselves when the Arameri threatened us with annihilation. But what Nahadoth implied—that some of my people had known the real reason for the Gods' War all along and had *hidden it from me*—no. That I could not, did not want to, believe.

There had always been whispers about me. Doubts. My Amn hair, my Amn eyes. My Amn mother, who might have inculcated me with her Arameri ways. I had fought so hard to win my people's respect. I thought I had succeeded.

"No," I whispered. "My grandmother would have told me..." Wouldn't she?

"So many secrets surround you," the Nightlord whispered. "So many lies, like veils. Shall I strip them away for you?" His hand touched my hip. I could not help jumping. His nose brushed mine, his breath tickling my lips. "You want me."

If I had not already been trembling, I would have begun. "N-no."

"So many lies." On the last word, his tongue licked out to brush my lips. Every muscle in my body seemed to tighten; I could not help whimpering. I saw myself on the green grass again, under him, pinned by him. I saw myself on a bed—the very bed on which I sat. I saw him take me on my mother's bed, his face savage and his movements violent, and I did not own him or control him. How had I ever dared to imagine that I might? He used me and I was helpless, crying out in pain and want. I was his and he devoured me, relishing my sanity as he tore it apart and swallowed it in oozing chunks. He would destroy me and I would love every minute of it.

"Oh gods—" The irony of my oath was lost on me. I reached

up, burying my hands in his black aura to push at him. I felt cool night air and thought my hands would just go on, touching nothing. Instead I encountered solid flesh, a warm body, cloth. I clutched at the latter to remind me of reality and danger. It was so hard not to pull him closer. "Please don't. Please, oh gods, please don't."

He still loomed over me. His mouth still brushed mine, so that I felt his smile. "Is that a command?"

I was shaking with fear and desire and effort. The last finally paid off as I managed to turn my face away from his. His cool breath tickled my neck and I felt it down my whole body, the most intimate of caresses. I had never wanted a man so much, never in my whole life. I had never been so afraid.

"Please," I said again.

He kissed me, very lightly, on my neck. I tried not to moan and failed miserably. I *ached* for him. But then he sighed, rose, and walked over to the window. The black tendrils of his power lingered on me a moment longer; I had been almost buried in his darkness. But as he moved away the tendrils released me—reluctantly, it seemed—and settled back into the usual restlessness of his aura.

I wrapped my arms around myself, wondering if I would ever stop shivering.

"Your mother was a true Arameri," said Nahadoth.

That shocked me out of desire, as suddenly as a slap.

"She was all that Dekarta wanted and more," he continued. "Their goals were never the same, but in every other way, she was more than a match for her father. He loves her still."

I swallowed. My legs were shaky so I did not stand, but I made myself straighten from the hunch that I had unconsciously adopted. "Then why did he kill her?"

"You think it was him?"

I opened my mouth to demand an explanation. But before I could, he turned to me. In the light from the window his body was a silhouette, except for his eyes. I saw them clearly, onyx-black and glittering with unearthly knowing and malice.

"No, little pawn," said the Nightlord. "Little tool. No more secrets, not without an alliance. That is for your safety as well as ours. Shall I tell you the terms?" Somehow I knew that he smiled. "Yes, I think I should. We want your life, sweet Yeine. Offer it to us and you'll have all the answers you want—and, too, the chance for revenge. That's what you truly want, isn't it?" A soft, cruel chuckle. "You're more Arameri than Dekarta sees."

I began to tremble again, not out of fear this time.

As before, he faded away, his image disappearing long before his presence did. When I could no longer feel him, I put away my mother's belongings and straightened the room so that no one would know I had been there. I wanted to keep the silver fruitstone, but I could think of nowhere safer to hide it than the compartment where it had lain undiscovered for decades. So I left it and the letters in their hiding place.

When I was finally done, I went back to my room. It took all my willpower not to run.

11

Mother

TʼVRIL TOLD ME THAT sometimes Sky eats people. It was built by the Enefadeh, after all, and living in a home built by angry gods necessarily entails some risk. On nights when the moon is black and the stars hide behind clouds, the stone walls stop glowing. Bright Itempas is powerless then. The darkness never lingers—a few hours at most—but while it lasts, most Arameri keep to their rooms and speak softly. If they must travel Sky's corridors, they move quickly and furtively, always watching their step. For you see, wholly at random, the floors open up and swallow the unwary. Searchers go into the dead spaces underneath, but no bodies are ever found.

I know now that this is true. But more important—

I know where the lost ones have gone.

*   *   *

"Please tell me about my mother," I said to Viraine.

He looked up from the contraption he was working on. It looked like a spidery mass of jointed metal and leather; I had no inkling of its purpose. "Tʼvril told me he sent you to her room last night," he said, shifting on his stool to face me. His expression was thoughtful. "What is it you're looking for?"

I made note: T'vril was not entirely trustworthy. But that did not surprise me; T'vril doubtless had his own battles to fight. "The truth."

"You don't believe Dekarta?"

"Would you?"

He chuckled. "You have no reason to believe me, either."

"I have no reason to believe anyone in this whole reeking Amn warren. But since I cannot leave, I have no choice but to crawl through the muck."

"Oh, my. You almost sound like her." To my surprise he seemed pleased by my rudeness. Indeed, he began smiling, though with an air of condescension. "Too crude, though. Too straightforward. Kinneth's insults were so subtle that you wouldn't realize she'd called you dirt until hours afterward."

"My mother never insulted anyone unless she had good reason. What did you say to provoke her?"

He paused for only a heartbeat, but I noted with satisfaction that his smile faded.

"What do you want to know?" he asked.

"Why did Dekarta have my mother killed?"

"The only person who could answer that question is Dekarta. Do you plan to talk to him?"

Eventually, I would. But two could play the game of answering a question with a question. "Why did she come here, that last night? The night Dekarta finally realized she wasn't coming back?"

I had expected the surprise in Viraine's face. What I had not expected was the cold fury that followed swiftly on its heels.

"Who have you been talking to? The servants? Sieh?"

Sometimes the truth can throw an opponent off-balance. "Nahadoth."

He flinched, and then his eyes narrowed. "I see. He'll kill you, you know. That's his favorite pastime, to toy with any Arameri foolish enough to try and tame him."

"Scimina—"

"—has no intention of taming him. The more monstrous he becomes, the happier she is. He spread the last fool who fell in love with him all over the centeryard, I hear."

I remembered Nahadoth's lips on my throat and fought to suppress a shudder, only half-succeeding. Death as a consequence of lying with a god wasn't something I had considered, but it did not surprise me. A mortal man's strength had limits. He spent himself and slept. He could be a good lover, but even his best skills were only guesswork—for every caress that sent a woman's head into the clouds, he might try ten that brought her back to earth.

Nahadoth would bring me into the clouds and keep me there. He would drag me further, into the cold airless dark that was his true domain. And if I suffocated there, if my flesh burst or my mind broke...well. Viraine was right; I'd have only myself to blame.

I gave Viraine a rueful smile, letting him see my very real fear. "Yes, Nahadoth probably will kill me—if you Arameri don't beat him to it. If that troubles you, you could always help me by answering my questions."

Viraine fell silent for a long moment, his thoughts unfathom-able behind the mask of his face. Finally he surprised me again, rising from his workbench and going to one of the enormous windows. From this one we could see the whole of the city and the mountains beyond.

"I can't say I remember the night well," he said. "It was twenty years ago. I had only just come to Sky then, newly posted by the Scriveners' College."

"Please tell me all you can recall," I said.

*   *   *

Scriveners learn several mortal tongues as children, before they begin learning the gods' language. This helps them understand the flexibility of language and of the mind itself, for there are many concepts that exist in some languages that cannot even be approximated in others. This is how the gods' tongue works; it allows the conceptualization of the impossible. And this is why the best scriveners can never be trusted.

*   *   *

"It was raining that night. I remember because rain doesn't often touch Sky; the heaviest clouds usually drop below us. But Kinneth got soaked just between her carriage and the entrance. There was a trail of water along the floor of every corridor she walked."

Which meant that he had watched her pass, I realized. Either he'd been lurking in a side corridor while she went by, or he'd followed close enough in her wake that the water hadn't dried. Hadn't Sieh said Dekarta emptied the hallways that night? Viraine must have disobeyed that order.

"Everyone knew why she had come, or thought they did. No

one expected that marriage to last. It seemed unfathomable that a woman so strong, a woman raised to rule, would give it all up for nothing." In the reflection of the glass, Viraine looked up at me. "No offense meant."

For an Arameri, it was almost polite. "None taken."

He smiled thinly. "But it *was* for him, you see. The reason she came that night. Her husband, your father; she didn't come to reclaim her position, she came because *he* had the Walking Death, and she wanted Dekarta to save him."

I stared at him, feeling slapped.

"She even brought him with her. One of the forecourt servants glanced inside the coach and saw him in there, sweating and feverish, probably in the third stage. The journey alone must have stressed him physically, accelerating the disease's course. She gambled everything on Dekarta's aid."

I swallowed. I'd known that my father had contracted the Death at some point. I'd known that my mother had fled from Sky at the height of her power, banished for the crime of loving beneath herself. But that the two events were linked— "She must have succeeded, then."

"No. When she left to return to Darr, she was angry. Dekarta was in such a fury as I've never seen; I thought there would be deaths. But he simply ordered that Kinneth was to be struck from the family rolls, not only as his heir—that had already been done—but as an Arameri altogether. He ordered me to burn off her blood sigil, which can be done from a distance, and which I did. He even made a public announcement. It was the talk of society—the first time any fullblood has been disowned in, oh, centuries."

I shook my head slowly. "And my father?"

"As far as I could tell, he was still sick when she left."

But my father had survived the Walking Death. Surviving was not unheard of, but it was rare, especially among those who had reached third stage.

Perhaps Dekarta had changed his mind? If he had ordered it, the palace physicians would have ridden out after the carriage, caught up to it and brought it back. Dekarta could have even ordered the Enefadeh to—

Wait.

Wait.

"So that's why she came," Viraine said. He turned from the window to face me, sober. "For him. There's no grand conspiracy to it, and no mystery—any servant who'd been here long enough could've told you this. So why were you so anxious to know that you'd ask *me*?"

"Because I thought you'd tell me more than a servant," I replied. I struggled to keep my voice even, so that he would not know my suspicions. "If sufficiently motivated."

"Is that why you goaded me?" He shook his head and sighed. "Well. It's good to see you've inherited *some* Arameri qualities."

"They seem to be useful here."

He offered a sardonic incline of the head. "Anything else?"

I was dying to know more, but not from him. Still, it would not do to appear hasty.

"Do you agree with Dekarta?" I asked, just to make conversation. "That my mother would have been more harsh in dealing with that heretic?"

"Oh, yes." I blinked in surprise, and he smiled. "Kinneth was like Dekarta, one of the few Arameri who actually took our role as Itempas's chosen seriously. She was death on unbelievers. Death on anyone, really, who threatened the peace—or her power." He shook his head, his smile nostalgic now. "You think Scimina's bad? Scimina has no vision. Your mother was purpose incarnate."

He was enjoying himself again, reading the discomfort on my face like a sigil. Perhaps I was still young enough to see her through the worshipful eyes of childhood, but the ways I'd heard my mother described since coming to Sky simply did not fit my memories. I remembered a gentle, warm woman, full of wry humor. She could be ruthless, oh yes—as befitted the wife of any ruler, especially under the circumstances in Darr at the time. But to hear her compared favorably against Scimina and praised by Dekarta...that was not the same woman who had raised me. That was another woman, with my mother's name and background but an entirely different soul.

Viraine specialized in magics that could affect the soul. *Did you do something to my mother?* I wanted to ask. But that would have been far, far too simple an explanation.

"You're wasting your time, you know," Viraine said. He spoke softly, and his smile had faded during my long silence. "Your mother is dead. You're still alive. You should spend more time trying to stay that way, and less time trying to join her."

Was that what I was doing?

"Good day, Scrivener Viraine," I said, and left.

* * *

I got lost then, figuratively and literally.

Sky is not generally an easy place in which to get lost. The corridors all look the same, true. The lifts get confused sometimes, carrying riders where they *want* to be rather than where they *intend* to go. (I'm told this was especially a problem for love-sick couriers.) Still, the halls are normally thick with servants who are happy to aid anyone wearing a highblood mark.

I did not ask for help. I knew this was foolish, but some part of me did not want direction. Viraine's words had cut deep, and as I walked through the corridors I worried at the wounds with my thoughts.

It was true that I had neglected the inheritance contest in favor of learning more about my mother. Learning the truth would not bring the dead back to life, but it could certainly get me killed. Perhaps Viraine was right, and my behavior reflected some suicidal tendency. It had been less than a turn of the seasons since my mother's death. In Darr I would have had time and family to help me mourn properly, but my grandfather's invitation had cut that short. Here in Sky I hid my grief—but that did not mean I felt it any less.

In this frame of mind I stopped and found myself at the palace library.

T'vril had shown me this on my first day in Sky. Under ordinary circumstances I would have been awed; the library occupied a space larger than the temple of Sar-enna-nem, back in my land. Sky's library contained more books, scrolls, tablets, and spheres than I had seen in my entire life. But I had been in need of a more peculiar kind of knowledge since my arrival in Sky, and the accumulated lore of the Hundred Thousand Kingdoms could not help me with that.

Still...for some reason, I now felt drawn to the place.

I wandered through the library's entrance hall and was

greeted only by the sounds of my own faintly echoing footsteps. The ceiling was thrice the height of a man, braced by enormous round pillars and a maze of floor-to-ceiling bookcases. Both cases and pillars were covered by shelf upon shelf of books and scrolls, some accessible only by the ladders that I saw in each corner. Here and there were tables and chairs, where one might lounge and read for hours.

Yet there seemed to be no one else around, which surprised me. Were the Arameri so inured to luxury that they took even this treasure trove for granted? I stopped to examine a wall of tomes as thick as my head, then I realized I couldn't read a single one. Senmite—the Amn language—had become the common tongue since the Arameri's ascension, but most nations were still allowed their own languages so long as they taught Senmite, too. These looked like Teman. I checked the next wall; Kenti. Somewhere in the place there was probably a Darren shelf, but I had no idea of where to begin finding it.

"Are you lost?"

I jumped, and turned to see a short, plump old Amn woman a few feet away, peering around the curve of a pillar. I hadn't noticed her at all. By the sour look on her face, she'd probably thought herself alone in the library, too.

"I—" I realized I had no idea what to say. I hadn't come in for any purpose. To stall, I said, "Is there a shelf here in Darren? Or at least, where are the Senmite books?"

Wordlessly, the old woman pointed right behind me. I turned and saw three shelves of Darren books. "The Senmite starts around the corner."

Feeling supremely foolish, I nodded thanks and studied the

Darren shelf. For several minutes I stared at them before realizing that half were poetry, and the other half collections of tales I'd heard all my life. Nothing useful.

"Are you looking for something in particular?" The woman stood right beside me now. I started a bit, since I hadn't heard her move.

But at her question, I suddenly realized there *was* something I could learn from the library. "Information about the Gods' War," I said.

"Religious texts are in the chapel, not here." If anything, now the woman looked more sour. Perhaps she was the librarian, in which case I might have offended her. It was clear the library saw little enough traffic as it was without being mistaken for someplace else.

"I don't want religious texts," I said quickly, hoping to placate her. "I want...historical accounts. Death records. Journals, letters, scholarly interpretations...anything written at the time."

The woman narrowed her eyes at me for a moment. She was the only adult I'd seen in Sky who was shorter than me, which might have comforted me somewhat if not for the blatant hostility in her expression. I marveled at the hostility, for she was dressed in the same simple white uniform as most of the servants. Usually all it took was the sight of the fullblood mark on my brow to make them polite to the point of obsequiousness.

"There are some things like that," she said. "But any *complete* accounts of the war have been heavily censored by the priests. There might be a few untouched resources left in private collections—it's said Lord Dekarta keeps the most valuable of these in his quarters."

I should have known. "I'd like to see anything you have." Nahadoth had made me curious. I knew nothing of the Gods' War that the priests hadn't told me. Perhaps if I read the accounts myself, I could sift some truth from the lies.

The old woman pursed her lips, thoughtful, and then gestured curtly for me to follow her. "This way."

I followed her through the winding aisles, my awe growing as I realized just how truly big the place was. "This library must hold all the knowledge of the world."

My dour companion snorted. "A few millennia worth, from a few pockets of humanity, nothing more. And that picked and sorted, trimmed and twisted to suit the tastes of those in power."

"There's truth even in tainted knowledge, if one reads carefully."

"Only if one knows the knowledge is tainted in the first place." Turning another corner, the old woman stopped. We had reached some sort of nexus amid the maze. Before us, several bookcases had been arranged back-to-back as a titanic six-sided column. Each bookcase was a good five feet wide, tall and sturdy enough to help support the ceiling that was twenty feet or more above; the whole structure rivaled the trunk of a centuries-old tree. "There is what you want."

I took a step toward the column and then stopped, abruptly uncertain. When I turned back, I realized the old woman was watching me with a disconcertingly intent gaze. Her eyes were the color of low-grade pewter.

"Excuse me," I said, spurred by some instinct. "There's a lot here. Where would you suggest I begin?"

She scowled and said "How should I know?" before turning away. She vanished amid the stacks before I could recover from the shock of such blatant rudeness.

But I had more important concerns than one cranky librarian, so I turned my attention back to the column. Choosing a shelf at random, I skimmed the spines for titles that sounded interesting, and began my hunt.

Two hours later—I had moved to the floor in the interim, spreading books and scrolls around myself—exasperation set in. Groaning, I flung myself back amid the circle of books, sprawling over them in a way that would surely incense the librarian if she saw me. The old woman's comments had made me think there would be little mention of the Gods' War, but this was anything but the case. There were complete eyewitness accounts of the war. There were accounts of accounts, and critical analyses of those accounts. There was so much information, in fact, that if I had begun reading that day and continued without stopping, it would have taken me months to read it all.

And try as I might, I could not sift the truth from what I'd read. All of the accounts cited the same series of events: the weakening of the world, in which every living thing from forests to strong young men had grown ill and begun to die. The three-day storm. The shattering and re-formation of the sun. On the third day the skies had gone quiet, and Itempas appeared to explain the new order of the world.

What was missing were the events leading up to the war. Here I could see the priests had been busy, for I could find no descriptions of the gods' relationship prior to the war. There were no mentions of customs or beliefs in the days of the Three. Those few texts that even touched on the subject simply cited what Bright Itempas had told the first Arameri: Enefa was instigator and villain, Nahadoth her willing coconspirator, Lord Itempas the hero betrayed and then triumphant. And I had wasted more time.

Rubbing my tired eyes, I debated whether to try again the next day or just give up altogether. But as I mustered my strength to get up, something caught my eye. On the ceiling. I could see, from this angle, where two of the bookcases joined to form the column. But they were not actually joined; there was a gap between them perhaps six inches wide. Puzzled, I sat up and peered closer at the column. It appeared as it always had, a set of huge, heavily laden bookcases arranged back-to-back in a rough circle, joined tight with no gaps.

Another of Sky's secrets? I got to my feet.

The trick was amazingly simple, once I took a good look. The bookcases were made of a heavy, dark wood that was naturally black in color—probably Darren, I guessed belatedly; once upon a time we'd been famous for it. Through the gaps I could see the backs of the other bookcases, also blackwood. Because the edges of the gaps were black, and the backs of the bookcases were black, the gaps themselves were all but invisible, even from a few steps away. But knowing the gaps were there...

I peered through the nearest gap and saw a wide, white-floored space corraled by the bookcases. Had someone tried to hide this space? But that made no sense; the trick was so simple that someone, probably many someones, must have found the inner column before. That suggested the goal was not to conceal, but to misdirect—to prevent casual browsers and passersby from finding whatever was within the column. Only those who

knew the visual trick was there, or who spent enough time looking for information, would find it.

The old woman's words came back to me. *If one knows the
knowledge is tainted in the first place* . . . Yes. Plain to see, if one
knew something was there to find.

The gap was narrow. I was grateful for once to be boy-shaped,
because that made it easy to wriggle between the shelves. But
then I stumbled and nearly fell, because once I was inside the
column, I saw what it *truly* hid.

* * *

*And then I heard a voice, except it wasn't a voice, and he asked,
"Do you love me?"*

*And I said, "Come and I will show you," and opened my arms.
He came to me and pulled me hard against him, and I did not see
the knife in his hand. No, no, there was no knife; we had no need
of such things. No, there was a knife, later, and the taste of blood
was bright and strange in my mouth as I looked up to see his terrible,
terrible gaze* . . .

But what did it mean that he made love to me first?

* * *

I stumbled back against the opposite wall, struggling to breathe
and think around blazing terror and inexplicable nausea and
the yawning urge to clutch my head and scream.

* * *

The final warning, yes. I am not usually so dense, but you must
understand. It was a bit much to deal with.

* * *

"Do you need help?"

My mind latched on to the voice of the old librarian with

the ferocity of a drowning victim. I must have looked a sight as I whipped around to face her; I was swaying on my feet, my mouth hanging open and dumb, my hands outstretched and forming claws in front of me.

The old woman, who stood bracketed by one of the bookcase gaps, gazed in at me impassively.

With an effort, I closed my mouth, lowered my hands, and straightened from the bizarre half crouch into which I'd sunk. I was still shaking inside, but some semblance of dignity was returning to me.

"I . . . I, no," I managed after a moment. "No. I'm . . . all right."

She said nothing, just kept watching me. I wanted to tell her to go away, but my eyes were drawn back to the thing that had shocked me so.

Across the back of a bookcase, the Bright Lord of Order gazed at me. It was just artwork—an Amn-style embossing, gold leaf layered onto an outline chiseled in a white marble slab. Still, the artist had captured Itempas in astounding, life-size detail. He stood in an elegant warrior's stance, His form broad and power-fully muscled, His hands resting on the hilt of a huge, straight sword. Eyes like lanterns pinned me from the solemn perfection of His face. I had seen renderings of Him in the priests' books, but not like this. They made Him slimmer, thin-featured, like an Amn. They always drew Him smiling, and they never made His expression so cold.

I put my hands behind me to push myself upright—and felt more marble under my fingers. When I turned, the shock was not so great this time. I half-expected what I saw: inlaid obsid-ian and a riot of tiny, starlike diamonds, all of it forming a lithe, sensual figure. His hands were flung outstretched from his sides, nearly lost amid the flaring cloak of hair and power. I could not see the exulting? screaming? figure's face, for it was tilted upward, dominated by that open, howling mouth. But I knew him anyhow.

Except...I frowned in confusion, reaching up to touch what might have been a swirl of cloth, or a rounded breast.

"Itempas forced him into a single shape," said the old woman, her voice very soft. "When he was free, he was all things beautiful and terrible." I had never heard a more fitting description.

But there was a third slab to my right. I saw it from the corner of my eye. Had seen it from the moment I'd slipped between the shelves. Had avoided looking at it, for reasons that had nothing to do with my rational self and everything to do with what I now, deep down in the unreasoning core of my instincts, suspected.

I made myself turn to face the third slab, while the old woman watched me.

Compared to her brothers, Enefa's image was demure. Undramatic. In gray marble profile she sat, clad in a simple shift, her face downcast. Only on closer observation did one notice the subtleties. Her hand held a small sphere—an object immediately recognizable to anyone who had ever seen Sieh's orrery. (And I understood, now, why he treasured his collection so much.) Her posture, taut with ready energy, more *crouch* than *sit*. Her eyes, which despite her downturned face glanced up, sidelong, at the viewer. There was something about her gaze that was...not seductive. It was too frank for that. Nor wary. But...*evaluative*. Yes. She looked at me and through me, measuring all that she saw.

With a shaking hand, I reached up to touch her face. More rounded than mine, prettier, but the lines were the same as what I saw in mirrors. The hair was longer, but the curl was right. The artist had set her irises with pale green jade. If the skin had been brown instead of marble... I swallowed, trembling harder still.

"We hadn't intended to tell you yet," said the old woman. Right behind me now, though she should've been too fat to fit through the gap. Would've been, if she had been human. "Pure chance that you decided to come to the library now. I suppose I could've found a way to steer you elsewhere, but..." I heard rather than saw her shrug. "You would have found out eventually."

I sank to the floor, huddling against the Itempas wall as if He would protect me. I was cold all over, my thoughts screaming and skittering every which way. Making that first, crucial connection had broken my ability to make others.

This is how madness feels, I understood.

"Will you kill me?" I whispered to the old woman. There was no mark on her forehead. I had missed that, still used to the absence of a mark, not its presence. I should have noticed. She'd had a different shape in my dream, but I knew her now: Kurue the Wise, leader of the Enefadeh.

"Why would I do that? We've invested far too much in creating you." A hand fell on my shoulder; I twitched. "But you're no good to us insane."

So I was not surprised to feel darkness close over me. I relaxed and, grateful, let it come.

12

Sanity

Once upon a time there was a
Once upon a time there was a
Once upon a time there was a
Stop this. It's undignified.

*   *   *

ONCE UPON A TIME THERE WAS A little girl who had two older siblings. The oldest was dark and wild and glorious, if somewhat uncouth. The other was filled with all the brightness of all the suns that ever were, and he was very stern and upright. They were much older than her, and very close to one another even though in the past they had fought viciously. "We were young and foolish then," said Second Sibling, whenever the little girl asked him about it.

"Sex was more fun," said First Sibling.

This sort of statement made Second Sibling very cross, which of course was why First Sibling said it. In this way did the little girl come to know and love them both.

* * *

This is an approximation, you realize. This is what your mortal mind can comprehend.

* * *

Thus went the little girl's childhood. They had no parents, the three of them, and so the little girl raised herself. She drank glimmering stuff when she was thirsty and lay down in soft places when she got tired. When she was hungry, First Sibling showed her how to draw sustenance from energies that suited her, and when she was bored Second Sibling taught her all the lore that had come into being. This was how she came to know names. The place in which they lived was called EXISTENCE—as opposed to the place from which they had come, which was a great shrieking mass of nothingness called MAELSTROM. The toys and foods she conjured were POSSIBILITY, and what a delightful substance that was! With it she could build anything she needed, even change the nature of EXISTENCE—though she quickly learned to ask before doing this, because Second Sibling got upset when she altered his carefully ordered rules and processes. First Sibling did not care.

Over time it came to be that the little girl spent more time with First Sibling than with Second, because Second did not seem to like her as much. "This is difficult for him," First Sibling said, when she complained. "We have been alone, he and I, for so very long. Now you are here, and that changes everything. He does not like change."

This the little girl had already come to understand. And this was why her siblings so often fought with each other, because First Sibling loved change. Often First Sibling would grow bored with EXISTENCE and transform it, or turn it inside out just to see the other side. Second Sibling would rage at First Sibling whenever this happened, and First Sibling would laugh at his fury, and before the little girl could blink they would be on each other, tearing and blasting, until something changed and then they would be clutching and gasping, and whenever this happened the little girl would patiently wait for them to finish so they could play with her again.

In time the little girl became a woman. She had learned to live with her two siblings, each in their own way—dancing wild with First Sibling and growing adept at discipline alongside Second. Now she made her own way beyond their peculiarities. She had stepped in between her siblings during their battles, fighting them to measure her strength and loving them when the fighting turned to joy. She had, though they did not know it, gone off to create her own separate EXISTENCES, where sometimes she pretended that she had no siblings. There she could arrange POSSIBILITY into stunning new shapes and meanings that she was sure neither of her siblings could have created themselves. In time she grew adept at this, and her creations so pleased her that she began to bring them into the realm where her siblings lived. She did this subtly at first, taking great care to fit them into Second Sibling's orderly spaces and arrangements in a way that might not offend him.

First Sibling, as usual delighted by anything new, urged her to do far more. However, the woman found that she had developed a taste for some of Second Sibling's order. She incorporated First Sibling's suggestions, but gradually, purposefully, observing how each minute change triggered others, sometimes causing growth in unexpected and wonderful ways. Sometimes the changes destroyed everything, forcing her to start over. She mourned the loss of her toys, her treasures, but she always began the process again. Like First Sibling's darkness and Second Sibling's light, this particular gift was something only she could master. The compulsion to do it was as essential to her as breathing, as much a part of her as her own soul.

Second Sibling, once he got over his annoyance at her tinkering, asked her about it. "It is called 'life,'" she said, liking the sound of the word. He smiled, pleased, for to name a thing is to give it order and purpose, and he understood then that she had done so to offer him respect.

But it was to First Sibling that she went for help with her most ambitious experiment. First Sibling was, as she had expected, eager to assist—but to her surprise, there was a sober warning as well. "If this works, it will change many things. You realize that, don't you? Nothing in our lives will ever be the same." First Sibling paused, waiting to see that she understood, and abruptly she did. Second Sibling did not like change.

"Nothing can stay the same forever," she said. "We were not made to be still. Even he must realize that."

First Sibling only sighed and said no more.

The experiment worked. The new life, mewling and shaking and uttering vehement protests, was beautiful in its unfinished way, and the woman knew that what she had begun was good and right. She named the creature "Sieh," because that was the sound of the wind. And she called his type of being a "child," meaning that it had the potential to grow into something like themselves, and meaning, too, that they could create more of them.

And as always with life, this minute change triggered many, many others. The most profound of them was something even she had not anticipated: they became a family. For a time, they were all happy with that—even Second Sibling.

But not all families last.

*   *   *

So there was love, once.

More than love. And now there is more than hate. Mortals have no words for what we gods feel. *Gods* have no words for such things.

But love like that doesn't just disappear, does it? No matter how powerful the hate, there is always a little love left, underneath.

Yes. Horrible, isn't it?

*   *   *

When the body suffers an assault, it often reacts with a fever. Assaults to the mind can have the same effect. Thus I lay shivering and insensible for the better part of three days.

A few moments from this time appear in my memory as still-life portraits, some in color and some in shades of gray. A solitary figure standing near my bedroom window, huge and alert with inhuman vigilance. Zhakkarn. Blink and the same image returns in negative: the same figure, framed by glowing white walls and a black rectangle of night beyond the window. Blink and there is another image: the old woman from the library standing over me, peering carefully into my eyes. Zhakkarn stands in the background, watching. A thread of conversation, disconnected from any image.

"If she dies—"

"Then we start over. What's a few more decades?"

"Nahadoth will be displeased."

A rough, rueful laugh. "You have a great gift for understatement, sister."

"Sieh, too."

"That is Sieh's own fault. I warned him not to get attached, the little fool."

Silence for a moment, full of reproach. "There is nothing foolish about hope."

Silence in reply, though this silence feels faintly of shame.

One of the images in my head is different from the others. This one is dark again, but the walls, too, have gone dark, and there is a *feeling* to the image, a sense of ominous weight and pressure and low, gathering rage. Zhakkarn stands away from the window this time, near a wall.

Her head is bowed in respect. In the foreground stands Nahadoth, gazing down at me in silence. Once again his face has transformed, and I understand now that this is because Itempas can only control him so much. He must change; he *is* Change. He could allow me to see his fury, for it weighs the very air, making my skin itch. Instead he is expressionless. His skin has turned warm brown and his eyes are layered shades of black, and his lips make me crave soft, ripe fruit. The perfect face for seducing lonely Darre girls—though it would work better if his eyes held any warmth.

He says nothing that I recall. When my fever breaks at last and I awaken, he is gone and the weight of rage has lifted—though it never goes away entirely. That, too, Bright Itempas cannot control.

*   *   *

Dawn.

I sat up, feeling heavy and thick-headed. Zhakkarn, still near the window, glanced back at me over her shoulder.

"You're awake." I turned to see Sieh curled in a chair beside the bed. Bonelessly he unfolded himself and came to me, touching my forehead. "The fever's broken. How do you feel?"

I responded with the first coherent thought my mind could muster. "What am I?"

He lowered his eyes. "I'm...not supposed to tell you."

I pushed away the covers and got up. For a moment I was dizzy as blood rushed to my head and away, but then it passed and I stumbled toward the bathroom.

"I want you both out of here by the time I'm done," I said over my shoulder.

Neither Sieh nor Zhakkarn responded. In the bathroom I stood over the sink for several painful moments, debating whether to vomit, though the emptiness of my stomach eventually settled the matter. My hands shook while I bathed and dried myself, and drank some water straight from the tap. I came out of the bathroom naked and was not at all surprised to find both Enefadeh still there. Sieh had drawn up his knees to sit on the edge of my bed, looking young and troubled. Zhakkarn had not moved from the window.

"The words must be phrased as a command," she said, "if you truly want us to leave."

"I don't care what you do." I found underthings and put them on. In the closet I took the first outfit I saw, an elegant

Amn sheath-dress with patterns meant to disguise my minimal curves. I picked boots that didn't match it and sat down to work them onto my feet.

"Where are you going?" Sieh asked. He touched my arm, anxious. I shook my arm as I would to get rid of an insect, and he drew back. "You don't even know, do you? Yeine—"

"Back to the library," I said, though I picked that at random because he'd been right; I hadn't had a destination in mind other than *away.*

"Yeine, I know you're upset—"

"*What am I?*" I stood with one boot on and rounded on him. He flinched, possibly because I'd bent to scream the words into his face. "*What? What? What am I, gods damn you? What*—"

"Your body is human," interrupted Zhakkarn. Now it was my turn to flinch. She stood near the bed, gazing at me with the same impassivity she'd always shown, though there was something subtly protective in the way she stood behind Sieh. "Your mind is human. The soul is the only change."

"What does that mean?"

"It means you're the same person you always were." Sieh looked both subdued and sullen. "An ordinary mortal woman."

"I look like her."

Zhakkarn nodded. She might have been reporting on the weather. "The presence of Enefa's soul in your body has had some influence."

I shivered, feeling ill again. Something inside me that was not me. I rubbed at my arms, resisting the urge to use my nails. "Can you take it out?"

Zhakkarn blinked, and I sensed that for the first time I'd surprised her. "Yes. But your body has grown accustomed to two souls. It might not survive having only one again."

Two souls. Somehow that was better. I was not an empty thing animated solely by some alien force. Something in me, at least, was me. "Can you try?"

"Yeine—" Sieh reached for my hand, though he seemed to think better of it when I stepped back. "Even we don't know what would happen if we take the soul out. We thought at first that her soul would simply consume yours, but that clearly hasn't happened."

I must have looked confused.

"You're still sane," said Zhakkarn.

Something inside me, *eating me*. I half-fell onto the bed, dry-heaving unproductively for several moments. The instant this passed, I pushed myself up and paced, limping with my one boot. I could not be still. I rubbed at my temples, tugged at my hair, wondering how much longer I would *stay* sane with such thoughts in my mind.

"And you're still *you*," Sieh said urgently, half-following me as I paced. "You're the daughter Kinneth would have had. You don't have Enefa's memories or personality. You don't think like her. That means you're strong, Yeine. That comes from *you*, not her."

I laughed wildly; it sounded like a sob. "How would you know?"

He stopped walking, his eyes soft and mournful. "If you were her," he said, "you would love me."

I stopped, too, pacing and breathing.

"And me," said Zhakkarn. "And Kurue. Enefa loved all her children, even the ones who eventually betrayed her."

I did not love Zhakkarn or Kurue. I let out the breath I'd held.

But I was shaking again, though part of that was from hunger. Sieh's hand brushed mine, tentative. When I did not pull away this time, he sighed and took hold of me, pulling me back to the bed to sit down.

"You could have gone your whole life never knowing," he said, reaching up to stroke my hair. "You would have grown older and loved some mortal, maybe had mortal children and loved those, too, and died in your sleep as a toothless old woman. That was what we wanted for you, Yeine. It's what you would have had if Dekarta hadn't brought you here. That forced our hand."

I turned to him. This close, the impulse was too strong to resist. I cupped his cheek in my hand and leaned up to kiss his forehead. He started in surprise but then smiled shyly, his cheek warming under my palm. I smiled back. Viraine had been right; he was so easy to love.

"Tell me everything," I whispered.

He flinched as if struck. Perhaps the magic that bound him to obey Arameri commands had some physical effect; perhaps it even hurt. Either way, there was a different kind of pain in his eyes as he realized I had issued the command deliberately.

But I had not been specific. He could have told me anything—the history of the universe from its inception, the number of colors in a rainbow, the words that cause mortal flesh to shatter like stone. I had left him that much freedom.

Instead, he told me the truth.

13

Ransom

WAIT. SOMETHING HAPPENED BEFORE THAT. I don't mean to get things so mixed up; I'm sorry, it's just hard to think. It was the morning after I found the silver apricotstone, three days before. Wasn't it? Before I went to Viraine, yes. I got up that morning and readied myself for the Salon, and found

*　　*　　*

a servant waiting for me when I opened the door.

"Message for you, Lady," he said, looking immensely relieved. I had no idea how long he'd been standing out there. Servants in Sky knocked only when the matter was urgent.

"Yes?"

"Lord Dekarta isn't feeling well," he said. "He will not be joining you for today's Consortium session, should you choose to attend."

T'vril had intimated that Dekarta's health played a factor in his attendance at the sessions, though I was surprised to hear it now: he had seemed fine the day before. And I was surprised he'd bothered to send word. But I hadn't missed that last bit;

a subtle reprimand for my skipping the session the day before. Suppressing annoyance, I said, "Thank you. Please convey my wishes for a swift recovery back to him."

"Yes, Lady." The servant bowed and left.

So I went to the highbloods' gate and transferred myself down to the Salon. As I had expected, Relad was not there. As I had feared, Scimina was. Once again she smiled at me, and I merely nodded back, and then we sat beside each other, silent, for the next two hours.

The session was shorter than usual that day because there was only a single item on the agenda: the annexation of the small island nation Irt by a larger kingdom called Uthr. The Archerine, former ruler of Irt—a stocky, red-haired man who reminded me vaguely of T'vril—had come to lodge a protest. The king of Uthr, apparently unconcerned about this challenge to his authority, had sent only a proxy on his behalf: a boy who looked not much older than Sieh, also red-haired. Both the Irti and the Uthre were offshoots of the Ken race, a fact that apparently had done nothing to foster genial relations between them.

The core of the Archerine's appeal was that Uthr had filed no petition to begin a war. Bright Itempas detested the chaos of war, so the Arameri controlled it strictly. The lack of a petition meant the Irti had had no warning of their neighbor's aggressive intent, no time to arm, and no right to defend themselves in any way that would have caused deaths. Without the petition, any enemy soldiers killed would be treated as murders and prosecuted as such by the law-keeping arm of the Itempan Order. Of course, the Uthre could not legally kill, either—and they hadn't. They had simply marched into the Irtin capital in over-whelming numbers, literally forced its defenders to their knees, and booted the Archerine out into the street.

My heart went out to the Irti, though it was clear to me they had no hope of succeeding in their appeal. The Uthre boy defended his people's aggression simply: "They weren't strong enough to hold their land against us. We have it now. It's better that a strong ruler hold power here than a weak one, isn't it?"

And that was what the whole matter boiled down to. What was *right* mattered far less than what was *orderly*, and the Uthre had proven their ability to keep things orderly by the simple fact that they'd taken Irt without shedding a drop of blood. That was how the Arameri would see it, and the Order, too, and I could not imagine the Nobles' Consortium daring to disagree.

In the end, to no one's surprise, they did not: the Irt appeal was rejected. No one even proposed sanctions against Uthr. They would keep what they had stolen, because making them give it back was too messy.

I could not help frowning as the final vote was read. Scimina, glancing over at me, let out a soft amused snort that reminded me of where I was; quickly I schooled my expression back to blankness.

When the session ended and she and I descended the steps, I kept my eyes forward so that I would not have to look at her, and I turned toward the bathroom so I would not have to travel back to Sky with her. But she said, "Cousin," and at that point I had no choice but to stop and see what in the unknown demons' names she wanted.

"When you've had time to settle in back at the palace, would you be interested in having lunch with me?" She smiled. "We could get to know each other better."

"If you don't mind," I said carefully, "no."

She laughed beautifully. "I see what Viraine meant about you! Well, then; if you won't come out of courtesy, perhaps curiosity will draw you. I have news of your homeland, Cousin, that I think will interest you greatly." She turned and began walking toward the gate. "I'll see you in an hour."

"What news?" I called after her, but she did not stop or turn back.

My fists were still clenched by the time I got to the bathroom, which was why I reacted badly to the sight of Ras Onchi sitting in one of the parlor's plush chairs. I stopped, my hand reaching automatically for a knife that was not in its usual place on my back. I'd chosen to strap it to my calf, under my full skirts, since it was not the Arameri way to go armed in public.

"Have you learned yet what an Arameri should know?" she asked, before I could recover.

I paused, then pushed the bathroom's door firmly closed. "Not yet, Auntie," I said at last. "Though I'm not likely to, since I'm not truly Arameri. Perhaps you could tell me, and stop riddling about."

She smiled. "So very Darre you are, impatient and sharp-tongued. Your father must have been proud."

I flushed, confused, because that had sounded suspiciously like a compliment. Was this her way of letting me know that she was on my side? She wore Enefa's symbol around her neck... "Not really," I said, slowly. "My father was a patient, cool-headed man. My temper comes from my mother."

"Ah. It must serve you well, then, in your new home."

"It serves me well everywhere. Now will you *please* tell me what this is about?"

She sighed, her smile fading. "Yes. There isn't much time. Forgive me, Lady." With an effort that made her knees crack—I winced in sympathy—she pushed herself up out of the chair. I wondered how long she'd been sitting there. Did she wait for me after every session? Again I regretted skipping the previous day.

"Do you wonder why Uthr didn't file a war petition?" she asked.

"I imagine because they didn't need to," I said, wondering what this had to do with anything. "It's nearly impossible to get a petition approved. The Arameri haven't allowed a war in a hundred years or more. So the Uthre gambled on being able to conquer Irt without bloodshed, and fortunately they were successful."

"Yes." Ras grimaced. "There will be more of these 'annexations,' I imagine, now that the Uthre have shown the world how to do it. 'Peace above all; this is the way of the Bright.'"

I marveled at the bitterness in her tone. If a priest had heard her, she'd have been arrested for heresy. If any other Arameri had heard her—I shuddered, imagining her skinny frame walking onto the Pier with Zhakkarn's spear at her back.

"Careful, Auntie," I said softly. "You won't live to a ripe old age, saying such things out loud."

Ras laughed softly. "True enough. I'll be more careful." She sobered. "But think of this, Lady Not-Arameri: maybe the Uthre didn't bother to petition because they knew another petition had *already* been approved—quietly, mingled in with other edicts the Consortium has passed in the past few months."

I froze, frowning. "*Another* petition?"

She nodded. "As you said, there hasn't been a successful petition for a century, so of course two petitions would never be approved back-to-back. And perhaps the Uthre even knew that other petition was more likely to pass, since it served the purposes of someone with a great deal of power. Some wars, after all, are useless without death."

I stared at her, too thrown to hide my confusion or shock. An approved war petition should have been the talk of the entire nobility. It should have taken the Consortium weeks to discuss it, much less approve it. How could anyone get a petition through without half the world hearing of it?

"Who?" I asked. But I was already beginning to suspect.

"No one knows the petition's sponsor, Lady, and no one knows what lands are involved, either as invader or target. But Uthr borders Tema on its eastern side. Uthr is small—bigger now—but their ruling family and the Teman Triadice have links of marriage and friendship going back generations."

And Tema, I realized with a belated chill, was one of the nations beholden to Scimina.

Scimina, then, had sponsored the war petition. And she had kept its approval quiet, though that had probably required a masterwork of political maneuvering. Perhaps helping Uthre conquer Irt had been part of that. But that left two very crucial questions: *why* had she done it? And what kingdom would soon fall victim to the attack?

Relad's warning: *If you love anyone, anything, beware.*

My mouth and hands went dry. I now wanted, very badly, to go and see Scimina.

"Thank you for this," I said to Ras. My voice was higher than usual; my mind was already elsewhere, racing. "I'll make good use of the information."

She nodded and then hobbled her way out, patting my arm in passing. I was too lost in thought to say good-bye, but then I recalled myself and turned, just as she opened the door to leave.

"What is it that an Arameri should know, Auntie?" I asked. It was something I had wondered since our first meeting.

She paused, glanced back at me. "How to be cruel," she said very softly. "How to spend life like currency and wield death itself as a weapon." She lowered her eyes. "Your mother told me that, once. I've never forgotten it."

I stared at her, dry-mouthed.

Ras Onchi bowed to me, respectfully. "I will pray," she said, "that you never learn this for yourself."

*   *   *

Back in Sky.

I had regained most of my composure by the time I went in search of Scimina's apartment. Her quarters were not far from my own, as all fullbloods in Sky are housed on the topmost level of the palace. She had gone one step further and claimed one of Sky's greater spires as her domain, which meant that the lifts did me no good. With a passing servant's aid I found the carpeted stairs leading up the spire. The stairway was not a great height—perhaps three stories—but my thighs were burning by the time I reached the landing, and I wondered why she'd chosen to live in such a place. The fitter highbloods would have no trouble and the servants had no choice, but I could not imagine someone as infirm as, say, Dekarta, making the climb. Perhaps that was the idea.

The door swung open at my knock. Inside I found myself in a vaulted corridor, lined on either side by statues, windows, and vases of some sort of flowering plant. The statues were of no one I recognized: beautiful young men and women naked and in artful poses. At the end the corridor opened out into a circular chamber that was furnished with cushions and low tables—no chairs. Scimina's guests were clearly meant to either stand or sit on the floor.

At the center of the circular room, a couch sat on an elevated dais. I wondered whether it was intentional on Scimina's part that this place felt so much like a throne room.

Scimina was not present, though I could see another corridor just beyond the dais, ostensibly leading into the apartment's more private chambers. Assuming she meant to keep me waiting, I sighed and settled myself, looking around. That was when I noticed the man.

He sat with his back propped against one of the room's wide windows, his posture not so much casual as insolent, with one leg drawn up and his head lolling to the side. It took me a moment to realize he was naked, because his hair was very long and draped over his shoulder, covering most of his torso. It took me another moment to understand, with a jarring chill, that this was Nahadoth.

Or at least, I thought it was him. His face was beautiful as usual, but strange somehow, and I realized for the first time that it was *still*—just one face, one set of features, and not the endlessly shifting melange that I usually saw. His eyes were brown, and not the yawning pits of black I recalled; his skin was pale, but it was a human pallor like that of an Amn, and not the glow of moonshine or starlight. He watched me lazily, unmoving except to blink, a faint smile curving lips that were just a shade too thin for my tastes.

"Hello," he said. "It's been a while."

I had just seen him the night before.

"Good morning, Lord Nahadoth," I said, using politeness to cover my unease. "Are you... well?"

He shifted a little—just enough for me to see the thin silver collar 'round his neck and the chain that dangled from it. Abruptly I understood. *By day I am human*, Nahadoth had said. No power save Itempas Himself could chain the Nightlord at night, but by day he was weak. And... different. I searched his face but saw none of the madness that had been there my first night in Sky. What I saw instead was calculation.

"I am very well," he said. He touched his tongue to his lips, which made me think of a snake testing the air. "Spending the afternoon with Scimina is usually enjoyable. Though I do grow bored so easily." He paused, just for a breath. "Variety helps."

There was no doubt as to what he meant—not with his eyes stripping my clothing as I stood there. I think he meant for his words to unnerve me, but instead, strangely, they cleared my thoughts.

"Why does she chain you?" I asked. "To remind you of your weakness?"

His eyebrows rose a touch. There was no true surprise in his expression, just a momentary heightening of interest. "Does it bother you?"

"No." But I saw at once by the sharpening of his eyes that he knew I was lying.

He sat forward, the chain making the faintest of sounds, like distant chimes. His eyes, human and hungry and so very, very cruel, stripped me anew, though not sexually this time. "You're not in love with him," he said, thoughtful. "You're not that stupid. But you want him."

I did not like this, but I had no intention of admitting it. There was something in this Nahadoth that reminded me of a bully, and one did not show weakness before that.

While I considered my response, however, his smile widened.

"You can have me," he said.

I worried, for the briefest of instants, that I would find the thought tempting. I needn't have worried; all I felt was revulsion. "Thank you, but no."

He ducked his eyes in a parody of polite embarrassment. "I understand. I'm just the human shell, and you want something more. I don't blame you. But..." And here he glanced up at me through his lashes. Never mind bully; what lurked in his face was *evil*, pure and plain. Here was the sadistic glee that had gloried in my terror that first night, all the more disturbing because this time it was sane. This version of Nahadoth gave truth to the priests' warning tales and children's fears of the dark.

And I did not like being alone in the room with him. Not one bit.

"You do realize," he drawled, "that you can never have him? Not that way. Your weak mortal mind and flesh would shatter like eggshells under the onslaught of his power. There wouldn't be enough left of you to send home to Darr."

I folded my arms and gazed pointedly at the corridor beyond Scimina's couch-throne. If she kept me waiting much longer I was going to leave.

"Me, though..." Abruptly he was on his feet and across the room and entirely too close. Startled, I lost my pose of indifference and tried to face him and stumble back all at once. I was too slow; he caught me by the arms. I had not realized until then how very *big* he was, taller than me by more than a head and well-muscled. In his night form I barely noticed his body; now I was very, very aware of it, and all the danger that it posed.

He demonstrated this by spinning me around and pinning me again from behind. At this I struggled, but his fingers tightened on my arms until I cried out, my eyes watering from the pain. When I stopped struggling, his grip eased.

"I can give you a taste of him," he whispered in my ear. His breath was hot on my neck; all over my body my skin crawled. "I could ride you all day—"

"Let go of me right now." I gritted the command through my teeth and prayed it would work.

His hands released me, but he did not move away. I danced away instead, and hated myself for it when I turned to face his smile. It was cold, that smile, which made the whole situation somehow worse. He wanted me—I could see that plainly enough now—but sex was the least of it. My fear and disgust pleased him, as had my pain when he'd bruised my arms.

And worst of all, I saw him relish the moment when I realized he had not lied. I had forgotten: night was the time not just of seducers but rapists; not just passion but violence. This creature *was* my taste of the Nightlord. Bright Itempas help me if I were ever insane enough to want more.

"Naha." Scimina's voice made me jump and spin. She stood beside the couch, one hand on her hip, smiling at me. How long had she been there, watching? "You're being rude to my guest. I'm sorry, Cousin; I should have shortened his leash."

I was feeling anything but gracious. "I haven't the patience for these games, Scimina," I snapped, too angry and, yes, frightened to be tactful. "State your business and let's be done."

Scimina lifted an eyebrow, amused by my rudeness. She smiled over at Nahadoth—no, *Naha*, I decided. The god's name did not fit this creature. He went to stand beside her, his back to me. She grazed the knuckles of one hand along his nearer arm and smiled. "Made your heart race a bit, did he? Our Naha can have that effect on the inexperienced. You're welcome to borrow him, by the way. As you've seen, he's nothing if not exciting."

I ignored this—but I did not miss the way Naha looked at her, beyond her line of sight. She was a fool to take that thing into her bed.

And I was a fool to keep standing there. "Good day, Scimina."

"I thought you might be interested in a rumor I heard," Scimina said to my back. "It concerns your homeland."

I paused, Ras Onchi's warning suddenly ringing in my mind.

"Your promotion has won your land new enemies, Cousin. Some of Darr's neighbors find you more threatening than even Relad or I. I suppose that's understandable—we were born to this, and have no antiquated ethnic loyalties."

I turned back, slowly. "You are Amn."

"But Amn superiority is accepted the world over; there is nothing surprising about us. You, however, are from a race that has never been more than savages, no matter how prettily we dress you."

I could not ask her outright about the war petition. But perhaps— "What are you saying? That someone may attack Darr simply because I've been claimed by the Arameri?"

"No. I'm saying someone may attack Darr because you still *think* like a Darren, though you now have access to Arameri power."

My order to my assigned nations, I realized. So that was the excuse she meant to use. I had forced them to resume trade with Darr. Of course it would be seen as favoritism—and those who saw it as such would be completely right. How could I not help my people with my new power and wealth? What kind of woman would I be if I thought only of myself?

An Arameri woman, whispered a little, ugly voice in the back of my mind.

Naha had moved to embrace Scimina from behind, the picture of an amorous lover. Scimina absently stroked his arms while he gazed murder at the back of her head.

"Don't feel bad, Cousin," Scimina said. "It wouldn't have mattered what you did, really. Some people would've always hated you, simply because you don't fit their image of a ruler. It's a shame you didn't take anything after Kinneth, other than those eyes of yours." She closed her eyes, leaning back against Naha's body, the picture of contentment. "Of course the fact that you *are* Darre doesn't help. You went through their warrior initiation, yes? Since your mother wasn't Darre, who sponsored you?"

"My grandmother," I answered quietly. It did not surprise me that Scimina knew that much of the Darre's customs. Anyone could learn that by opening a book.

Scimina sighed and glanced back at Naha. To my surprise, he did not change his expression, and to my greater surprise, she smiled at the pure hate in his eyes.

"Do you know what happens in the Darre ceremony?" she asked him conversationally. "They were quite the warriors once, and matriarchal. We forced them to stop conquering their neighbors and treating their men like chattel, but like most of these darkling races, they cling to their little traditions in secret."

"I know what they once did," Naha said. "Capture a youth of an enemy tribe, circumcise him, nurse him back to health, then use him for pleasure."

I had schooled my face to blankness. Scimina laughed at this, lifting a lock of Naha's hair to her lips while she watched me.

"Things have changed," she said. "Now the Darre aren't permitted to kidnap and mutilate their boys. Now a girl just survives alone in the forest for a month, and then comes home to be deflowered by some man her sponsor has chosen. Still barbaric, and something we stop whenever we hear about it, but it happens, especially among the women of their upper class. And the part they think they've hidden from us is this: the girl must either defeat him in public combat and therefore control the encounter, or be defeated—and learn how it feels to submit to an enemy."

"I would like that," Naha whispered. Scimina laughed again, slapping his arm playfully.

"How predictable. Be silent now." Her eyes slid to me, side-long. "The ritual seems the same in principle, does it not? But so much has changed. Now Darre men no longer fear women—or respect them."

It was a statement, not a question; I knew better than to answer.

"Really, when you consider it, the earlier ritual was the more civilized. That ritual taught a young warrior not only how to survive but also how to respect an enemy, how to nurture. Many girls later married their captives, didn't they? So they even learned to love. The ritual now... well, what *does* it teach you? I cannot help but wonder."

* * *

It taught me to do whatever was necessary to get what I wanted, you evil bitch.

* * *

I did not answer, and after a moment Scimina sighed.

"So," she said, "there are new alliances being formed on Darr's borders, meant to counter Darr's perceived new strength. Since Darr in fact *has* no new strength, that means the entire region is becoming unstable. Hard to say what will happen under circumstances like that."

My fingers itched for a sharpened stone. "Is that a threat?"

"Please, Cousin. I'm merely passing the information along. We Arameri must look out for one another."

"I appreciate your concern." I turned to leave, before my temper slipped any further. But this time it was Naha's voice that stopped me.

"Did you win?" he asked. "At your warrior initiation? Did you beat your opponent, or did he rape you in front of a crowd of spectators?"

I knew better than to answer. I really did. But I answered anyway.

"I won," I said, "after a fashion."

"Oh?"

If I closed my eyes, I would see it. Six years had passed since that night, but the smell of the fire, of old furs and blood, of my own reek after a month living rough, was still vivid in my mind.

"Most sponsors choose a man who is a poor warrior," I said softly. "Easy for a girl barely out of childhood to defeat. But I was to be *ennu*, and there were doubts about me because I was half Amn. Half Arameri. So my grandmother chose the strongest of our male warriors instead."

I had not been expected to win. Endurance would have been sufficient to be marked as a warrior; as Scimina had guessed, many things had changed for us. But endurance was not sufficient to be *ennu*. No one would follow me if I let some man use me in public and then crow about it all over town. I needed to win.

"He defeated you," Naha said. He breathed the words, hungry for my pain.

I looked at him, and he blinked. I wonder what he saw in my eyes in that moment.

"I put on a good show," I said. "Enough to satisfy the requirements of the ritual. Then I stabbed him in the head with a stone knife I had hidden in my sleeve."

The council had been upset about that, especially once it became clear I had not conceived. Bad enough I had killed a man, but to also lose his seed and the strength it might have given future Darre daughters? For a while victory had made things worse for me. *She is no true Darre,* went the whispers. *There is too much death in her.*

I had not meant to kill him, truly. But in the end, we were warriors, and those who valued my Arameri murderousness had outnumbered my doubters. They made me *ennu* two years later.

The look on Scimina's face was thoughtful, measuring. Naha, however, was sober, his eyes showing some darker emotion that I could not name. If I had to put a word to it, it might have been bitterness. But that was not so surprising, was it? I was not so Darre as, and so much more Arameri than, I seemed. It was something I had always hated about myself.

"He's begun to wear a single face for you, hasn't he?" Naha asked. I knew at once who "he" was. "That's how it starts. His voice grows deeper or his lips fuller; his eyes change their shape. Soon he's something out of your sweetest dreams, saying all the right things, touching all the right places." He pressed his face into Scimina's hair, as if seeking comfort. "Then it's only a matter of time."

I left, goaded by fear and guilt and a creeping, hateful sense that no matter how Arameri I was, it was not enough to help me survive this place. Not Arameri enough by far. That is when I went to Viraine, and that is what led me to the library and the secret of my two souls, and that is how I ended up here, dead.

14

The Walking Dead

WE CURED YOUR FATHER," said Sieh. "That was your mother's price. In exchange she allowed us to use her unborn child as the vessel for Enefa's soul."

I closed my eyes.

He took a deep breath in my silence. "Our souls are no different from yours. We expected Enefa's to travel onward after she died, in the usual manner. But when Itempas...When Itempas killed Enefa, he kept something. A piece of her." It was difficult to catch, but he was rushing his words ever so slightly. Distantly I considered soothing him. "Without that piece, all life in the universe would have died. Everything Enefa created—everything except Nahadoth and Itempas himself. It is the last vestige of her power. Mortals call it the Stone of Earth."

Against my closed eyelids images formed. A small, ugly lump of bruise-dark flesh. An apricotstone. My mother's silver necklace.

"With the Stone still in this world, the soul was trapped here, too. Without a body it drifted, lost; we only discovered what had happened centuries later. By the time we found it the soul had been battered, eroded, like a sail left on a mast through a storm. The only way to restore it was to house it again in flesh." He sighed. "I will admit the thought of nurturing Enefa's soul in the body of an Arameri child was appealing on many levels."

I nodded. That I could certainly understand.

"If we can restore the soul to health," Sieh said, "then there is a chance it can be used to free us. The thing that subdues us in this world, trapping us in flesh and binding us to the Arameri, is the Stone. Itempas took it not to preserve life, but so that he could use Enefa's power against Nahadoth—two of the Three against one. But he could not wield it himself; the Three are all too different from one another. Only Enefa's children can use Enefa's power. A godling like me, or a mortal. In the war, it was both—some of my siblings, and one Itempan priestess."

"Shahar Arameri," I said.

The bed moved slightly with his nod. Zhakkarn was a silent, watching presence. I drew Zhakkarn's face with my mind, matching it against the face I'd seen in the library. Zhakkarn's face was framed like Enefa's, with the same sharp jaw and high cheekbones. It was in all three of them, I realized, though they didn't look like siblings or even members of the same race. All of Enefa's children had kept some feature, some tribute, to their mother's looks. Kurue had the same frank, dissecting gaze. Sieh's eyes were the same jade color.

Like mine.

"Shahar Arameri." Sieh sighed. "As a mortal, she could wield only a fraction of the Stone's true power. Yet she was the one who struck the deciding blow. Nahadoth would have avenged Enefa that day, if not for her."

"Nahadoth says you want my life."

Zhakkarn's voice, with a hint of irritation: "He told you that?"

Sieh's voice, equally irritated, though at Zhakkarn: "He can only defy his own nature for so long."

"Is it true?" I asked.

Sieh was silent for so long that I opened my eyes. He winced at the look on my face; I did not care. I was through with evasions and riddles. I was not Enefa. I did not *have* to love him.

Zhakkarn unfolded her arms, a subtle threat. "You haven't agreed to ally with us. You could give this information to Dekarta."

I gave her the same look that I had Sieh. "Why," I said, enunciating each word carefully, "would I possibly betray you to *him*?"

Zhakkarn's eyes flicked over to Sieh. Sieh smiled, though there was little humor in it. "I told her you'd say that. You do have one advocate among us, Yeine, however little you might believe it."

I said nothing. Zhakkarn was still glaring at me, and I knew better than to look away from a challenge. It was a pointless challenge on both sides—she would have no choice but to tell me if I commanded her, and I would never earn her trust merely by my words. But my whole world had just been shattered, and I knew of no other way to learn what I needed to know.

"My mother sold me to you," I said, mostly to Zhakkarn. "She was desperate, and perhaps I would even make the same choice in her position, but she still did it and at the moment I am not feeling well-inclined towards any Arameri. You and your kind are gods; it doesn't surprise me that you would play with mortal lives like pieces in a game of *nikkim*. But I expect better of human beings."

"You were made in our image," she said coldly.

An unpleasantly astute point.

There were times to fight, and times to retreat. Enefa's soul inside me changed everything. It made the Arameri my enemies in a far more fundamental way, because Enefa had been Itempas's enemy and they were his servants. Yet it did not automatically make the Enefadeh my allies. I was not actually Enefa, after all.

Sieh sighed to break the silence. "You need to eat," he said, and got up. He left my bedroom; I heard the apartment door open and close.

I had slept nearly three days. My angry declaration that I would leave had been a bluff; my hands were shaking, and I did not trust my ability to walk far if I tried. I looked down at my unsteady hand and thought sourly that if the Enefadeh had infected me with a goddess's soul, the least they could have done was give me a stronger body in the process.

"Sieh loves you," said Zhakkarn.

I put my hand on the bed so it would no longer shake. "I know."

"No, you don't." The sharpness in Zhakkarn's voice made me look up. She was still angry, and I realized now that it had nothing to do with the alliance. She was angry about how I'd treated Sieh.

"What would you do, if you were me?" I asked. "Surrounded by secrets, with your life dependent on the answers?"

"I would do as you have done." That surprised me. "I would use every possible advantage I had to gain as much information as I could, and I would not apologize for doing so. But I am not the mother Sieh has missed for so long."

I could tell already that I was going to become very, very sick of being compared to a goddess.

"Neither am I," I snapped.

"Sieh knows that. And yet he loves you." Zhakkarn sighed. "He is a child."

"He's older than you, isn't he?"

"Age means nothing to us. What matters is staying true to one's nature. Sieh has devoted himself fully to the path of childhood. It is a difficult one."

I could imagine, though it made no sense to me. Enefa's soul seemed to bring me no special insight into the tribulations of godhood.

"What do you want me to do?" I asked. I felt weary, though that might've been the hunger. "Shall I cuddle him to my breast when he comes back, and tell him everything will be all right? Should I do the same for you?"

"You should not hurt him again," she said, and vanished.

I gazed at the spot where she had stood for a long while. I was still staring at it when Sieh returned, setting a platter in front of me.

"The servants here don't ask questions," he said. "Safer that way. So T'vril didn't know you'd been unwell until I showed up and asked for food. He's tearing a strip out of the servants assigned to you right now."

The platter held a Darren feast. Maash paste and fish rolled in callena leaves, with a side of fire-toasted golden peppers. A shallow boat of serry relish and thin, crisp-curled slices of meat. In my land it would've been the heart of a particular species of sloth; this was probably beef. And a true treasure: a whole roasted gran banana. My favorite dessert, though how T'vril had found that out I would never know.

I picked up a leafroll, and my hand trembled with more than hunger.

"Dekarta doesn't mean for you to win the contest," Sieh said softly. "That isn't why he's brought you here. He intends for *you* to choose between Relad and Scimina."

I looked sharply at him, and recalled the conversation I'd overheard between Relad and Scimina in the solarium. Was this what Scimina had meant? "Choose between them?"

"The Arameri ritual of succession. To become the next head of the family, one of the heirs must transfer the master sigil—the mark Dekarta wears—from Dekarta's brow to his own. Or her own. The master sigil outranks all the rest; whoever wears it has absolute power over us, the rest of the family, and the world."

"The rest of the family?" I frowned. They had hinted at this before, when they altered my own sigil. "So that's it. What do the blood sigils really do? Allow Dekarta to read our thoughts? Burn out our brains if we refuse to obey?"

"No, nothing so dramatic. There are some protective spells built in for highbloods, to guard against assassins and the like, but among the family they simply compel loyalty. No one who wears a sigil can act against the interests of the family head. If not for measures like that, Scimina would have found a way to undermine or kill Dekarta long ago."

The leafroll smelled too good. I bit off a piece, making myself chew slowly as I mulled over Sieh's words. The fish was strange— some local species, similar to but not the same as the speckled ui usually used. Still good. I was ravenous, but I knew better than to bolt my food after days without.

"The Stone of Earth is used in the succession ritual. Someone—an Arameri, by Itempas's own decree—must wield its power to transfer the master sigil."

"An Arameri." Another puzzle piece slipped into place. "Anyone in Sky can do this? Everyone, down to the lowliest servant?"

Sieh nodded slowly. I noticed he did not blink when he was intent on something. A minor slip.

"Any Arameri, however distant from the Central Family. For just one moment, that person becomes one of the Three."

It was obvious in his wording. That person. For one moment.

It would be like striking a match, I imagined, having that much power course through mortal flesh. A bright flare, perhaps a few seconds of steady flame. And then...

"Then that person dies," I said.

Sieh gave me his unchildlike smile. "Yes."

Clever, so clever, my Arameri foremothers. By forcing all relatives however distant to serve here, they had in place a virtual army of people who could be sacrificed to wield the Stone. Even if each used it only for a moment, the Arameri—the highbloods, at least, who would die last—could still approximate the power of a goddess for a considerable time.

"So Dekarta means for me to be that mortal," I said. "Why?"

"The head of this clan must have the strength to kill even loved ones." Sieh shrugged. "It's easy to sentence a servant to die, but what about a friend? A husband?"

"Relad and Scimina barely knew I was alive before Dekarta brought me here. Why did he choose me?"

"That, only he knows."

I was growing angry again, but this was a frustrated, directionless sort of anger. I'd thought the Enefadeh had all the answers. Of course it wouldn't be that easy.

"Why in the Maelstrom would *you* use me, anyhow?" I asked, annoyed. "Doesn't that put Enefa's soul too close to the very people who would destroy it if they could?"

Sieh rubbed his nose, abruptly looking abashed. "Ah . . . well . . . that was my idea. It's always easier to hide something right under a person's nose, you see? And Dekarta's love for Kinneth was well known; we thought that would make you safe. No one expected him to kill her—certainly not after twenty years. All of us were caught off guard by that."

I made myself take another bite of the leafroll, chewing on more than its fragrant wrapping. No one had expected my mother's death. And yet, some part of me—the still-grieving, angry part of me—felt they should have known. They should have warned her. They should have prevented it.

"But listen." Sieh leaned forward. "The Stone is what's left of Enefa's body. Because you possess Enefa's soul, you can wield the Stone's power in ways that no one but Enefa herself could do. If *you* held the Stone, Yeine, you could change the shape of the universe. You could set us free like that." He snapped his fingers.

"Then die."

Sieh lowered his eyes, his enthusiasm fading. "That wasn't the original plan," he said, "but yes."

I finished the leafroll and looked at the rest of the plate without enthusiasm. My appetite had vanished. But anger—

slow-building and fierce, almost as hot as my anger over my mother's murder—was beginning to take its place.

"*You* mean for me to lose the contest, too," I said softly.

"Well . . . yes."

"What will you offer me? If I accept this alliance?"

He grew very still. "Protection for your land through the war that would follow our release. And favor forever after our victory. We keep our vows, Yeine, believe me."

I believed him. And the eternal blessing of four gods was indeed a powerful temptation. That would guarantee safety and prosperity for Darr, if we could get through this time of trial. The Enefadeh knew my heart well.

But then, they thought they already knew my soul.

"I want that and one thing more," I said. "I'll do as you wish, Sieh, even if it costs me my life. Revenge against my mother's killer is worth that. I'll take up the Stone and use it to set you free, and die. But not as some humbled, beaten sacrifice." I glared at him. "I want to win this contest."

His lovely green eyes went wide.

"Yeine," he began, "that's impossible. Dekarta and Relad and Scimina . . . they're all against you. You haven't got a chance."

"You're the instigator of this whole plot, aren't you? Surely the god of mischief can think of a way."

"*Mischief*, not politics!"

"You should go and tell the others my terms." I made myself pick up the fork and eat some relish.

Sieh stared at me, then finally let out a shaky laugh. "I don't believe this. You're crazier than Naha." He got to his feet and rubbed a hand over his hair. "You—gods." He seemed not to notice the strangeness of his oath. "I'll talk to them."

I inclined my head formally. "I shall await your answer."

Muttering in his strange language, Sieh summoned his yellow ball and left through the bedroom wall.

They would accept, of course. Whether I won or lost, they would get the freedom they wanted—unless, of course, I chose not to give it to them. So they would do whatever it took to keep me agreeable.

Reaching for another leafroll, I concentrated on chewing slowly so that my ill-used stomach would not rebel. It was important that I recover quickly. I would need my strength in the time to come.

15

Hatred

I SEE MY LAND BELOW ME. It passes underneath, as if I am flying. High ridges and misty, tangled valleys. Occasional fields, even rarer towns and cities. Darr is so green. I saw many lands as I traveled across High North and Senm on the way to Sky, and none of them seemed half as green as my beautiful Darr. Now I know why.

* * *

I slept again. When I woke, Sieh still had not returned, and it was night. I did not expect an answer from the Enefadeh anytime soon. I had probably annoyed them by my refusal to trudge obediently to death. If I were them, I would keep me waiting awhile.

Almost as soon as I woke, there was a knock at the door. When I went to answer, a bony-faced servant boy stood very straight and said, with painful formality, "Lady Yeine. I bear a message."

Rubbing sleep from my eyes, I nodded permission for him to continue, and he said, "Your grandsire requests your presence."

And suddenly I was very, very awake.

*   *   *

The audience chamber was empty this time. Just me and Dekarta. I knelt as I had that first afternoon, and laid my knife on the floor as was customary. I did not, to my own surprise, contemplate using it to kill him. Much as I hated him, his blood was not what I wanted.

"Well," he said from his throne. His voice sounded softer than before, though that may have been a trick of perception on my part. "Have you enjoyed your week as an Arameri, Granddaughter?"

Had it been only a week?

"No, Grandfather," I said. "I have not."

He uttered a single laugh. "But now, perhaps, you understand us better. What do you think?"

This I had not expected. I looked at him from where I knelt, and wondered what he was up to.

"I think," I said slowly, "the same thing that I thought before I came here: that the Arameri are evil. All that has changed is that now I believe most of you are mad as well."

He grinned, wide and partially toothless. "Kinneth said much the same thing to me once. She included herself, however."

I resisted the immediate urge to deny this. "Maybe that's why she left. Maybe, if I stay long enough, I'll become as evil and mad as the rest of you."

"Maybe." There was a curious gentleness in the way he said this that threw me. I could never read his face. Too many lines.

Silence rose between us for the next several breaths. It plateaued; stalled; broke.

"Tell me why you killed my mother," I said.

His smile faded. "I am not one of the Enefadeh, Grand-daughter. You cannot command answers from me."

Heat washed through me, followed by cold. I rose slowly to my feet. "You loved her. If you had hated her, feared her, that I could have understood. But you loved her."

He nodded. "I loved her."

"She was crying when she died. We had to wet her eyelids to get them open—"

"You will be silent."

In the empty chamber, his voice echoed. The edge of it sawed against my temper like a dull knife.

"And you love her *still*, you hateful old bastard." I stepped forward, leaving my knife on the floor. I did not trust myself with it anymore. I moved toward my grandfather's highbacked not-throne, and he drew himself up, perhaps in anger, perhaps in fear. "You love her and mourn her; it's your own fault and you *mourn* her, and you want her back. Don't you? But if Itempas is listening, if he cares at all about order and righteousness or any of the things the priests say, then I pray to him now that you keep loving her. That way you'll feel her loss the way I do. You'll feel that agony until you die, and I pray that's a long, long time from now!"

By this point I stood before Dekarta, bent down, my hands on the armrests of his chair. I was close enough to see the color of his eyes at last—a blue so pale that it was barely a color at all. He was a small, frail man now, whatever he'd been in his prime. If I blew hard, I might break his bones.

But I did not touch him. Dekarta did not deserve mere physical pain any more than he deserved a swift death.

"Such hate," he whispered. Then, to my shock, he smiled. It looked like a death rictus. "Perhaps you are more like her than I thought."

I stood up straight and told myself that I was not drawing back.

"Very well," said Dekarta, as if we'd just exchanged pleasant small talk. "We should get down to business, Granddaughter. In seven days' time, on the night of the fourteenth, there will be a ball here in Sky. It will be in your honor, to celebrate your elevation to heir, and some of the most noteworthy citizens of the world will join us as guests. Is there anyone in particular you'd like invited?"

I stared at him and heard an entirely different conversation. *In seven days the most noteworthy citizens in the world will gather to watch you die.* Every mote of intuition in my body understood: the succession ceremony.

His question hovered unanswered in the air between us.

"No," I said softly. "No one."

Dekarta inclined his head. "Then you are dismissed, Granddaughter."

I stared at him for a long moment. I might never again have the chance to speak with him like this, in private. He had not told me why he'd killed my mother, but there were other secrets that he might be willing to divulge. He might even know the secret of how I might save myself.

But in the long silence I could think of no questions to ask, no way to get at those secrets. So at last I picked up my knife and walked out of the room, and tried not to feel a sense of shame as the guards closed the door behind me.

*　　*　　*

This turned out to be the start of a very bad night.

*　　*　　*

I stepped inside my apartment and found that I had visitors.

Kurue had appropriated the chair, where she sat with her fingers steepled, a hard look in her eyes. Sieh, perched on the edge of my parlor's couch, sat with his knees drawn up and his eyes downcast. Zhakkarn stood sentinel near the window, impassive as ever. Nahadoth—

I felt his presence behind me an instant before he put his hand through my chest.

"Tell me," he said into my ear, "why I should not kill you."

I stared at the hand through my chest. There was no blood, and as far as I could tell there was no wound. I fumbled for his hand and found that it was immaterial, like a shadow. My fingers passed through his flesh and waggled in the translucence of his fist. It did not hurt exactly, but it felt as though I'd plunged my fingers into an icy stream. There was a deep, aching coldness between my breasts.

He could withdraw his hand and tear out my heart. He could leave his hand in place but make it tangible, and kill me as surely as if he'd punched through blood and bone.

"Nahadoth," Kurue said in a warning tone.

Sieh jumped up and came to my side, his eyes wide and frightened. "Please don't kill her. Please."

"She's one of them," he hissed in my ear. His breath was cold as well, making the flesh of my neck prickle in goose bumps. "Just another Arameri convinced of her own superiority. We *made* her, Sieh, and she dares to command us? She has no right to carry my sister's soul." His hand curled into a claw, and suddenly I realized it was not my flesh that he meant to damage.

Your body has grown used to containing two souls, Zhakkarn had said. *It might not survive having only one again.*

But at that realization, completely to my own surprise, I burst into laughter.

"Do it," I said. I could hardly breathe for laughing, though that might've been some effect of Nahadoth's hand. "I never wanted this thing in me in the first place. If you want it, take it!"

"Yeine!" Sieh clutched my arm. "That could kill you!"

"What difference does it make? You want to kill me anyway. So does Dekarta—he's got it all planned, seven days from now. My only real choice lies in *how* I die. This is as good as any other method, isn't it?"

"Let's find out," Nahadoth said.

Kurue sat forward. "Wait, what did she—"

Nahadoth drew his hand back. It seemed to take effort; the arm moved through my flesh slowly, as if through clay. I could not be more certain because I was shrieking at the top of my lungs. Instinctively I lunged forward, trying to escape the pain, and in retrospect this made things worse. But I could not think, all my reason having been subsumed by agony. It felt as though I was being torn apart—as, of course, I was.

But then something happened.

*   *   *

Above, a sky out of nightmare. I could not say if it was day or night. Both sun and moon were visible, but it was hard to say which was which. The moon was huge and cancerously yellow. The sun was a bloody distortion, nowhere near round. There was a single cloud in the sky and it was black—not dark gray with rain but black, like a drifting hole in the sky. And then I realized it was a hole, because something fell through—

Tiny figures, struggling. One of them was white and blazing, the other black and smoking; as they tumbled, I could see fire and hear cracks like thunder all around them. They fell and fell and smashed into the earth nearby. The ground shook, a great cloud of dust and debris kicked up from the impact; nothing human could have survived such a fall, but I knew they were not—

I ran. All around me were bodies—not dead, I understood with the certainty of a dream, but dying. The grass was dry and dessicated, crackling beneath my bare feet. Enefa was dead. Everything was dying. Leaves fell around me like heavy snow. Ahead, just through the trees—

"Is this what you want? Is it?" Inhuman fury in that voice, echoing through the forest shadows. Following it came a scream of such agony as I have never imagined—

I ran through the trees and stopped at the edge of a crater and saw—

O Goddess, I saw—

*   *   *

"Yeine." A hand slapped my face lightly. "Yeine!"

My eyes were open. I blinked because they were dry. I was on my knees on the floor. Sieh crouched before me, his eyes wide with concern. Kurue and Zhakkarn were watching, too, Kurue looking worried and Zhakkarn soldier-still.

I did not think. I swung around and looked at Nahadoth, who stood with one hand—the one that had been in my body—still raised. He stared down at me, and I realized he somehow knew what I had seen.

"I don't understand." Kurue rose from the desk chair. Her hand, on the chair's back, tightened. "It's been twenty years. The soul should be able to survive extraction by now."

"No one has ever put a god's soul into a mortal," said Zhakkarn. "We knew there was a risk."

"Not of *this*!" Kurue pointed at me almost accusingly. "Will the soul even be usable now, contaminated with this mortal filth?"

"Be silent!" Sieh snapped, whipping around to glare at her. His voice dropped suddenly, a young man's again; instant puberty. "How dare you? I have told you time and again—mortals are as much Enefa's creations as we ourselves."

"Leftovers," Kurue retorted. "Weak and cowardly and too stupid to look beyond themselves for more than five minutes. Yet you and Naha will insist on putting your trust in them—"

Sieh rolled his eyes. "Oh, *please*. Tell me, Kurue, which of your proud, god-only plans has gotten us free?"

Kurue turned away in resentful silence.

I barely saw all this. Nahadoth and I were still staring at each other.

"Yeine." Sieh's small, soft hand touched my cheek, coaxing my head around to face him. His voice had returned to a childish treble. "Are you all right?"

"What happened?" I asked.

"We're not certain."

I sighed and pulled away from him, trying to get to my feet. My body felt hollowed out, stuffed with cotton. I slipped and settled onto my knees again, and cursed.

"Yeine—"

"If you're going to lie to me again, don't bother."

A muscle worked in Sieh's jaw; he glanced at his siblings. "It's true, Yeine. We *aren't* certain. But . . . for some reason . . . Enefa's soul has not healed as much as we hoped it would in the time since we put it in you. It's whole," and here he glanced at Kurue significantly. "Enough to serve its purpose. But it's very fragile—too fragile to be drawn out safely."

Safely for the soul, he meant, not for me. I shook my head, too tired to laugh.

"No telling how much damage has been done," Kurue muttered, turning away to pace the room's small confines.

"An unused limb withers," Zhakkarn said softly. "She had her own soul, and no need for another."

Which I would happily have told you, I thought sourly, *if I'd been able to protest at the time.*

But what in the Maelstrom did all this mean for me? That the Enefadeh would make no further attempt to draw the soul from my body? Good, since I had no desire to experience that pain ever again. But it also meant that they were committed to their plan now, because they couldn't get the thing out of me otherwise.

Was that, then, why I had all these strange dreams and visions? Because a goddess's soul had begun to rot inside me?

Demons and darkness. Like a compass needle seeking north, I swung back around to look at Nahadoth. He turned away.

"What did you say earlier?" Kurue suddenly demanded. "About Dekarta."

That particular concern seemed a million miles away. I pulled myself back to it, the here and now, and tried to push from my mind that terrible sky and the image of shining hands gripping and twisting flesh.

"Dekarta is throwing a ball in my honor," I replied, "in one week. To celebrate my designation as one of the possible heirs." I shook my head. "Who knows? Maybe it's just a ball."

The Enefadeh looked at each other.

"So soon," murmured Sieh, frowning. "I had no idea he would do it this soon."

Kurue nodded to herself. "Canny old bastard. He'll probably have the ceremony at dawn the morning after."

"Could this mean he's discovered what we've done?" asked Zhakkarn.

"No," Kurue said, looking at me, "or she'd be dead and the soul would already be in Itempas's hands."

I shuddered at the thought and finally pushed myself to my feet. I did not turn to Nahadoth again.

"Are you done being angry with me?" I asked, brushing wrinkles out of my skirt. "I think we have unfinished business."

16

Sar-enna-nem

T HE PRIESTS DO MENTION THE GODS' WAR sometimes, mainly
as a warning against heresy. Because of Enefa, they say. Because
of the Betrayer, for three days people and animals lay helpless
and gasping for air, hearts gradually slowing and bellies bloat-
ing as their bowels ceased to function. Plants wilted and died in
hours; vast fertile plains turned to gray desert. Meanwhile the
sea we now call Repentance boiled, and for some reason all the
tallest mountains were split in half. The priests say that was the
work of the godlings, Enefa's immortal offspring, who each took
sides and battled across the earth. Their fathers, the lords of the
sky, mostly kept their fight up there.

Because of Enefa, the priests say. They do not say, because
Itempas killed her.

When the war finally ended, most of the world was dead.
What remained was forever changed. In my land, hunters pass
down legends of beasts that no longer exist; harvest songs praise
staples long lost. Those first Arameri did a great deal for the survivors, the priests are careful to note. With the magic of their

war-prisoner gods they replenished the oceans, sealed the mountains, healed the land. Though there was nothing to be done for the dead, they saved as many as they could of the survivors.

For a price.

The priests don't mention that, either.

*　*　*

There had in fact been very little business to discuss. In light of the looming ceremony, the Enefadeh needed my cooperation more than ever, and so—with palpable annoyance—Kurue agreed to my condition. We all knew there was little chance I could become Dekarta's heir. We all knew the Enefadeh were merely humoring me. I was content with that, so long as I did not think about it too deeply.

Then one by one they vanished, leaving me with Nahadoth. He was the only one, Kurue had said, who had the power to carry me to and from Darr in the night's few remaining hours. So in the silence that fell, I turned to face the Nightlord.

"How?" he asked. The vision, he meant, of his defeat.

"I don't know," I said. "But it's happened before. I had a dream once, of the old Sky. I saw you destroy it." I swallowed, chilled. "I thought it was just a dream, but if what I just saw is what really happened..." Memories. I was experiencing Enefa's memories. Dearest Skyfather, I did not want to think about what that meant.

His eyes narrowed. He wore that face again—the one I feared because I could not help wanting it. I fixed my eyes on a point just above his shoulder.

"It is what happened," he said slowly. "But Enefa was dead by then. She never saw what he did to me."

And I wish I hadn't. But before I could speak, Nahadoth took a step toward me. I very quickly took a step back, and he stopped.

"You fear me now?"

"You did try to rip out my soul."

"And yet you still desire me."

I froze. Of course he would have sensed that. I said nothing, unwilling to admit weakness.

Nahadoth moved past me to the window. I shivered as he passed; a tendril of his cloak had curled 'round my calf for just an instant in a cool caress. I wondered if he was even aware of this.

"What exactly do you hope to accomplish in Darr?" he asked.

I swallowed, glad to be on another subject. "I need to speak with my grandmother. I thought of using a sigil sphere, but I don't understand such things. There could be a way for others to eavesdrop on our conversation."

"There is."

It gave me no pleasure to be right. "Then the questions must be asked in person."

"What questions?"

"Whether it's true what Ras Onchi and Scimina said, about Darr's neighbors arming for war. I want to hear my grandmother's assessment of the situation. And...I hope to learn..." I felt inexplicably ashamed. "More about my mother. Whether she was like the rest of the Arameri."

"I have told you already: she was."

"You will forgive me, Lord Nahadoth, if I do not trust you."

He turned slightly, so that I could see the side of his smile. "She was," he repeated, "and so are you."

The words, in his cold voice, hit me like a slap.

"She did this, too," he continued. "She was your age, perhaps younger, when she began asking questions, questions, so many questions. When she could not get answers from us with politeness, she commanded them—as you have done. Such hate there was in her young heart. Like yours."

I fought the urge to swallow, certain he would hear it.

"What sort of questions?"

"Arameri history. The war between my siblings and I. Many things."

"Why?"

"I have no idea."

"You didn't ask?"

"I didn't care."

I took a deep breath and forced my sweaty fists to unclench. This was his way, I reminded myself. There had been no need for him to say anything about my mother; he just knew it was the way to unsettle me. I had been warned. Nahadoth didn't like to kill outright. He teased and tickled until you lost control, forgot the danger, and opened yourself to him. He made you ask for it.

After I had been silent for a few breaths, Nahadoth turned to me. "The night is half over. If you mean to go to Darr, it should be now."

"Oh. Ah, yes." Swallowing, I looked around the room, anywhere but at him. "How will we travel?"

In answer, Nahadoth extended his hand.

I wiped my hand unnecessarily on my skirt, and took it.

The blackness that surrounded him flared like lifting wings, filling the room to its arched ceiling. I gasped and would have stepped back, but his hand became a vice on my own. When I looked at his face I felt ill: his eyes had changed. They were all black now, iris and whites alike. Worse, the shadows nearest his body had deepened, so much that he was invisible beyond his extended hand.

I stared into the abyss of him and could not bring myself to go closer.

"If I meant to kill you," he said, and his voice was different, too, echoing, shadowed, "it would already be too late."

There was that. So I looked up into those terrible eyes, mustered my courage, and said, "Please take me to Arrebaia, in Darr. The temple of Sar-enna-nem."

The blackness at his core expanded so swiftly to envelop me that I had no time to cry out. There was an instant of unbearable cold and pressure, so great I thought it would crush me. But it stopped short of pain, and then even the cold vanished. I opened my eyes and saw nothing. I stretched out my hands—including the hand that I knew he held—and felt nothing. I cried out and heard only silence.

Then I stood on stone and breathed air laden with familiar scents and felt warm humidity soak into my skin. Behind me spread the stone streets and walls of Arrebaia, filling the plateau on which we stood. It was later in the night than it had been at Sky, I could tell, because the streets were all but empty. Before me rose stone steps, lined on either side by standing lanterns, at the top of which were the gates to Sar-enna-nem.

I turned back to Nahadoth, who had reverted to his usual, just-shy-of-human appearance.

"Y-you are welcome in my family's home," I said. I was still shivering from our mode of travel.

"I know." He strode up the steps. Caught off guard, I stared at his back for ten steps before remembering myself and trotting to follow.

Sar-enna-nem's gates are heavy, ugly wood-and-metal affairs—a more recent addition to the ancient stone. It took at least four women to work the mechanism that swung them open, which made a vast improvement over the days when the gates had been made of stone and needed twenty openers. I had arrived unannounced, in the small hours of the morning, and knew that this meant upsetting the entire guardstaff. We had not been attacked in centuries, but my people prided themselves on vigilance nonetheless.

"They might not let us in," I murmured, drawing alongside the Nightlord. I was hard-pressed to keep up; he was taking the steps two at a time.

Nahadoth said nothing in reply and did not slow his pace. I heard the loud, echoing sound of the great latch lifting, and then the gates swung open—on their own. I groaned, realizing what he'd done. Of course there were shouts and running feet as we passed through, and as we stepped onto the grassy patch that served as Sar-enna-nem's forecourt, two clusters of guards came running forth from the ancient edifice's doors. One was the gate company—just men, since it was a lowly position that required only brute strength.

The other company was the standing guard, composed of women and those few men who had earned the honor, distinguished by white silk tunics under the armor. This one was led by a familiar face: Imyan, a woman from my own Somem tribe. She shouted in our language as she reached the forecourt, and the company split to surround us. Very quickly we were surrounded by a ring of spears and arrows pointed at our hearts.

No—their weapons were pointed at *my* heart, I noticed. Not a single one of them had aimed at Nahadoth.

I stepped in front of Nahadoth to make it easier for them, and to signal my friendliness. For a moment it felt strange to speak in my own tongue. "It's good to see you, Captain Imyan."

"I don't know you," she said curtly. I almost smiled. As girls we had gotten into all manner of mischief together; now she was as committed to her duty as I.

"You laughed the first time you saw me," I said. "I'd been trying to grow my hair longer, thinking to look like my mother. You said it looked like curly tree moss."

Imyan's eyes narrowed. Her own hair—long and beautifully Darre-straight—had been arranged in an efficient braids-and-knot behind her head. "What are you doing here, if you're Yeine-*ennu*?"

"You know I'm no longer *ennu*," I said. "The Itempans have been announcing it all week, by word of mouth and by magic. Even High North should've heard by now."

Imyan's arrow wavered for a moment longer, then slowly came down. Following her lead, the other guards lowered their weapons as well. Imyan's eyes shifted to Nahadoth, then back to me, and for the first time there was a hint of nervousness in her manner. "And this?"

"You know me," Nahadoth said in our language.

No one flinched at the sound of his voice. Darren guards are too well-trained for that. But I saw not a few exchanged looks of unease among the group. Nahadoth's face, I noticed belatedly, had begun to waver again, a watery blur that shifted with the torchlight shadows. So many new mortals to seduce.

Imyan recovered first. "Lord Nahadoth," she said at last. "Welcome back."

Back? I stared at her, then at Nahadoth. But then a more familiar voice greeted me, and I let out a breath of tension I hadn't realized that I felt.

"You are indeed welcome," said my grandmother. She came down the short flight of steps that led to Sar-enna-nem's living quarters, and the guards parted before her: a shorter-than-average elderly woman still clad in a sleeping tunic (though she'd taken the time to strap on her knife, I noted). Tiny as she was—I had unfortunately inherited her size—she exuded an air of strength and authority that was almost palpable.

She inclined her head to me as she came. "Yeine. I've missed you, but not so much that I wanted to see you back so soon." She glanced at Nahadoth, then back at me. "Come."

And that was that. She turned to head into the columned entrance, and I moved to follow—or would have, had Nahadoth not spoken.

"Dawn is closer, here, to this part of the world," he said. "You have an hour."

I turned, surprised on several levels. "You aren't coming?"

"No." And he walked away, off to the side of the forecourt. The guards moved out of his way with an alacrity that might have been amusing under other circumstances.

I watched him for a moment, then moved to follow my grandmother.

*   *   *

Another tale from my childhood occurs to me here.

It is said the Nightlord cannot cry. No one knows the reason for this, but of the many gifts that the forces of the Maelstrom bestowed upon their darkest child, the ability to cry was not one of them.

Bright Itempas can. Legends say his tears are the rain that some-times falls while the sun still shines. (I have never believed this legend, because it would mean Itempas cries rather frequently.)

Enefa of the Earth could cry. Her tears took the form of the yellow, burning rain that falls around the world after a volcano has erupted. It still falls, this rain, killing crops and poisoning water. But now it means nothing.

Nightlord Nahadoth was firstborn of the Three. Before the others appeared, he spent countless aeons as the only living thing in all of existence. Perhaps that explains his inability. Perhaps, amid so much loneliness, tears become ultimately useless.

*   *   *

Sar-enna-nem was once a temple. Its main entrance is a vast and vaulted hall supported by columns hewn whole from the earth, erected by my people in a time long before we knew of such Amn innovations as scrivening or clockwork. We had our own techniques back then. And the places we built to honor the gods were magnificent.

After the Gods' War, my ancestors did what had to be done. Sar-enna-nem's Twilight and Moon Windows, once famed for their beauty, were bricked up, leaving only the Sun. A new temple, dedicated exclusively to Itempas and untainted by the devotion once offered to his siblings, was built some ways to the south; that is the current religious heart of the city. Sar-enna-nem was repurposed as nothing more than a hall of govern-ment, from which our warrior council issued edicts that I, as *ennu*, once implemented. Any holiness was long gone.

The hall was empty, as befitted the late hour. My grand-mother led me to the raised plinth where, during the day, the Warriors' Council members sat on a circle of thick rugs. She took a seat; I took one opposite.

"Have you failed?" she asked.

"Not yet," I replied. "But that is only a matter of time."

"Explain," she said, so I did. I will admit I edited the account somewhat. I did not tell her of the hours I wasted in my mother's chambers weeping. I did not mention my dangerous thoughts about Nahadoth. And I most certainly did not speak of my two souls.

When I was done, she sighed, the only sign of her concern. "Kinneth always believed Dekarta's love for her would safeguard you. I cannot say I ever liked her, but over the years I grew to trust her judgment. How could she have been so wrong?"

"I'm not certain she was," I said softly. I was thinking of Nahadoth's words about Dekarta, and my mother's murder: *You think it was him?*

I had spoken with Dekarta since then. I had seen his eyes while he spoke of my mother. Could a man like him murder someone he loved so much?

"What did Mother tell you, Beba?" I asked. "About why she left the Arameri?"

My grandmother frowned, taken aback by my shift from

formality. We had never been close, she and I. She had been too old to become *ennu* when her own mother finally died, and none of her children had been girls. Though my father had managed against all odds to succeed her, becoming one of only three male *ennu* ever in our history, I was the closest thing to a daughter she would ever have. I, the half-Amn embodiment of her son's greatest mistake. I had given up on trying to earn her love years before.

"It was not something she spoke of much," Beba said, speaking slowly. "She said she loved my son."

"That couldn't possibly have been sufficient for you," I said softly.

Her eyes hardened. "Your father made it clear that it would have to be."

And then I understood: she had never believed my mother. "What do you think was the reason, then?"

"She was full of anger, your mother. She wanted to hurt someone, and being with my son allowed her to accomplish that."

"Someone in Sky?"

"I don't know. Why does this concern you, Yeine? It's now that matters, not twenty years ago."

"I think what happened then has bearing on now," I said, surprising myself—but it was true, I realized at last. Perhaps I had felt that all along. And with that opening, I readied my next attack. "Nahadoth has been here before, I see."

At this, my grandmother's face resumed its usual stern frown. "*Lord* Nahadoth, Yeine. We are not Amn here; we respect our creators."

"The guard have drilled in how to approach him. A shame I

wasn't included; I could have used that training myself before I went to Sky. When did he come here last, Beba?"

"Before you were born. He came to see Kinneth once. Yeine, this isn't—"

"Was it after Father recovered from the Walking Death?" I asked. I spoke softly, though the blood was pounding in my ears. I wanted to reach over and shake her, but I kept control. "Was that the night they did it to me?"

Beba's frown deepened, momentary confusion becoming alarm. "Did...to *you*? What are you talking about? You weren't even born at that point; Kinneth was barely pregnant. What did..."

And then she trailed off. I saw thoughts racing behind her eyes, which widened as they stared at me. I spoke to those thoughts, teasing out the knowledge that I sensed behind them.

"Mother tried to kill me when I was born." I knew why, now, but there was more truth here, something I hadn't discovered yet. I could feel it. "They didn't trust her alone with me for months. Do you remember?"

"Yes," she whispered.

"I know she loved me," I said. "And I know that sometimes women go mad in childbearing. Whatever it was that made her fear me then—" I nearly choked on the obfuscation. I had never been a good liar. "—it faded and she became a good mother thereafter. But you must have wondered, Beba, what it was that she feared so. And my father must have wondered..."

I trailed off then, as awareness struck. *Here* was a truth I had not considered—

"No one wondered."

I jumped and whirled. Nahadoth stood fifty feet away at the entrance of Sar-enna-nem, framed by its triangle design. With the moonlight behind him he was a stark silhouette, but as always, I could see his eyes.

"I killed anyone who saw me with Kinneth that night," he said. We both heard him as clearly as if he stood right beside us. "I killed her maid, and the child who came to serve us wine, and the man who sat with your father while he recovered from the sickness. I killed the three guards who tried to eavesdrop on this old woman's orders." He nodded toward Beba, who stiffened. "After that, no one dared to wonder about you."

So you've decided to talk? I would have asked him, but then my grandmother did something so unexpected, so incredible, so stupid, that the words stopped in my throat. She leapt to her feet and moved in front of me, drawing her knife.

"What did you do to Yeine?" she cried. I had never in my life seen her so angry. "What foulness did the Arameri put you up to? She is *mine*, she belongs to *us*, you had no right!"

Nahadoth laughed then, and the whiplashing rage in that sound sent a chill down my spine. Had I thought him merely an embittered slave, a pitiable creature burdened by grief? I was a fool.

"You think this temple protects you?" he hissed. Only then did I realize he had not actually stepped over the threshold. "Have you forgotten that your people once worshipped *me* here, too?"

He stepped into Sar-enna-nem.

The rugs beneath my knees vanished. The floor, which had been planks of wood, disintegrated; underneath was a mosaic of polished semiprecious tiles, stones of every color interspersed with squares of gold. I gasped as the columns shuddered and the bricks exploded into nothingness and suddenly I could *see* the Three Windows, not just Sun but Moon and Twilight, too. I had never realized they were meant to be viewed together. We had lost so much. And all around us stood the statues of beings so perfect, so alien, so *familiar*, that I wanted to weep for all of Sieh's lost brothers and sisters, Enefa's loyal children, slaughtered like dogs for trying to avenge their mother's murder. *I understand. All of you, I understand so much—*

And then the torchlight went out and the air creaked and I turned to see that Nahadoth had changed as well. Night's darkness now filled that end of Sar-enna-nem, but it was not like my first night in Sky. Here, fueled by the residue of ancient devotion, he showed me all he had once been: first among gods, sweet dream and nightmare incarnate, all things beautiful and terrible. Through a hurricane swirl of blue-black unlight I caught a glimpse of moon-white skin and eyes like distant stars; then they warped into something so unexpected that my brain refused to interpret it for an instant. But the library embossing had warned me, hadn't it? A woman's face shone at me from the darkness, proud and powerful and so breathtaking that I yearned for *her* as much as I had for *him*, and it did not seem strange at all that I did so. And then the face shifted again into something that in no way resembled human, something tentacled and toothed and hideous, and I screamed. Then there was only darkness where his face should have been, and that was most frightening of all.

He stepped forward again. I felt it: an impossible, invisible vastness moved with him. I heard the walls of Sar-enna-nem groan, too flimsy to contain such power. The whole world could not contain this. I heard the sky above Darr rumble with thunder; the ground beneath my feet trembled. White teeth gleamed amid the darkness, sharp like wolves'. That was when I knew I had to act, or the Nightlord would kill my grandmother right before my eyes.

Right before my—

* * *

Right before my eyes she lies, sprawled and naked and bloody
this is not flesh this is all you can comprehend
but it means the same thing as flesh, she is dead and violated, her perfect form torn in ways that should not be possible, should not be *and who has done this? Who could have*
what did it mean that he made love to me before driving the knife home?
and then it hits: betrayal. I had known of his anger, but never once did I imagine . . . never once had I dreamt . . . I had dismissed her fears. I thought I knew him. I gather her body to mine and will all of creation to make her live again. We are not built for death. But nothing changes, nothing changes, *there was a hell that I built long ago and it was a place where everything remained the same forever because I could imagine nothing more horrific, and* now I am there.
Then others come, our children, and all react with equal horror
in a child's eyes, a mother is god
but I can see nothing of their grief through the black mist of my own. I lay her body down but my hands are covered in her blood, our blood, sister lover pupil teacher friend otherself, and when I lift my head to scream out my fury, a million stars turn black and die. No one can see them, but they are my tears.

*   *   *

I blinked.

Sar-enna-nem was as it had been, shadowed and quiet, its splendor hidden again beneath bricks and dusty wood and old rugs. I stood in front of my grandmother, though I did not remember getting up or moving. Nahadoth's human mask was back in place, his aura diminished to its usual quiet drift, and once again he was staring at me.

I covered my eyes with one hand. "I can't take much more of this."

"Y-Yeine?" My grandmother. She put a hand on my shoulder. I barely noticed.

"It's happening, isn't it?" I looked up at Nahadoth. "What you expected. Her soul is devouring my own."

"No," said Nahadoth very softly. "I don't know what this is."

I stared at him and could not help myself. All the shock and fear and anger of the past few days bubbled up, and I burst out laughing. I laughed so loudly that it echoed from Sar-enna-nem's distant ceiling; so long that my grandmother peered at me in concern, no doubt wondering if I had gone mad. I probably had, because suddenly my laughter turned to screaming and my mirth ignited as white-hot rage.

"How can you not know?" I shrieked at Nahadoth. I had lapsed into Senmite again. "You're a god! How can you not *know?*"

His calm stoked my fury higher. "I built uncertainty into this universe, and Enefa wove that into every living being. There will always be mysteries beyond even we gods' understanding—"

I launched myself at him. In the interminable second that my mad rage lasted, I saw that his eyes flicked to my approaching fist and widened in something very like amazement. He had plenty of time to block or evade the blow. That he did not was a complete surprise.

The smack of it echoed as loud as my grandmother's gasp.

In the ensuing silence, I felt empty. The rage was gone. Horror had not yet arrived. I lowered my hand to my side. My knuckles stung.

Nahadoth's head had turned with the blow. He lifted a hand to his lip, which was bleeding, and sighed.

"I must work harder to keep my temper around you," he said. "You have a memorable way of chastising me."

He lifted his eyes, and suddenly I knew he was remembering the time I had stabbed him. *I have waited so long for you,* he had said then. This time, instead of kissing me, he reached out and touched my lips with his fingers. I felt warm wetness and reflexively licked, tasting cool skin and the metallic salt of his blood.

He smiled, his expression almost fond. "Do you like the taste?"

*   *   *

Not of your blood, no.

But your finger was another matter.

*   *   *

"Yeine," said my grandmother again, breaking the tableau. I took a deep breath, marshaled my wits, and turned back to her.

"Are the neighboring kingdoms allying?" I asked. "Are they arming for war?"

She swallowed before nodding. "We received formal notice this week, but there had been earlier signs. Our merchants and diplomats were expelled from Menchey almost two months ago.

They say old Gemd has passed a conscription law to boost the ranks of his army, and he's accelerated training for the rest. The council believes he'll march in a week, maybe less."

Two months ago. I had been summoned to Sky only a short while before that. Scimina had guessed my purpose the instant Dekarta summoned me.

And it made sense she had chosen to act through Menchey. Menchey was Darr's largest and most powerful neighbor, once our greatest enemy. We had been at peace with the Mencheyev since the Gods' War, but only because the Arameri had been unwilling to grant either land permission to annihilate the other. But as Ras Onchi had warned me, things had changed.

Of course they had submitted a formal war petition. They would want the right to shed our blood.

"I would hope we had begun to muster forces as well, in the time since," I said. It was no longer my place to give orders; I could only suggest.

My grandmother sighed. "As best we could. Our treasury is so depleted we can barely afford to feed them, much less train and equip. No one will lend us funds. We've resorted to asking for volunteers—any woman with a horse and her own weapons. Men as well, if they're not yet fathers."

It was very bad if the council had resorted to recruiting men. By tradition men were our last line of defense, their physical strength bent toward the single and most important task of protecting our homes and children. This meant the council had decided that our only defense was to defeat the enemy, period. Anything else meant the end of the Darre.

"I'll give you what I can," I said. "Dekarta watches everything I do, but I have wealth now, and—"

"No." Beba touched my shoulder again. I could not remember the last time she had touched me without reason. But then, I had never seen her leap to protect me from danger, either. It pained me that I would die young and never truly know her.

"Look to yourself," she said. "Darr is not your concern, not any longer."

I scowled. "It will always be—"

"You said yourself they would use us to hurt you. Look what's happened just from your effort to restore trade."

I opened my mouth to protest that this was merely their excuse, but before I could, Nahadoth's head turned sharply east.

"The sun comes," he said. Beyond Sar-enna-nem's entry arch, the sky was pale; night had faded quickly.

I cursed under my breath. "I *will* do what I can." Then, on impulse, I stepped forward and wrapped my arms around her and held her tight, as I had never dared to do before in my whole life. She held stiff against me for a moment, surprised, but then sighed and rested her hands on my back.

"So much like your father," she whispered. Then she pushed me away gently.

Nahadoth's arm folded around me, surprisingly gentle, and I found my back pressed against the human solidity of the body within his shadows. Then the body was gone and so was Sar-enna-nem, and all was cold and darkness again.

I reappeared in my room in Sky, facing the windows. The sky here was still mostly dark, though there was a hint of pale against the distant horizon. I was alone, to my surprise, but also to my relief. It had been a very long, very difficult day. Without undressing I lay down—but sleep did not come immediately. I lay where I was awhile, reveling in the silence, letting my mind rest. Like bubbles in still water, two things rose to the surface of my thoughts.

My mother had regretted her bargain with the Enefadeh. She had sold me to them, but not without qualm. I found it perversely comforting that she had tried to kill me at birth. That seemed like her, choosing to destroy her own flesh and blood rather than let it be corrupted. Perhaps she had only decided to accept me on *her* terms—later, without the heady rush of new motherhood to color her feelings. When she could look into my eyes and see that one of the souls in them was my own.

The other thought was simpler, yet far less comforting.

Had my father known?

17

Relief

During those nights, those dreams, I saw through a thousand eyes. Bakers, blacksmiths, scholars, kings—ordinary and extraordinary, I lived their lives every night. But as with all dreams, I now remember only the most special.

In one, I see a darkened, empty room. There is almost no furniture. An old table. A messy, half-ragged pile of bedding in one corner. A marble beside the bedding. No, not a marble; a tiny, mostly blue globe, its nearer face a mosaic of brown and white. I know whose room this is.

"Shhh," says a new voice, and abruptly there are people in the room. A slight figure, half-draped across the lap of another body that is larger. And darker. "Shhh. Shall I tell you a story?"

"Mmm," says the smaller one. A child. "Yes. More beautiful lies, Papa, please."

"Now, now. Children are not so cynical. Be a proper child, or you will never grow big and strong like me."

"I will never be like you, Papa. That is one of your favorite lies."

I see tousled brown hair. A hand strokes it, long-fingered and graceful. The father? "I have watched you grow these long ages. In ten thousand years, a hundred thousand..."

"And will my sun-bright father open his arms when I have grown so great, and welcome me to his side?"

A sigh. "If he is lonely enough, he might."

"I don't want him!" Fitfully, the child moves away from the stroking hand and looks up. His eyes reflect the light like those of some nocturnal beast. "I will never betray you, Papa. Never!"

"Shhh." The father bends, laying a gentle kiss on the child's forehead. "I know."

And the child flings himself forward then, burying his face in soft darkness, weeping. The father holds him, rocking him gently, and begins to sing. In his voice I hear echoes of every mother who has ever comforted her child in the small hours, and every father who has ever whispered hopes into an infant's ear. I do not understand the pain I perceive, wrapped around both of them like chains, but I can tell that love is their defense against it.

It is a private moment; I am an intruder. I loosen invisible fingers, and let this dream slip through them and away.

* * *

I felt the poor sleep keenly when I dragged myself awake well into the next day. The inside of my head felt muddy, congealed. I sat on the edge of the bed with my knees drawn up, gazing through the windows at a bright, clear noon sky and thinking, *I am going to die.*

I am going to DIE.

In seven days—no, six now.

Die.

I am ashamed to admit that this litany went on for some time. The seriousness of my situation had not sunk in before; impending death had taken second place to Darr's jeopardy and a celestial conspiracy. But now I had no one yanking on my soul to distract me, and all I could think of was death. I was not yet twenty years old. I had never been in love. I had not mastered the nine forms of the knife. I had never—gods. I had never really *lived*, beyond the legacies left to me by my parents: *ennu*, and Arameri. It seemed almost incomprehensible that I was doomed, and yet I was.

Because if the Arameri did not kill me, I had no illusions about the Enefadeh. I was the sheath for the sword they hoped to draw against Itempas, their sole means of escape. If the succession ceremony was postponed, or if by some miracle I succeeded in becoming Dekarta's heir, I was certain the Enefadeh would simply kill me. Clearly, unlike other Arameri, I had no protection against harm by them; doubtless that was one of the alterations they had applied to my blood sigil. And killing me might be the easiest way for them to free Enefa's soul with minimal harm. Sieh might mourn the necessity of my death, but no one else in Sky would.

So I lay on the bed and trembled and wept and might have continued to do so for the rest of the day—one-sixth of my remaining life—if there had not come a knock at the door.

That pulled me back to myself, more or less. I was still wearing the clothes I'd slept in from the day before; my hair was mussed; my face was puffy and my eyes red. I hadn't bathed. I opened the door a crack to see T'vril, to my great dismay, with a tray of food in one hand.

"Greetings, Cousin—" He paused, took a second look at me, and scowled. "What in demons happened to you?"

"N-nothing," I mumbled, then tried to close the door. He slapped it open with his free hand, pushing me back and stepping inside. I would have protested, but the words died in my throat as he looked me up and down with an expression that would have made my grandmother proud.

"You're letting them win, aren't you?" he asked.

I think my mouth might have dropped open. He sighed. "Sit down."

I closed my mouth. "How do you—"

"I know nearly everything that happens in this place, Yeine. The upcoming ball, for example, and what will happen afterward. Halfbloods usually aren't told, but I have connections." He gently took me by the shoulders. "You've found out, too, I suspect, which is why you're sitting here going to rot."

On another occasion I would have been pleased that he'd finally called me by my name. Now I shook my head dumbly and rubbed my temples where a weary ache had settled. "T'vril, you don't—"

"Sit *down*, you silly fool, before you pass out and I have to call Viraine. Which, incidentally, you don't want me to do. His remedies are effective but highly unpleasant." He took my hand and guided me over to my table.

"I came because they told me you hadn't ordered breakfast or a midday meal, and I thought you might be starving yourself again." Sitting me and the tray down, he picked up a dish of some sort of sectioned fruit, speared a piece on a fork, and thrust this at my face until I ate it. "You seemed a sensible girl when you first came here. Gods know this place has a way of knocking the sense out of a person, but I never expected you to yield so easily. Aren't you a warrior, or something like that? The rumors have you swinging through trees half-naked with a spear."

I glared at him, affront cutting through my muddle. "That's the stupidest thing you've ever said to me."

"So you're not dead yet. Good." He took my chin between his fingers, peering into my eyes. "And they haven't defeated you yet. Do you understand?"

I jerked away from him, clinging to my anger. It was better than despair, if just as useless. "You don't know what you're talking about. My people . . . I came here to help them, and instead they're in *more* danger because of me."

"Yes, so I've heard. You do realize that both Relad and Scimina are consummate liars, don't you? Nothing you've done caused this. Scimina's plans were set in motion long before you ever arrived in Sky. That's how this family does things." He held a hunk of cheese to my mouth. I had to bite off a piece, chew it, and swallow just to get his hand out of the way.

"If that's—" He pushed more fruit at me; I batted the fork aside and the fruit flew off somewhere near my bookcases. "If that's true, then you know there's nothing I can do! Darr's enemies are preparing to attack. My land is weak; we can't fight off one army, let alone however many are gathering against us!"

He nodded, sober, and held up a new chunk of fruit for me. "That sounds like Relad. Scimina is usually more subtle. But it could be either of them, frankly. Dekarta hasn't given them much time to work, and they both get clumsy under pressure."

The fruit tasted like salt in my mouth. "Then tell me—" I blinked back tears. "What am I supposed to do, T'vril? You say I'm letting them win, but *what else can I do?*"

T'vril set down the dish and took my hands, leaning forward. I realized suddenly that his eyes were green, though a deeper shade than my own. I had never before considered the fact that we were relatives. So few of the Arameri felt human to me, much less like family.

"You fight," he said, his voice low and intent. His hands gripped my own fiercely enough to hurt. "You fight in whatever way you can."

It might have been the strength of his grip, or the urgency of his voice, but abruptly I realized something. "You want to be heir yourself, don't you?"

He blinked in surprise, and then a rueful smile crossed his face. "No," he said. "Not really. No one would want to be heir under these conditions; I don't envy you that. But..." He looked away, toward the windows, and I saw it in his eyes: a terrible frustration that must have been burning in him all his life. The unspoken knowledge that he was just as smart as Relad or Scimina, just as strong, just as deserving of power, just as capable of leadership.

And if the chance were ever given to him, he would fight to keep it. To use it. He would fight even if he had no hope of victory, because to do otherwise was to concede that the stupid, arbitrary assignment of fullblood status had anything to do with logic; that the Amn truly were superior to all other races; that he deserved to be nothing more than a servant.

As I deserved to be nothing more than a pawn. I frowned.

T'vril noticed. "That's better." He put the dish of fruit in my hands and stood up. "Finish eating and get dressed. I want to show you something."

*   *   *

I had not realized that it was a holiday. Fire Day; some Amn celebration I'd heard of, but never paid much attention to. When T'vril brought me out of my room, I heard the sounds of laughter and Senmite music drifting through the corridors. I had never liked the music of this continent; it was strange and arrhythmic, full of eerie minors, the sort of thing only people with refined tastes were supposed to be able to comprehend or enjoy.

I sighed, thinking we were headed in that direction. But T'vril cast a grim look that way and shook his head. "No. You don't want to attend *that* celebration, Cousin."

"Why not?"

"That party is for highbloods. You'd certainly be welcome, and as a halfblood I could go, too, but I would suggest that you avoid social events with our fullblooded relatives if you actually want to enjoy yourself. They have ... odd notions of what constitutes fun." His grim look warned me off further questioning. "This way."

He led me in the complete opposite direction, down several levels and angling toward the palace's heart. The corridors were bustling with activity, though I saw only servants as we walked, all of them moving so hurriedly that they barely had time to bob a greeting at T'vril. I doubt they even noticed me.

"Where are they all going?" I asked.

T'vril looked amused. "To work. I've scheduled everyone on rotating short shifts, so they've probably waited until the last minute to leave. Didn't want to miss any of the fun."

"Fun?"

"Mmm-hmm." We rounded a curve and I saw a wide set of translucent doors before us. "Here we are; the centeryard. Now, you're friendly with Sieh so I imagine the magic will work for you, but if it doesn't—if I disappear—just return to the hall and wait, and I'll come back out to get you."

"What?" I was growing used to feeling stupid.

"You'll see." He pushed the doors open.

The scene beyond was almost pastoral—*would* have been if I hadn't known I was in the middle of a palace hovering a half mile above the earth. We looked into some sort of vast atrium at the center of the palace, in which rows of tiny cottages bordered a cobblestone path. It surprised me to realize that the cottages were made, not of the pearly material that comprised the rest of the palace, but of ordinary stone and wood and brick. The style of the cottages varied wildly from that of the palace, too—the first sharp angles and straight lines I'd seen—and from cottage to cottage. Many of the designs were foreign to my eye, Tokken and Mekatish and others, including one with a striking bright-gold rooftop that might have been Irtin. I glanced up, realizing that the centeryard sat within a vast cylinder in the body of the palace; directly above was a circle of perfectly clear blue sky.

But the whole place was silent and still. I saw no one in or around the cottages; not even wind stirred.

T'vril took my hand and pulled me over the threshold—and I gasped as the stillness broke. In a moment's flicker there were suddenly *many* people about, all around us, laughing and milling and exclaiming in a cacophony of joy that would not have startled me so much if it hadn't come out of nowhere. There was music, too, more pleasant than the Senmite but still nothing I was used to. It came from much closer, somewhere in the middle of the cottages. I made out a flute and a drum, and a babel of languages—the only one I recognized was Kenti—before someone grabbed my arm and spun me around.

"Shaz, you came! I thought—" The Amn man who'd caught my hand started when he saw my face, then paled further. "Oh, demons."

"It's all right," I said quickly. "An honest mistake." From behind I could pass for Tema, Narshes, or half the other northern races—and it had not escaped me that he'd called me by a boy's name. That was clearly not the source of his horror. His eyes had locked on my forehead and the fullblood circle there.

"It's all right, Ter." T'vril came up beside me and put a hand on my shoulder. "This is the new one."

Relief restored color to the man's face. "Sorry, miss," he said, bobbing a greeting to me. "I just...well." He smiled sheepishly. "You understand."

I reassured him again, though I was not entirely sure that I did understand. The man wandered off after that, leaving T'vril and I to ourselves—inasmuch as we could be alone amid such a horde. I could see now that everyone present wore lowblood marks; they were all servants. There must have been nearly a thousand people in the centeryard's sprawling space. T'vril was so good at keeping them unobtrusive that I'd had no idea there were this many servants in Sky, though I suppose I should have guessed they would outnumber the highbloods.

"Don't blame Ter," T'vril said. "Today's one of the few days we can be free of rank considerations. He wasn't expecting to see that." He nodded toward my forehead.

"What is this, T'vril? Where did these people...?"

"A little favor from the Enefadeh." He gestured toward the entrance we'd just walked through, and upward. There was a faint, glasslike sheen to the air all around the centeryard, which I had not noticed before. We stood within a huge, transparent bubble of—something. Magic, whatever it was.

"No one with a mark higher than quarterblood sees anything, even if they pass through the barrier," T'vril said. "An exception was made for me, and, as you saw, we can bring others through if we choose. This means we can celebrate without highbloods coming here to ogle our 'quaint common-folk customs' like we're animals in a zoo."

I understood at last, and smiled as I did. It was probably only one of many small rebellions that the lowblood servants quietly fomented against their higher-born relations. If I stayed in Sky longer I would probably see others...

But, of course, I would not live long enough for that.

That thought sobered me at once, despite the music and gaiety around me. T'vril flashed me a grin and let go my hand. "Well, you're here now. Enjoy yourself for a while, hmm?" And almost at the moment he let me go, a woman grabbed him and pulled him into the mass of people. I saw a flash of his red hair among other heads, and then he was gone.

I stood where he'd left me, feeling oddly bereft. The servants celebrated on around me, but I was not part of it. Nor could I relax amid so much noise and chaos, however joyous. None of these people were Darre. None of them were under threat of execution. None of them had gods' souls stuffed into their bodies, tainting all that they thought and felt.

Yet T'vril had brought me here in an attempt to cheer me up, and it would've been churlish to leave right away. So I looked around for some quiet spot where I might sit out of the way. My eyes caught on a familiar face—or at least, it seemed familiar at first. A young man watched me from the steps of one of the cottages, smiling as if he knew *me*, at least. He was a little older than me, pretty-faced and slender, Tema-looking but with completely un-Tema eyes of faded green—

I caught my breath and went over to him. "Sieh?"

He grinned. "Glad to see you out."

"You're..." I gaped a moment longer, then closed my mouth. I had known all along that Nahadoth was not the only one among the Enefadeh who could change his form. "So this is your doing?" I gestured at the barrier, which now I could see above us as well, like a dome.

He shrugged. "T'vril's people do favors for us all year; it's fitting we should pay them back. We slaves must stick together."

There was a bitterness in his tone that I had not heard before. It felt oddly comforting in comparison with my own mood, so I sat down on the steps beside him, near his legs. Together we watched the celebration in silence for a long while. After a time I felt his hand touch my hair, stroking it, and that comforted me further still. Whatever form he took, he was still the same Sieh.

"They grow and change so fast," he said softly, his eyes on a group of dancers near the musicians. "Sometimes I hate them for that."

I glanced up at him in surprise; this was a strange mood indeed for him. "You gods are the ones who made us this way, aren't you?"

He glanced at me, and for a jarring, painful instant I saw confusion on his face. Enefa. He had spoken as if I was Enefa.

Then the confusion passed, and he shared with me a small, sad smile. "Sorry," he said.

I could not feel bitter about it, given the sorrow in his face. "I do seem to look like her."

"That's not it." He sighed. "It's just that sometimes—well, it feels like she died only yesterday."

The Gods' War had occurred over two thousand years before, by most scholars' reckonings. I turned away from Sieh and sighed, too, at the width of the gulf between us.

"You're not like her," he said. "Not really."

I didn't want to talk about Enefa, but I said nothing. I drew up my knees and rested my chin on them. Sieh resumed stroking my hair, petting me like a cat.

"She was reserved like you, but that's the only similarity. She was... cooler than you. Slower to anger—although she had the same *kind* of temper as you, I think, magnificent when it finally blew. We tried hard not to anger her."

"You sound like you were afraid of her."

"Of course. How could we not be?"

I frowned in confusion. "She was your mother."

Sieh hesitated, and in it I heard an echo of my earlier thoughts about the gulf between us. "It's... difficult to explain."

I hated that gulf. I wanted to breach it, though I had no idea if it was even possible. So I said, "Try."

His hand paused on my hair, and then he chuckled, his voice warm. "I'm glad you're not one of my worshippers. You'd drive me mad with your demands."

"Would you even bother answering any prayers that I made?" I could not help smiling at the idea.

"Oh, of course. But I might sneak a salamander into your bed to get back at you."

I laughed, which surprised me. It was the first time all day that I'd felt human. It didn't last long as laughs went, but when it passed, I felt better. On impulse, I shifted to lean against his legs, putting my head on his knee. His hand never left my hair.

"I needed no mother's milk when I was born." Sieh spoke slowly, but I did not sense a lie this time. I think it was just difficult for him to find the right words. "There was no need to protect me from danger or sing me lullabies. I could hear the songs between the stars, and I was more dangerous to the worlds I visited than they could ever be to me. And yet, compared to the Three, I was weak. Like them in many ways, but obviously inferior. Naha was the one who convinced her to let me live and see what I might become."

I frowned. "She was going to...kill you?"

"Yes." He chuckled at my shock. "She killed things all the time, Yeine. She was death as well as life, the twilight along with the dawn. Everyone forgets that."

I turned to stare at him, which made him draw his hand back from my hair. There was something in that gesture—something regretful and hesitant, not befitting a god at all—that suddenly angered me. It was there in his every word. However incomprehensible relationships between gods might be, he had been a child and Enefa his mother, and he had loved her with any child's abandon. Yet she had almost killed him, as a breeder culls a defective foal.

Or as a mother smothers a dangerous infant...

No. That had been entirely different.

"I'm beginning to dislike this Enefa," I said.

Sieh started in surprise, stared at me for a long second, then burst out laughing. It was infectious, though nonsensical; humor born of pain. I smiled as well.

"Thank you," Sieh said, still chuckling. "I hate taking this form; it always makes me maudlin."

"Be a child again." I liked him better that way.

"Can't." He gestured toward the barrier. "This takes too much of my strength."

"Ah." I wondered suddenly which was the default state for him: the child? Or this world-weary adult who slipped out whenever he let his guard down? Or something else altogether? But that seemed too intimate and possibly painful a question to ask, so I did not. We fell silent awhile longer, watching the servants dance.

"What will you do?" Sieh asked.

I lay my head back on his knee and said nothing.

Sieh sighed. "If I knew how to help you, I would. You know that, don't you?"

The words warmed me more than I'd expected. I smiled. "Yes. I know, though I can't say I understand it. I'm just a mortal like the rest of them, Sieh."

"Not like the rest."

"Yes." I looked at him. "However...*different* I might be—"

I did not like saying it aloud. No one stood near enough to us to overhear, but it seemed foolish to take chances. "You said it yourself. Even if I lived to be a hundred, my life would still be only an eyeblink of yours. I should be nothing to you, like these others." I nodded toward the throng.

He laughed softly; the bitterness had returned. "Oh, Yeine. You really don't understand. If mortals were truly nothing to us, our lives would be so much easier. And so would yours."

I could say nothing to that. So I fell silent, and he did, too, and around us the servants celebrated on.

*   *   *

It was nearly midnight by the time I finally left the centeryard. The party was still in full swing, but T'vril left with me and walked me to my quarters. He'd been drinking, though not nearly as much as some I'd seen. "Unlike them, I have to be clearheaded in the morning," he said, when I pointed this out.

At the door of my apartment we stopped. "Thank you," I said, meaning it.

"You didn't enjoy yourself," he said. "I saw: you didn't dance all evening. Did you even have a glass of wine?"

"No. But it did help." I groped for the right words. "I won't deny a part of me spent the whole time thinking, *I'm wasting one-sixth of my remaining life.*" I smiled; T'vril grimaced. "But to spend that time surrounded by so much joy... it did make me feel better."

There was such compassion in his eyes. I found myself wondering, again, why he helped me. I supposed it made a difference that he had some fellow feeling for me, perhaps even liked me. It was touching to think so, and perhaps that was why I reached

221

up to cup his cheek. He blinked in surprise, but he did not draw back. That pleased me, too, and so I yielded to impulse.

"I'm probably not pretty by your standards," I ventured. His cheek felt slightly scratchy under my fingers, and I remembered that men of the island peoples tended to grow beards. I found the idea exotic and intriguing.

A half-dozen thoughts flickered across T'vril's face in the span of a breath, then settled with his slow smile. "Well, I'm not by yours, either," he said. "I've seen those showhorses you Darre call men."

I chuckled, abruptly nervous. "And we are, of course, relatives..."

"This is Sky, Cousin." Amazing how that explained everything.

I opened the door to my apartment, then took his hand and pulled him inside.

He was strangely gentle—or perhaps it only seemed strange to me because I had little experience to compare him against. I was surprised to find that he was even paler beneath his clothing, and his shoulders were covered in faint spots, like those of a leopard but smaller and random. He felt normal enough against me, lean and strong, and I liked the sounds that he made. He did try to give me pleasure, but I was too tense, too aware of my own loneliness and fear, so there were no stormwinds for me. I did not mind so much.

I was unused to having someone in my bed, so afterward I slept restlessly. Finally in the small hours of the morning I got up and went into the bathroom, hoping that a bath would settle me to sleep. While water filled the tub, I ran more in the sink and splashed my face, then stared at myself in the mirror. There were new lines of strain around my eyes, making me look older. I touched my mouth, suddenly melancholy for the girl I had been just a few months before. She had not been innocent—no leader of any people can afford that—but she had been happy, more or less. When was the last time I'd felt happiness? I could not recall.

Suddenly I was annoyed with T'vril. At least pleasure would have relaxed me and perhaps pulled my mood out of its grim track. At the same time it bothered me to feel such disappointment because I liked T'vril, and the fault was as much mine as his.

But on the heels of this, unbidden, came an even more disturbing thought—one that I fought for long seconds, caught between morbid, forbidden-thrill fascination and superstitious fear.

I knew why I had found no satisfaction with T'vril.

Never whisper his name in the dark

No. This was stupidity. No, no, no.

unless you want him to answer.

There was a terrible, mad recklessness inside me. It whirled and crashed in my head, a cacophony of not-quite-thought. I could actually see it manifest as I stared into the mirror; my own eyes stared back at me, too wide, the pupils too large. I licked my lips, and for a moment they were not mine. They belonged to some other woman, much braver and stupider than me.

The bathroom was not dark because of the glowing walls, but darkness took many forms. I closed my eyes and spoke to the blackness beneath my lids.

"Nahadoth," I said.

My lips barely moved. I had given the word only enough breath to make it audible, and no more. I didn't even hear myself over the running water and the pounding of my heart. But I waited. Two breaths. Three.

Nothing happened.

For an instant I felt utterly irrational disappointment. This was followed swiftly by relief, and fury at myself. What in the Maelstrom was wrong with me? I had never in my life done anything so foolish. I must have been losing my mind.

I turned away from the mirror—and as I did the glowing walls went dark.

"What—" I began, and a mouth settled over mine.

Even if logic hadn't told me who it was, that kiss would have. There was no taste to it, only wetness and strength, and a hungry, agile tongue that slid around mine like a snake. His mouth was cooler than T'vril's had been. But a different kind of heat coiled through me in response, and when hands began to explore my body I could not help arching up to meet them. I breathed harder as the mouth finally relinquished mine and moved down my neck.

I knew I should have stopped him. I knew this was his favorite way to kill. But when unseen ropes lifted me and pinned me to the wall, and fingers slipped between my thighs to play a subtle music, thinking became impossible. That mouth, *his* mouth, was everywhere. He must have had a dozen of them. Every time I moaned or cried out, he kissed me, drinking down the sound like wine. When I could restrain myself his face pressed into my hair; his breath was light and quick in my ear. I tried to reach up,

I think to embrace him, but nothing was there. Then his fingers did something new and I was screaming, screaming at the top of my lungs, except that he had covered my mouth again and there was no sound, no light, no movement; he had swallowed it all. There was nothing but pleasure, and it seemed to go on for an eternity. If he had killed me right then and there, I would have died happy.

And then it was gone.

I opened my eyes.

I sat slumped on the bathroom floor. My limbs felt weak, shaky. The walls were glowing again. Steaming water filled the tub beside me to the brim; the taps were closed. I was alone.

I got up and bathed, then returned to bed. T'vril murmured in his sleep and threw an arm over me. I curled against him and told myself for the rest of the night that I was still trembling because of fear, nothing else.

18

The Oubliette

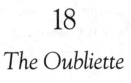

THERE ARE THINGS I KNOW NOW that I did not before.

Like this: In the instant Bright Itempas was born, he attacked the Nightlord. Their natures were so opposed that at first this seemed destined and unavoidable. For countless eternities they battled, each occasionally achieving victory only to be later overthrown. Only gradually did both come to understand that such battle was pointless; in the grand scale of things, it was an eternal stalemate.

Yet in the process, completely by accident, they created many things. To the formless void that Nahadoth birthed, Itempas added gravity, motion, function, and time. For every great star killed in the cross fire, each god used the ashes to create something new—more stars, planets, sparkling colored clouds, marvels that spiraled and pulsed. Gradually, between the two of them, the universe took shape. And as the dust of their battling cleared, both gods found that they were pleased.

Which of them made the first overture to peace? I imagine there were false starts at first—broken truces and the like. How long before hatred turned to tolerance, then respect and trust, then something more? And once it finally did, were they as passionate in love as they had been in war?

There is a legendary romance in this. And most fascinating to me, most frightening, is that *it isn't over yet.*

* * *

T'vril left for work at dawn. We exchanged few words and a silent understanding: the previous night had just been comfort between friends. It was not as awkward as it could have been; I got the sense he expected nothing else. Life in Sky did not encourage more.

I slept awhile longer and then lay awake in bed for a time, thinking.

My grandmother had said Menchey's armies would march soon. With so little time, I could think of few strategies that had any real chance of saving Darr. The best I could do was delay the attack. But how? I could seek allies in the Consortium, perhaps. Ras Onchi spoke for half of High North; perhaps she would know—no. I had watched both my parents and Darr's warrior council devote years to the quest for allies; if there were friends to be had, they would have made themselves known by now. The best I could do were individual sympathizers like Onchi—welcome, but ultimately useless.

So it would have to be something else. Even a few days' reprieve would be enough; if I could delay the attack until after the succession ceremony, then my bargain with the Enefadeh would take effect, earning Darr four godly protectors.

Assuming they won their battle.

So: all or nothing. But risky odds were better than none, so

I would chase them with all I had. I rose and went in search of Viraine.

He was not in his laboratory. A slim young servant woman was, cleaning. "He's at the oubliette," she told me. Since I had no idea what this was, or where, she gave me directions and I set out for Sky's lowermost level. And I wondered, as I walked, at the look of disgust that had been on the servant woman's face.

I emerged from the lift amid corridors that felt oddly dim. The walls' glow was muted in a strange way—not as bright as I'd grown used to, flatter somehow. There were no windows and, most curious, no doors, either. Apparently even servants did not live this far down. My footsteps echoed from ahead as I walked, so I was not surprised to emerge from the corridor into an open space: a vast, oblong chamber whose floor sloped toward a peculiar metal grate several feet in diameter. Nor was I surprised to find Viraine near this grate, gazing steadily at me as I entered. He had probably heard me the moment I stepped off the lift.

"Lady Yeine." He inclined his head, for once not smiling. "Shouldn't you be at the Salon?"

I hadn't been to the Salon in days, or reviewed my assigned nations' records, either. It was hard to care about these duties, considering. "I doubt the world will falter for my absence, now or in the next five days."

"I see. What brings you here?"

"I was looking for you." My eyes were drawn toward the grate in the floor. It looked like an exceptionally ornate sewer grate, apparently leading to some sort of chamber under the floor. I could see light glowing from within that was brighter than the ambient light of the room Viraine and I stood in—but that odd sense of flatness, of *grayness*, was even stronger here. The light underlit Viraine's face in a way that should have sharpened the angles and shadows in his expression, but instead it stripped them away.

"What is this place?" I asked.

"We're below the palace proper, actually in the support column that elevates us above the city."

"The column is hollow?"

"No. Only this space here at the top." He watched me, his eyes trying to gauge something I could not fathom. "You didn't attend the celebration yesterday."

I was not certain whether the highbloods knew about the servants' celebration and ignored it, or whether it was a secret. In case of the latter I said, "I haven't been in a celebratory mood."

"If you had come, this would be less of a surprise to you." He gestured toward the grate at his feet.

I stayed where I was, suffused with a sudden sense of dread. "What are you talking about?"

He sighed, and abruptly I realized he was in an ugly sort of mood himself. "One of the highlights of the Fire Day celebration. I'm often asked to provide entertainment. Tricks and the like."

"Tricks?" I frowned. From what I knew, scrivening was far too powerful and dangerous to be risked on tricks. One miswritten line and gods knew what could go wrong.

"Tricks. Of the sort that generally require a human 'volunteer.'" He gave me a thin smile as my jaw dropped. "Highbloods are difficult to entertain, you see—you being the natural exception. The rest..." He shrugged. "A lifetime of indulging all manner of whims sets the bar for entertainment rather high. Or low."

From the grate at his feet, and the chamber beyond, I heard a hollow, strained moan that chilled both my souls.

"What in the gods' names have you done?" I whispered.

"The gods have nothing to do with it, my dear." He sighed, gazing into the pit. "Why were you looking for me?"

I forced my eyes, and my mind, away from the grate. "I...I need to know if there's a way to send a message to someone, from Sky. Privately."

The look he gave me would have been withering under ordinary circumstances, but I could see that whatever was in the oubliette had taken the edge off his usual sardonic attitude. "You do realize spying on such communications is one of my routine duties?"

I inclined my head. "I suspected as much. That's why I'm asking you. If there's a way to do it, you would know." I swallowed, then privately chided myself for allowing nervousness to show. "I'm prepared to compensate you for your trouble."

In the strange gray light, even Viraine's surprise was muted. "Well, well." A tired smile stretched across his face. "Lady Yeine, perhaps you're a true Arameri after all."

"I do what's necessary," I said flatly. "And you know as well as I do that I don't have time to be more subtle."

At that his smile faded. "I know."

"Then help me."

"What message do you want to send, and to whom?"

"If I wanted half the palace to know, I wouldn't ask how to send it privately."

"I'm asking because the only way to send such a message is through me, Lady."

I paused then, unpleasantly surprised. But it made sense as I considered it. I had no idea how messaging crystals worked in detail, but like any sigil-based magic their function simply mimicked what any competent scrivener could do.

But I did not like Viraine, for reasons I could not fully understand myself. I had seen the bitterness in his eyes, heard the contempt in his voice on those occasions that he spoke of Dekarta or the other highbloods. Like the Enefadeh, he was a weapon and probably just as much a slave. Yet there was something about him that simply made me uneasy. I suspected it was that he seemed to have no loyalties; he was on no one's side except his own. That meant he could be relied upon to keep my secrets, if I made it worth his while. But what if there was more benefit for him in divulging my secrets to Dekarta? Or worse— Relad and Scimina? Men who served anyone could be trusted by no one.

He smirked as he watched me consider. "Of course, you could always ask Sieh to send the message for you. Or Nahadoth. I'm sure *he'd* do it, if sufficiently motivated."

"I'm sure he would," I replied coolly…

*   *   *

The Darren language has a word for the attraction one feels to danger: *esui*. It is *esui* that makes warriors charge into hopeless battles and die laughing. *Esui* is also what draws women to lovers who are bad for them—men who would make poor fathers, women of the enemy. The Senmite word that comes closest is "lust," if one includes the variations "bloodlust" and "lust for life," though these do not adequately capture the layered nature of *esui*. It is glory, it is folly. It is everything not sensible, not rational, not safe at all—but without *esui*, there is no point in living.

It is *esui*, I think, that draws me to Nahadoth. Perhaps it is also what draws him to me.

But I digress.

*   *   *

"...but then it would be a simple matter for some other highblood to command my message out of him."

"Do you honestly think I would bother getting involved with your schemes? After living between Relad and Scimina for two decades?" Viraine rolled his eyes. "I don't care which of you ends up succeeding Dekarta."

"The next family head could make your life easier. Or harder." I said it in a neutral tone; let him hear promises or threats as he pleased. "I would think the whole world cares who ends up on that stone seat."

"Even Dekarta answers to a higher power," Viraine said. While I wondered what in the gods' names that meant in the context of our discussion, he gazed into the hole beyond the metal grate, his eyes reflecting the pale light. Then his expression changed to something that immediately made me wary. "Come," he said. He gestured at the grate. "Look."

I frowned. "Why?"

"I'm curious about something."

"What?"

He said nothing, waiting. Finally I sighed and went to the grate's edge.

At first I saw nothing. Then there was another of those hol-

low groans, and someone shuffled into view, and it took everything I had not to run away and throw up.

Take a human being. Twist and stretch his limbs like clay.
Add new limbs, designed for gods know what purpose. Bring
some of his innards out of his body, yet leave them working.
Seal up his mouth and—Skyfather. God of all gods.

And the worst was this: I could still see intelligence and
awareness in the distorted eyes. They had not even allowed him
the escape of insanity.

I could not conceal my reaction entirely. There was a fine
sheen of sweat on my brow and upper lip when I looked up to
meet Viraine's intent gaze.

"Well?" I asked. I had to swallow before I could speak. "Is
your curiosity satisfied?"

The way he was looking at me would have disturbed me even
if we hadn't stood above the tortured, mutilated evidence of his
power. There was a kind of lust in his eyes that had nothing
to do with sex, and everything to do with—what? I could not
guess, but it reminded me, unpleasantly, of the human form
Nahadoth. He made my fingers itch for a knife the same way.

"Yes," he said softly. There was no smile on his face, but I could
see a high, triumphant gleam in his eyes. "I wanted to know
whether you had any chance, any at all, before I assisted you."

"And your verdict is . . . ?" But I knew already.

He gestured into the pit. "Kinneth could have looked at that
thing without batting an eyelash. She could have done the deed
herself and enjoyed it—"

"You lie!"

"—or pretended to enjoy it well enough that the difference

wouldn't have mattered. She had what it took to defeat Dekarta. You don't."

"Maybe not," I snapped. "But at least I still have a soul. What did you trade yours for?"

To my surprise, Viraine's glee seemed to fade. He looked down into the pit, the gray light making his eyes seem colorless and older than Dekarta's.

"Not enough," he said, and walked away. He moved past me into the corridor, heading for the lift.

I did not follow. Instead I went to the far wall of the chamber, sat down against it, and waited. After what seemed an eternity of gray silence—broken only by the faint, occasional suffering sounds of the poor soul in the pit—I felt a familiar shudder ripple through the palace's substance. I waited awhile, counting the minutes until I judged that sunset's light had faded enough from the evening sky. Then I got up and went to the corridor, my back to the oubliette. The gray light painted my shadow along the floor in a thin, attenuated line. I made certain my face was in that shadow before I spoke. "Nahadoth."

The walls dimmed before I turned. Yet the room was brighter than it should have been, because of the light from the oubliette. For some reason, his darkness had no effect on it.

He watched me, inscrutable, his face even more inhumanly perfect in the colorless light.

"Here," I said, and moved past him to the oubliette. The prisoner within was looking up at me, perhaps sensing my intent. It did not bother me to look at him this time as I pointed into the pit.

"Heal him," I said.

234

I expected a furious response. Or amusement, or triumph; there really was no way to predict the Nightlord's reaction to my first command. What I did not expect, however, was what he said.

"I can't."

I frowned at him; he gazed into the oubliette dispassionately. "What do you mean?"

"Dekarta gave the command that caused this."

And because of his master sigil, I could countermand no orders that Dekarta gave. I closed my eyes and sent a brief prayer for forgiveness to—well. Whichever god cared to listen.

"Very well, then," I said, and my voice sounded very small in the open chamber. I took a deep breath. "Kill him."

"I can't do that, either."

That jolted me, badly. "Why in the Maelstrom not?"

Nahadoth smiled. There was something strange about the smile, something that unnerved me even more than usual, but I could not allow myself to dwell on it. "The succession will take place in four days," he said. "Someone must send the Stone of Earth to the chamber where this ritual takes place. This is tradition."

"What? I don't—"

Nahadoth pointed into the pit. Not at the shuffling, whimpering creature there, but slightly away from it. I followed his finger and saw what I had not before. The floor of the oubliette glowed with that strange gray light, so different from that of the palace's walls. The spot where Nahadoth pointed seemed to be where the light was concentrated, not so much brighter as simply *more gray*. I stared at it and thought that I saw a darker shadow embedded in the translucent palacestuff. Something small.

All this time it had been right beneath my feet. The Stone of Earth.

"Sky exists to contain and channel its power, but here, so close, there is always some leakage." Nahadoth's finger shifted slightly. "That power is what keeps him alive."

My mouth was dry. "And...and what did you mean about... sending the Stone to the ritual chamber?"

He pointed up this time, and I saw that the ceiling of the oubliette chamber had a narrow, rounded opening at its center, like a small chimney. The narrow tunnel beyond went straight up, as far as the eye could see.

"No magic can act upon the Stone directly. No living flesh can come near it without suffering ill effects. So even for a relatively simple task, like moving the Stone from here to the chamber above, one of Enefa's children must spend his life to wish it there."

I understood at last. Oh, gods, it was monstrous. Death would be a relief to the unknown man in the pit, but the Stone some-how prevented that. To earn release from that twisted prison of flesh, the man would have to collaborate in his own execution.

"Who is he?" I asked. Below, the man had managed at last to sit down, though with obvious discomfort. I heard him weeping quietly.

"Just another fool caught praying to an outlawed god. This one happens to be a distant Arameri relation—they leave a few free to bring new blood into the clan—so he was doubly doomed."

"H-he could..." I could not think. *Monstrous.* "He could send the Stone away. Wish it into a volcano, or some frozen waste."

"Then one of us would simply be sent to retrieve it. But he won't defy Dekarta. Unless he sends the Stone properly, his lover will share his fate."

In the pit, the man uttered a particularly loud moan—as close to a wail as his warped mouth could manage. Tears filled my eyes, blurring the gray light.

"Shhh," Nahadoth said. I looked at him in surprise, but he was still gazing into the pit. "Shhh. It will not be long. I'm sorry."

When Nahadoth saw my confusion, he gave me another of those strange smiles that I did not understand, or did not want to understand. But that was blindness on my part. I kept thinking that I knew him.

"I always hear their prayers," said the Nightlord, "even if I'm not allowed to answer."

*   *   *

We stood at the foot of the Pier, gazing down at the city half a mile below.

"I need to threaten someone," I said.

I had not spoken since the oubliette. Nahadoth had accompanied me to the Pier, me meandering, him following. (The servants and highbloods gave us both a wide berth.) He said nothing now, though I felt him there beside me.

"The Minister of Mencheyev, a man named Gemd, who probably leads the alliance against Darr. Him."

"To threaten, you must have the power to cause harm," Nahadoth said.

I shrugged. "I've been adopted into the Arameri. Gemd has already assumed I have such power."

"Beyond Sky, your right to command us ends. Dekarta will

never give you permission to harm a nation which has not offended him."

I said nothing.

Nahadoth glanced at me, amused. "I see. But a bluff won't hold this man long."

"It doesn't have to." I pushed away from the railing and turned to him. "It only needs to hold him for four more days. And I can use your power beyond Sky ... if you let me. Will you?"

Nahadoth straightened as well, to my surprise lifting a hand to my face. He cupped my cheek, drew a thumb along the bottom curve of my lips. I will not lie: this made me think dangerous thoughts.

"You commanded me to kill tonight," he said.

I swallowed. "For mercy."

"Yes." That disturbing, alien look was in his eyes again, and finally I could name it: understanding. An almost human compassion, as if for that instant he actually thought and felt like one of us.

"You will never be Enefa," he said. "But you have some of her strength. Do not be offended by the comparison, little pawn." I started, wondering again if he could read minds. "I do not make it lightly."

Then Nahadoth stepped back. He spread his arms wide, revealing the black void of his body, and waited.

I stepped inside him and was enfolded in darkness. It might have been my imagination, but it seemed warmer this time.

19

Diamonds

YOU ARE INSIGNIFICANT. One of millions, neither special nor
unique. I did not ask for this ignominy, and I resent the comparison.

Fine. I don't like you, either.

* * *

We appeared in a stately, brightly lit hall of white and gray
marble, lined by narrow rectangular windows, under a chande-
lier. (If I had never seen Sky, I would have been impressed.) At
both ends of the hall were double doors of polished dark wood;
I assumed we faced the relevant set. From beyond the open windows I could hear merchants crying their wares, a baby fussing,
a horse's neigh, womens' laughter. City life.

No one was around, though the evening was young. I
knew Nahadoth well enough by now to suspect that this was
deliberate.

I nodded toward the doors. "Is Gemd alone?"

"No. With him are a number of guards, colleagues, and advisors."

Of course. Planning a war took teamwork. I scowled and then caught myself: I could not do this angry. My goal was delay—peace, for as long as possible. Anger would not help.

"Please try not to kill anyone," I murmured, as we walked toward the door. Nahadoth said nothing in response, but the hall grew dimmer, the flickering torchlit shadows sharpening to razor fineness. The air felt heavy.

This my Arameri ancestors had learned, at the cost of their own blood and souls: the Nightlord cannot be controlled. He can only be unleashed. If Gemd forced me to call on Nahadoth's power—

Best to pray that would not be necessary.

I walked forward.

The doors flung themselves open as I came to them, slamming against the opposite walls with an echoing racket that would bring half Gemd's palace guard running if they had any competence. It made for a suitably stunning entrance as I strode through, greeted by a chorus of surprised shouts and curses. Men who had been seated around a wide, paper-cluttered table scrambled to their feet, some groping for weapons and others staring at me dumbly. Two of them wore deep-red cloaks that I recognized as Tok warrior attire. So that was one of the lands Menchey had allied with. At the head of this table sat a man of perhaps sixty years: richly dressed, salt-and-pepper-haired, with a face like flint and steel. He reminded me of Dekarta, though only in manner; the Mencheyev were High North people, too, and they looked more like Darre than Amn. He half-stood, then hovered where he was, more angry than surprised.

I fixed my gaze on him, though I knew that Menchey, like

Darr, was ruled more by its council than its chieftain. In many ways we were merely figureheads, he and I. But in this confrontation, he would be the key.

"Minister," I said, in Senmite. "Greetings."

His eyes narrowed. "You're that Darre bitch."

"One of many, yes."

Gemd turned to one of his men and murmured something; the man hurried away. To supervise the guards and figure out how I'd gotten in, no doubt. Then Gemd turned back, his look appraising and wary.

"You're not among many now," he said slowly. "Or are you? You couldn't have been foolish enough to come alone."

I caught myself just before I would have looked around. Of course Nahadoth would choose not to appear. The Enefadeh had pledged to help me, after all, and having the Nightlord looming behind me like an overgrown shadow would have undermined what little authority I had in these men's eyes.

But Nahadoth was there. I could feel him.

"I have come," I said. "Not entirely alone. But then, no Arameri is ever fully alone, is she?"

One of his men, almost as richly dressed as Gemd, narrowed his eyes. "You're no Arameri," he said. "They didn't even acknowledge you until these last few months."

"Is that why you've decided to form this alliance?" I asked, stepping forward. A few of the men tensed, but most did not. I am not very intimidating. "I can't see how that makes much sense. If I'm so unimportant to the Arameri, then Darr is no threat."

"Darr is always a threat," growled another man. "You man-eating harlots—"

"Enough," said Gemd, and the man subsided.

Good; not wholly a figurehead, then.

"So this is not about the Arameri adopting me, then?" I eyed the man Gemd had silenced. "Ah, I see. This is about old grudges. The last war between our peoples was more genera-tions back than any of us can count. Are Mencheyev memories so long?"

"Darr claimed the Atir Plateau in that war," Gemd said qui-etly. "You know we want it back."

I knew, and I knew that was a stupid, stupid reason to start a war. The people who lived on the Atir didn't even speak the Mencheyev tongue anymore. None of this made any sense, and that was enough to make my temper rise.

"Who is it?" I asked. "Which of my cousins is pulling your strings? Relad? Scimina? Some sycophant of theirs? Who are you whoring for, Gemd, and how much have you charged to bend forward?"

Gemd's jaw tightened but he said nothing. His men were not so well-trained; they bristled and glared daggers. Not all of them, though. I noted which ones looked uncomfortable, and knew that they were the ones through whom Scimina or another of my relatives had chosen to work.

"You are an uninvited guest, Yeine-*ennu*," Gemd said. "Lady Yeine, I should say. You are interrupting my business. Say what you've come to say, and then please leave."

I inclined my head. "Call off your plans to attack Darr."

Gemd waited for a moment. "Or?"

I shook my head. "There is no alternative, Minister. I've learned a great deal from my Arameri relatives these last few days, including the art of wielding absolute power. We do not give ultimatums. We give orders, and those are obeyed."

The men turned to look at one another, their expressions ranging from fury to incredulity. Two kept their faces blank: the richly dressed man at Gemd's side and Gemd himself. I could see calculation in their eyes.

"You don't have absolute power," said the man beside Gemd. He kept his tone neutral, a sign that he was uncertain. "You haven't even been named heir."

"True," I said. "Only the Lord Dekarta holds total power over the Hundred Thousand Kingdoms. Whether they thrive. Whether they falter. Whether they are obliterated and forgotten." Gemd's brow tightened at that, not quite a frown. "Grandfather has this power, but he may of course choose to delegate it to those of us in Sky who have his favor."

I let them wonder whether I had earned that favor or not. It probably sounded like a sign of favor that I had been summoned to Sky and named a fullblood.

Gemd glanced at the man beside him before saying, "You must realize, Lady Yeine, that once plans have been set in motion, they can be difficult to stop. We will need time to discuss your . . . order."

"Of course," I said. "You have ten minutes. I'll wait."

"Oh for—" This was from another man, younger and bigger, one of the ones I had marked for an Arameri tool. He looked at me as if I were excrement on the bottom of his shoe. "Minister, you cannot seriously be considering this ridiculous demand!"

Gemd glared at him, but the silent reprimand clearly had no impact. The younger man stepped away from the table and came toward me, his whole posture radiating menace. Every Darre woman is taught to deal with such behavior from men. It is an animal trick that they use, like dogs ruffling their fur and growling. Only rarely is there actual threat behind it, and a woman's strength lies in discerning when the threat is real and when it is just hair and noise. For now the threat was not real, but that could change.

He stopped before me and turned back to his fellows, pointing at me. "Look at her! They probably had to call a scrivener just to confirm she came out of an Arameri cunt—"

"Rish!" Gemd looked furious. "Sit down."

The man—Rish—ignored him and turned back to me, and abruptly the threat became real. I saw it in the way he positioned himself, angling his body to put his right hand near my right side. He meant to backhand me. I had an instant to decide whether to dodge or reach for my knife—

And in that sliver of time, I felt the power around me coalesce, malice-hard and sharp as crystal.

*　　*　　*

That this analogy occurred to me should have been a warning.

*　　*　　*

Rish swung. I held still, tense for the blow. Three inches from my face Rish's fist seemed to glance off something no one could see—and when it did, there was a high hard clacking sound, like stone striking stone.

Rish drew his hand away, startled and perhaps puzzled by his failure to put me in my place. He looked at his fist, on which a patch of shining, faceted black had appeared about the knuckles.

I was close enough to see the flesh around this patch blistering, beading with moisture like meat cooked over a flame. Except it was not burning, but *freezing*; I could feel the waft of cold air from where I stood. The effect was the same, however, and as the flesh withered and crisped away as if it had been charred, what appeared underneath was not raw flesh, but stone.

I was surprised that Rish took so long to begin screaming.

All the men in the room reacted to Rish's cry. One stumbled back from the table and nearly fell over a chair. Two others ran over to Rish to try and help him. Gemd moved to help as well, but some powerful preservative instinct must have risen in the well-dressed man beside him; he grabbed Gemd by the shoulder to halt him. That turned out to be wise, because the first of the men who reached Rish—one of the Toks—grabbed Rish's wrist to see what was the matter.

The black was spreading swiftly; nearly the whole hand was now a glittering lump of black crystal in the rough shape of a fist. Only the tips of Rish's fingers remained flesh, and they transformed even as I watched. Rish fought the Tok, maddened with agony, and the Tok grabbed Rish's fist in an effort to hold him still. Almost immediately he jerked away, as if the stone had been too cold to touch—and then the Tok, too, stared at his palm, and the black blotch that was now spreading there.

Not merely crystal, I realized, in the part of my mind that was not frozen in horror. The black substance was too pretty to be quartz, too flawless and clear in its faceting. The stone caught the light like diamond, because that was what their flesh had become. Black diamond, the rarest and most valuable of all.

The Tok began to scream. So did several others of the men in the room.

Through it all I remained still and kept my face impassive.

* * *

He shouldn't have tried to hit me. He deserved what he got. He shouldn't have tried to hit me.

And the man who tried to help him? What did that one deserve?

They are all my enemies, my people's enemies. They should not have... they should not... Oh, gods. Gods.

The Nightlord cannot be controlled, child. He can only be unleashed. And you asked him not to kill.

* * *

I could not show weakness.

So while the two men flailed and screamed, I stepped around them and walked up to the table. Gemd looked at me, his mouth distorted with disgust and disbelief.

I said, "Take all the time you like to discuss my order." Then I turned to leave.

"W-wait." Gemd. I paused, not allowing my eyes to linger on the two men. Rish was almost half diamond now, the stone creeping over his arm and chest, down one leg and up the side of his neck. He lay on the floor, no longer screaming, though he still keened in a low, agonized voice. Perhaps his throat had turned to diamond already. The other man was reaching toward his comrades, begging for a sword so he could cut off his arm. A young fellow—one of Gemd's heirs, to judge by his features— drew his blade and edged close, but then another man grabbed him and hauled him back. Another wise decision; flecks of black no larger than a grain of sand sparkled on the floor around the two men. Bits of Rish's flesh, transformed and cast about by his flailing. As I watched, the Tok fell onto his good hand, and his thumb touched one of the flecks. It, too, began to change.

"Stop this," Gemd murmured.

"I did not start it."

He cursed swiftly in his language. "Stop it, gods damn you! What kind of monster are you?"

I could not help laughing. That there was no humor in it, only bitter self-loathing, would be lost on them.

"I'm an Arameri," I said.

One of the men behind us abruptly fell silent, and I turned. Not the Tok; he was still shrieking while blackness ate its way down his spine. The diamond had spread to encompass Rish's mouth and was consuming the whole lower half of his face. It seemed to have stopped on his torso, though it was working its way down his remaining leg. I suspected it would stop altogether once it had consumed the nonvital parts of his body, leaving him mutilated and perhaps mad, but alive. I had, after all, asked Nahadoth not to kill.

I averted my eyes, lest I give myself away by throwing up.

"Understand this," I said. The horror in my heart had crept into my voice; it lent me a deeper timbre, and a hint of resonance, that I had not possessed before. "If letting these men die will save my people, then they will die." I leaned forward, putting my hands on the table. "If killing everyone in this room, everyone in this *palace*, will save my people, then know, Gemd: I will do it. You would, too, if you were me."

He had been staring at Rish. Now his eyes jerked toward me,

and I saw realization and loathing flicker through them. Was there a hint of self-loathing amid that hatred? Had he believed me when I'd said *you would, too*? Because he would. Anyone would, I understood now. There was nothing we mortals would not do when it came to protecting our loved ones.

I would tell myself that for the rest of my life.

"Enough." I barely heard Gemd over the screams, but I saw his mouth move. "Enough. I'll call off the attack."

"And disband the alliance?"

"I can speak only for Menchey." There was something broken in his tone. He did not meet my eyes. "The others may choose to continue."

"Then warn them, Minister Gemd. The next time I'm forced to do this, two hundred will suffer instead of two. If they press the issue, two thousand. You chose this war, not I. I will not fight fairly."

Gemd looked at me in mute hatred. I held his eyes awhile longer, then turned to the two men, one of whom still shuddered and whimpered on the floor. The other, Rish, seemed catatonic. I walked over to them. The glimmering, deadly black flecks did not harm me, though they crunched under my feet.

Nahadoth could stop the magic, I was certain. He could probably even restore the men to wholeness—but Darr's safety depended on my ability to strike fear into Gemd's heart.

"Finish it," I whispered.

The black surged and consumed each of the men in seconds. Chill vapors rose around them as their final screams mingled with the sounds of flesh crackling and bone snapping, then all of it died away. In the men's place lay two enormous, faceted gems in the rough shape of huddled figures. Beautiful, and quite valuable, I guessed; if nothing else, their families would live well from henceforth. If the families chose to sell their loved ones' remains.

I passed between the diamonds on my way out. The guards who had come in behind me moved out of my way, some of them stumbling in their haste. The doors swung shut behind me, quietly this time. When they were closed, I stopped.

"Shall I take you home?" asked Nahadoth. Behind me.

"Home?"

"Sky."

Ah, yes. Home, for Arameri.

"Let's go," I said.

Darkness enveloped me. When it cleared, we were in Sky's forecourt again, though at the Garden of the Hundred Thousand this time rather than the Pier. A path of polished stones wound between neat, orderly flower beds, each overhung with a different type of exotic tree. In the distance, through the leaves, I could see the starry sky and the mountains that met it.

I walked through the garden until I found a spot with an unimpeded view, beneath a miniature satinbell tree. My thoughts turned in slow, lazy spirals. I was growing used to the cool feel of Nahadoth behind me.

"My weapon," I said to him.

"As you are mine."

I nodded, sighing into a breeze that lifted my hair and set the leaves of the satinbell a-rustle. As I turned to face Nahadoth, a scud of cloud passed across the moon's crescent. His cloak seemed to inhale in that dim instant, growing impossibly until it almost eclipsed the palace in rippling waves of black. Then the cloud passed, and it was just a cloak again.

I felt like that cloak all of a sudden—wild, out of control, giddily alive. I lifted my arms and closed my eyes as another breeze gusted. It felt so good.

"I wish I could fly," I said.

"I can gift you with that magic, for a time."

I shook my head, closing my eyes to sway with the wind. "Magic is wrong." I knew that oh, so well now.

He said nothing to that, which surprised me until I thought deeper. After witnessing so many generations of Arameri hypocrisy, perhaps he no longer cared enough to complain.

It was tempting, so tempting, to stop caring myself. My mother, Darr, the succession; what did any of it matter? I could forget all of that so easily, and spend the remainder of my life—all four days of it—indulging any whim or pleasure I wanted.

Any pleasure, except one.

"Last night," I said, lowering my arms at last. "Why didn't you kill me?"

"You're more useful alive."

I laughed. I felt light-headed, reckless. "Does that mean I'm the only person in Sky who has nothing to fear from you?" I knew it was a stupid question before I finished speaking, but I do not think I was entirely sane in that moment.

Fortunately, the Nightlord did not answer my stupid, dangerous question. I glanced back at him to gauge his mood and saw that his nightcloak had changed again. This time the wisps had spun long and thin, drifting through the garden like layers of campfire smoke. The ones nearest me curled inward, surrounding me on all sides. I was reminded of certain plants in my homeland, which grew teeth or sticky tendrils to ensnare insects.

And at the heart of this dark flower, my bait: his glowing face, his lightless eyes. I stepped closer, deeper into his shadow, and he smiled.

"You wouldn't have had to kill me," I said softly. I ducked my head and looked up at him through my lashes, curving my body in silent invitation. I had seen prettier women do this all my life, yet never dared myself. I lifted a hand and moved it toward his chest, half-expecting to touch nothing and be snatched forward into darkness. But this time there was a body within the shadows, startling in its solidity. I could not see it, or my own hand where I touched him, but I could feel skin, smooth and cool beneath my fingertips.

Bare skin. Gods.

I licked my lips and met his eyes. "There's a great deal you could have done without compromising my . . . usefulness."

Something in his face changed, like a cloud across the moon: the shadow of the predator. His teeth were sharper when he spoke. "I know."

Something in me changed, too, as the wild feeling went still. That look in his face. Some part of me had been waiting for it.

"Would you?" I licked my lips again, swallowed around sudden tightness in my throat. "Kill me? If . . . I asked?"

There was a pause.

When the Lord of Night touched my face, fingertips tracing my jaw, I thought I was imagining things. There was an unmistakable tenderness in the gesture. But then, just as tenderly, the hand slid farther down and curled around my neck. As he leaned close, I closed my eyes.

"Are you asking?" His lips brushed my ear as he whispered.

I opened my mouth to speak and could not. All at once I was trembling. Tears welled in my eyes, spilled down my face onto his wrist. I wanted to speak, to ask, so badly. But I just stood there, trembling and crying, while his breath tickled my ear. In and out. Three times.

Then he released my neck, and my knees buckled. I fell forward, and suddenly I was buried in the soft, cool dark of him, pressed against a chest I could not see, and I began sobbing into it. After a moment, the hand that had almost killed me cupped the nape of my neck. I must have bawled for an hour, though maybe it was less. I don't know. He held me tight the whole time.

20

The Arena

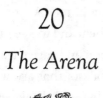

ALL THAT REMAINS OF THE TIME before the Gods' War is whispered myth and half-forgotten legend. The priests are quick to punish anyone caught telling these tales. There was nothing before Itempas, they say; even in the age of the Three, he was first and greatest. Still, the legends persist.

For example: it is said that once people made sacrifices of flesh to the Three. They would fill a room with volunteers. Young, old, female, male, poor, wealthy, healthy, infirm; all the variety and richness of humanity. On some occasion that was sacred to all Three—this part has been lost with time—they would call out to their gods and beg them to partake of the feast.

Enefa, it is said, would claim the elders and the ill—the epitome of mortality. She would give them a choice: healing or gentle, peaceful death. The tales say more than a few chose the latter, though I cannot imagine why.

Itempas took then what he takes now—the most mature and noble, the brightest, the most talented. These became his priests, setting duty and propriety above all else, loving him and submitting to him in all things.

Nahadoth preferred youths, wild and carefree—though he would claim the odd adult, too. Anyone willing to yield to the moment. He seduced them and was seduced by them; he reveled in their lack of inhibition and gave them everything of himself.

The Itempans fear talk of that age will lead people to yearn for it anew and turn to heresy. I think perhaps they overestimate the danger. Try as I might, I cannot imagine what it was like to live in a world like that, and I have no desire to return to it. We have enough trouble with one god now; why in the Maelstrom would we want to live again under three?

*   *   *

I wasted the next day, a quarter of my remaining life. I had not meant to. But I had not returned to my rooms until nearly dawn, my second night of little sleep, and my body demanded recompense by sleeping past noon. I had dreams of a thousand faces, representing millions, all distorted with agony or terror or despair. I smelled blood and burned flesh. I saw a desert littered with fallen trees because it had once been a forest. I woke up weeping; such was my guilt.

Late that afternoon there was a knock at the door. Feeling lonely and neglected—not even Sieh had come to visit—I went to answer, hoping it was a friend.

It was Relad.

"What in the names of every useless god have you done?" he demanded.

*　　*　　*

The arena, Relad had told me. Where the highbloods played at war.

That was where I would find Scimina, who had somehow found out about my efforts to counter her meddling. He had said it between curses and profanities and much maligning of my inferior halfbreed bloodlines, but that much I understood. *What* Scimina had found out Relad did not seem to know, which gave me some hope . . . but not much.

I was shaking with tension when I emerged from the lift amid a crowd of backs. Those nearest the lift had made some space, perhaps after being jostled from behind by new arrivals too many times, but beyond that was a solid wall of people. Most were white-clad servants; a few were better dressed, bearing the marks of quarter- or eighthbloods. Here and there I rubbed against brocade or silk as I gave up politeness and just started pushing my way through. It was slow going because most of them towered over me, and because they were wholly riveted on whatever was happening at the center of the room.

From where I could hear screaming.

I might never have gotten there if someone hadn't glanced back, recognized me, and murmured to someone else nearby. The murmur rippled through the crowd, and abruptly I found myself the focus of dozens of silent, pent stares. I stumbled to a halt, unnerved, but the way ahead abruptly cleared as they moved aside for me. I hurried forward, then stopped in shock.

On the floor knelt a thin old man, naked, chained in a pool of blood. His white hair, long and lank, hung 'round his face, obscuring it, though I could hear him panting raggedly for breath. His skin was a webwork of lacerations. If it had just been his back, I would have thought him flogged, but it was not just his back. It was his legs, his arms, his cheeks and chin. He was kneeling; I saw cuts on the soles of his feet. He pushed himself upright awkwardly, using the sides of his wrists, and I saw that a round red hole in the back of each showed bone and tendon clearly.

Another heretic? I wondered, confused.

"I wondered how much blood I would have to draw before someone went running for you," said a savage voice beside me, and as I turned something came at my face. I raised my hands instinctively and felt a thin line of heat cross my palms; something had cut me.

I did not pause long enough to assess the damage, springing back and drawing my knife. My hands still worked, though blood made the hilt slippery. I shifted it to a defensive grip and crouched, ready to fight.

Across from me stood Scimina, gowned in shining green satin. The flecks of blood that had sprayed across her dress looked like tiny ruby jewels. (There were flecks on her face as well, but those just looked like blood.) In her hands was something that I did not at first realize was a weapon—a long, silver wand, ornately decorated, perhaps three feet in length. But at the tip was a short double-edged blade, thin as a surgeon's scalpel, made of glass. Too short and strangely weighted to be a spear, more like an elaborate fountain pen. Some Amn weapon?

Scimina smirked at my drawn blade, but instead of raising her own weapon, she turned away and resumed pacing around the circle that the crowd had formed, with the old man at its center. "How like a barbarian. You can't use a knife against me, Cousin; it would shatter. Our blood sigils prevent all life-threatening attacks. Honestly, you're so ignorant. What are we going to do with you?"

I stayed in my crouch and kept hold of my knife anyway, pivoting to keep her in sight as she walked. As I did so, I saw faces among the crowd that I recognized. Some of the servants who'd been at the Fire Day party. A couple of Dekarta's courtiers. T'vril, white-lipped and stiff; his eyes fixed on me in something that might have been warning. Viraine, standing forward from the rest of the crowd; he had folded his arms and stood gazing into the middle distance, looking bored.

Zhakkarn and Kurue. Why were they there? They were watching me, too. Zhakkarn's expression was hard and cold; I had never seen her show anger so clearly before. Kurue was furious, too, her nostrils flared and hands tight at her sides. The look in her eyes would have flayed me if it could. But Scimina was already flaying someone, so I focused on the greater threat for the moment.

"Sit up!" Scimina barked, and the old man jerked upright as if on strings. I could see now that there were fewer cuts on his torso, though as I watched Scimina walked past him and flicked the wand, and another long, deep slice opened on the old man's abdomen. He cried out again, his voice hoarse, and opened eyes he'd shut in reaction to the pain. That was when I caught my breath, because the old man's eyes were green and sharpfold and then I realized how the shape of his face would be familiar if he were sixty years younger and dearest gods, dearest Skyfather, it was *Sieh*.

"Ah," Scimina said, interpreting my gasp. "That does save time.

257

You were right, T'vril; she *is* sweet on him. Did you send one of your people to fetch her? Tell the fool to be quicker next time."

I glared at T'vril, who clearly had not sent for me. His face was paler than usual, but that strange warning was still in his eyes. I almost frowned in confusion, but I could feel Scimina's gaze like a vulture, hovering over my facial expressions and ready to savage the emotions they revealed.

So I schooled myself to calmness, as my mother had taught me. I rose from my fighting crouch, though I only lowered my knife to my side and did not sheathe it. Scimina probably would not know, but among Darre, this was disrespect—a sign that I did not trust her to behave like a woman.

"I'm here now," I said to her. "State your purpose."

Scimina uttered a short, sharp laugh, never ceasing her pacing. "State my purpose. She sounds so martial, doesn't she?" She looked around the crowd; no one answered her. "So *strong*. Tiny, ill-bred, pathetic little thing that she is—*what do you THINK my purpose is, you fool?*" She shouted this last at me, her fists clenched at her sides, the odd wand-weapon quivering. Her hair, up in an elaborate coif that was still lovely, was coming undone. She looked exquisitely demented.

"I think you want to be Dekarta's heir," I said softly, "and the gods help all the world if you succeed."

Quick as wind, Scimina went from a screaming madwoman to smiling charm. "True. And I meant to begin with your land, stomping it ever so thoroughly out of existence. In fact I should have begun doing so already, if not for the fact that the alliance I so carefully put together in that region is now falling apart." She resumed pacing, glancing back at me over her shoulder, turning the wand delicately in her hands. "I thought at first the problem might be that old High North woman you've been meeting at the Salon. But I looked into that; she's only given you information, and most of it useless. So you've done something else. Would you care to explain?"

My blood went cold. What had Scimina done to Ras Onchi? Then I looked at Sieh, who had recovered himself somewhat, though he still looked weak and dazed from pain. He was not healing, which made no sense. I had stabbed Nahadoth in the heart and it had been barely a nuisance. Yet it had taken time for him to heal, I recalled with a sudden chill. Perhaps, if left alone for a while, Sieh would recover as well. Unless...Itempas had trapped the Enefadeh in human form to suffer all the horrors of mortality. They were eternal, powerful—but not invulnerable. Did the horrors of mortality include death? Sweat stung the cuts on my hands. There were things I was not prepared to endure.

But then the palace shuddered. For an instant I wondered if this tremor signified some new threat, and then I remembered. Sunset.

"Oh demons," Viraine muttered into the silence. An instant later I and every other person in the room was thrown sprawling in a blast of wind and bitter, painful cold.

It took me a moment to struggle upright, and when I did, my knife was gone. The room was chaos around me; I heard groans of pain, curses, shouts of alarm. When I glanced toward the lift, I could see several people crowding its opening, trying to cram their way in. I forgot all of this, though, when I looked toward the center of the room.

It was difficult to see Nahadoth's face. He crouched near Sieh, his head bowed, and the blackness of his aura was as it had been my first night in Sky, so dark that it hurt the mind. I focused instead on the floor, where the chains that had held Sieh lay shattered, their tips glistening with frost. Sieh himself I could not see entirely—only one of his hands, dangling limp, before Nahadoth's cloak swept around him, swallowing him into darkness.

"Scimina." There was that hollow, echoing quality to Nahadoth's voice again. Was the madness upon him? No; this was just pure, plain rage.

But Scimina, who had also been knocked to the floor, got to her high-heeled feet and composed herself. "Nahadoth," she said, more calmly than I would have imagined. Her weapon was gone, too, but she was a true Arameri, unafraid of the gods' wrath. "How good of you to join us at last. Put him down."

Nahadoth stood and flicked his cloak back. Sieh, a young man now, whole and clothed, stood beside him glaring defiantly at Scimina. Somewhere deep inside me, a knot of tension relaxed.

"We had an agreement," Nahadoth said, still in that voice echoing with murder.

"Indeed," Scimina said, and now it was her smile that frightened me. "You'll serve as well as Sieh for this purpose. Kneel." She pointed at the bloody space and its empty chains.

For an instant the sense of power in the room swelled, like pressure against the eardrums. The walls creaked. I shuddered beneath it, wondering if this was it. Scimina had made some error, left some opening, and now Nahadoth would crush us all like insects.

But then, to my utter shock, Nahadoth moved away from Sieh and went to the center of the room. He knelt.

Scimina turned to me, where I still half-lay on the floor. Shamed, I got to my feet. I was surprised to see that there was still an audience around us, though it was now sparse—T'vril, Viraine, a handful of servants, perhaps twenty highbloods. I suppose the highbloods took some inspiration from Scimina's fearlessness.

"This will be an education for you, Cousin," she said, still in that sweet, polite tone that I was coming to hate. She resumed pacing, watching Nahadoth with an expression that was almost avid. "Had you been raised here in Sky, or taught properly by your mother, you would know this...but allow me to explain. It is difficult to damage an Enefadeh. Their human bodies repair themselves constantly and swiftly, through the benevolence of our Father Itempas. But they *do* have weaknesses, Cousin; one must simply understand these. Viraine."

Viraine had gotten to his feet as well, though he seemed to be favoring his left wrist. He eyed Scimina warily. "You'll take responsibility with Dekarta?"

She swung on him so fast that if the wand had still been in her hand, Viraine might have suffered a mortal wound. "Dekarta will be dead in days, Viraine. *He* is not whom you should fear now."

Viraine stood his ground. "I'm simply doing my job, Scimina, and advising you on the consequences. It may be weeks before he's useful again—"

Scimina made a sound of savage frustration. "*Does it look as though I care?*"

There was a pent moment, the two of them facing each other, during which I honestly thought Viraine had a chance. They were both fullbloods. But Viraine was not in line for the succession, and Scimina was—and in the end, Scimina was right. It was no longer Dekarta's will that mattered.

I looked at Sieh, who was staring at Nahadoth with an unreadable expression on his too-old face. Both were gods more ancient than life on earth. I could not imagine such a length of existence. A day of pain was probably nothing to them... but not to me.

"Enough," I said softly. The word carried in the vaulted space of the arena. Viraine and Scimina both looked at me in surprise. Sieh, too, swung around to stare at me, puzzled. And Nahadoth—no. I could not look at him. He would think me weak for this.

Not weak, I reminded myself. *Human. I am still that, at least.*

"Enough," I said again, lifting my head with what remained of my pride. "Stop this. I'll tell you whatever you want to know."

"Yeine," said Sieh, sounding shocked.

Scimina smirked. "Even if you weren't the sacrifice, Cousin, you could never have been my Uncle's heir."

I glared at her. "I will take that as a compliment, Cousin, if *you* are the example I should follow."

Scimina's face tightened, and for a moment I thought she would spit at me. Instead she turned away and resumed circling Nahadoth, though slower now. "Which member of the alliance did you approach?"

"Minister Gemd, of Menchey."

"Gemd?" Scimina frowned at this. "How did you persuade him? He was more eager for the chance than all the others."

I took a deep breath. "I brought Nahadoth with me. His persuasive powers are...formidable, as I'm sure you know."

Scimina barked a laugh—but her gaze was thoughtful as she glanced at me, then at him. Nahadoth gazed into the middle distance, as he had since kneeling. He might have been contemplating matters beyond human reckoning, or the dyes in T'vril's pants.

"Interesting," Scimina said. "Since I'm certain Uncle would not have commanded the Enefadeh to do this for you, that means our Nightlord decided to help you on his own. How on earth did you manage that?"

I shrugged, though abruptly I felt anything but relaxed. Stupid, stupid. I should have realized the danger in this line of questioning. "He seemed to find it amusing. There were...several deaths." I tried to look uneasy and found that it was not difficult. "I had not intended those, but they were effective."

"I see." Scimina stopped, folding her arms and tapping her fingers. I did not like the look in her eyes, even though it was directed at Nahadoth. "And what else did you do?"

I frowned. "Else?"

"We keep a tight leash on the Enefadeh, Cousin, and Nahadoth's is tightest of all. When he leaves the palace, Viraine knows of it. And Viraine tells me he left twice, on two separate nights."

Demons. Why in the Father's name hadn't the Enefadeh told me? Damned secret keeping— "I went to Darr, to see my grandmother."

"For what purpose?"

To understand why my mother sold me to the Enefadeh—

263

I jerked my thoughts off that path and folded my arms. "Because I missed her. Not that *you* would understand something like that."

She turned to gaze at me, a slow, lazy smile playing about her lips, and I suddenly realized I had made a mistake. But what? Had my insult bothered her that much? No, it was something else.

"You did not risk your sanity traveling with the Nightlord just to exchange pleasantries with some old hag," Scimina said. "Tell me why you really went there."

"To confirm the war petition and the alliance against Darr."

"And? That's all?"

I thought fast, but not fast enough. Or perhaps it was my unnerved expression that alerted her, because she *tsk*ed at me. "You're keeping secrets, Cousin. And I mean to have them. Viraine!"

Viraine sighed and faced Nahadoth. An odd look, almost pensive, passed over his face. "This would not have been my choice," he said softly.

Nahadoth's eyes flicked to him and lingered for a moment; there was a hint of surprise in his expression. "You must do as your lord requires." Not Dekarta. Itempas.

"This is not his doing," Viraine said, scowling. Then he seemed to recall himself, throwing Scimina one last glare and shaking his head. "Fine, then."

He reached into a pocket of his cloak and went to crouch beside Nahadoth, setting on his thigh a small square of paper on which had been drawn a spidery, liquid gods' sigil. Somehow—I refused to think deeply about how—I knew a line was missing from it. Then Viraine took out a brush with a capped tip.

I felt queasy. I stepped forward, lifting a bloodied hand to protest—and then stopped as my eyes met Nahadoth's. His face was impassive, the glance lazy and disinterested, but my mouth went dry anyhow. He knew what was coming better than I did. He knew I could stop it. But the only way I could do that was to risk revealing the secret of Enefa's soul.

Yet the alternative...

Scimina, observing this exchange, laughed—and then, to my revulsion, she came over to take me by the shoulder. "I commend you on your taste, Cousin. He *is* magnificent, isn't he? I have often wondered if there was some way... but, of course, there isn't."

She watched as Viraine set the square of paper on the floor beside Nahadoth, in one of the few spots unmarred by Sieh's blood. Viraine then uncapped the brush, hunched over the square, and very carefully drew a single line.

Light blazed down from the ceiling, as if someone had opened a colossal window at high noon. There *was* no opening in the ceiling, though; this was the power of the gods, who could defy the physical laws of the human realm and create something out of nothing. After the relative dimness of Sky's soft pale walls, this was too bright. I raised a hand in front of my watering eyes, hearing murmurs of discomfort from our remaining audience.

Nahadoth knelt at the light's center, his shadow stark amid the chains and blood. I had never seen his shadow before. At first the light seemed to do him no harm—but that was when I realized what had changed. I *hadn't* seen his shadow before. The living nimbus that surrounded him ordinarily did not allow it, constantly twisting and lashing and overlapping itself. It was not his nature to contrast his surroundings; he blended in. But now the nimbus had become just long black hair, draping over his back. Just a voluminous cloak cascading over his shoulders. His whole body was still.

And then Nahadoth uttered a soft sound, not quite a groan, and the hair and cloak began to boil.

"Watch closely," murmured Scimina in my ear. She had moved behind me, leaning against my shoulder like a dear companion. I could hear the relish in her voice. "See what your gods are made of."

Knowing she was there kept my face still. I did not react as the surface of Nahadoth's back bubbled and ran like hot tar, wisps of black curling into the air around him and evaporating with a rattling hiss. Nahadoth slowly slumped forward, pressed down as if the light crushed him beneath unseen weight. His hands landed in Sieh's blood and I saw that they, too, boiled, the unnaturally white skin rippling and spinning away in pale, fungoid tendrils. (Distantly, I heard one of the onlookers retch.) I could not see his face beneath the curtain of sagging, melting hair—but did I want to? He had no true form. I knew that everything I had seen of him was just a shell. But dearest Father, I had *liked* that shell and thought it beautiful. I could not bear to see the ruin of it now.

Then something white showed through his shoulder. At first I thought it was bone, and my own gorge rose. But it was not bone; it was skin. Pale like T'vril's, though devoid of spots, shifting now as it pushed up through the melting black.

And then I saw—

*   *   *

And did not see.

*A shining form (that my mind would not see) stood over a shape-less black mass (that my mind could not see) and plunged hands into the mass again and again. Not tearing it apart. Pummeling—pounding—*brutalizing *it into shape. The mass screamed, struggling desperately, but the shining hands held no mercy. They plunged again and hauled out arms. They crushed formless black until it became legs. They thrust into the middle and dragged out a torso, hand up to the wrist in its abdomen, gripping to impose a spine. And last was torn forth a head, barely human and bald, unrecognizable. Its mouth was open and shrieking, its eyes mad with agony beyond any mortal endurance. But of course, this was not a mortal.*

This is what you want, *snarls the shining one, his voice savage, but these are not words and I do not hear them. It is knowledge; it is in my head.* This abomination that she created. You would choose her over me? Then take her "gift"—take it—take it and never forget that you—chose—this—

The shining one is weeping, I notice, even as he commits this vio-lation.

And somewhere inside me someone was screaming, but it was not me, although I was screaming, too. And neither of us could be heard over the screams of the new-made creature on the ground, whose suf-fering had only begun—

*   *   *

The arm wrenched its way out of Nahadoth with a sound that reminded me of cooked meat. That same juicy, popping sound when one tears off a joint. Nahadoth, on his hands and knees, shuddered all over as the extra arm flailed blindly and then found purchase on the ground beside him. I could see now that it was pale, but not the moon-white I was used to. This was a far more mundane, human white. This was his daytime self, tearing through the godly veneer that covered it at night, in a grisly parody of birth.

He did not scream, I noticed. Beyond that initial abortive sound, Nahadoth remained silent even though another body ripped its way out of his. Somehow that made it worse, because his pain was so obvious. A scream would have eased my horror, if not his agony.

Beside him, Viraine watched for a moment, then closed his eyes, sighing.

"This could take hours," said Scimina. "It would go faster if this were true sunlight, of course, but only the Skyfather can command that. This is just a paltry imitation." She threw Viraine a contemptuous look. "More than enough for my purposes, though, as you can see."

I kept my jaw clenched tight. Across the circle, through the shaft of light and the haze created by Nahadoth's steaming godflesh, I could see Kurue. She looked at me once, bitter, and then away. Zhakkarn kept her eyes on Nahadoth. It was a warrior's way to acknowledge suffering, and thus respect it; she would not look away. Neither would I. But gods, gods.

It was Sieh who caught and held my gaze as he walked forward into the pool of light. It did not harm him; it was not his weakness. He knelt beside Nahadoth and gathered the disintegrating head to his chest, wrapped his arms around the heaving shoulders—all three of them. Through it all Sieh watched me, with a look that others probably interpreted as hatred. I knew otherwise.

Watch, those green eyes, so like mine yet so much older, said. *See what we endure. And then set us free.*

I will, I said back, with all my soul and Enefa's, too. *I will.*

* * *

I did not know. No matter what else happened, Itempas loved Naha. I never thought that could turn to hate.

What in the infinite hells makes you think that was hate?

* * *

I glanced at Scimina and sighed.

"Are you trying to nauseate me into answering?" I asked. "Add a new mess to the floor? That's all this farce is going to do."

She leaned back from me, lifting an eyebrow. "No compassion for your ally?"

"The Nightlord is *not* my ally," I snapped. "As everyone in this den of nightmares has repeatedly warned me, he is a monster. But since he's no different from the rest of you who want me dead, I thought I might at least use his power to help my people."

Scimina looked skeptical. "And what help did he provide? You made the effort in Menchey the next night."

"None; dawn came too quickly. But..." I faltered here, remembering my grandmother's arms and the smell of the humid Darren air that night. I *did* miss her, and Darr itself, and all the peace I had once known there. Before Sky. Before my mother's death.

I lowered my eyes and let my very real pain show. Only that would appease Scimina.

"We spoke of my mother," I said, softer. "And other things, personal things—none of which should have any importance to you." With this I glared at her. "And even if you roast that creature all night, I will not share those things with you."

Scimina gazed at me for a long moment, her smile gone, her eyes dissecting my face. Between and beyond us, Nahadoth finally made another sound through his teeth, an animal snarl. There were more hideous tearing sounds. I made myself not care by hating Scimina.

Finally she sighed and stepped away from me. "So be it," she said. "It was a feeble attempt, Cousin; you must have realized it had almost no chance of succeeding. I'm going to contact Gemd and tell him to resume the attack. They'll take control of your capital and crush any resistance, though I'll tell them to hold off on slaughtering your people—more than necessary—for the time being."

So there it was, laid plain: I would have to do her bidding, or she would unleash the Mencheyev to wipe my people out of existence. I scowled. "What guarantee do I have that you won't kill them anyway?"

"None whatsoever. After this foolishness, I'm tempted to do it just for spite. But I'd rather the Darre survive, now that I think about it. I imagine their lives won't be pleasant. Slavery rarely is—though we'll call it something else, of course." She glanced at Nahadoth, amused. "But they will be alive, Cousin, and where there is life, there is hope. Isn't that worth something to you? Worth a whole world, perhaps?"

I nodded slowly, though my innards clenched in new knots. I would not grovel. "It will do for now."

"For now?" Scimina stared at me, incredulous, then began to laugh. "Oh, Cousin. Sometimes I wish your mother were still alive. She at least could have given me a real challenge."

I had lost my knife, but I was still Darre. I whipped around and hit her so hard that one of her heeled shoes came off as she sprawled across the floor.

"Probably," I said, as she blinked away shock and what I hoped was a concussion. "But my mother was civilized."

Fists tight enough to sting at my sides, I turned my back on the whole arena and walked out.

21

First Love

I ALMOST FORGOT. When I first arrived in Sky, T'vril informed me that the highbloods sometimes gather for dinner in one of the fancier halls. This happened once during my time there, but I chose not to attend. There are rumors about Sky, you see. Some of them are exaggerations, and many are true, as I discovered. But there is one rumor I hoped never to confirm.

The Amn were not always civilized, the rumors remind us. Once, like High North, Senm was also a land of barbarians, and the Amn were simply the most successful of these. After the Gods' War they imposed their barbarian ways on the whole world and judged the rest of us by how thoroughly we adopted them—but they did not export all of their customs. Every culture has its ugly secrets. And once, the rumors say, Amn elites prized the taste of human flesh above all other delicacies.

Sometimes I am more afraid of the blood in my veins than the souls in my flesh.

*   *   *

When Nahadoth's torture ended, the clouds resumed moving across the night sky. They had been still, a caul over the moon that glimmered with arcs of color like weak, sickly rainbows. When the clouds finally moved on, something in me relaxed.

I had half-expected the knock at the door when it came, so I called enter. In the glass's reflection I saw T'vril, hovering uncertainly in the doorway.

"Yeine," he said, then faltered to silence.

I left him floundering in it for a while before saying, "Come in."

He stepped inside, just enough to allow the door to shut. Then he just looked at me, perhaps waiting for me to speak. But I had nothing to say to him, and eventually he sighed.

"The Enefadeh can endure pain," he said. "They've dealt with far worse over the centuries, believe me. What I wasn't sure of was *your* endurance."

"Thank you for your confidence."

T'vril winced at my tone. "I just knew you cared for Sieh. When Scimina started in on him, I thought..." He looked away, spread his hands helplessly. "I thought it would be better for you not to see."

"Because I'm so weak-willed and sentimental that I'd blabber all my secrets to save him?"

He scowled. "Because you're not like the rest of us. I thought you would do what you could to save a friend in pain, yes. I wanted to spare you that. Hate me for it if you like."

I turned to him, privately amazed. T'vril still saw me as the innocent, noble-hearted girl who had been so grateful for his kindness that first day in Sky. How many centuries ago had that been? Not quite two weeks.

"I don't hate you," I said.

T'vril exhaled, then came over to join me at the window. "Well... Scimina was furious when you left, as you might imagine."

I nodded. "Nahadoth? Sieh?"

"Zhakkarn and Kurue took them away. Scimina lost interest in us and left shortly after you did."

"'Us'?"

He paused for a second, and I could almost hear him cursing to himself under his breath. After a moment he said, "Her original plan was to play that little game with the servants."

"Ah, yes." I felt myself growing angry again. "That's when you suggested she use Sieh instead?"

He spoke tightly. "As I said, Yeine, the Enefadeh can survive Scimina's amusement. Mortals usually don't. You aren't the only one I need to protect."

Which made it no more right—but understandable. Like so much in Sky, wrong but *understandable*. I sighed.

"I offered myself first."

I started. T'vril was gazing out the window, a rueful smile on his face. "As Lady Yeine's friend, I said, if you'll forgive me for presuming. But she said I wasn't any better than the rest of the servants." His smile faded; I saw the muscles ripple along his jaw.

Dismissed again, I realized. *Not even his pain is good enough for the Central Family.* Yet he could not complain too much; his unimportance had saved him a great deal of suffering.

"I have to go," T'vril said. He lifted a hand, hesitated, then put it on my shoulder. The gesture, and the hesitancy, reminded me of Sieh. I put my own hand over his. I would miss him—ironic, since I was the one slated to die.

"Of course you're my friend," I whispered. His hand tightened for a moment, then he went to the door to leave.

Before he could, I heard a startled murmur from him; the voice that responded was familiar, too. I turned, and as T'vril stepped out Viraine stepped in.

"My apologies," he said. "May I come in?" He did not close the door, I noted, in case I said no.

For a moment I stared at him, amazed at his audacity. I had no doubt that he had magically enabled Scimina's torture of Sieh, just as he had Nahadoth's. That was his true role here, I understood now—to facilitate all the evil that our family dreamt up, especially where it concerned the gods. He was the Enefadeh's keeper and driver, wielder of the Arameri whip.

But an overseer is not solely to blame for a slave's misery. Sighing, I said nothing. Apparently deciding this constituted acceptance, Viraine let the door close and came over. Unlike T'vril, there was nothing resembling apology in his expression, just the usual guarded Arameri coolness.

"It was unwise of you to interfere in Menchey," he said.

"So I've been reminded."

"If you had trusted me—"

My mouth fell open in pure incredulity.

"If you had trusted me," Viraine said again, with a hint of stubbornness, "I would have helped you."

I almost laughed. "For what price?"

Viraine fell silent for a moment, then moved to stand beside me, almost exactly where T'vril had been. He felt very different, though. Warmer, most noticeably. I could feel his body heat from where I stood, a foot away.

"Have you chosen an escort for the ball?"

"Escort?" The question threw me entirely. "No. I've barely thought about the ball; I may not even attend."

"You must. Dekarta will compel you magically if you don't come on your own."

Of course. Viraine would be the one to impose the compulsion, no doubt. I shook my head, sighing. "Fine, then. If Grandfather is set on humiliating me, there's nothing I can do but endure it. But I see no reason to inflict the same on an escort."

He nodded slowly. That should have been my warning. I had never seen Viraine be anything but brisk in his mannerisms, even when relaxed.

"You might enjoy the night, at least a little," he said, "if I were your escort."

I was silent for so long that he turned to face my stare and laughed. "Are you so unused to being courted?"

"By people who aren't interested in me? Yes."

"How do you know I'm not?"

"Why *would* you be?"

"Do I need a reason?"

I folded my arms. "Yes."

Viraine raised his eyebrows. "I must apologize again, then. I hadn't realized I'd made such a poor impression on you over the past few weeks."

"Viraine—" I rubbed my eyes. I was tired—not physically

but emotionally, which was worse. "You've been very helpful, true, but I can't call you anything like kind. I've even doubted your sanity at times. Not that this makes you any different from other Arameri."

"Guilty as judged." He laughed again. That felt wrong, too. He was trying too hard. He seemed to realize it, because abruptly he sobered.

"Your mother," he said, "was my first lover."

My hand twitched toward my knife. It was on the side farthest from him. He did not see.

After a moment passed with no apparent reaction from me, Viraine seemed to relax somewhat. He lowered his eyes, gazing at the lights of the city far below. "I was born here, like most Arameri, but the highbloods sent me off to the Litaria—the scrivening college—at the age of four, when my gift for languages was noticed. I was just twenty when I returned, the youngest master ever approved by the program. Brilliant, if I may say, but still very young. A child, really."

I was not yet twenty myself, but of course barbarians grow up faster than civilized folk. I said nothing.

"My father had died in the interim," he continued. "My mother—" He shrugged. "Disappeared some night. That sort of thing happens here. It was just as well. I was granted fullblood status when I returned, and she was a lowblood. If she were still alive, I would no longer be her son." He glanced at me, after a pause. "That will sound heartless to you."

I shook my head, slowly. "I've been in Sky long enough."

He made a soft sound, somewhere between amusement and

cynicism. "I had a harder time getting used to this place than you," he said. "Your mother helped me. She was…like you in some ways. Gentle on the surface, something entirely different underneath."

I glanced at him, surprised by this description.

"I was smitten, of course. Her beauty, her wit, all that power…" He shrugged. "But I would have been content to admire her from afar. I wasn't *that* young. No one was more surprised than I when she offered me more."

"My mother wouldn't do that."

Viraine just looked at me for a moment, during which I glared back at him.

"It was a brief affair," he said. "Just a few weeks. Then she met your father and lost interest in me." He smiled thinly. "I can't say I was happy about that."

"I told you—" I began with some heat.

"You didn't know her," he said softly. It was that softness that silenced me. "No child knows her parents, not truly."

"You didn't know her, either." I refused to think about how childish that sounded.

For a moment there was such sorrow in Viraine's face, such lingering pain, that I knew he was telling the truth. He had loved her. He had been her lover. She had gone off to marry my father, leaving Viraine with only memories and longing. And now fresh grief burned in my soul, because he was right—I *hadn't* known her. Not if she could do something like this.

Viraine looked away. "Well. You wanted to know my reason for offering to escort you. You aren't the only one who mourns

Kinneth." He took a deep breath. "If you change your mind, let me know." He inclined his head, then headed for the door.

"Wait," I said, and he stopped. "I told you before: my mother did nothing without reason. So why did she take up with you?"

"How should I know?"

"What do you *think*?"

He considered a moment, then shook his head. He was smiling again, hopelessly. "I think I don't want to know. And neither do you."

He left. I stared at the closed door for a long time.

Then I went looking for answers.

*   *   *

I went first to my mother's room, where I took the chest of letters from behind the bed's headboard. When I turned with it in my hands, I found my unknown maternal grandmother gazing directly at me from within her portrait. "Sorry," I muttered, and left again.

It was not difficult to find an appropriate corridor. I simply wandered until a sense of nearby, familiar power tickled my awareness. I followed that sense until, before an otherwise nondescript wall, I knew I had found a good spot.

The gods' language was not meant to be spoken by mortals, but I had a goddess's soul. That had to be good for something.

"*Atadie*," I whispered, and the wall opened up.

I went through two dead spaces before finding Sieh's orrery. As the wall closed behind me, I looked around and noticed that the place looked starkly bare compared to the last time I'd seen it. Several dozen or so of the colored spheres lay scattered on the floor, unmoving, a few showing cracks or missing chunks. Only a handful floated in their usual places. The yellow ball was nowhere to be seen.

Beyond the spheres, Sieh lay on a gently curved hump of palace-stuff, with Zhakkarn crouched beside him. Sieh was younger than I had seen him in the arena, but still too old: long-legged and lanky, he must have been somewhere in late adolescence. Zhakkarn, to my surprise, had removed her headkerchief; her hair lay in close-curled, flattened ringlets about her head. Rather like mine, except that it was blue-white in color.

They were both staring at me. I crouched beside them, setting down the chest. "Are you all right?" I asked Sieh.

Sieh struggled to sit up, but I could see in his movements how weak he was. I moved to help, but Zhakkarn had him, bracing his back with one big hand. "Amazing, Yeine," Sieh said. "You opened the walls by yourself? I'm impressed."

"Can I help you?" I asked. "Somehow?"

"Play with me."

"Play—" But I trailed off as Zhakkarn caught my eye with a stern look. I thought a moment, then stretched out my hands, palms up. "Put your hands over mine."

He did so. His hands were larger than mine, and they shook like an old man's. So much wrongness. But he grinned. "Think you're fast enough?"

I slapped at his hands, and scored. He moved so slowly that I could've recited a poem in the process. "Apparently I am."

"Beginner's luck. Let's see you do it again." I slapped at his hands again. He moved faster this time; I almost missed. "Ha!

All right, third time's the charm." I slapped again, and this time did miss.

Surprised, I looked up at him. He grinned, visibly younger, though not by much. A year, perhaps. "See? I told you. You're slow."

I could not help smiling as I understood. "Do you think you might be up for tag?"

It was midnight. My body wanted sleep, not games, which made me sluggish. That worked in Sieh's favor, especially once he recovered enough to actually run. Then he chased me all over the chamber, amusing himself since I presented very little real challenge. It was doing him such noticeable good that I kept at it until he finally called a halt and we both flopped on the floor, panting. He looked, at last, normal—a spindly boy of nine or ten, beautiful and carefree. I no longer questioned why I loved him.

"Well, that was fun," Sieh said at last. He sat up, stretched, and began beckoning the dead spheres to himself. They rolled across the floor to him, where he picked them up, petted them fondly, then lifted them into the air, giving each a practiced twist before releasing it to float away. "So what's in the chest?"

I glanced at Zhakkarn, who had not joined in our play. I suspected children's games did not mesh well with the essence of battle. She nodded to me once, and this time it was approving. I flushed and looked away.

"Letters," I said, putting my hand on my mother's chest. "They are..." I hesitated, inexplicably reticent. "My father's letters to my mother, and some unsent drafts from her to him. I think..."

I swallowed. My throat was suddenly tight, and my eyes stung. There is no logic to grief.

Sieh ignored me, brushing my hand out of the way before opening the chest. I regained my composure while he took out each letter, skimmed it, and laid it on the ground, eventually standing up to enlarge the pattern. I had no idea what he was doing as he finally set the last letter into the corner of a great square some five paces by five, with a smaller square off to the side for my mother's letters. Then he stood and folded his arms to stare down at the whole mess.

"There are some missing," said Zhakkarn. I started to find her looming behind me, gazing down at the pattern as well.

Puzzled, I went to look myself, but could not read either my mother's fine script or my father's more sprawling hand from this distance. "How can you tell?"

"They both refer to prior letters," Zhakkarn said, pointing here and there at certain pages.

"And the pattern is broken in too many places," Sieh added, stepping lightly between the pages to crouch and peer more closely at the letters. "Both of them were creatures of habit, your parents. Once a week they wrote, regular as clockwork, over the span of a year. But there are six—no, seven weeks missing. No apologies after the missing weeks, and that is where I see references to the prior letters." He glanced back at me over his shoulder. "Did anyone besides you know this chest was there? Wait, no, it's been twenty years; half the palace might've known."

I shook my head, frowning. "They were hidden. The place *seemed* undisturbed—"

"That might only mean it happened so long ago that the dust

had time to settle." Sieh straightened, turning to me. "What is it you were expecting to find here?"

"Viraine—" I set my jaw. "Viraine says he was my mother's lover."

Sieh raised his eyebrows and exchanged a look with Zhakkarn. "I'm not certain I would use any part of the word 'love' in what she did to him."

In the face of such casual confirmation, I could not protest. I sat down heavily.

Sieh flopped down on his belly beside me, propping himself on his elbows. "What? Half of Sky is in bed with the other half at any given time."

I shook my head. "Nothing. It's just . . . a bit much to take."

"He's not your father or anything like that, if you're worried."

I rolled my eyes and raised my brown Darre hand. "I'm not."

"Pleasure is often used as a weapon," Zhakkarn said. "There's no love in that."

I frowned at her, surprised by this notion. I still did not like the idea of my mother lying with Viraine, but it helped to think of it as strategy. But what had she hoped to gain? What did Viraine know that no one else in Sky knew? Or rather, what would the younger, smitten Viraine—new to Sky, overconfident, eager to please—have been more likely to say than any other Arameri?

"Something about magic," I murmured to myself. "That must be what she was trying to get out of him. Something about . . . you?" I glanced over at Zhakkarn.

Zhakkarn shrugged. "If she learned any such secrets, she never used them."

"Hmm. What else is Viraine in charge of, here?"

"Magic use," Sieh said, ticking off fingers. "Everything from the routine to, well, us. Information dissemination—he's Dekarta's liaison to the Itempan Order. He oversees all important ceremonies and rituals..."

Sieh trailed off. I looked at him and saw surprise on his face. I glanced at Zhakkarn, who looked thoughtful.

Ceremonies and rituals. A flicker of excitement stirred in my belly as I realized what Sieh meant. I sat up straighter. "When was the last succession?"

"Dekarta's was about forty years ago," Zhakkarn said.

My mother had been forty-five at her death. "She would have been too young to understand what was happening at the ceremony."

"She wasn't at the ceremony," Sieh said. "Dekarta ordered me to play with her that day, to keep her busy."

That was surprising. Why would Dekarta have kept my mother, his heir, away from the ceremony that she would one day have to undertake herself? A bright child could have been made to understand its purpose. Was it that they meant to kill a servant in the course of the ceremony? But this was Sky; servants died all the time. I couldn't imagine any Arameri, much less my grandfather, denying that harsh reality even to a child.

"Did anything unusual happen at that ceremony?" I asked. "Did you make a play for the Stone that time?"

"No, we weren't ready. It was a routine succession, like the hundred others that have occurred since our imprisonment."

Sieh sighed. "Or so I'm told, since I wasn't there. None of us were, except Nahadoth. They always make him attend."

I frowned. "Why just him?"

"Itempas attends the ceremony," said Zhakkarn. While I gaped at her, trying to shape my mind around the idea of the Skyfather *here, right here, coming here,* Zhakkarn went on. "He makes his greetings personally to the new Arameri ruler. Then he offers Nahadoth freedom, though only if he serves Itempas. Thus far, Naha has refused, but Itempas knows it is in his nature to change his mind. He will keep asking."

I shook my head, trying to rid myself of the lingering sense of reverence that a lifetime of training had inculcated in me. The Skyfather, at the succession ceremony. At *every* succession ceremony. He would be there to see me die. He would put his blessing on it.

Monstrous. All my life, I had worshipped him.

To distract myself from my own whirling thoughts, I pinched the bridge of my nose with my fingers. "So who was the sacrifice last time? Some other hapless relative dragged into the family nightmare?"

"No, no," said Sieh. He got up, stretched again, then bent double and began to stand on his hands, wobbling alarmingly. He spoke in between puffing breaths. "An Arameri clan head... must be willing to kill... every person in this palace... if Itempas should require it. To prove themselves, usually... the prospective head must... sacrifice someone *close.*"

I considered this. "So I was chosen because neither Relad nor Scimina is close to anyone?"

Sieh wobbled too much, tumbled to the ground, then rolled upright at once, examining his nails as if the fall hadn't happened. "Well, I suppose. No one's really sure why Dekarta chose you. But for Dekarta himself, the sacrifice was Ygreth."

The name teased my memory with familiarity, though I could not immediately place it with a face. "Ygreth?"

Sieh looked at me in surprise. "His wife. Your maternal grandmother. Kinneth didn't tell you?"

22

Such Rage

ARE YOU STILL ANGRY WITH ME?

No.

That was quick.

Anger is pointless.

I disagree. I think anger can be very powerful under the right circumstances. Let me tell you a story to illustrate. Once upon a time there was a little girl whose father murdered her mother.

How awful.

Yes, you understand that sort of betrayal. The little girl was very young at the time, so the truth was hidden from her. Perhaps she was told her mother abandoned the family. Perhaps her mother vanished; in their world, such things happened. But the little girl was very clever, and she had loved her mother dearly. She pretended to believe the lies, but in reality, she bided her time.

When she was older, wiser, she began to ask questions—but not of her father, or anyone else who claimed to care for her. These could not be trusted. She asked her slaves, who hated her already. She asked an innocent young scrivener who was smitten with her, brilliant and easy to manipulate. She asked her enemies, the heretics, whom her family had persecuted for generations. None of them had any reason to lie, and between them all she pieced together the truth. Then she set all her mind and heart and formidable will on vengeance... because that is what a daughter does when her mother has been murdered.

Ah, I see. But I wonder; did the little girl love her father?

I wonder that, too. Once, certainly, she must have; children cannot help loving. But what of later? Can love turn to hate so easily, so completely? Or did she weep inside even as she set herself against him? I do not know these things. But I do know that she set in motion a series of events that would shake the world even after her death, and inflict her vengeance on all humankind, not just her father. Because in the end, we are all complicit.

All of you? That seems a bit extreme.

Yes. Yes, it is. But I hope she gets what she wants.

*   *   *

This, then, was the Arameri succession: a successor was chosen by the family head. If she was the sole successor, she would be required to convince her most cherished person to willingly die on her behalf, wielding the Stone and transferring the master sigil to her brow. If there was more than one successor, they competed to force the designated sacrifice to choose one or the other. My mother had been sole heir; whom would she have been forced to kill, had she not abdicated? Perhaps she had cultivated Viraine as a lover for more than one reason. Perhaps she could have convinced Dekarta himself to die for her. Perhaps this was why she had never come back after her marriage, after my conception.

So many pieces had fallen into place. More yet floated, indistinct. I could feel how close I was to understanding it all, but would I have time? There was the rest of the night, the next day, and another whole night and day beyond that. Then the ball, and the ceremony, and the end.

More than enough time, I decided.

"You can't," Sieh said again urgently, trotting along beside me. "Yeine, Naha needs to heal, just as I did. He can't do that with mortal eyes shaping him—"

"I won't look at him, then."

"It's not that simple! When he's weak, he's more dangerous than ever; he has trouble controlling himself. You shouldn't—" His voice dropped an octave suddenly, breaking like that of a youth in puberty, and he cursed under his breath and stopped. I walked on, and was not surprised when I heard him stamp the floor behind me and shout, "You are the stubbornest, most infuriating mortal I've ever had to put up with!"

"Thank you," I called back. There was a curve up ahead; I stopped before rounding it. "Go and rest in my room," I said. "I'll read you a story when I get back."

What he snarled in reply, in his own tongue, needed no translation. But the walls did not fall in, and I did not turn into a frog, so he couldn't have been that angry.

Zhakkarn had told me where to find Nahadoth. She had looked at me for a long time before saying it, reading my face with eyes that had assessed a warrior's determination since the dawn of time. That she'd told me was a compliment—or a warning. Determination could easily become obsession. I did not care.

In the middle of the lowermost residential level, Zhakkarn had said, Nahadoth had an apartment. The palace was perpetually shadowed here by its own bulk, and in the center there would be no windows. All the Enefadeh had dwellings on that level, for those unpleasant occasions when they needed to sleep and eat and otherwise care for their semimortal bodies. Zhakkarn had not mentioned why they'd chosen such an unpleasant location, but I thought I knew. Down there, just above the oubliette, they could be closer to Enefa's Stone than to Itempas's usurped sky. Perhaps the lingering feel of her presence was a comfort, given that they suffered so much in her name.

The level was silent when I stepped out of the lift alcove. None of the palace's mortal complement lived here—not that I blamed them. Who would want the Nightlord for a neighbor? Unsurprisingly, the level seemed unusually gloomy; the palace walls did not glow so brightly here. Nahadoth's brooding presence permeated the whole level.

But when I rounded the last curve, I was briefly blinded by a flash of unexpected brightness. In the afterimage of that flash I had seen a woman, bronze-skinned and silver-haired, almost as tall as Zhakkarn and sternly beautiful, kneeling in the corridor as if to pray. The light had come from the wings on her back, covered in mirror-bright feathers of overlapping precious metals. I had seen her once before, this woman, in a dream—

Then I blinked my watering eyes and looked again, and the light was gone. In its place, heavyset, plain Kurue was laboriously climbing to her feet, glaring at me.

"I'm sorry," I said, for the interruption of whatever meditations a goddess required. "But I need to speak with Nahadoth."

There was only one door in this corridor, and Kurue stood in front of it. She folded her arms. "No."

"Lady Kurue, I don't know when I'll have another chance to ask these things—"

"What, precisely, does 'no' mean in your tongue? Clearly you don't understand Senmite—"

But before our argument could escalate, the apartment door slid aside a fraction. I could see nothing through that sliver, only darkness. "Let her speak," said Nahadoth's deep voice from within.

Kurue's scowl deepened. "Naha, no." I started a little; I had never heard anyone contradict him. "It's her fault you're in this condition."

I flushed, but she was right. Yet there was no answer from within the chamber. Kurue's fists clenched, and she glared into the darkness with a very ugly look.

"Would it help if I wore a blindfold?" I asked. There was something in the air that hinted at a long-standing anger beyond just this brief exchange. Ah, but of course—Kurue hated mortals, quite rightly blaming us for her enslaved condition. She thought Nahadoth was being foolish over me. Most likely she was right about that, too, being a goddess of wisdom. I did not feel offended when she looked at me with new contempt.

"It isn't just your eyes," Kurue said. "It's your expectations, your fears, your desires. You mortals want him to be a monster and so he becomes one—"

"Then I will want nothing," I said. I smiled as I said it, but I was annoyed now. Perhaps there was wisdom in her blind hatred of humankind. If she expected the worst from us, then we could never disappoint her. But that was beside the point. She was in my way, and I had business to complete before I died. I would command her aside if I had to.

She stared at me, perhaps reading my intentions. After a moment she shook her head and made a dismissive gesture. "Fine, then. You're a fool. And so are you, Naha; you both deserve each other." With that, she walked away, muttering as she rounded a corner. I waited until the sound of her footfalls stopped—not fading, but simply vanishing—then turned to face the open door.

"Come," said Nahadoth from within.

I cleared my throat, abruptly nervous. Why did he frighten me at all the wrong times? "Begging your pardon, Lord Nahadoth," I said, "but perhaps I'd better stay out here. If it's true that just my *thoughts* can harm you—"

"Your thoughts have always harmed me. All your terrors, all your needs. They push and pull at me, silent commands."

I stiffened, horrified. "I never meant to add to your suffering."

There was a pause, during which I held my breath.

"My sister is dead," Nahadoth said very softly. "My brother has gone mad. My children—the handful who remain—hate and fear me as much as they revere me."

And I understood: what Scimina had done to him was nothing. What was a few moments' suffering beside the centuries of grief and loneliness that Itempas had inflicted on him? And here I was, fretting over my own small addition.

I opened the door and stepped inside.

Within the chamber, the darkness was absolute. I lingered near the door for a moment, hoping my eyes would adjust, but they did not. In the silence after the door closed I made out the sound of breathing, slow and even, some ways away.

I put out my hands and began groping my way blindly toward the sound, hoping gods had no great need of furniture. Or steps.

"Stay where you are," Nahadoth said. "I am...not safe to be near." Then, softer, "But I am glad you came."

This was the other Nahadoth, then—not the mortal, but not the mad beast of a cold winter's tale, either. This was the Nahadoth who had kissed me that first night, the one who actually seemed to like me. The one I had the fewest defenses against.

I took a deep breath and tried to concentrate on the soft empty dark.

"Kurue is right. I'm sorry. It's my fault Scimina punished you."

"She did it to punish *you.*"

I winced. "Even worse."

He laughed softly, and I felt a breeze stir past me, soft as a warm summer night. "Not for me."

Point. "Is there anything I can do to help you?"

I felt the breeze again, and this time it tickled the tiny hairs on my skin. I had a sudden image of him standing just behind me, holding me close and exhaling into the curve of my neck.

There was a soft, hungry sound from the other side of the

room, and abruptly lust filled the space around me, powerful and violent and not remotely tender. Oh, gods. I quickly fixed my thoughts again on darkness, nothing, darkness, my mother. Yes.

It seemed to take a long time, but eventually that terrible hunger faded.

"It would be best," he said with disturbing gentleness, "if you make no effort to help."

"I'm sorry—"

"You are mortal." That seemed to say it all. I lowered my eyes, ashamed. "You have a question about your mother."

Yes. I took a deep breath. "Dekarta killed *her* mother," I said. "Was that the reason she gave, when she agreed to help you?"

"I am a slave. No Arameri would confide in me. As I told you, all she did was ask questions at first."

"And in return, you asked for her help?"

"No. She still wore the blood sigil. She could not be trusted."

Involuntarily I raised a hand to my own forehead. I continually forgot the mark was there. I had forgotten that it was a factor in Sky politics as well. "Then how—"

"She bedded Viraine. Prospective heirs are usually told about the succession ceremony, but Dekarta had commanded that the details be kept from her. Viraine knew no better, so he told Kinneth how the ceremony usually goes. I assume that was enough for her to figure out the truth."

Yes, it would have been. She had suspected Dekarta already—and Dekarta had feared her suspicions, it seemed. "What did she do, once she knew?"

"She came to us and asked how she might be made free of her

mark. If she could act against Dekarta, she said, she would be willing to use the Stone to set us free."

I caught my breath, amazed at her daring—and her fury. I had come to Sky willing to die to avenge my mother, and only fortune and the Enefadeh had made that possible. My mother had created her own vengeance. She had betrayed her people, her heritage, even her god, all to strike a blow against one man.

Scimina was right. I was nothing compared to my mother.

"You told me only I could use the Stone to free you," I said. "Because I possess Enefa's soul."

"Yes. This was explained to Kinneth. But since the opportunity had presented itself... We suggested to her that being disowned would get her free of the sigil. And we aimed her toward your father."

Something in my chest turned to water. I closed my eyes. So much for my parents' fairy-tale romance.

"Did she...agree from the start to have a child for you?" I asked. My voice sounded very soft in my own ears, but the room was quiet. "Did she and my father...*breed* me for you?"

"No."

I could not bring myself to believe him.

"She hated Dekarta," Nahadoth continued, "but she was still his favorite child. We told her nothing of Enefa's soul and our plans, because we did not trust her."

More than understandable.

"All right," I said, trying to marshal my thoughts. "So she met my father, who was one of Enefa's followers. She married him knowing he would help her achieve her goal, and also knowing the marriage would get her thrown out of the family. That got her free of the sigil."

"Yes. And as a test of her intentions, it proved to us that she was sincere. It also partially achieved her goal: when she left, Dekarta was devastated. He mourned her as if she'd died. His suffering seemed to please her."

I understood. Oh, how I understood.

"But then...then Dekarta used the Walking Death to try to kill my father." I said it slowly. Such a convoluted patchwork to piece together. "He must have blamed my father for her leaving. Maybe he convinced himself that she'd come back if Father was dead."

"Dekarta did not unleash the Death on Darr."

I stiffened. "What?"

"When Dekarta wants magic done, he uses us. None of us sent the plague to your land."

"But if you didn't—"

No. Oh, no.

There was another source of magic in Sky besides the Ene-fadeh. Another who could wield the gods' power, albeit weakly. The Death had killed only a dozen people in Darr that year; a minor outbreak by all the usual standards. The best a mortal murderer could do.

"Viraine," I whispered. My hands clenched into fists. "*Viraine*."

He had played the martyr so well—the innocent used and abused by my scheming mother. Meanwhile he had tried to murder my father, knowing she would blame Dekarta and not him. *He* had waited in the corridors like a vulture while she came to plead with Dekarta for her husband's life. Perhaps he had revealed himself to her afterward and commiserated with her over Dekarta's refusal. To lay the groundwork for wooing her back? Yes, that felt like him.

And yet my father had not died. My mother had not returned to Sky. Had Viraine pined for her all these years, hating my father—hating *me* for thwarting his plans? Had Viraine been the one to raid my mother's chest of letters? Perhaps he had burned any that referred to him, hoping to forget his youthful folly. Perhaps he'd kept them, fantasizing that the letters contained some vestige of the love he'd never earned.

I would hunt him down. I would see his white hair fall around his face in a red curtain.

There was a faint, skittering sound nearby, like pebbles on the hard Skystuff floor. Or claw tips—

"Such rage," the Nightlord breathed, his voice all deep crevasses and ice. And he was close, all of a sudden, so close. Right behind me. "Oh, yes. Command me, sweet Yeine. I am your weapon. Give the word, and I will make the pain he inflicted on me tonight seem kind."

My anger was gone, frozen away. Slowly I took a deep breath, then another, calming myself. No hatred. No fear of whatever the Nightlord had become thanks to my carelessness. I fixed my mind on the dark and the silence, and did not answer. I did not dare.

After a very long while I heard a faint, disappointed sigh. Farther away this time; he had returned to the other side of the room. Slowly I allowed my muscles to unclench.

Dangerous to continue this line of questioning right now. So many secrets to discover, so many pit-traps of emotion. I pushed aside thoughts of Viraine, with an effort.

"My mother wanted to save my father," I said. Yes. That was a good thing to understand. She must have grown to love him, however strangely the relationship had begun. I knew he'd loved her. I remembered seeing it in his eyes.

"Yes," said Nahadoth. His voice was as calm as before my lapse. "Her desperation made her vulnerable. Of course we took advantage."

I almost grew angry, but caught myself in time.

"Of course. So you persuaded her then to allow Enefa's soul into her child. And…" I took a deep breath. Paused, marshaling my strength. "My father knew?"

"I don't know."

If the Enefadeh did not know what my father thought of the matter, then no one here would know. I dared not go back to Darr to ask Beba.

So I chose to believe that Father knew and loved me anyway. That Mother, beyond her initial misgivings, had chosen to love me. That she had kept the ugly secrets of her family from me out of some misguided hope that I would have a simple, peaceful destiny in Darr… at least until the gods came back to claim what was theirs.

I needed to stay calm, but I could not hold it all in. I closed my eyes and began to laugh. So many hopes had been rested on me.

"Am I allowed none of my own?" I whispered.

"What would you want?" Nahadoth asked.

"What?"

"If you could be free." There was something in his voice that I did not understand. Wistfulness? Yes, and something more.

Kindness? Fondness? No, that was impossible. "What would you want for yourself?"

The question made my heart ache. I hated him for asking it. It was his fault that my wishes would never come true—his fault, and my parents', and Dekarta's, and even Enefa's.

"I'm tired of being what everyone else has made me," I said. "I want to be myself."

"Don't be a child."

I looked up, startled and angry, though of course there was nothing to see. "What?"

"You are what your creators and experiences have made you, like every other being in this universe. Accept that and be done; I tire of your whining."

If he had said it in his usual cold voice, I would have walked out in affront. But he truly did sound tired, and I remembered the price he had paid for my selfishness.

The air stirred nearby again, soft, almost a touch. When he spoke, he was closer. "The future, however, is yours to make—even now. Tell me what you want."

It was something I had never truly thought about, beyond vengeance. I wanted...all the usual things that any young woman wanted. Friends. Family. Happiness for those I loved.

And also...

I shivered, though the chamber was not cold. The very strangeness of this new thought made me suspicious. Was this some sign of Enefa's influence?

Accept that and be done.

"I..." I closed my mouth. Swallowed. Tried again. "I want...something different for the world." Ah, but the world would indeed be different after Nahadoth and Itempas were done with it. A pile of rubble, with humanity a red ruin underneath. "Something better."

"What?"

"I don't know." I clenched my fists, struggling to articulate what I felt, surprised by my own frustration. "Right now, everyone is...afraid." Closer, yes. I kept at it. "We live at the gods' mercy and shape our lives around your whims. Even when your quarrels don't involve us, we die. What would we be like if...if you just...went away?"

"More would die," said the Nightlord. "Those who worship us would be frightened by our absence. Some would decide it was the fault of others, while those who embrace the new order would resent any who keep the old ways. The wars would last centuries."

I felt the truth of his words in the pit of my belly, and it left me queasy with horror. But then something touched me—hands, cool and light. He rubbed my shoulders, as if to soothe me.

"But eventually, the battles would end," he said. "When a fire burns out, new things grow in its wake."

I felt no lust or rage from him—probably because, for the moment, he felt none from me. He was not like Itempas, unable to accept change, bending or breaking everything around him to his will. Nahadoth bent himself to the will of others. For a moment the thought made me sad.

"Are you ever yourself?" I asked. "Truly yourself, not just the way others see you?"

The hands went still, then withdrew. "Enefa asked me that once."

"I'm sorry—"

"No." There was sorrow in his voice. It never faded, for him. How terrible to be a god of change and endure grief unending.

"When I am free," he said, "I will choose who shapes me."

"But..." I frowned. "That isn't freedom."

"At the dawn of reality I was myself. There was nothing and no one else to influence me—only the Maelstrom that had given birth to me, and it did not care. I tore open my flesh and spilled out the substance of what became your realm: matter and energy and my own cold, black blood. I devoured my mind and reveled in the novelty of pain."

Tears sprang to my eyes. I swallowed hard and tried to will them away, but abruptly the hands returned, lifting my chin. Fingers stroked my eyes shut, brushing the tears away.

"When I am free I will choose," he said again, whispering, very close. "You must do the same."

"But I will never be—"

He kissed me silent. There was longing in that kiss, tangy and bittersweet. Was that my own longing, or his? Then I understood, finally: it didn't matter.

But oh gods, oh goddess, it was so good. He tasted like cool dew. He made me thirsty. Just before I began to want more, he pulled back. I fought not to feel disappointment, for fear of what it would do to us both.

"Go and rest, Yeine," he said. "Leave your mother's schemes to play themselves out. You have your own trials to face."

And then I was in my apartment, sitting on the floor in a square of moonlight. The walls were dark, but I could see easily because the moon, bright though just a sliver, was low in the sky. Well past midnight, probably only an hour or two before dawn. This was becoming a habit for me.

Sieh sat in the big chair near my bed. Seeing me, he uncurled from it and moved onto the floor beside me. In the moonlight his pupils were huge and round, like those of an anxious cat.

I said nothing, and after a moment he reached up and pulled me down so that my head rested in his lap. I closed my eyes, drawing comfort from the feel of his hand on my hair. After a time, he began to sing me a lullaby that I had heard in a dream. Relaxed and warm, I slept.

23

Selfishness

TELL ME WHAT YOU WANT, the Nightlord had said.

Something better for the world, I had replied.

But also...

*   *   *

In the morning I went to the Salon early, before the Consortium session began, hoping to find Ras Onchi. Before I could, I saw Wohi Ubm, the other High North noblewoman, arriving on the Salon's wide, colonnaded steps.

"Oh," she said after an awkward introduction and my inquiry. I knew then, the instant I saw the pitying look in her eyes. "You haven't heard. Ras died in her sleep just these two nights past." She sighed. "I still can't believe it. But, well; she was old."

I went back to Sky.

*   *   *

I walked through the corridors awhile, thinking about death.

Servants nodded as they passed me and I nodded back. Courtiers—my fellow highbloods—either ignored me or stared in open curiosity. Word must have spread that I was finished as an heir candidate, publicly defeated by Scimina. Not all of the stares were kind. I inclined my head to them anyhow. Their pettiness was not mine.

On one of the lower levels I surprised T'vril on a shadowed balcony, dangling a clipboard from one finger and watching a passing cloud. When I touched him, he started guiltily (fortunately catching the clipboard), which I took to mean he had been thinking about me.

"The ball will begin at dusk tomorrow night," he said. I had moved to stand at the railing beside him, absorbing the view and the comfort of his presence in silence. "It will continue until dawn the next morning. That's tradition, before a succession ceremony. Tomorrow is a new moon—a night that was once sacred to the followers of Nahadoth. So they celebrate through it."

Petty of them, I thought. Or petty of Itempas.

"Immediately after the ball, the Stone of Earth will be sent through the palace's central shaft to the ritual chamber, in the solarium spire."

"Ah. I heard you warning the servants about this last week."

T'vril turned the clipboard in his fingers gently, not looking at me. "Yes. A fleeting exposure supposedly does no harm, but..." He shrugged. "It's a thing of the gods. Best to stay away."

I could not help it; I laughed. "Yes, I agree!"

T'vril looked at me oddly, a small uncertain smile on his lips. "You seem...comfortable."

I shrugged. "It isn't my nature to spend all my time fretting. What's done is done." Nahadoth's words.

T'vril shifted uncomfortably, flicking a few stray windblown hairs out of his face. "I'm...told that an army gathers along the pass that leads from Menchey into Darr."

I steepled my fingers and gazed at them, stilling the voice that cried out within myself. Scimina had played her game well. If I did not choose her, I had no doubt she had left instructions for Gemd to begin the slaughter. Gemd might do it anyhow once I set the Enefadeh free, but I was counting on the world being preoccupied with survival amid the outbreak of another Gods' War. Sieh had promised that Darr would be kept safe through the cataclysm. I wasn't sure I entirely trusted that promise, but it was better than nothing.

For what felt like the hundredth time, I considered and discarded the idea of approaching Relad. Scimina's people were on the ground; her knife was at Darr's throat. If I chose Relad at the ceremony, could he act before that knife cut a fatal wound? I could not bet my people's future on a man I didn't even respect.

Only the gods could help me now.

"Relad has confined himself in his quarters," T'vril said, obviously thinking along the same lines as me. "He receives no calls, lets no one in, not even the servants. The Father knows what he's eating—or drinking. There are bets among the highbloods that he'll kill himself before the ball."

"I suppose there's little else interesting here to bet on."

T'vril glanced at me, perhaps deciding whether to say more. "There are also bets that *you* will kill *yourself*."

I laughed into the breeze. "What are the odds? Do you think they'd let me bet, too?"

T'vril turned to face me, his eyes suddenly intent. "Yeine—if, if you—" He faltered silent and looked away; his voice had choked on the last word.

I took his hand and held it while he bowed his head and trembled and fought to keep control of himself. He led and protected the servants here; tears would have made him feel weak. Men have always been fragile that way.

After a few moments he took a deep breath. His voice was higher than usual as he said, "Shall I escort you to the ball tomorrow night?"

When Viraine had offered the same thing, I had hated him. With T'vril, the offer made me love him a little more. "No, T'vril. I want no escort."

"It could help. To have a friend there."

"It could. But I will not ask such a thing of my few friends."

"You aren't asking. I'm offering—"

I stepped closer, leaning against his arm. "I'll be fine, T'vril."

He regarded me for a long while, then shook his head slowly. "You will, won't you? Ah, Yeine. I'll miss you."

"You should leave this place, T'vril. Find yourself a good woman to take care of you and keep you in silks and jewelry."

T'vril stared at me, then burst out laughing, not strained at all this time. "A Darre woman?"

"No, are you mad? You've seen what we're like. Find some Ken girl. Maybe those pretty spots of yours will breed true."

"Pretty—*freckles*, you barbarian! They're called freckles."

"Whatever." I lifted his hand, kissed the back of it, and let him go. "Good-bye, my friend."

I left him there, still laughing, as I walked away.

* * *

But...?

But that was not all I wanted.

* * *

That conversation helped me decide on my next move. I went looking for Viraine.

I had been of two minds about confronting him ever since the previous night's conversation with Nahadoth. I believed now that Viraine, not Dekarta, had killed my mother. I still did not understand it; if he had loved her, why kill her? And why now, twenty years after she'd broken his heart? Part of me craved understanding.

The other part of me did not care why he'd done it. This part of me wanted blood, and I knew that if I listened to it I might do something foolish. There would be blood aplenty when I got my vengeance on the Arameri; all the horror and death of a second Gods' War unleashed. That much blood should have been enough for me...but I would not be alive to see it. We are selfish that way, we mortals.

So I went to see Viraine.

He did not answer when I knocked at the door to his workshop, and for a moment I wavered, debating whether to pursue the matter further. Then I heard a faint, muffled sound from within.

Doors in Sky do not lock. For highbloods, rank and politics provide more than enough security, as only those who are immune to retaliation dare invade another's privacy. I, condemned to die in slightly more than a day, was thus immune, and so I slid the door open, just a bit.

I did not see Viraine at first. There was the workbench

where I had been marked, its surface empty this time. All of the benches were empty, in fact, which seemed strange to me. So were the animal cages at the back of the room, which was stranger yet. Only then did I spot Viraine—in part because he stood so still and in part because with his white hair and garments, he matched his pristine, sterile workplace so thoroughly.

He was near the large crystal globe at the back of the chamber. I thought at first that he leaned against it in order to peer into its translucent depths. Perhaps this was how he had spied on me, in my lone, abortive communication with my assigned nations. But then I noticed that he stood slumped, one hand braced against the globe's polished surface, head hanging. I could not see his free hand through the white curtain of his hair, but there was something about its furtive movements that rang an instant note of recognition within me. He sniffed, and that confirmed it: alone in his workshop, on the eve of his god's once-in-a-lifetime reaffirmation of triumph, Viraine was crying.

It was weakness unbecoming of a Darre woman that this quieted my anger. I had no idea why he was crying. Perhaps all his evils had revived the tatters of his conscience for one moment. Perhaps he had stubbed his toe. But in the moment that I stood there, watching him weep as T'vril had managed not to, I could not help wondering: what if even one of those tears was for my mother? So few people had mourned her besides me.

I slid the door shut and left.

*　　*　　*

Foolish of me.

Yes. Even then, you resisted the truth.

Do I know it?

Now, yes. Then, you did not.

Why—

You're dying. Your soul is at war. And another memory preoccupies you.

Tell me what you want, the Nightlord had said.

* * *

Scimina was in her quarters, being fitted for her ball gown. It was white—a color that did not suit her well. There was not enough contrast between the material and her pale skin, and the overall result made her look faded. Still, the gown was lovely, made of some shining material that had been further enhanced by tiny diamonds studding the bodice and the lines of the skirt. They caught the light as she turned on her dais for the tailors.

I waited patiently while she issued instructions to them. On the far side of the room, the human version of Nahadoth sat on a windowsill, gazing out at the early-afternoon sun. If he heard me enter, he did not look up to acknowledge it.

"I confess I'm curious," Scimina said, turning to me at last. I felt a fleeting, petty sense of pleasure at the sight of a large bruise on her jaw. Was there no magic to quickly heal such small wounds? A shame. "What could bring you here to visit me? Do you plan to plead for your nation?"

I shook my head. "There would be no point."

She smiled, almost kindly. "True. Well, then. What do you want?"

"To take you up on an offer," I said. "I hope that it still stands?"

Another small satisfaction: the blank look on her face. "What offer would that be, Cousin?"

I nodded past her, at the still figure in the window. He was clothed, I saw, in a simple black shirt and pants, and a plain iron collar for once. That was good. I found him more distasteful nude. "You said that I was welcome to borrow your pet sometime."

Beyond Scimina, Naha turned to stare at me, his brown eyes wide. Scimina did, too, for a moment, and then she burst out laughing.

"I see!" She shifted her weight to one side and put a hand on her hip, much to the consternation of the tailors. "I can't argue with your choice, Cousin. He's much more fun than T'vril. But—forgive me—you seem such a small creature. And my Naha is so very...strong. Are you certain?"

Her insults wafted past me like air; I barely noticed. "I am."

Scimina shook her head, bemused. "Very well. I have no use for him at the moment anyhow; he's weak today. Probably just right for you, though—" She paused then, glancing at the windows. Checking the position of the sun. "Of course you know to beware sunset."

"Of course." I smiled, drawing a momentary frown from her. "I have no wish to die earlier than necessary."

Something like suspicion flickered in Scimina's eyes for a moment, and I felt tension in the pit of my belly. But she finally shrugged.

"Go with her," she said, and Nahadoth rose.

"For how long?" he asked, his voice neutral.

"Until she's dead." Scimina smiled and opened her arms in a magnanimous gesture. "Who am I to deny a last request? But while you're at it, Naha, see to it that she does nothing too strenuous—nothing that would incapacitate her, at least. We need her fit, two mornings from now."

The iron chain had been connected to a nearby wall. It fell away with Scimina's words. Naha picked up the loose end, then stood watching me, his expression unreadable.

I inclined my head to Scimina. She ignored me, returning her attention to the tailors' work with a snarl of irritation; one of them had pinned the hem badly. I left, not caring whether Nahadoth followed now or later.

*　　*　　*

What would I want, if I could be free?

Safety for Darr.

My mother's death given meaning.

Change, for the world.

And for myself...

I understand now. I have chosen who will shape me.

*　　*　　*

"She's right," Naha said, when we stood together in my apartment. "I'm not much use at the moment." He said it blandly, with no emotional inflection, but I guessed his bitterness.

"Fine," I said. "I'm not interested anyhow." I went to stand at the window.

Silence behind me for a long moment, and then he came over. "Something's changed." The light was wrong to see his reflection, but I could imagine his suspicious expression. "You're different."

"A lot has happened since you and I last met."

He touched my shoulder. When I did not throw off his hand, he took hold of the other, then turned me gently to face him. I let him. He stared at me, trying to read my eyes, perhaps trying to intimidate me.

Except, up close, he was anything but intimidating. Deep lines

of weariness marked paths from his sunken eyes; the eyes themselves were bloodshot, even more ordinary looking than before. His
posture was slouched and strange. Belatedly I understood: he could
barely stand. Nahadoth's torture had taken its toll on him as well.

My face must have shown my pity, because abruptly he
scowled and straightened. "Why did you bring me here?"

"Sit down," I said, gesturing to the bed. I tried to turn back to
the window, but his fingers tightened on my shoulders. If he had
been at his best, he would have hurt me. I understood that now.
He was a slave, a whore, not even allowed part-time control of
his own body. The only power he had was what little he could
exert over his lovers, his users. That wasn't much.

"Are you waiting for him?" he asked. The way he said "him"
held a treasure's worth of resentment. "Is that it?"

I reached up and detached his hands from my shoulders,
pushing them away firmly. "Sit down. Now."

The "now" forced him to let go of me, walk the few steps to the
bed, and sit down. He did it glaring the whole way. I turned back
to the window and let his hate splash uselessly against my back.

"Yes," I said. "I'm waiting for him."

A stunned pause. "You're in love with him. You weren't
before, but you are now. Aren't you?"

*   *   *

You resist the truth.

*   *   *

I considered the question.

"In love with him?" I said it slowly. The phrase felt strange
when I thought about it, like a poem that has been read too
often. "In love with him."

*   *   *

Another memory preoccupies you.

*   *   *

I was surprised to hear real fear in Naha's voice. "Don't be a fool. You don't know how often I've woken up beside a corpse. If you're strong, you can resist him."

"I know. I've said no to him before."

"Then…" Confusion.

I had a sudden epiphany as to what his life had been like: this other, unwanted Nahadoth. Every day a plaything of the Arameri. Every night—not sleep but oblivion, as close to death as any mortal can come short of the event itself. No peace, no true rest. Every morning a chilling surprise: mysterious injuries. Dead lovers. And the soul-grinding knowledge that it would never, ever end.

"Do you dream?" I asked.

"What?"

"Dream. At night, while you're… within him. Do you?"

Naha frowned for a long moment, as if he was trying to figure out the trick in my question. Finally he said, "No."

"Not at all?"

"I have… flashes, sometimes." He gestured vaguely, looking away from me. "Memories, maybe. I don't know what they are."

I smiled, feeling sudden warmth toward him. He was like me. Two souls, or at least two selves, in a single body. Perhaps that was where the Enefadeh had gotten the idea.

"You look tired," I said. "You should get some sleep."

He frowned. "No. I sleep enough at night—"

"Sleep now," I said, and he crumpled onto his side so swiftly that I might have laughed under other circumstances. I walked over to the bed, lifted his legs onto it and arranged him for comfort, then knelt beside it, putting my mouth near his ear.

"Have pleasant dreams," I commanded. The frown that had been on his face altered subtly, smoothing and softening.

Satisfied, I got to my feet and went back to the window, to wait.

*   *   *

Why can't I remember what happened next?

You are remembering—

No, why can't I remember it *now*? As I talk through it, it comes back to me, but only then. Without that there's an empty space. A great dark hole.

You are remembering.

*   *   *

The instant the sun's red curve sank below the horizon, the room shook, and with it the whole palace. This close, the vibration was powerful enough to make my teeth rattle. A line seemed to sweep the room, moving outward from behind me, and when this line passed, the room was darker. I waited, and when the hairs prickled on the back of my neck, I spoke. "Good evening, Lord Nahadoth. Are you feeling better?"

My only answer was a low, shuddering exhalation. The evening sky was still heavily stroked with sunlight, golds and reds and violets as deep as jewels. He was not himself yet.

I turned. He was sitting up. He still looked human, ordinary, but I could see his hair wafting around him, though there was no breeze. As I watched it thickened, lengthened, darkened, spinning itself into the cloak of night. Fascinating, and beautiful. He had averted his face from the lingering sunlight and did not see me approach until I was right there. Then he looked up, raising a hand as if to shield himself. *From me?* I wondered, and smiled.

The hand trembled as I watched. I took it, reassured by the cool dryness of his skin. (His skin was brown now, I noticed. My doing?) Beyond the hand his eyes watched me, black now, and unblinking. Unthinking, like those of a beast.

I cupped his cheek and willed him sane. He blinked, frowned slightly, then stared at me as his confusion cleared. His hand in mine became still.

When I judged the moment right, I let go his hand. Unfastened my blouse, and slipped it off my shoulders. I unhitched the skirt and let it fall, along with my underclothes. Naked, I waited, an offering.

24

If I Ask

—AND THEN—THEN—

You remember.

No. No, I don't.

Why are you afraid?

I don't know.

Did he hurt you?

I don't remember!

You do. Think, child. I made you stronger than this. What were the sounds? The scents? What do the memories feel like?

Like . . . like summer.

Yes. Humid, thick, those summertime nights. Did you know—the earth absorbs all the day's heat, and gives it back in the dark hours. All that energy just hovers in the air, waiting to be used. It slickens the skin. Open your mouth and it curls around your tongue.

I remember. *Oh, gods, I remember.*

I knew you would.

*　　*　　*

The shadows in the room seemed to deepen as the Nightlord rose to his feet. He loomed over me, and for the first time I could not see his eyes in the dark.

"Why?" he asked.

"You never answered my question."

"Question?"

"Whether you would kill me, if I asked."

I won't pretend I wasn't afraid. That was part of it—my pounding heart, the quickness of my breath. *Esui*, the thrill of danger. But then he reached out, so slowly that I worried I was dreaming, and trailed his fingertips up my arm. Just that one touch and my fear became something entirely different. Gods. *Goddess.*

White teeth flashed at me, startling in the darkness. Oh, yes, this was far beyond mere danger.

"Yes," he said. "If you asked, I would kill you."

"Just like that?"

"You seek to control your death as you cannot control your life. I ... understand this." So much unspoken meaning in that brief pause. I wondered, suddenly, whether the Nightlord had ever yearned to die.

"I didn't think you wanted me to control my death."

"No, little pawn." I tried to concentrate on his words while his hand continued its slow journey up my arm, but it was difficult. I am only human. "It is Itempas's way to force his will upon others. I have always preferred *willing* sacrifices."

He drew one fingertip along my collarbone now, and I nearly

moved away because it felt almost unbearably good. I did not because I had seen his teeth. One did not run from a predator.

"I…I knew you would say yes." My voice shook. I was babbling. "I don't know how, but I knew. I knew…" *That I was more than a pawn to you.* But no, that part I could not say.

"I must be what I am." He said it as if the words made sense. "Now. *Are* you asking?"

I licked my lips, hungry. "Not to die. But—for you. Yes. I'm asking for you."

"To have me is to die," he warned me, even as he grazed my breast with the backs of his fingers. The knuckles caught on my already-taut nipple and I could not help gasping. The room got darker.

But one thought pushed up through the desire. It was the thought that had motivated me to do this mad thing, because in spite of everything I was not suicidal. I wanted to live for whatever pittance of time I had left. In the same way I hated the Arameri, yet I sought to understand them; I wanted to prevent a second Gods' War, yet I also wanted the Enefadeh freed. I wanted so many things, each of them contradictory, all of them together impossible. I wanted them anyway. Perhaps Sieh's childishness had infected me.

"Once you took many mortal lovers," I said. My voice was more breathy than it should have been. He leaned close to me and inhaled, as if scenting it. "Once you claimed them by the dozen, and they all lived to tell the tale."

"That was before centuries of human hatred made me a monster," said the Nightlord, and for a moment his voice was sad. I had used the same word for him myself, but it felt strange and wrong to hear him say it. "Before my brother stole whatever tenderness there once was in my soul."

And just like that, my fear faded.

"No," I said.

His hand paused. I reached up and caught it, my fingers tangling in his.

"Your tenderness isn't gone, Nahadoth. I've seen it. I've tasted it." I pulled his hand up, up, to touch my lips. I felt his fingers twitch, as if in surprise. "You're right about me; if I must die, I want to die on my own terms. There are so many things I will never do—but *this* I can have. You." I kissed his fingers. "Will you show me that tenderness again, Nightlord? Please?"

From the corner of my eye I saw movement. When I turned my head there were black lines, curling and random, etching their way along the walls, the windows, the floor. The lines flowed out from Nahadoth's feet, spreading, overlapping. I caught a glimpse of strange, airy depths within the lines; a suggestion of drifting mist and deep, endless chasms. He let out a low, soughing breath, and it curled around my tongue.

"I need so much," he whispered. "It has been so long since I shared that part of myself, Yeine. I hunger—I always hunger. I devour myself with hunger. But Itempas has betrayed me, and you are not Enefa, and I...I am...afraid."

Tears stung my eyes. Reaching up, I cupped his face in my hands and pulled him down to me. His lips were cool, and this time they tasted of salt. I thought I felt him shiver. "I will give you all I can," I said, when we parted.

He pressed his forehead against mine; he was breathing hard. "You must say the words. I will try to be what I was, I will try, but—" He groaned softly, desperate. "Say the words!"

I closed my eyes. How many of my Arameri ancestors had said these words and died? I smiled. It would be a death befitting a Darre, if I joined them.

"Do with me as you please, Nightlord," I whispered.

Hands seized me.

I do not say *his* hands because there were too many of them, gripping my arms and grasping my hips and tangling in my hair. One even curled 'round my ankle. The room was almost entirely dark. I could see nothing except the window and the sky beyond, where the sun's light had finally faded completely. Stars spun as I was lifted and lowered until I felt the bed underneath my back.

Then we fed each other's hunger. Wherever I wanted to be touched, he touched; I don't know how he knew. Whenever I touched him, there was a delay. I would cup emptiness before it became a smooth muscled arm. I would wrap my legs around nothing and only then find hips settled there, taut with ready energy. In this way I shaped him, making him suit my fantasies; in this way he chose to be shaped. When heavy, thick warmth pushed into me, I had no idea whether this was a penis or some entirely different phallus that only gods possessed. I suspect the latter, since no mere penis can fill a woman's body the way he filled mine. Size had nothing to do with it. This time he let me scream.

"Yeine…" Through the haze of my own body heat I was aware of few things. The clouds, racing across the stars. The black lines, webbing the room's ceiling, widening and melding into one great yawning abyss. The rising urgency of Nahadoth's movements. There was pain now, because I wanted it. "Yeine. Open yourself to me."

I had no idea what he meant; I could not think. But he gripped my hair and slid a hand under my hips, pulling me tighter against him in a way that sent me spiraling again. "Yeine!"

Such need in him. Such wounds—two of them, raw and unhealing, for two lost lovers. So much more than one mortal girl could ever satisfy.

And yet in my madness, I tried. I couldn't; I was only human. But for that moment I yearned to be more, give more, because I loved him.

I loved him.

Nahadoth arched up, away from me. In the last starlight I caught a glimpse of a smooth, perfect body, taut-muscled and sleek with sweat all the way down to where it joined with mine. He had flung back his hair in an arc. His face was all tight-clenched eyes and open mouth and that delicious near-agony expression men make when the moment strikes. The black lines joined, and nothingness enclosed us.

Then we fell.

—no, no, we *flew*, not downward but forward, into the dark. There were streaks within this darkness, thin random lines of white and gold and red and blue. I put out my hand in fascination and snatched it back when something stung the fingertips. I looked and found them wet with glimmering stuff that spun with tiny orbiting motes. Then Nahadoth cried out, his body shuddering, and now we went *up*—

—past endless stars, past countless worlds, through layers of light and glowing cloud. Up and up we went, our speed impossible, our size incomprehensible. We left the light behind and kept going, passing through stranger things than mere worlds. Geometric shapes that twisted and gibbered. A white landscape of frozen explosions. Shivering lines of *intention* that turned to chase us. Vast, whalelike beings with terrifying eyes and the faces of long-lost friends.

I closed my eyes. I had to. Yet the images continued, because in this place I had no eyelids to close. I was immense, and still growing. I had a million legs, two million arms. I don't know what I became in that place Nahadoth took me, because there are things no mortal is meant to do or be or comprehend, and I encompassed all of them.

Something familiar: that darkness which is Nahadoth's quintessence. It surrounded me, pressed in, until I had no choice but to yield to it. I felt things in me—sanity? self?—stretch, growing so taut that a touch would break them. This was the end, then. I was not afraid, not even when I became aware of a sound: a titanic, awful roar. I cannot describe it except to say something of that roar was in Nahadoth's voice as he shouted again. I knew then that his ecstasy had taken us beyond the universe, and now we approached the Maelstrom, birthplace of gods. It would tear me apart.

Then, just when the roar had become so terrible that I knew I could bear no more, we stopped. Hovered, pent.

And then we fell again through gibbering strangeness and layered dark and whirlpools of light and dancing globes toward one globe in particular, blue-green and beautiful. There was a new roaring as we streaked down through air, trailing white-hot fire. Something glowing and pale reared up, puny then enormous, all spikes and white stone and treachery—*Sky, it was Sky*—and it swallowed us whole.

I think I screamed again as, naked, skin steaming, I smashed into my bed. The shock wave of impact swept the room; the sound of it was the Maelstrom come to earth. I knew no more.

25

A Chance

HE SHOULD'VE KILLED ME THAT NIGHT. It would have been easier.

That's selfish of you.

What?

He gave you his body. He gave you pleasure no mortal lover can match. He fought his own nature to keep you alive, and you wish he hadn't bothered.

I didn't mean—

Yes, you did. Oh, child. You think you love him? You think you're worthy of his love?

I can't speak for him. But I know what I feel.

Don't be a—

And I know what I hear. Jealousy does not become you.

What?

This is why you're so angry with me, isn't it? You're just like Itempas, you can't bear to share—

Be silent!

—but it isn't necessary. Don't you see? He has never stopped loving you. He never will. You and Itempas will always hold his heart in your hands.

...Yes. That is true. But I am dead, and Itempas is mad.

And I am dying. Poor Nahadoth.

Poor Nahadoth, and poor us.

*　　*　　*

I woke slowly, aware first of warmth and comfort. Sunlight shone against the side of my face, red through one of my eyelids. A hand rubbed my back in little arcs.

I opened my eyes and did not understand what I saw at first. A white, rolling surface. I had fleeting memories of something else like it—*frozen explosions*—and then the memories swam away, deeper into my consciousness and out of reach. For a moment understanding lingered: I was mortal, not ready for some knowledge. Then even that vanished, and I was myself again. I was wearing a plush robe. I was sitting in someone's lap. Frowning, I lifted my head.

Nahadoth's daytime form gazed back at me with frank, too-human eyes.

I did not think, half-falling and half-leaping off his lap and rolling to my feet. He rose with me and a taut moment passed, me staring, him just standing there.

The moment broke when he turned to the small nightstand, on which sat a gleaming silver tea service. He poured, the small liquid sound making me flinch for reasons I did not understand, and then held the cup forward, offering it to me.

I stood naked before him, an offering—

Gone, like fish in a pond.

"How do you feel?" he asked. I flinched again, not sure I

understood the words. How did I feel? Warm. Safe. Clean. I lifted a hand, sniffed my wrist; I smelled of soap.

"I bathed you. I hope you'll forgive the liberty." Low, soft, his voice, as if he spoke to a skittish mare. He looked different from the day before—healthier for one, but also browner, like a Darre man. "You were so deeply asleep that you didn't wake. I found the robe in the closet."

I hadn't known I had a robe. Belatedly it came to me that he was still holding out the cup of tea. I took it, more out of politeness than any real interest. When I sipped, I was surprised to find it lukewarm and rich with cooling mint and calmative herbs. It made me realize I was thirsty; I drank it down greedily. Naha held out the pot, silently offering more, and I let him pour.

"What a wonder you are," he murmured, as I drank. Noise. He was staring and it bothered me. I looked away to shut him out and savored the tea.

"You were ice cold when I woke up, and filthy. There was something—soot, I think—all over you. The bath seemed to warm you up, and that helped, too." He jerked his head toward the chair where we'd been sitting. "There wasn't anywhere else, so—"

"The bed," I said, and flinched again. My voice was hoarse, my throat raw and sore. The mint helped.

For an instant Naha paused, his lips quirking with a hint of his usual cruelty. "The bed wouldn't have worked."

Puzzled, I looked past him, and caught my breath. The bed was a wreck, sagging on a split frame and broken legs. The mattress looked as though it had been hacked by a sword and then set afire. Loose goosedown and charred fabric scraps littered the room.

It was more than the bed. One of the room's huge glass windows had spiderwebbed; only luck that it hadn't shattered. The vanity mirror had. One of my bookcases lay on the floor, its contents scattered but intact. (I saw my father's book there, with great relief.) The other bookcase had been shattered into kindling, along with most of the books on it.

Naha took the empty teacup from my hand before I could drop it. "You'll need to get one of your Enefadeh friends to fix this. I kept the servants out this morning, but that won't work for long."

"I...I don't..." I shook my head. So much of what had happened was dreamlike in my memory, more metaphysical than actual. I remembered falling. There was no hole in the ceiling. Yet, the bed.

Naha said nothing as I moved about the room, my slippered feet crunching on glass and splinters. When I picked up a shard of the mirror, staring at my own face, he said, "You don't look as much like the library mural as I'd first thought."

That turned me around to face him. He smiled at me. I had thought him human, but no. He had lived too long and too strangely, knew too much. Perhaps he was more like the demons of old, half mortal and half something else.

"How long have you known?" I asked.

"Since we met." His lips quirked. "Though that can't properly be called a 'meeting,' granted."

He had stopped and stared at me, that first evening in Sky. I'd forgotten in the rush of terror afterward. Then later in Scimina's quarters— "You're a good actor."

"I have to be." His smile was gone now. "Even then, I wasn't sure. Not until I woke up and saw this." He gestured around the devastated room. "And you there beside me, alive."

I didn't expect to be. But I was, and now I would have to deal with the consequences.

"I'm not her," I said.

"No. But I'll wager you're a part of her, or she's a part of you. I know a little about these things." He ran a hand through his unruly black locks. Just hair, and not the smokelike curls of his godly self, but his meaning was plain.

"Why haven't you told anyone?"

"You think I would do that?"

"Yes."

He laughed, though there was a hard edge to the sound. "And you know me so well."

"You would do anything to make your life easier."

"Ah. Then you *do* know me." He flopped down in the chair— the only intact piece of furniture in the room—one leg tossed over one arm. "But if you know that much, Lady, then you should be able to guess why I would never tell the Arameri of your...uniqueness."

I put down the shard of mirror and went to him. "Explain," I commanded, because I might pity him, but I would never like him.

He shook his head, as if chiding me for my impatience. "I, too, want to be free."

I frowned. "But if the Nightlord is ever freed..." What did happen to a mortal soul buried within a god's body? Would he sleep and never awaken? Would some part of him continue, trapped and aware inside an alien mind? Or would he simply cease to exist?

He nodded, and I realized all of those thoughts and more must have occurred to him over the centuries. "He has promised to destroy me, should the day ever come."

And this Naha would rejoice on that day, I realized with a chill. Perhaps he had tried to kill himself before, only to be resurrected the next morning, trapped by magic meant to torment a god.

Well, if all went as planned, he would be free soon.

I rose and went to the remaining undamaged window. The sun was high in the sky, past noon. My last day of life was half over. I was trying to think of how to spend my remaining time when I felt a new presence in the room, and turned. Sieh stood there, looking from the bed to me to Naha, and back again.

"You seem well," I said, pleased. He was properly young again, and there was a grass stain on one of his knees. The look in his eyes, though, was far from childish as he focused on Naha. When his pupils turned to ferocious slits—I saw the change this time—I knew I'd have to intervene. I went to Sieh, deliberately stepping into his line of sight, and opened my arms to invite him near.

He put his arms around me, which at first seemed affectionate until he picked me up bodily and put me behind him, then turned to face Naha.

"Are you all right, Yeine?" he asked, sinking into a crouch. It was not a fighter's crouch; it was closer to the movement of an animal gathering itself to spring. Naha returned his gaze coolly.

I put my hand on his wire-tight shoulder. "I'm fine."

"This one is dangerous, Yeine. We do not trust him."

"Lovely Sieh," said Naha, and there was that cruel edge in his voice again. He opened his arms in a mockery of my own gesture. "I've missed you. Come; give your father a kiss."

Sieh hissed, and I had a moment to wonder whether I had a chance in the infinite hells of holding him. Then Naha laughed and sat back in the chair. Of course he would know exactly how far to push.

Sieh looked as though he was still considering something dire when it finally occurred to me to distract him. "Sieh." He did not look at me. "*Sieh*. I was with your father last night."

He swung around to look at me, so startled that his eyes reverted to human at once. Beyond him, Naha chuckled softly.

"You couldn't have been," said Sieh. "It's been centuries since—" He paused and leaned close. I saw his nostrils twitch delicately once, twice. "Skies and earth. You *were* with him."

Self-conscious, I surreptitiously sniffed the collar of my robe. Hopefully it was something only gods could detect. "Yes."

"But he...that should've..." Sieh shook his head sharply. "Yeine, oh, Yeine, do you know what this means?"

"It means your little experiment worked better than you thought," said Naha. In the shadows of the chair, his eyes glittered, reminding me just a little of his other self. "Perhaps you could give her a try, too, Sieh. You must get tired of perverted old men."

Sieh tensed all over, his hands forming fists. I marveled that he allowed such taunts to work on him—but perhaps that was another of his weaknesses. He had bound himself by the laws of childhood; perhaps one of those laws was *no child shall hold his temper when bullied.*

I touched his chin and turned his face back around to me. "The room. Could you...?"

"Oh. Yes." Pointedly turning his back on Naha, he looked around the room and said something in his own language, fast and high-pitched. The room was abruptly restored, just like that.

"Handy," I said.

"No one's better at cleaning up messes than me." He flashed me a quick grin.

Naha got up and went to browse one of the restored bookshelves, studiously ignoring us. Belatedly it occurred to me that he had been different before Sieh appeared—solicitous, respectful, almost kind. I opened my mouth to thank him for that, then thought better of it. Sieh had been careful to conceal that side of himself from me, but I had seen the signs of a crueler streak within him. There was very old, very bad blood between these two, and such things were rarely one-sided.

"Let's go somewhere else to talk. I have a message for you." Breaking my reverie, Sieh pulled me to the nearest wall. We stepped through it into the dead space beyond.

After a few chambers, Sieh sighed, opened his mouth, closed it, then finally decided to speak. "The message I carry is from Relad. He wants to see you."

"Why?"

"I don't know. But I don't think you should go."

I frowned. "Why not?"

"Think, Yeine. You aren't the only one facing death tomorrow. When you appoint Scimina heir, the first thing she'll do is kill her baby brother, and he knows it. What if he decides that killing *you*—right now, before the ceremony—is the best way to earn himself a few extra days of life? It would be futile, of course; Dekarta's seen what's happened with Darr. He'll just designate someone else the sacrifice, and tell that person to choose Scimina. But desperate men do not always think rationally."

Sieh's reasoning made sense—but something else did not. "Relad ordered you to bring me this message?"

"No, he asked. And he *asks* to see you. He said, 'If you see her, remind her that I am not my sister; I have never done her harm. I know she listens to you.'" Sieh scowled. "*Remind her*—that was the only part he commanded. He knows how to speak to us. He left me the choice deliberately."

I stopped walking. Sieh got a few paces ahead before he noticed, and turned to me with a puzzled look. "And why did you choose to tell me?" I asked.

A shadow of unease passed over his face; he lowered his eyes. "It's true that I shouldn't have," he said slowly. "Kurue wouldn't have allowed it, if she'd known. But what Kurue doesn't know..." A faint smile crossed Sieh's face. "Well, it *can* hurt her, but we'll just have to hope that doesn't happen."

I folded my arms, waiting. He still hadn't answered my question, and he knew it.

Sieh looked annoyed. "You're no fun anymore."

"Sieh."

"Fine, fine." He slid his hands into his pockets and shrugged with total nonchalance, but his voice was serious. "You agreed to help us, that's all. That makes you our ally, not our tool. Kurue is wrong; we shouldn't hide things from you."

I nodded. "Thank you."

"Thank me by not mentioning it to Kurue. Or Nahadoth or Zhakkarn, while you're at it." He paused, then smiled at me with sudden amusement. "Though it seems Nahadoth has his own secrets to hide with you."

My cheeks grew hot. "It was my decision." I blurted the words, irrationally compelled to explain. "I caught him by surprise, and—"

"Yeine, please. You're not about to try and tell me you 'took advantage of him' or anything like that, are you?"

As I had been about to say exactly that, I fell silent.

Sieh shook his head and sighed. I was startled to see an odd sort of sadness in his smile. "I'm glad, Yeine—more glad than you know. He's been so alone since the war."

"He isn't alone. He has you."

"We comfort him, yes, and keep him from completely letting go of his sanity. We can even be his lovers, though for us the experience is . . . well, as *strenuous* as it was for you." I blushed again, though some of that was at the disquieting thought of Nahadoth lying with his own children. But the Three had been siblings, after all. The gods did not live by our rules.

As if hearing that thought, Sieh nodded. "It's equals he needs, not pity offerings from his children."

"I'm not equal to any of the Three, Sieh, no matter whose soul is in me."

He grew solemn. "Love can level the ground between mortals and gods, Yeine. It's something we've learned to respect."

I shook my head. This was something I had understood from the moment the mad impulse to make love to a god had come over me. "He doesn't love me."

Sieh rolled his eyes. "I love you, Yeine, but sometimes you can be such a mortal."

Taken aback, I fell silent. Sieh shook his head and called one of his floating orbs out of nowhere, batting it back and forth in his hands. This one was blue-green, which teased my memories mercilessly. "So what do you plan to do about Relad?"

"What—oh." So dizzying, this constant switch between matters mundane and divine. "I'll meet with him."

"Yeine—"

"He won't kill me." In my mind's eye, I saw Relad's face from two nights ago, framed by the doorway of my room. He had come to tell me of Sieh's torture, which even T'vril had not done. Surely he'd realized that if Scimina forced me to give up my secrets, she would win the contest. So why had he done it?

I had a private theory, based on that brief meeting in the solarium. I believed that somewhere deep down, Relad was even less of an Arameri than T'vril—perhaps even less than me. Somewhere amid all that bitterness and self-loathing, hidden behind a thousand protective layers, Relad Arameri had a soft heart.

Useless for an Arameri heir, if it was true. Beyond useless— dangerous. But because of it, I was willing to chance trusting him.

"I could still choose him," I said to Sieh, "and he knows that. It would make no sense, because it would guarantee my people's suffering. But I could do it. I'm his last hope."

"You sound very sure of that," Sieh said dubiously.

I had the sudden urge to tousle Sieh's hair. He might even enjoy it given his nature, but he would not enjoy the thought that triggered the impulse: Sieh really was a child in one fundamental way. He did not understand mortals. He had lived among us for centuries, millennia, and yet he had never been one of us. He did not know the power of hope.

"I am very sure," I said. "But I would be grateful if you'd come with me."

He looked surprised, though immediately he took my hand. "Of course. But why?"

"Moral support. And in case I'm horribly, horribly wrong."

He grinned, and opened another wall that would take us there.

*   *   *

Relad's apartment was as large as Scimina's, and each was three times the size of mine. If I had seen their apartments my first day in Sky, I would have immediately understood that I was not a true contender for Dekarta's rule.

The configuration of his quarters was entirely different from Scimina's, however: a huge, open chamber with a short stair near the back leading up to a loft area. The main floor was dominated by a square depression set into the floor, in which a world map had been formed of beautifully colored ceramic tiles. Aside from this the chamber was surprisingly austere, with only a few pieces of furniture, a side bar heavily laden with alcohol bottles, and a small bookshelf. And Relad, who stood by the map looking stiff and formal and uncomfortably sober.

"Greetings, Cousin," he said as I came in, and then he paused, glaring at Sieh. "I invited only Yeine."

I put a hand on Sieh's shoulder. "He was concerned that you meant me harm, Cousin. Do you?"

"What? Of course not!" The look of surprise on Relad's face reassured me. In fact, everything about this little scene suggested he was set to charm me, and one did not charm expendable people. "Why in the Maelstrom would I? You're no good to me dead."

I set my smile and decided to let this tactless remark slide. "That's good to know, Cousin."

"Don't mind me," Sieh said. "I'm just a fly on the wall."

Relad made an effort and ignored him. "Can I get you something? Tea? A drink?"

"Well, since you asked—" Sieh began, before I squeezed his shoulder hard. I didn't want to push Relad, at least not yet.

"Thank you, no," I said. "Though I appreciate the offer. I also appreciate your warning, Cousin, the night before last." I stroked Sieh's hair.

Relad wrestled for an appropriate response for a full three seconds before finally muttering, "It was nothing."

"Why did you invite me here?"

"I have an offer to make." He gestured vaguely at the floor.

I looked down at the world map in the floor, my eyes automatically finding High North and the tiny corner of it that was Darr. Four polished, flattened white stones sat ranged around Darr's borders—one in each of the three kingdoms that I'd suspected were part of the alliance, plus a second stone in

Menchey. At Darr's heart sat a single marbled-gray stone, probably representing our pathetic troop strength. But just south of Menchey, along the coast where the continent met the Repentance Sea, were three pale yellow stones. I could not guess what those were.

I looked up at Relad. "Darr is all I care about right now. Scimina has offered me my people's lives. Is that what you're offering?"

"Potentially more than that." Relad stepped down into the map-depression, walking over to stand just below High North. His feet were in the middle of the Repentance Sea, which struck me as irrationally amusing for a moment.

"The white are your enemies, as I'm certain you've guessed; Scimina's pawns. These"—he pointed at the yellow stones— "are mine."

I frowned, but before I could speak, Sieh snorted. "You have no allies in High North, Relad. You've ignored the whole continent for years. Scimina's victory is the result of your own neglect."

"I know that," Relad snapped, but then he turned to face me. "It's true I have no friends in High North. Even if I did, the kingdoms there all hate your land, Cousin. Scimina's simply facilitating what they've been itching to do for generations."

I shrugged. "High North was a land of barbarians once, and we Darre were among the most barbaric. The priests may have civilized us since, but no one can erase the past."

Relad nodded dismissively; he didn't care and it showed. He really was terrible at being charming. He pointed at the yellow stones again. "Mercenaries," he said. "Mostly Ken and Min pirates, some Ghor nightfighters, and a contingent of Zhurem City strikemen. I can order them to fight for you, Cousin."

I stared at the yellow stones and was reminded of my earlier thought about mortals and the power of hope.

Sieh hopped down into the map-depression and peered at the yellow stones as if he could see the actual forces they represented. He whistled. "You must've bankrupted yourself to hire so many and get them to High North in time, Relad. I didn't realize you'd acquired that much capital over the years." He glanced back at Relad and me over his shoulder. "But these are too far away to get to Darr by tomorrow. Scimina's friends are already on their way."

Relad nodded, watching me. "My forces are close enough to attack Menchey's capital tonight, and even stage a strike on Tokland the day after. They're fully equipped, rested, and well supplied. Their battle plans were drawn up by Zhakkarn herself." He folded his arms, a bit defensively. "With Menchey under attack, half your enemies will turn back from the assault on Darr. That will leave the Zarenne and the Atir rebels for your people to contend with, and they'll still be outnumbered two to one. But it will give the Darre a fighting chance."

I threw Relad a sharp look. He had gauged me well on this—surprisingly well. Somehow he had realized that it was not the prospect of war that frightened me; I was a warrior, after all. But an *unwinnable* war, against enemies who would not only take spoils but destroy our spirits, if not our lives...that I could not stomach.

Two-to-one odds were winnable. Hard, but winnable.

I glanced at Sieh, who nodded. My instincts told me Relad's offer was legitimate, but he knew Relad's capabilities and would warn me of any trickery. I think we were both surprised that Relad had managed this at all.

"You should abstain from drinking more often, Cousin," I said softly.

Relad smiled, utterly without humor. "It wasn't intentional, I assure you. It's just that impending death tends to sour even the best wine."

I understood completely.

There was another of those awkward silences, and then Relad stepped forward, proferring his hand. Surprised, I took it. We were agreed.

*   *   *

Later, Sieh and I walked slowly back to my room. He took me on a new route this time, passing through parts of Sky that I had not seen in the two weeks since my arrival. Among other wonders, he showed me a high, narrow chamber—not a dead space, but still sealed off and forgotten for some reason—whose ceiling looked like an accident in the gods' construction design. The pale Skystuff hung in attenuated extrusions like cave stalactites, though far more delicate and graceful. A few were close enough to touch; some ended barely inches below the ceiling. I could not fathom the purpose of the chamber until Sieh led me to a panel on the wall.

When I touched it, a slot opened on the ceiling, letting in a sharp, startling gust of ice-cold air. I shivered, but forgot my discomfort when the ceiling extrusions began to sing, stroked into vibration by the wind. It was like no music I'd ever heard, wavering and alien, a cacophony too beautiful to call merely noise. I didn't let Sieh touch the panel to shut off the air until I began to lose the feeling in my fingers.

In the silence that fell, during which I crouched against the wall and blew on my hands to warm them, Sieh crouched in front of me, staring at me intently. I was too cold to notice at first, but then he suddenly leaned forward and kissed me. Startled, I froze, but there was nothing unpleasant about it. It was the kiss of a child, spontaneous and unconditional. Only the fact that he was not a child made me uncomfortable.

Sieh pulled back, and sighed ruefully at the expression on my face. "Sorry," he said, and settled down beside me.

"Don't apologize," I said. "Just tell me what that was for." I realized that was an inadvertent command and added, "Will you?"

He shook his head, playing shy, and pressed his face into my arm. I liked having his warmth there, but I didn't like his silence. I pulled away, forcing him to sit up or risk falling over.

"Yeine!"

"Sieh."

He sighed, looking annoyed, and shifted to sit cross-legged. For a moment I thought he'd just sit there and sulk, but finally he said, "I just don't think it's fair, that's all. Naha got to taste you, but I didn't."

That *did* make me uncomfortable. "Even in my barbarian land, women do not take children as lovers."

The annoyance grew in his expression. "I told you before, I don't want *that* from you. I'm talking about this." He sat up on his knees abruptly and leaned toward me. I flinched away, and he stopped, waiting. It occurred to me that I loved him, trusted him with my very soul. Shouldn't I trust him with a kiss? So after a deep breath, I relaxed. Sieh waited until I gave him a minute nod, and a moment longer than that—making sure. Then he leaned in and kissed me again.

And this time it was different, because I could taste *him*— not Sieh the sweaty, slightly dirty child, but the Sieh beneath the human mask. It is…difficult to describe. A sudden burst of something refreshing, like ripe melon, or maybe a waterfall. A torrent, a current; it rushed into me and through me and back into him so swiftly that I barely had time to draw breath. Salt. Lightning. That hurt enough that I almost pulled away, but distantly I felt Sieh's hands tighten painfully on my arms. Before I could yelp, cold wind shot through me, soothing both the jolt and my bruises.

Then Sieh pulled back. I stared at him, but his eyes were still shut. Uttering a deep, satisfied sigh, he shifted to sit beside me again, lifting my arm and pulling it 'round himself proprietarily.

"What…was that?" I asked, when I had recovered somewhat.

"Me," he said. Of course.

"What do I taste like?"

Sieh sighed, snuggling against my shoulder, his arms looping around my waist. "Soft, misty places full of sharp edges and hidden colors."

I could not help it; I giggled. I felt light-headed, like I'd drunk too much of Relad's liqueur. "That's not a taste!"

"Of course it is. You tasted Naha, didn't you? He tastes like falling to the bottom of the universe."

That stopped my giggling, because it was true. We sat awhile longer, not speaking, not thinking—or at least I was not. It was, after the constant worry and scheming of the past two weeks, a moment of pure bliss. Perhaps that was why, when I did think again, it was of a different kind of peace.

"What will happen to me?" I asked. "After."

He was a clever child; he knew what I meant at once.

"You'll drift for a time," he said very softly. "Souls do that when they're first freed from flesh. Eventually they gravitate toward places that resonate with certain aspects of their nature. Places that are safe for souls lacking flesh, unlike this realm."

"The heavens and the hells."

He shrugged, just a little, so that it would not jostle either of us. "That's what mortals call them."

"Is that not what they are?"

"I don't know. What does it matter?" I frowned, and he sighed. "I'm not mortal, Yeine, I don't obsess over this the way your kind does. They're just...places for life to rest, when it's not being alive. There are many of them because Enefa knew your kind needed variety." He sighed. "That was why Enefa's soul kept drifting, we think. All the places she made, the ones that resonated best with her, vanished when she died."

I shivered, and thought I felt something else shiver deep within me.

"Will...will both our souls find a place, she and I? Or will hers drift again?"

"I don't know." The pain in his voice was quiet, inflectionless. Another person would have missed it.

I rubbed his back gently. "If I can," I said, "if I have any control over it... I'll take her with me."

"She may not want to go. The only places left now are the ones her brothers created. Those don't fit her much."

"Then she can stay inside me, if that's better. I'm no heaven, but we've put up with each other this long. We're going to have to talk, though. All these visions and dreams must go. They're really quite distracting."

Sieh lifted his head and stared at me. I kept a straight face for as long as I could, which was not long. Of course he managed it longer than me. He had centuries more of practice.

We dissolved into laughter there on the floor, wrapped around each other, and thus ended the last day of my life.

*   *   *

I went back to my apartment alone, about an hour before dusk. When I got inside, Naha was still sitting in the big chair as if he hadn't moved all day, although there was an empty food tray on the nightstand. He started as I walked in; I suspected he had been napping, or at least daydreaming.

"Go where you like for the remainder of the day," I told him. "I'd like to be alone awhile."

He did not argue as he got to his feet. There was a dress on my bed—a long, formal gown, beautifully made, except that it was a drab gray in color. There were matching shoes and accessories sitting beside it.

"Servants brought those," Naha said. "You're to wear them tonight."

"Thank you."

He moved past me on his way out, not looking at me. At the room's threshold I heard him stop for a moment. Perhaps he turned back. Perhaps he opened his mouth to speak. But he said nothing, and a moment later I heard the apartment's door open and close.

I bathed and got dressed, then sat down in front of the windows to wait.

26

The Ball

I SEE MY LAND BELOW ME.

On the mountain pass, the watchtowers have already been overrun. The Darren troops there are dead. They fought hard, using the pass's narrowness to make up for their small numbers, but in the end there were simply too many of the enemy. The Darre lasted long enough to light the signal fires and send a message: *The enemy is coming.*

The forests are Darr's second line of defense. Many an enemy has faltered here, poisoned by snakes or weakened by disease or worn down by the endless, strangling vines. My people have always taken advantage of this, seeding the forests with wise-women who know how to hide and strike and fade back into the brush, like leopards.

But times have changed, and this time the enemy has brought a special weapon—a scrivener. Once this would have been unheard of in High North; magic is an Amn thing, deemed cowardly by most barbarian standards. Even for those nations willing to try cowardice, the Amn keep their scriveners too expensive to hire. But of course, that is not a problem for an Arameri.

(Stupid, stupid me. I have money. I could have sent a scrivener to fight on Darr's behalf. But in the end, I am still a barbarian; I did not think of it, and now it is too late.)

The scrivener, some contemporary of Viraine's, draws sigils on paper and pastes these to a few trees, and steps back. A column of white-hot fire sears through the forest in an unnaturally straight line. It goes for miles and miles, all the way to the stone walls of Arrebaia, which it smashes against. Clever; if they had set the whole forest afire, it would have burned for months. This is just a narrow path. When it has burned enough, the scrivener sets down more godwords, and the fire goes out. Aside from crumbling, charred trees and the unrecognizable corpses of animals, the way is clear. The enemy can reach Arrebaia within a day.

There is a stir at the edge of the forest. Someone stumbles out, blinded and half-choked by smoke. A wisewoman? No, this is a man—a *boy*, not even old enough to sire daughters. What is he doing out here? We have never allowed boys to fight. And the knowledge comes: my people are desperate. Even children must fight, if we are to survive.

The enemy soldiers swarm over him like ants. They do not kill him. They chain him in a supply cart and carry him along as they march. When they reach Arrebaia, they mean to put him on display to strike at our hearts—oh, and how it will. Our men have always been our treasures. They may slit his throat on the steps of Sar-enna-nem, just to rub salt in the wound.

I should have sent a scrivener.

* * *

The ballroom of Sky: a vast, high-ceilinged chamber whose walls were even more vividly mother-of-pearl than the rest of the palace, and tinted a faint rose hue. After the unrelenting white of the rest of Sky, that touch of color seemed almost shockingly vivid. Chandeliers like the starry sky turned overhead; music drifted through the air, complicated Amn stuff, from the sextet of musicians on a nearby dais. The floors, to my surprise, were something other than Skystuff: clear and golden, like dark polished amber. It could not possibly have been amber since there were no seams, and that would have required a chunk of amber the size of a small hill. But that was what it looked like.

And people, filling this glorious space. I was stunned to see the enormous number present, all of them granted special dispensation to stay in Sky for this one night. There must have been a thousand people in the room: preening highbloods and the most officious of the Salon's officials, kings and queens of lands far more important than mine, famous artists and courtesans, everybody who was anybody. I had spent the past few days wholly absorbed in my own troubles, so I had not noticed carriages coming and going all day, as they must have been to bring so many to Sky. My own fault.

I would have happily gone into the room and merged with the crowd as best I could. They all wore white, which was traditional for formal events in Sky. Only I wore a color. But I wouldn't have been able to disappear in any case, because when I entered the room and stopped at the top of the stairs, a servant nearby—clad in a strange white formal livery that I'd never seen before—cleared his throat and bellowed, loudly enough to make me wince, "The Lady Yeine Arameri, chosen heir of Dekarta, benevolent guardian of the Hundred Thousand Kingdoms! Our guest of honor!"

This obliged me to stop at the top of the steps, as every eye in the room turned to me.

I had never stood before such a horde in my life. Panic filled me for a moment, along with the utter conviction that *they knew*. How could they not? There was polite, restrained applause. I saw smiles on many faces, but no true friendliness. Interest, yes—the kind of interest one holds for a prize heifer that is soon to be slaughtered for the plates of the privileged. *What will she taste like?* I imagined in their gleaming, avid regard. *If only we could have a bite.*

My mouth went dry. My knees locked, which was the only thing that stopped me from turning on my uncomfortably high heels and running out of the room. That, and one other realization: that my parents had met at an Arameri ball. Perhaps in this very room. My mother had stood on the same steps and faced her own roomful of people who hated and feared her behind their smiles.

She would have smiled back at them.

So I fixed my eyes on a point just above the crowd. I smiled, and lifted my hand in a polite and regal wave, and hated them back. It made the fear recede, so that I could then descend the steps without tripping or worrying whether I looked graceful.

Halfway down I looked across the ballroom and saw Dekarta on a dais opposite the door. Somehow they had hauled his huge stone chair-not-throne from the audience chamber. He watched me from within its hard embrace with his colorless eyes.

I inclined my head. He blinked. *Tomorrow*, I thought. *Tomorrow*.

The crowd opened and closed around me like lips.

I made my way through sycophants who attempted to curry favor by making small talk, and more honest folk who merely gave me cool or sardonic nods. Eventually I reached an area where the crowd thinned, which happened to be near a refreshment table. I got a glass of wine from the attendant, drained it, got another, and then spotted arched glass doors to one side. Praying they would open and were not merely decorative, I went to them and found that they led outside, to a wide patio where a few guests had already congregated to take in the magically warmed night air. Some whispered to one another as I went past, but most were too engrossed in secrets or seduction or any of the usual activities that take place in the shadowy corners of such events. I stopped at the railing only because it was there, and spent a while willing my hand to stop shaking so I could drink my wine.

A hand came around me from behind, covering my own and helping me steady the glass. I knew who it was even before I felt that familiar cool stillness against my back.

"They mean for this night to break you," said the Nightlord. His breath stirred my hair, tickled my ear, and set my skin tingling with half a dozen delicious memories. I closed my eyes, grateful for the simplicity of desire.

"They're succeeding," I said.

"No. Kinneth made you stronger than that." He took the glass from my hand and lifted it out of my sight, as if he meant to drink it himself. Then he returned the glass to me. What had been white wine—some incredibly light vintage that had hardly any color and tasted of flowers—was now a red so dark that it seemed black in the balcony light. Even when I raised the glass to the sky, the stars were only a faint glimmer through a lens of deepest burgundy. I sipped experimentally, and shivered as the taste moved over my tongue. Sweet, but with a hint of almost metallic bitterness, and a salty aftertaste like tears.

"And we have made you stronger," said Nahadoth. He spoke into my hair; one of his arms slid around me from behind, pulling me against him. I could not help relaxing against him.

I turned in the half circle of his arm and stopped in surprise. The man who gazed down at me did not look like Nahadoth, not in any guise I'd ever seen. He looked human, Amn, and his hair was a rather dull blond nearly as short as mine. His face was handsome enough, but it was neither the face he wore to please me nor the face that Scimina had shaped. It was just a face. And he wore white. That, more than anything else, shocked me silent.

Nahadoth—because it *was* him, I *felt* that, no matter what he looked like—looked amused. "The Lord of Night is not welcome at any celebration of Itempas's servants."

"I just didn't think..." I touched his sleeve. It was just cloth—something finely made, part of a jacket that looked vaguely military. I stroked it and was disappointed when it did not curl around my fingers in welcome.

"I made the substance of the universe. Did you think white thread would be a challenge?"

That startled me into a laugh, which startled me silent in the next instant. I had never heard him joke before. What did it mean?

He lifted a hand to my cheek, sobering. It struck me that though he was pretending to be human, he was nothing like his daytime self. Nothing about him was human beyond his appearance—not his movements, not the speed with which he shifted from one expression to another, especially not his eyes. A human mask simply wasn't enough to conceal his true nature. It was so obvious to my eyes that I marveled the other people out on the balcony weren't screaming and running, terrified to find the Nightlord so close.

"My children think I am going mad," he said, stroking my face ever so gently. "Kurue tells me I risk all our hopes over you. She's right."

I frowned in confusion. "My life is still yours. I'll abide by our agreement, even though I've lost the contest. You acted in good faith."

He sighed, to my surprise leaning forward to rest his forehead against mine. "Even now you speak of your life as a commodity, sold for our 'good faith.' What we have done to you is obscene."

I had no idea what to say to that; I was too stunned. It occurred to me, in a flash of insight, that *this* was what Kurue feared—Nahadoth's fickle, impassioned sense of honor. He had gone to war to vent his grief over Enefa; he had kept himself and his children enslaved out of sheer stubbornness rather than forgive Itempas. He could have dealt with his brother differently, in ways that wouldn't have risked the whole universe and destroyed so many lives. But that was the problem: when the Nightlord cared for something, his decisions became irrational, his actions extreme.

And he was beginning, against all reason, to care for me.

Flattering. Frightening. I could not guess what he might do in such a circumstance. But, more important, I realized what this meant in the short term. In only a few hours, I would die, and he would be left to mourn yet again.

How strange that this thought made my own heart ache, too.

I cupped the Nightlord's face between my hands and sighed, closing my eyes so that I could feel the person beneath the mask. "I'm sorry," I said. And I was. I had never meant to cause him pain.

He did not move, and neither did I. It felt good, leaning against his solidity, resting in his arms. It was an illusion, but for the first time in a long while, I felt safe.

I don't know how long we stood there, but we both heard it when the music changed. I straightened and looked around; the handful of guests who had been on the patio with us had gone inside. That meant it was midnight—time for the main dance of the evening, the highlight of the ball.

"Do you want to go in?" Nahadoth asked.

"No, of course not. I'm fine out here."

"They dance to honor Itempas."

I looked at him, confused. "Why should I care about that?"

His smile made me feel warm inside. "Have you turned from the faith of your ancestors so completely?"

"My ancestors worshipped *you*."

"And Enefa, and Itempas, and our children. The Darre were one of the few races who honored us all."

I sighed. "It's been a long time since those days. Too much has changed."

"*You* have changed."

I could say nothing to that; it was true.

On impulse, I stepped away from him and took his hands, pulling him into dancing position. "To the gods," I said. "All of them."

It was so gratifying to surprise him. "I have never danced to honor myself."

"Well, there you are." I shrugged, and waited for the start of a new chorus before pulling him to step with me. "A first time for everything."

Nahadoth looked amused, but he moved easily in time with me despite the complicated steps. Every noble child learned such dances, but I had never really liked them. Amn dances reminded me of the Amn themselves—cold, rigid, more concerned with appearance than enjoyment. Yet here, on a dark balcony under a moonless sky, partnered by a god, I found myself smiling as we wheeled back and forth. It was easy to remember the steps with him exerting gentle guiding pressure against my hands and back. Easy to appreciate the grace of the timing with a partner who glided like the wind. I closed my eyes, leaning into the turns, sighing in pleasure as the music swelled to match my mood.

When the music stopped, I leaned against him and wished the night would never end. Not just because of what awaited me come dawn.

"Will you be with me tomorrow?" I asked, meaning the true Nahadoth, not his daytime self.

"I am permitted to remain myself by daylight for the duration of the ceremony."

"So that Itempas can ask you to return to him."

His breath tickled my hair, a soft, cold laugh. "And this time I shall, but not the way he expects."

I nodded, listening to the slow, strange pulse of his heart. It sounded distant, echoing, as if I heard it across miles. "What will you do if you win? Kill him?"

His moment of silence warned me before the actual answer came. "I don't know."

"You still love him."

He did not answer, though he stroked my back once. I didn't fool myself. It was not me he meant to reassure.

"It's all right," I said. "I understand."

"No," he said. "No mortal could understand."

I said nothing more, and he said nothing more, and thus did the long night pass.

I had endured too many nights with little sleep. I must've fallen asleep standing there, because suddenly I was blinking and lifting my head, and the sky was a different color—a hazy gradient of soupy black through gray. The new moon hovered just above the horizon, a darker blotch against the lightening sky.

Nahadoth's fingers squeezed again gently, and I realized he'd woken me. He was gazing toward the balcony doors. Viraine stood there, and Scimina, and Relad. Their white garments seemed to glow, casting their faces into shadow.

"Time," said Viraine.

I searched inside myself and was pleased to find stillness rather than fear.

"Yes," I said. "Let's go."

Inside, the ball was still in full swing, though there were fewer people dancing now than I had last seen. Dekarta's throne stood empty on the other side of the throng. Perhaps he had left early to prepare.

Once we entered Sky's quiet, preternaturally bright halls, Nahadoth let his guise slip; his hair lengthened and his clothing changed color between one step and another. Pale-skinned again; too many of my relatives around, I supposed. We rode a lift upward, emerging on what I now recognized as Sky's topmost floor. As we exited, I saw the doors to the solarium standing open, the manicured forest beyond shadowed and quiet. The only light came from the palace's central spire, which jutted up from the solarium's heart, glowing like the moon. A fainter path ran from our feet into the trees, directly toward the spire's base.

But I was distracted by the figures who stood on either side of the door.

Kurue I recognized at once; I had not forgotten the beauty of her gold-silver-platinum wings. Zhakkarn, too, was magnificent in silver armor traced with molten sigils, her helm shining in the light. I had last seen that armor in a dream.

The third figure, between them, was at once less impressive and more strange: a sleek, black-furred cat like the leopards of my homeland, though significantly larger. And no forest had given birth to this leopard, whose fur rippled like waves in an unseen wind, iridescent to matte to a familiar, impossibly deep blackness. So he did look like his father, after all.

I could not help smiling. *Thank you*, I mouthed. The cat bared its teeth back in what could never have been misinterpreted as a snarl, and winked one green, slitted eye.

I had no illusions about their presence. Zhakkarn was not in full battle armor just to impress us with its shine. The second

Gods' War was about to begin, and they were ready. Sieh—well, maybe Sieh was here for me. And Nahadoth...

I looked back at him over my shoulder. He was not watching me or his children. Instead his gaze had turned upward, toward the top of the spire.

Viraine shook his head, apparently deciding not to protest. He glanced at Scimina, who shrugged; at Relad, who glared at him as if to say *Why would I possibly care?*

(Our eyes met, mine and Relad's. He was pale, sweat beading his upper lip, but he nodded to me just slightly. I returned the nod.)

"So be it," Viraine said, and all walked into the solarium, toward that central spire.

27

The Ritual of the Succession

AT THE TOP OF THE SPIRE was a room, if it could be called that.

The space was enclosed in glass, like an oversize bell jar. If not for a faint reflective sheen it would have seemed as though we stood in the open air, atop a spire sheared flat at the tip. The floor of the room was the same white stuff as the rest of Sky, and it was perfectly circular, unlike every other room I'd seen in the palace in the past two weeks. That marked the room as a space sacred to Itempas.

We stood high above the great white bulk of the palace. From the odd angle I could just glimpse the forecourt, recognizing it by the green blot of the Garden and the jut of the Pier. I had never realized that Sky itself was circular. Beyond that, the earth was a darkened mass, seeming to curve 'round us like a great bowl. Circles within circles within circles; a sacred place indeed.

Dekarta stood opposite the room's floor entrance. He was leaning heavily on his beautiful Darrwood cane, which he had doubtless needed to get up the steep spiral staircase that led into the room. Behind and above him, predawn clouds covered the sky, bunched and rippled like strings of pearls. They were as gray and ugly as my gown—except in the east, where the clouds had begun to glow yellow-white.

"Hurry up," Dekarta said, nodding toward points around the room's circumference. "Relad there. Scimina there, across from him. Viraine, to me. Yeine, here."

I did as I was bidden, moving to stand before a simple white plinth that rose from the floor, about as high as my chest. There was a hole in its surface perhaps a handspan wide; the shaft that led from the oubliette. A few inches above this shaft a tiny dark object floated, unsupported, in the air. It was withered, misshapen, closely resembling a lump of dirt. *This* was the Stone of Earth? This?

I consoled myself with the fact that at least the poor soul in the oubliette was dead now.

Dekarta paused then, glaring behind me at the Enefadeh. "Nahadoth, you may take your customary position. The rest of you—I did not command your presence."

To my surprise, Viraine answered. "It would serve well to have them here, my Lord. The Skyfather might be pleased to see his children, even these traitors."

"No father is pleased to see children who have turned on him." Dekarta's gaze drifted to me. I wondered if it was me he saw, or just Kinneth's eyes in my face.

"I want them here," I said.

There was no visible reaction from him beyond a tightening of his already-thin lips. "Such good friends they are, to come and watch you die."

"It would be harder to face this without their support, Grandfather. Tell me, did you allow Ygreth any company when you murdered her?"

He drew himself straight, which was rare for him. For the first time I saw a shadow of the man he had been, tall and haughty as any Amn, and formidable as my mother; it startled me to see the resemblance at last. He was too thin for the height now, though; it only emphasized his unhealthy gauntness. "I will not explain my actions to you, Granddaughter."

I nodded. From the corner of my eye I saw the others watching. Relad looked anxious; Scimina, annoyed. Viraine—I could not read him, but he watched me with an intensity that puzzled me. I could not spare thought for it, however. This was perhaps my last chance to find out why my mother had died. I still believed Viraine had done the deed, yet that still made no sense; he'd loved her. But if he had been acting on Dekarta's orders...

"You don't need to explain," I replied. "I can guess. When you were young, you were like these two—" I gestured to Relad and Scimina. "Self-absorbed, hedonistic, cruel. But not as heartless as they, were you? You married Ygreth, and you must have cared for her, or your mother wouldn't have designated her your sacrifice when the time came. But you loved power more, and so you made the trade. You became clan head. And your daughter became your mortal enemy."

Dekarta's lips twitched. I could not tell if this was a sign of emotion, or the palsy that seemed to afflict him now and again. "Kinneth loved me."

"Yes, she did." Because that was the kind of woman my mother had been. She could hate and love at once; she could use one to conceal and fuel the other. She had been, as Nahadoth said, a true Arameri. Only her goals had been different.

"She loved you," I said, "and I think you killed her."

This time I was certain that pain crossed the old man's face. It gave me a moment's satisfaction, though no more than that. The war was lost; this skirmish meant nothing in the grand scale of things. I would die. And while my death would fulfill the desires of so many—my parents, the Enefadeh, myself—I could not face it in such clinical terms. My heart was full of fear.

In spite of myself I turned and looked at the Enefadeh, ranged behind me. Kurue would not meet my eyes, but Zhakkarn did, and she gave me a respectful nod. Sieh: he uttered a soft feline croon that was no less anguished for its inhumanity. I felt tears sting my eyes. Foolishness. Even if I weren't destined to die today, I would be only a hiccup in his endless life. And I was the one who was dying, yet I would miss him terribly.

Finally I looked at Nahadoth, who had hunkered down on one knee behind me, framed by the gray cloud-chains. Of course they would force him to kneel, here in Itempas's place. But it was me he watched, and not the brightening eastern sky. I had expected his expression to be impassive, but it was not. Shame and sorrow and a rage that had shattered planets were in his eyes, along with other emotions too unnerving to name.

Could I trust what I saw? Did I dare? After all, he would soon be powerful again. What did it cost him to pretend love now and thus motivate me to follow through with their plan?

I lowered my eyes, pained. I had been in Sky so long that I no longer trusted even myself.

"I did not kill your mother," Dekarta said.

I started and turned to him. He'd spoken so softly that for a moment I thought I'd misheard. "What?"

"I didn't kill her. I would never have killed her. If she had not hated me I would have begged her to return to Sky, even bring you along." To my shock, I saw wetness on Dekarta's cheeks; he was crying. And glaring at me through his tears. "I would even have tried to love you, for her sake."

"Uncle," said Scimina; her tone bordered on the insolent, practically vibrating with impatience. "While I can appreciate your kindness toward our cousin—"

"Be silent," Dekarta snarled at her. His diamond-pale eyes fixed on her so sharply that she actually flinched. "You don't know how close I came to killing you when I heard of Kinneth's death."

Scimina went stiff, echoing Dekarta's own posture. Predictably she did not obey his order. "That would have been your privilege, my lord. But I had no part in Kinneth's death; I paid no attention to her or this mongrel daughter of hers. I don't even know why you chose her as today's sacrifice."

"To see if she was a true Arameri," Dekarta said very softly. His eyes drifted back to mine. It took three full heartbeats for me to realize what he meant, and the blood drained from my face as I did.

"You thought *I* killed her," I whispered. "Father of All, you honestly believed that."

"Murdering those we love best is a long tradition in our family," Dekarta said.

*   *   *

Beyond us, the eastern sky had grown very bright.

*   *   *

I spluttered. It took me several tries to muster a coherent sentence through my fury, and when I did it was in Darre. I only realized it when Dekarta looked more confused than offended by my curses. "I am not Arameri!" I finished, fists clenched at my sides. "You eat your own young, you feed on suffering, like monsters out of some ancient tale! I will never be one of you in anything but blood, and if I could burn that out of myself I would!"

"Perhaps you aren't one of us," Dekarta said. "Now I see that you are innocent, and by killing you I only destroy what remains of her. There is a part of me which regrets this. But I will not lie, Granddaughter. There is another part of me that will rejoice in your death. You took her from me. She left Sky to be with your father, and to raise you."

"Do you wonder why?" I gestured around the glass chamber, at gods and blood relatives come to watch me die. "*You killed her mother.* What did you think she would do, get over it?"

For the first time since I had met him, there was a flicker of humanity in Dekarta's sad, self-deprecating smile. "I suppose I did. Foolish of me, wasn't it?"

I could not help it; I echoed his smile. "Yes, Grandfather. It was."

Viraine touched Dekarta's shoulder then. A patch of gold had grown against the eastern horizon, bright and warning. Dawn was coming. The time for confessions had passed.

Dekarta nodded, then gazed at me for a long, silent moment

before speaking. "I'm sorry," he said very softly. An apology that covered many transgressions. "We must begin."

*   *   *

Even then, I did not say what I believed. I did not point at Viraine and name him my mother's killer. There was still time. I could have asked Dekarta to see to him before completing the succession, as a last tribute to Kinneth's memory. I don't know why I didn't— No. I do. I think in that moment, vengeance and answers ceased to have meaning for me. What difference would it make to know why my mother had died? She would still be dead. What good did it do me to punish her killer? I would be dead, too. Would any of this give meaning to my death, or hers?

There is always meaning in death, child. You will understand, soon.

*   *   *

Viraine began a slow circuit of the room. He raised his hands, lifted his face, and—still walking—began to speak.

"Father of the sky and of the earth below you, master of all creation, hear your favored servants. We beg your guidance through the chaos of transition."

He stopped in front of Relad, whose face looked waxy in the gray light. I did not see the gesture that Viraine made, but Relad's sigil suddenly glowed white, like a tiny sun etched upon his forehead. He did not wince or show any sign of pain, though the light made him look paler still. Nodding to himself, Viraine moved on around the room, now passing behind me. I turned my head to follow him; for some reason it bothered me to have him out of sight.

"We beg your assistance in subduing your enemies." Behind

me, Nahadoth had turned his face away from the rising dawn. The black aura around him had begun to wisp away, as it had on the night of Scimina's torture. Viraine touched Nahadoth's forehead. A sigil appeared out of nowhere, also white-hot, and Nahadoth hissed as if this caused him further pain. But the leaking of his aura stopped, and when he lifted his head, panting, the dawn's light no longer seemed to bother him. Viraine moved on.

"We beg your blessing upon your newest chosen," he said, and touched Scimina's forehead. She smiled as her sigil ignited, the white light illuminating her face in stark angles and eager, fierce planes.

Viraine came to stand before me then, with the plinth between us. As he passed behind it, my eyes were again drawn to the Stone of Earth. I had never dreamt it would look so singularly unimpressive.

The lump shivered. For just an instant, a perfect, beautiful silver seed floated there before fading back into the dark lump.

If Viraine had been looking at me in that moment, all might have been lost. I understood what had happened and realized the danger all in a single icy bolt of intuition, and it showed on my face. The Stone was like Nahadoth, like all the gods bound here on earth; its true form was hidden behind a mask. The mask made it seem ordinary, unimportant. But for those who looked upon it and expected more—especially those who knew its true nature—it would become more. It would change its shape to reflect all that they knew.

I was condemned, and the Stone was to be my executioners' blade. I should have seen it as a menacing, terrible thing. That

I saw beauty and promise was a clear warning to any Arameri that I intended to do more than just die today.

Fortunately Viraine was not looking at me. He had turned to face the eastern sky, as had everyone else in the room. I looked from face to face, seeing pride, anxiety, expectation, bitterness. The last was Nahadoth, who alone besides me did not look at the sky. His gaze found mine instead, and held it. Perhaps that was why we alone were not affected as the sun crested the distant horizon, and power made the whole world shiver like a jolted mirror.

* * *

From the instant the sun sinks out of mortal sight until the last light fades: that is twilight. From the instant the sun crests the horizon 'til it no longer touches earth: that is dawn.

* * *

I looked around in surprise, and caught my breath as before me, the Stone blossomed.

That was the only word that could fit what I saw. The ugly lump shivered, then *unfolded*, layers peeling away to reveal light. But this was not the steady white light of Itempas, nor the wavering unlight of Nahadoth. This was the strange light I had seen in the oubliette, gray and unpleasant, somehow leaching the color from everything nearby. There was no shape to the Stone now, not even the silver apricotseed. It was a star, shining, but somehow strengthless.

Yet I felt its true power, radiating at me in waves that made my skin crawl and my stomach churn. I stepped back inadvertently, understanding now why T'vril had warned off the servants. There was nothing wholesome in this power. It was part of the Goddess of Life, but she was dead. The Stone was just a grisly relic.

"Name your choice to lead our family, Granddaughter," said Dekarta.

I turned away from the Stone, though its radiance made that side of my face itch. My sight went blurry for a moment. I felt weak. The thing was killing me and I hadn't even touched it.

"R-Relad," I said. "I choose Relad."

"What?" Scimina's voice, stunned and outraged. *"What did you say, you mongrel?"*

Movement behind me. It was Viraine; he had come around to my side of the plinth. I felt his hand on my back, supporting me when the Stone's power made me sway, dizzy. I took it as comfort and made a greater effort to stand. As I did so, Viraine shifted a bit and I caught a glimpse of Kurue. Her expression was grim, resolute.

I thought I understood why.

*   *   *

The sun, as was its wont, was moving quickly. Already half of its bulk was above the horizon line. Soon it would no longer be dawn, but day.

*   *   *

Dekarta nodded, unruffled by Scimina's sudden spluttering. "Take the Stone, then," he commanded me. "Make your choice real."

My choice. I lifted a shaking hand to take the Stone, and wondered if death would hurt. My choice.

"Do it," whispered Relad. He was leaning forward, his whole body taut. "Do it, do it, do it…"

"No!" Scimina again, a scream. I saw her lunge at me from the corner of my eye.

"I'm sorry," Viraine whispered behind me, and suddenly everything stopped.

I blinked, not sure what had happened. Something made me look down. There, poked through the bodice of my ugly dress, was something new: the tip of a knife blade. It had emerged from my body on the right side of my sternum, just beside the swell of my breast. The cloth around it was changing, turning a strange wet black.

Blood, I realized. The Stone's light stole the color even from that.

Lead weighed my arm. What had I been doing? I could not remember. I was very tired. I needed to lie down.

So I did.

And I died.

28

Twilight and Dawn

I REMEMBER WHO I AM NOW.

I have held on to myself, and I will not let that knowledge go.
I carry the truth within myself, future and past, inseparable.
I will see this through.

*   *   *

*In the glass-walled chamber, many things happen at once. I move
among my former companions, unseen, yet seeing all.*

*My body falls to the floor, unmoving but for the blood spreading
around it. Dekarta stares at me, perhaps seeing other dead women.
Relad and Scimina begin shouting at Viraine, their faces distorted.
I do not hear their words. Viraine, gazing down at me with a pecu-
liarly empty expression, shouts something as well, and all of the
Enefadeh are frozen in place. Sieh trembles, feline muscles bunched
and straining. Zhakkarn, too, quivers, her massive fists clenched.
Two of them make no effort to move, I notice, and because I notice,
I see them up close. Kurue stands straight, her expression calm but
resigned. There is a shadow of sorrow about her, hugging close like
the cloak of her wings, but it is not something the others can see.*

Nahadoth—ah. The shock in his expression is giving way to anguish as he stares at me. The me on the floor bleeding out, not the me who watches him. How can I be both? *I wonder fleetingly, before dismissing the question. It doesn't matter.*

What matters is that there is real pain in Nahadoth's eyes, and it is more than the horror of a lost chance at freedom. It is not a pure pain, though; he, too, sees other dead women. Would he mourn me at all if I did not carry his sister's soul?

That is an unfair question and small-hearted of me.

Viraine crouches and yanks the knife out of my corpse. More blood spills at this, but not much. My heart has already stopped. I have fallen onto my side, half-curled as if in sleep, but I am not a god. I will not wake up.

"Viraine." Someone. Dekarta. "Explain yourself."

Viraine gets to his feet, glancing at the sky. The sun is three-quarters above the horizon. A strange look crosses his face, a hint of fear. Then it is gone, and he looks down at the bloody knife in his hand and then lets it drop to the floor. The clattering sound is distant, but my vision focuses in close on his hand. My blood has splattered his fingers. They tremble just slightly.

"It was necessary," he says, half to himself. Then he pulls himself together and says, "She was a weapon, my lord. Lady Kinneth's last strike at you, with the collusion of the Enefadeh. There's no time to explain now, but suffice it to say that if she had touched the Stone, made her wish, all the world would have suffered for it."

Sieh has managed to straighten, perhaps because he has stopped trying to kill Viraine. His voice is lower in his cat form, a half snarl. "How did you know?"

"I told him."

369

N. K. Jemisin

Kurue.

The others stare at her, disbelieving. But she is a goddess. Even as a traitor she will not yield her dignity.

"You have forgotten yourselves," she says, looking at each of her fellow Enefadeh in turn. "We have been too long at the mercy of these creatures. Once we would never have stooped so low as to rely on a mortal—especially not a descendant of the very mortal who betrayed us." She looks at my corpse and sees Shahar Arameri. I carry the burdens of so many dead women. "I would rather die than beg her for my freedom. I would rather kill her and use her death to buy Itempas's mercy."

There is a held breath of silence, at her words. It is not shock; it is rage.

Sieh breaks it first, growling out soft, bitter laughter. "I see. You killed Kinneth."

All the humans in the room start, except Viraine. Dekarta drops his cane, because his gnarled hands have clenched into half fists. He says something. I do not hear it.

Kurue does not seem to hear him, either, though she inclines her head to Sieh. "It was the only sensible course of action. The girl had to die here, at dawn." She points at the Stone. "The soul will linger near its fleshly remnant. And in a moment Itempas will arrive to collect and destroy it at last."

"And our hopes with it," says Zhakkarn, her jaw tight.

Kurue sighs. "Our mother is dead, Sister. Itempas won. I hate it, too—but it's time we accepted this. What did you think would happen if we did manage to free ourselves? Just the four of us, against the Bright Lord and dozens of our brothers and sisters? And the Stone, you realize. We have no one to wield it for us, but Itempas has his Arameri pets. We would end up enslaved again, or worse. No."

370

Then she turns to glare at Nahadoth. How could I have failed to recognize the look in her eyes? It has always been there. She looks at Nahadoth the way my mother probably looked at Dekarta, with sorrow inseparable from contempt. That should have been enough to warn me.

"Hate me for it if you like, Naha. But remember that if you had only swallowed your foolish pride and given Itempas what he wanted, none of us would be here. Now I will give him what he wants, and he's promised to set me free for it."

Nahadoth speaks very softly. "You're the fool, Kurue, if you think Itempas will accept anything short of my capitulation."

He looks up then. I have no flesh in this vision, this dream, but I want to shiver. His eyes are black through black. The skin around them is crazed with lines and cracks, like a porcelain mask on the verge of shattering. What gleams through these cracks is neither blood nor flesh; it is an impossibly black glow that pulses like a heartbeat. When he smiles, I cannot see his teeth.

"Isn't that true . . . Brother?" His voice holds echoes of emptiness. He is looking at Viraine.

Viraine, half-silhouetted by the dawning sun, turns to Nahadoth— but it is my eyes he seems to meet. The watching, floating me. He smiles. The sorrow and fear in that smile is something that only I, out of this whole room, can possibly understand. I know this instinctively, though I do not know why.

Then, just before the sun's bottommost curve lifts free of the horizon, I recognize what I have seen in him. Two souls. Itempas, like both his siblings, also has a second self.

Viraine flings back his head and screams, and from his throat vomits hot, searing white light. It floods the room in an instant, blinding me. I imagine the people in the city below, and in the surrounding countryside, will see this light from miles away. They will think it is a sun come to earth, and they will be right.

In the brightness I hear the Arameri crying out, except Dekarta. He alone has witnessed this before. When the light fades, I look upon Itempas, Bright Lord of the Sky.

The library etching was surprisingly accurate, though the differences are profound. His face is even more perfect, with lines and symmetry that put mere etching to shame. His eyes are the gold of a blazing noonday sun. Though white like Viraine's, his hair is shorter and tighter-curled than even my own. His skin is darker, too, matte-smooth and flawless. (This surprises me, though it shouldn't. How it must gall the Amn.) I can see, in this first glance, why Naha loves him.

And there is love in Itempas's eyes, too, as he steps around my body and its nimbus of coagulating blood. "Nahadoth," he says, smiling and extending his hands. Even in my fleshless state, I shiver. The things his tongue does to those syllables! He has come to seduce the god of seduction, and oh, has he come prepared.

Nahadoth is abruptly free to rise to his feet, which he does. But he does not take the proferred hands. He walks past Itempas to where my body lies. My corpse is fouled with blood all along one side, but he kneels and lifts me anyhow. He holds me against himself, cradling my head so it does not flop back on my limp neck. There is no expression on his face. He simply looks at me.

If this gesture is calculated to offend, it works. Itempas lowers his hands slowly, and his smile fades.

"Father of All." Dekarta bows with precarious dignity, unsteady without his cane. "We are honored by your presence once again."

Murmurs from the sides of the room: Relad and Scimina make their greetings as well. I do not care about them. I exclude them from my perception.

For a moment I think Itempas will not answer. Then he says, still gazing at Nahadoth's back, "You still wear the sigil, Dekarta. Call a servant and finish the ritual."

"At once, Father. But . . ."

Itempas looks at Dekarta, who trails off under that burning-desert gaze. I do not blame him. But Dekarta is Arameri; gods do not frighten him for long.

"Viraine," he says. "You were . . . part of him."

Itempas lets him flounder to silence, then says, "Since your daughter left Sky."

Dekarta looks over at Kurue. "You knew this?"

She inclines her head, regal. "Not at first. But Viraine came to me one day and let me know I need not be damned to this earthly hell for all eternity. Our father could still forgive us, if we proved ourselves loyal." She glances at Itempas then, and even her dignity cannot hide her anxiety. She knows how fickle his favor can be. "Even then I wasn't certain, though I suspected. That was when I decided on my plan."

"But . . . that means . . ." Dekarta pauses then, realization-anger-resignation flickering across his face in quick succession. I can guess his thoughts: Bright Itempas orchestrated Kinneth's death.

My grandfather closes his eyes, perhaps mourning the death of his faith. "Why?"

"Viraine's heart was broken." And does the Father of All realize that his eyes turn to Nahadoth when he says this? Is he aware of what

373

this look reveals? "He wanted Kinneth back, and offered anything if I would help him achieve that goal. I accepted his flesh in payment."

"How predictable." I shift to myself, lying in Nahadoth's arms. Nahadoth speaks above me. "You used him."

"If I could have given him what he wanted, I would have," Itempas replies with a very human shrug. "But Enefa gave these creatures the power to make their own choices. Even we cannot change their minds when they're set on a given course. Viraine was foolish to ask."

The smile that curves Nahadoth's lips is contemptuous. "No, Tempa, that isn't what I meant, and you know it."

And somehow, perhaps because I am no longer alive and no longer thinking with a fleshly brain, I understand. Enefa is dead. Never mind that some remnant of her flesh and soul lingers; both are mere shadows of who and what she truly was. Viraine, however, took into himself the essence of a living god. I shiver as I realize: the moment of Itempas's manifestation was also the moment of Viraine's death. Had he known it was coming? So much of his strangeness became clear, in retrospect.

But before that, disguised by Viraine's mind and soul, Itempas could watch Nahadoth like a voyeur. He could command Nahadoth and thrill in his obedience. He could pretend to be doing Dekarta's will while manipulating events to exert subtle pressure on Nahadoth. All without Nahadoth's knowledge.

Itempas's expression does not change, but there is something about him now that suggests anger. A more burnished shade to his golden eyes, perhaps. "Always so melodramatic, Naha." He steps closer— close enough that the white glow which surrounds him clashes against Nahadoth's smoldering shadow. Where the two powers brush against each other, both light and dark vanish, leaving nothing.

"You clutch that piece of meat like it means something," Itempas *says.*

"She does."

"Yes, yes, a vessel, I know—but her purpose is served now. She has bought your freedom with her life. Will you not come take your reward?"

Moving slowly, Nahadoth sets my body down. I feel his rage coming before, apparently, anyone else. Even Itempas looks surprised when Nahadoth clenches his fists and slams them into the floor. My blood flies up in twin sprays. The floor cracks ominously, and some of the cracks run up the glass walls—though, fortunately, these only spiderweb and do not shatter. As if in compensation, the plinth at the center of the room shatters instead, spilling the Stone ignominiously onto the floor and peppering everyone with glittering white flecks.

"More," Nahadoth *breathes. His skin has cracked further; he is barely contained by the flesh that is his prison. When he rises and turns, his hands drip something too dark to be blood. The cloak that surrounds him lashes the air like miniature tornadoes.*

"She . . . was . . . more!" He is barely coherent. He lived countless ages before language. Perhaps his instinct is to forego speech altogether in moments of extremity, and just roar out his fury. *"More than a vessel. She was my last hope. And yours."*

Kurue—my vision swings toward her against my will—steps forward, opening her mouth to protest. Zhakkarn catches her arm in warning. Wise, I think, or at least wiser than Kurue. Nahadoth looks utterly demented.

But then, so does Itempas, as he stares down Nahadoth's rage. There is open lust in his eyes, unmistakable beneath the warrior's tension. But of course: how many aeons did they spend battling, raw violence giving way to stranger longings? Or perhaps Itempas has simply been so long without Nahadoth's love that he will take anything, even hate, in its place.

"Naha," he says gently. "Look at you. All this over a mortal?" He sighs, shaking his head. "I'd hoped that putting you here, amid the vermin that are our sister's legacy, would show you the error of your ways. Now I see that you are merely growing accustomed to captivity."

He steps forward then, and does what every other person in the room would have considered suicide: he touches Nahadoth. It is a brief gesture, just a light brush of his fingers against the cracked porcelain of Nahadoth's face. There is such yearning in that touch that my heart aches.

But does it matter anymore? Itempas has killed Enefa; he has killed his own children; he has killed me. He has killed something in Nahadoth as well. Can he not see that?

Perhaps he does, because his soft look fades, and after a moment he takes his hand away.

"So be it," he says, going cold. "I tire of this. Enefa was a plague, Nahadoth. She took the pure, perfect universe that you and I created and fouled it. I kept the Stone because I did care for her, whatever you might think . . . and because I thought it might help to sway you."

He pauses then, looking down at my corpse. The Stone has fallen into my blood, less than a handbreadth from my shoulder. Despite Nahadoth's care in setting me down, my head has flopped to one side. One arm is curled upward as if to try and cup the Stone closer. The image is ironic—a mortal woman, killed in the act of trying to lay claim to a goddess's power. And a god's lover.

I imagine Itempas will send me to an especially awful hell.

"But I think it's time our sister dies completely," Itempas says. I

cannot tell if he is looking at the Stone or at me. "Let her infestation die with her, and then our lives can be as they were. Have you not missed those days?"

(I notice Dekarta, who stiffens at this. Only he, of the three mortals, seems to realize what Itempas means.)

"I will hate you no less, Tempa," Nahadoth breathes, "when you and I are the last living things in this universe."

Then he is a roaring black tempest, streaking forward in attack, and Itempas is a crackle of white fire bracing to meet him. They collide in a concussion that shatters the glass in the ritual chamber. Mortals scream, their voices almost lost as cold, thin air howls in to fill the void. They fall to the floor as Nahadoth and Itempas streak away, upward—but my perception is drawn to Scimina for an instant. Her eyes fix on the knife that killed me, Viraine's knife, lying not far from her. Relad sprawls dazed amid glass shards and chunks of the broken plinth. Scimina's eyes narrow.

Sieh roars, his voice an echo of Nahadoth's battle cry. Zhakkarn turns to face Kurue, and her pike appears in one hand.

And at the center of it all, unnoticed, untouched, my body and the Stone lie still.

*   *   *

And here we are.

Yes.

You understand what has happened?

I'm dead.

Yes. In the presence of the Stone, which houses the last of my power.

Is that why I'm still here, able to see these things?

Yes. The Stone kills the living. You're dead.

You mean…I can come back to life? Amazing. How convenient that Viraine turned on me.

I prefer to think of it as fate.

So what now?

Your body must change. It will no longer be able to bear two souls within itself; that is an ability only mortals possess. I made your kind that way, gifted in ways that we are not, but I never dreamt it would make you so strong. Strong enough to defeat me, in spite of all my efforts. Strong enough to take my place.

What? No. I don't want your place. You are you. I am me. I have fought for this.

And fought well. But my essence, all that I am, is necessary for this world to continue. If I am not to be the one who restores that essence, then it must be you.

But—

I do not regret, Daughter, Little Sister, worthy heir. Neither should you. I only wish…

I know your wish.

Do you really?

Yes. They are blinded by pride, but underneath there is still love. The Three are meant to be together. I will see it done.

Thank you.

Thank *you*. And farewell.

*　　*　　*

I can ponder for an eternity. I am dead. I have all the time I want.

But I was never very patient.

*　　*　　*

In and around the glass room, which no longer has glass and probably no longer qualifies as a room, battle rages.

Itempas and Nahadoth have taken their fight to the skies they once shared. Above the motes they have become, dark streaks break the gradient of dawn, like strips of night layered over the morning. A blazing white beam, like the sun but a thousand times brighter, sears across these to shatter them. There is no point to this. It is daytime. Nahadoth would already be asleep within his human prison if not for Itempas's parole. Itempas can revoke that parole whenever he wishes. He must be enjoying himself.

Scimina has gotten Viraine's knife. She has flung herself on Relad, trying to gut him. He's stronger, but she has leverage and the strength of ambition on her side. Relad's eyes are wide with terror; perhaps he has always feared something like this.

Sieh, Zhakkarn, and Kurue feint and circle in a deadly metal-and-claw dance. Kurue has conjured a pair of gleaming bronze swords to defend herself. This contest, too, is foregone; Zhakkarn is battle incarnate, and Sieh has all the power of childhood's cruelty. But Kurue is wily, and she has the taste of freedom in her mouth. She will not die easily.

Amid all this, Dekarta moves toward my body. He stops and struggles to his knees; in the end he slips in my blood and half-falls on me, grimacing in pain. Then his expression hardens. He looks up into the sky, where his god fights, then down. At the Stone. It is the source of the Arameri clan's power; it is also the physical representation of their duty. Perhaps he hopes that by doing that duty, he will remind Itempas of the value of life. Perhaps he retains some smidgeon of faith. Perhaps it is simply that forty years ago, Dekarta killed his wife to prove his commitment. To do otherwise now would mock her death.

He reaches for the Stone.

It is gone.

But it was there, lying in my blood, a moment before. Dekarta frowns, looks around. His eyes are attracted by movement. The hole in my chest, which he can see through the torn cloth of my bodice: the raw lips of the wound are drawing together, pressing themselves closed. As the line of the wound shrinks, Dekarta catches a glimmer of thin gray light. Within me.

Then I am drawn forward, down—

Yes. Enough of this disembodied soul business. Time to be alive again.

* * *

I opened my eyes and sat up.

Dekarta, behind me, made a sound somewhere between choking and a gasp. No one else noticed as I got to my feet, so I turned to face him.

"Wh—what in every god's name—" His mouth worked. He stared.

"Not every god," I said. And because I was still me after all, I leaned down to smile in his face. "Just me."

Then I closed my eyes and touched my chest. Nothing beat beneath my fingers; my heart had been destroyed. Yet something was there, giving life to my flesh. I could feel it. The Stone. A thing of life, born of death, filled with incalculable potential. A seed.

"*Grow,*" I whispered.

29

The Three

As with any birth, there was pain.

I believe I screamed. I think that in that instant many things occurred. I have a vague sense of the sky wheeling overhead, cycling day through day and night and back to morning in the span of a breath. (If this happened, then what moved was not the sky.) I have a feeling that somewhere in the universe an uncountable number of new species burst into existence, on millions of planets. I am fairly certain that tears fell from my eyes. Where they landed, lichens and moss began to cover the floor.

I cannot be certain of any of this. Somewhere, in dimensions for which there are no mortal words, I was changing, too. This occupied a great deal of my awareness.

But when the changes were done, I opened my eyes and saw new colors.

The room practically glowed with them. The iridescence of the floor's Skystuff. Glints of gold from glass shards lying about the room. The blue of the sky—it had been a watery blue-white, but now it was such a vivid teal that I stared at it in wonder. It had never, at least in my lifetime, been so blue.

Next I noticed scent. My body had become something else, less a *body* than an *embodiment*, but its shape for the moment was still human, as were my senses. And something was different here, too. When I inhaled, I could taste the crisp, acrid thinness of the air, underlaid by the metallic scent of the blood that covered my clothing. I touched my fingers to this and tasted it. Salt, more metal, hints of bitter and sour. Of course; I had been unhappy for days before I died.

New colors. New scents in the air. I had never realized, before now, what it meant to live in a universe that had lost one-third of itself. The Gods' War had cost us so much more than mere lives.

No more, I vowed.

Around me the chaos had stopped. I did not want to talk, to think, but a sense of responsibility pushed insistently against my reverie. At last I sighed and focused on my surroundings.

To my left stood three shining creatures, stronger than the rest, more malleable in form. I recognized in them an essence of myself. They stared at me, weapons frozen in hand or on claw, mouths agape. Then one of them moulded himself into a different shape—a child—and came forward. His eyes were wide. "M-Mother?"

That was not my name. I would have turned away in disinterest had it not occurred to me that this would hurt him. Why did that matter? I didn't know, but it bothered me.

So instead I said, "No." On impulse, I reached out to stroke his hair. His eyes got even wider, then spilled over with tears. He pulled away from me then, covering his face. I did not know what to make of this behavior, so I turned to the others.

Three more to my right—or rather, two, and one dying. Also shining creatures, though their light was hidden within them, and their bodies were weaker and crude. And finite. The dying one expired as I watched, too many of his organs having been damaged to sustain life. I felt the rightness of their mortality even as I mourned it.

"What is this?" demanded one of them. The younger one, the female. Her gown and hands were splattered with her brother's blood.

The other mortal, old and close to death himself, only shook his head, staring at me.

Then suddenly two more creatures stood before me, and I caught my breath at the sight. I could not help myself. They were so beautiful, even beyond the shells they wore to interact with this plane. They were part of me, kin, and yet so very different. I had been born to be with them, to bridge the gap between them and complete their purpose. To stand with them now—I wanted to throw back my head and sing with joy.

But something was wrong. The one who felt like light and stillness and stability—he was whole, and glorious. Yet there was something unwholesome at his core. I looked closer and perceived a great and terrible loneliness within him, eating at his heart like a worm in an apple. That sobered me, softened me, because I knew what that kind of loneliness felt like.

The same blight was in the other being, the one whose nature called to everything dark and wild. But something more had been done to him; something terrible. His soul had been battered and crushed, bound with sharp-edged chains, then forced into a too-small vessel. Constant agony. He had gone down on one knee, staring at me through dull eyes and lank, sweat-soaked hair. Even his own panting caused him pain.

It was an obscenity. But a greater obscenity was the fact that the chains, when I followed them to their source, were *part of me*. So were three other leashes, one of which led to the neck of the creature who had called me Mother.

Revolted, I tore the chains away from my chest and willed them to shatter.

The three creatures to my left all gasped, folding in on themselves as power returned to them. Their reaction was nothing, however, compared to that of the dark being. For an instant he did not move, only widening his eyes as the chains loosened and fell away.

Then he flung his head back and screamed, and all existence shifted. On this plane, this manifested as a single, titanic concussion of sound and vibration. All sight vanished from the world, replaced by a darkness profound enough to drive weaker souls mad if it lasted for more than a heartbeat. It passed even more quickly than that, replaced by something new.

Balance: I felt its return like the setting of a dislocated joint. Out of Three had the universe been formed. For the first time in an age, Three walked again.

When all was still, I saw that my dark one was whole. Where once restless shadows had flickered in his wake, now he shone with an impossible negative radiance, black as the

Maelstrom. Had I thought him merely beautiful before? Ah, but now there was no human flesh to filter his cool majesty. His eyes glowed blue-black with a million mysteries, terrifying and exquisite. When he smiled, all the world shivered, and I was not immune.

Yet this shook me on an entirely different level, because suddenly memory surged through me. They were pallid, these memories, as of something half-forgotten—but they pushed at me, demanding acknowledgment, until I made a sound and shook my head and batted at the air in protest. They were part of me, and though I understood now that names were as ephemeral as form for my kind, those memories insisted upon giving the dark creature a name: Nahadoth.

And the bright one: Itempas.

And me—

I frowned in confusion. My hands rose in front of my face, and I stared at them as if I had never seen them. In a way, I had not. Within me was the gray light I had so hated before, transformed now into all the colors that had been stolen from existence. Through my skin I could see those colors dancing along my veins and nerves, no less powerful for being hidden. Not my power. But it was my flesh, wasn't it? Who was I?

"Yeine," said Nahadoth in a tone of wonder.

A shudder passed through me, the same feeling of balance I'd had a moment before. Suddenly I understood. It *was* my flesh, and my power, too. I was what mortal life had made me, what Enefa had made me, but all that was in the past. From henceforth I could be whomever I wanted.

"Yes," I said, and smiled at him. "That is my name."

*   *   *

Other changes were necessary.

Nahadoth and I turned to face Itempas, who watched us with eyes as hard as topaz.

"Well, Naha," he said, though the hate in his eyes was all for me. "I must congratulate you; this is a fine coup. I thought killing the girl would be sufficient. Now I see I should have obliterated her entirely."

"That would have taken more power than you possess," I said. A frown flickered across Itempas's face. He was so easy to read; did he realize that? He still thought of me as a mortal, and mortals were insignificant to him.

"You aren't Enefa," he snapped.

"No, I'm not." I could not help smiling. "Do you know why Enefa's soul lingered all these years? It wasn't because of the Stone."

His frown deepened with annoyance. What a prickly creature he was. What did Naha see in him? No, that was jealousy speaking. Dangerous. I would not repeat the past.

"The cycle of life and death flows from me and through me," I said, touching my breast. Within it, something—not quite a heart—beat strong and even. "Even Enefa never truly understood this about herself. Perhaps she was always meant to die at some point; and now, perhaps I am the only one of us who will never be truly immortal. But by the same token, neither can I truly die. Destroy me and some part will always linger. My soul, my flesh, perhaps only my memory—but it will be enough to bring me back."

"Then I simply wasn't thorough enough," Itempas said, and

his tone promised dire things. "I'll be sure to rectify that next time."

Nahadoth stepped forward. The dark nimbus that surrounded him made a faint crackling sound as he moved, and white flecks—moisture frozen out of the air—drifted to the floor in his wake.

"There will be no next time, Tempa," he said with frightening gentleness. "The Stone is gone and I am free. I will tear you apart, as I have planned for all the long nights of my imprisonment."

Itempas's aura blazed like white flames; his eyes glowed like twin suns. "I threw you broken to the earth once before, Brother, and I can do it again—"

"Enough," I said.

Nahadoth's answer was a hiss. He crouched, his hands suddenly monstrous claws at his sides. There was a blur of movement and suddenly Sieh was beside him, a feline shadow. Kurue moved as if to join Itempas, but instantly Zhakkarn's pike was at her throat.

None of them paid any attention to me. I sighed.

The knowledge of my power was within me, as instinctive as *how to think* and *how to breathe*. I closed my eyes and reached for it, and felt it uncurl and stretch within me, ready. Eager.

This was going to be fun.

The first blast of power that I sent through the palace was violent enough to stagger everyone, even my quarrelsome brothers, who fell silent in surprise. I ignored them and closed my eyes, tapping and shaping the energy to my will. There was so much! If I was not careful, I could so easily destroy rather than create.

On some level I was aware of being surrounded by colored light: cloudy gray, but also the rose of sunset and the white-green of dawn. My hair wafted in it, shining. My gown swirled about my ankles, an annoyance. A flick of my will and it became a Darren warrior's garments, tight-laced sleeveless tunic and practical calf-length pants. They were an impractical shining silver, but—well, I *was* a goddess, after all.

Walls—rough, brown, *tree-bark*—appeared around us. They did not completely enclose the room; here and there were gaps, though as I watched those filled. Branches nearby grew, split, and sprouted curling leaves. Above us the sky was still visible, though dimmer, thanks to the leafy canopy that now spread there. Through that canopy rose a titanic tree trunk, gnarling and curving high into the sky.

In fact the tree's topmost branches *pierced* the sky. If I looked down on this world from above I would see white clouds and blue seas and brown earth and a single magnificent tree, breaking the planet's smooth round curve. If I flew closer I would see roots like mountains, nestling the whole of Sky-the-city between the forks. I would see branches as long as rivers. I would see people on the ground below, shaken and terrified, crawling out of their homes and picking themselves up from the sidewalks to stare in awe at the great tree that had twined itself around the Skyfather's palace.

In fact I saw all of these things without ever opening my eyes. Then I did open them, to find my brothers and children staring at me.

"Enough," I said again. This time they paid attention. "This realm cannot endure another Gods' War. I will not permit it."

"You will not *permit*...?" Itempas clenched his fists, and I felt the heavy, blistering smolder of his power. For a moment it frightened me, and with good reason. He had bent the universe to his will at the beginning of time; he far outstripped me in experience and wisdom. I didn't even know how to fight as gods fought. He did not attack because there were two of us to his one, but that was the only thing holding him back.

Then there is hope, I decided.

As if reading my thoughts, Nahadoth shook his head. "No, Yeine." His eyes were black holes in his skull, ready to swallow worlds. The hunger for retribution curled off him like smoke. "He murdered Enefa even though he loved her. He'll have no qualms at all over you. We must destroy him, or be destroyed ourselves."

A quandary. I held no grudge against Itempas—he had murdered Enefa, not me. But Nahadoth had millennia of pain to expunge; he deserved justice. And worse, he was right. Itempas was mad, poisoned by his own jealousy and fear. One did not allow the mad to roam free, lest they hurt others or themselves.

Yet killing him was also impossible. Out of Three had the universe been made. Without all Three, it would all end.

"I can think of only one solution," I said softly. And even that was imperfect. After all, I knew from experience how much damage even a single mortal could inflict on the world, given enough time and power. We would just have to hope for the best.

Nahadoth frowned as he read my intention, but some of the hate flowed out of him. Yes; I had thought this might satisfy him. He nodded once in agreement.

Itempas stiffened as he realized what we meant to do. Language had been his invention; we had never really needed words. "I will not tolerate this."

"You will," I said, and joined my power with Nahadoth's. It was an easy fusion, more proof that we Three were meant to work together and not at odds. Someday, when Itempas had served his penance, perhaps we could truly be Three again. What wonders we would create then! I would look forward to it, and hope.

"You will serve," Nahadoth said to Itempas, and his voice was cold and heavy with the weight of law. I felt reality reshape itself. We had never really needed a separate language, either; any tongue would do, as long as one of us spoke the words. "Not a single family, but all the world. You will wander among mortals as one of them, unknown, commanding only what wealth and respect you can earn with your deeds and words. You may call upon your power only in great need, and only to aid these mortals for whom you hold such contempt. You will right all the wrongs inflicted in your name."

Nahadoth smiled then. This smile was not cruel—he was free and had no need of cruelty anymore—but neither was there mercy in him. "I imagine this task will take some time."

Itempas said nothing, because he could not. Nahadoth's words had taken hold of him, and with the aid of my power the words wove chains that no mortal could see or sever. He fought the chaining, once unleashing his power against ours in a furious blast, but it was no use. A single member of the Three could never hope to defeat the other two. Itempas had used those odds in his own favor long enough to know better.

But I could not leave it at that. A proper punishment was meant to redeem the culprit, not just assuage the victims.

"Your sentence can end sooner," I said, and my words, too, curved and linked and became hard around him, "if you learn to love truly."

Itempas glared at me. He had not been driven to his knees by the weight of our power, but it was a near thing. He stood now with back bowed, trembling all over, the white flames of his aura gone and his face sheened with a very mortal sweat. "I . . . will never . . . love you," he gritted through his teeth.

I blinked in surprise. "Why would *I* want your love? You're a monster, Itempas, destroying everything you claim to care for. I see such loneliness in you, such suffering—but all of it is your own doing."

He flinched, his eyes widening. I sighed, shook my head, and stepped close, lifting a hand to his cheek. He flinched again at my touch, though I stroked him until he quieted.

"But I am only one of your lovers," I whispered. "Haven't you missed the other?"

And as I had expected, Itempas looked at Nahadoth. Ah, the need in his eyes! If there had been any hope of it, I would have asked Nahadoth to share this moment with us. Just one kind word might have speeded Itempas's healing. But it would be centuries before Nahadoth's own wounds had healed enough for that.

I sighed. So be it. I would do what I could to make it easier for both of them, and try again when the ages had worked their magic. I had made a promise, after all.

"When you're ready to be among us again," I whispered to Itempas, "I, at least, will welcome you back." Then I kissed him, and filled that kiss with all the promise I could muster. But some of the surprise that passed between us was mine, for his mouth was soft despite its hard lines. Underneath that I could taste hot spices and warm ocean breezes; he made my mouth water and my whole body ache. For the first time I understood why Nahadoth loved him—and by the way his mouth hung open when I pulled back, I think he felt the same.

I looked over at Nahadoth, who sighed with too-human weariness. "He doesn't change, Yeine. He can't."

"He can if he wants to," I said firmly.

"You are naive."

Maybe I was. But that didn't make me wrong.

I kept my eyes on Itempas, though I went to Naha and took his hand. Itempas watched us like a man dying of thirst, within sight of a waterfall. It would be hard for him, the time to come, but he was strong. He was one of us. And one day, he would be ours again.

Power folded around Itempas like the petals of a great flower, scintillating. When the light faded, he was human—his hair no longer shining, his eyes merely brown. Handsome, but not perfect. Just a man. He fell to the floor, unconscious from the shock.

With that done, I turned to Nahadoth.

"No," he said, scowling.

"He deserves the same chance," I said.

"I promised him release already."

"Death, yes. I can give him more." I stroked Nahadoth's cheek, which flickered beneath my hand. His face changed every moment now, beautiful no matter how it looked—though the mortals probably would not have thought so, since some of his faces were not human. I was no longer human myself. I could accept all of Nahadoth's faces, so he had no need of any one in particular.

He sighed and closed his eyes at my touch, which both gratified and troubled me. He had been too long alone. I would have to take care not to exploit this weakness of his now, or he would hate me for it later.

Still, this had to be done. I said, "He deserves freedom, same as you."

He gave me a heavy sigh. But his sigh took the form of tiny black stars, surprisingly bright as they sparkled and multiplied and coalesced into a human form. For a moment a negative phantasm of the god stood before me. I willed it to life, and it became a man: Nahadoth's daytime self. He looked around, then stared at the shining being who had been his other half for so long. They had never met in all that time, but his eyes widened with realization.

"My gods," he breathed, too awed to realize the irony of his oath.

"Yeine—"

I turned to find Sieh beside me in his child form. He stood taut, his green eyes searching my face. "Yeine?"

I reached for him, then hesitated. He was not mine, despite my possessive feelings.

He reached up just as hesitantly, touching my arms and face in wonder. "You really . . . aren't her?"

"No. Just Yeine." I lowered my hand, letting him choose. I would respect his decision if he rejected me. But... "Was this what you wanted?"

"Wanted?" The look on his face would have gratified colder hearts than mine. He put his arms around me, and I pulled him close and held him tightly. "Ah, Yeine, you're still such a mortal," he whispered against my breast. But I felt him trembling.

Over Sieh's head, I looked at my other children. Stepchildren, perhaps; yes, that was a safer way to think of them. Zhakkarn inclined her head to me, a soldier acknowledging a new commander. She would obey, which was not quite what I wanted, but it would do for now.

Kurue, though, was another matter.

Gently disentangling myself from Sieh, I stepped toward her. Kurue dropped immediately to one knee and bowed her head.

"I will not beg your forgiveness," she said. Only her voice betrayed her fear; it was not its usual strong, clear tone. "I did what I felt was right."

"Of course you did," I said. "It was the wise thing to do." As I had done with Sieh, I reached out and stroked her hair. It was long and silver in this form of hers, like metal spun into curls. Beautiful.

I let it trail through my fingers as Kurue fell to the floor, dead.

"Yeine." Sieh, sounding stunned. For the moment I ignored him, because my eyes happened to meet Zhakkarn's as I looked up. She inclined her head again, and I knew then that I had earned a measure of her respect.

"Darr," I said.

"I'll see to things," Zhakkarn replied, and vanished.

The amount of relief I felt surprised me. Perhaps I had not left my humanity so very far behind after all.

Then I turned to face everyone in the chamber. A branch was growing across the room, but I touched it and it grew in a different direction, out of the way. "You, too," I said to Scimina, who blanched and stepped back.

"No," said Nahadoth abruptly. He turned to Scimina then and smiled; the room grew darker. "This one is mine."

"No," she whispered, taking another step back. If she could have bolted—another branch had covered the stairway entrance—I'm certain she would have, though of course that would have been pointless. "Just kill me."

"No more orders," Nahadoth said. He lifted a hand, the fingers curling as if to grip an invisible leash, and Scimina cried out as she was jerked forward, falling to her knees at his feet. She clutched at her throat, fingers scrabbling for some way to free herself, but there was nothing there. Naha leaned down, taking her chin in his fingers, and laid a kiss on her lips that was no less chilling for its tenderness. "I will kill you, Scimina, never fear. Just not yet."

I felt no pity. That, too, was a remnant of my humanity.

Which left only Dekarta.

He sat on the floor, where he had been thrown during the manifestation of my tree. When I went to him, I could see the throbbing ache in his hip, which was broken, and the unstable flutter of his heart. Too many shocks. It had not been a good night for him. But he smiled as I crouched before him, to my surprise.

"A goddess," he said, then barked out a single laugh that was remarkably free of bitterness. "Ah, Kinneth never did things by half measures, did she?"

In spite of myself, I shared his smile. "No. She didn't."

"So, then." He lifted his chin and regarded me imperiously, which would have worked better if he had not been panting due to his heart. "What of us, Goddess Yeine? What of your human kin?"

I wrapped my arms around my knees, balancing on my toes. I had forgotten to make shoes.

"You'll choose another heir, who will hold on to your power as best he can. Whether he succeeds or not, we will be gone, Naha and I, and Itempas will be useless to you. It should be interesting to see what mortals make of the world without our constant interference."

Dekarta stared at me in disbelief and horror. "Without the gods, every nation on this planet will rise up to destroy us. Then they'll turn on each other."

"Perhaps."

"*Perhaps?*"

"It will definitely happen," I said, "if your descendants are fools. But the Enefadeh have never been the Arameri's sole weapon, Grandfather; you know that better than anyone. You have more wealth than any single nation, enough to hire and equip whole armies. You have the Itempan priesthood, and they will be very motivated to spread your version of the truth, since they are threatened, too. And you have your own fine-honed viciousness, which has served well enough as a weapon all this time." I shrugged. "The Arameri can survive, and perhaps even retain power for a few generations. Enough, hopefully, to temper the worst of the world's wrath."

"There will be change," said Nahadoth, who was suddenly beside me. Dekarta drew back, but there was no malice in Nahadoth's eyes. Slavery was what had driven him half mad; already he was healing. "There must be change. The Arameri have kept the world still for too long, against nature. This must now correct itself in blood."

"But if you're clever," I added, "you'll get to keep most of yours."

Dekarta shook his head slowly. "Not me. I'm dying. And my heirs—they had the strength to rule as you say, but..." He glanced over at Relad, who lay open-eyed on the floor with a knife stuck in his throat. He had bled even more than I.

"Uncle—" Scimina began, but Nahadoth jerked her leash to silence her. Dekarta glanced once in her direction, then away.

"You have another heir, Dekarta," I said. "He's clever and competent, and I believe he's strong enough—though he will not thank me for recommending him."

I smiled to myself, seeing without eyes through the layers of Sky. Within, the palace was not so very different. Bark and branches had replaced the pearly Skystuff in places, and some of the dead spaces had been filled with living wood. But even this simple change was enough to terrify the denizens of Sky, highblood and low alike. At the heart of the chaos was T'vril, marshaling the palace's servants and organizing an evacuation.

Yes, he would do nicely.

Dekarta's eyes widened, but he knew an order when he heard one. He nodded, and in return, I touched him and willed his hip whole and his heart stable. That would keep him alive a few days longer—long enough to see the transition through.

"I...I don't understand," said the human Naha, as the godly

version and I got to our feet. He looked deeply shaken. "Why have you done this? What do I do now?"

I looked at him in surprise. "Live," I said. "Why else do you think I put you here?"

* * *

There was much more to be done, but those were the parts that mattered. You would have enjoyed all of it, I think—righting the imbalances triggered by your death, discovering existence anew. But perhaps there are interesting discoveries to be had where you've gone, too.

It surprises me to admit it, but I shall miss you, Enefa. My soul is not used to solitude.

Then again, I will never be *truly* alone, thanks to you.

* * *

Sometime after we left Sky and Itempas and the mortal world behind, Sieh took my hand. "Come with us," he said.

"Where?"

Nahadoth touched my face then, very gently, and I was awed and humbled by the tenderness in his gaze. Had I earned such warmth from him? I hadn't—but I would. I vowed this to myself, and lifted my face for his kiss.

"You have much to learn," he murmured against my lips when we parted. "I have so many wonders to show you."

I could not help grinning like a human girl. "Take me away, then," I said. "Let's get started."

So we passed beyond the universe, and now there is nothing more to tell.

* * *

Of this tale, anyhow.

APPENDIX
1

A Glossary of Terms

Altarskirt rose: A rare, specially bred variety of white rose, highly prized.

Amn: Most populous and powerful of the Senmite races.

Arameri: Ruling family of the Amn; advisors to the Nobles' Consortium and the Order of Itempas.

Arrebaia: Capital city of Darr.

Blood sigil: The mark of a recognized Arameri family member.

Bright, the: The time of Itempas's solitary rule after the Gods' War. General term for goodness, order, law, rightness.

Darkling: Those races that adopted the exclusive worship of Itempas only after the Gods' War, under duress. Includes most High Northern and island peoples.

Darr: A High North nation.

Dekarta Arameri: Head of the Arameri family.

Demon: Children of forbidden unions between gods/godlings and mortals. Extinct.

Enefa: One of the Three. The Betrayer. Deceased.

Enefadeh: Those who remember Enefa.

Gods: Immortal children of the Maelstrom. The Three.

Godling: Immortal children of the Three. Sometimes also referred to as gods.

Gods' Realm: Beyond the universe.

Gods' War: An apocalyptic conflict in which Bright Itempas claimed rulership of the heavens after defeating his two siblings.

Heavens, Hells: Abodes for souls beyond the mortal realm.

Heretic: A worshipper of any god but Itempas. Outlawed.

High North: Northernmost continent. A backwater.

Hundred Thousand Kingdoms: Collective term for the world since its unification under Arameri rule.

Irt: An island nation.

Islands, the: Vast archipelago east of High North and Senm.

Itempan: General term for a worshipper of Itempas. Also used to refer to members of the Order of Itempas.

Itempas: One of the Three. The Bright Lord; master of heavens and earth; the Skyfather.

Ken: Largest of the island nations, home to the Ken and Min peoples.

Kinneth Arameri: Only daughter of Dekarta Arameri.

Kurue: A godling, also called the Wise.

Lift: A magical means of transportation within Sky; a lesser version of the Vertical Gates.

Maelstrom: The creator of the Three. Unknowable.

Magic: The innate ability of gods and godlings to alter the material and immaterial world. Mortals may approximate this ability through the use of the gods' language.

Menchey: A High North nation.

A Glossary of Terms

Mortal realm: The universe, created by the Three.

Nahadoth: One of the Three. The Nightlord.

Narshes: A High North race whose homeland was conquered by the Tok several centuries ago.

Nobles' Consortium: Ruling political body of the Hundred Thousand Kingdoms.

Order of Itempas: The priesthood dedicated to Bright Itempas. In addition to spiritual guidance, also responsible for law and order, education, and the eradication of heresy. Also known as the Itempan Order.

Relad Arameri: Nephew of Dekarta Arameri, twin brother of Scimina.

Salon: Headquarters for the Nobles' Consortium.

Sar-enna-nem: Seat of the Darren *ennu* and the Warriors' Council.

Scimina Arameri: Niece of Dekarta Arameri, twin sister of Relad.

Scrivener: A scholar of the gods' written language.

Senm: Southernmost and largest continent of the world.

Senmite: The Amn language, used as a common tongue for all the Hundred Thousand Kingdoms.

Shahar Arameri: High Priestess of Itempas at the time of the Gods' War. Her descendants are the Arameri family.

Sieh: A godling, also called the Trickster. Eldest of all the godlings.

Sigil: An ideograph of the gods' language, used by scriveners to imitate the magic of the gods.

Sky: Largest city on the Senm continent. Also, the palace of the Arameri family.

Stone of Earth: An Arameri family heirloom.

Tema: A Senmite kingdom.

Time of the Three: Before the Gods' War.

Tokland: A High North nation.

T'vril Arameri: A grandnephew of Dekarta.

Uthr: An island nation.

Vertical Gate: A magical means of transportation between Sky (the city) and Sky (the palace).

Viraine Arameri: First Scrivener of the Arameri.

Walking Death: A virulent plague that appears in frequent epidemics. Affects only those of low social status.

Yeine Darr: A granddaughter of Dekarta and daughter of Kinneth.

Ygreth: Wife of Dekarta, mother of Kinneth. Deceased.

Zhakkarn of the Blood: A godling.

APPENDIX
2

A Clarification of Terms[1]

In the name of Itempas Skyfather, most Bright and peaceful.

The Conspirators, as they are properly called,[2] are like all gods in that they possess complete mastery over the material world[3] as well as most things spiritual. Though not omnipotent—only the Three, when united, were so gifted—their individual power is so great relative to that of mortals that the difference is academic. However, the Bright Lord in His wisdom has seen fit to greatly limit the power of the Conspirators as a punishment, thus enabling their use as tools for the betterment of mortalkind.

Their disparate natures impose further limitations, different

1. Initial compilation by First Scrivener and Order of the White Flame Ordinate Sefim Arameri, in the 55th year of the Bright. Subsequent revisions by First Scriveners Comman Knorn/Arameri (170), Latise Arameri (1144), Bir Get/Arameri (1721), and Viraine Derreye/Arameri (2224).

2. The subjects do not refer to themselves as such, but this terminology was agreed upon per the *Munae Scrivan*, 7th Reiterate, year 230 of the Bright.

3. Defined as *magic* per Litaria standard terminology, 1st progression.

for each individual. We refer to this as *affinity*, since gods' language appears to have no term for it. Affinities can be either material or conceptual, or some combination thereof.[4] An example of which is the Conspirator called Zhakkarn, who holds dominion over all things combat-related including weaponry (material), strategy (conceptual), and the martial arts (both). In actual battle she has the unique ability to replicate herself thousands of times over, becoming a literal one-woman army.[5] However, she has also been observed to avoid any gathering of mortals for peaceful purposes, such as holiday celebrations. Indeed, being near religious paraphernalia symbolizing peace, such as the white jade ring worn by our order's highest devotees, causes her acute discomfort.

As the Conspirators are in fact prisoners of war, and we of the family are in fact their jailors, understanding the concept of affinity is essential as it represents our only means of imposing discipline.

Additionally, we must understand the restrictions imposed upon them by Our Lord. The primary and common means by which the Conspirators have been limited is *corporeality*. It has been observed that a god's natural state is immaterial,[6] thus permitting the god to draw upon immaterial resources (e.g., the motion of heavenly bodies, the growth of living things) for sustenance and normal function. The Conspirators, however, are not permitted to enter the aetheric state and are instead required

4. See *On Magic*, volume 12.

5. As observed in the Pells War, the Ulan Uprising, and other occasions.

6. Hereinafter referred to as *aetheric* per Litaria standard terminology, 4th progression.

to maintain a physical locality at all times. This restricts their range of operability to the limits of their human senses, and it restricts their power to that which may be contained by this material form.[7] This restriction also requires them to ingest food and drink in the mortal fashion in order to maintain strength. Experiments[8] have shown that when deprived of sustenance or otherwise physically traumatized, the Conspirators' magical abilities diminish greatly or entirely until they have returned to health. Due to the Stone of Earth's role in their imprisonment, however, they perpetually retain the ability to regenerate aged or damaged flesh and revive from apparent death, even when their bodies are virtually destroyed. Therefore it is a misnomer to say that they have "mortal forms"; their physical bodies are only superficially mortal.

In the next chapter, we will discuss the specific peculiarities of each of the Conspirators, and the means by which each might be better controlled.

7. Scrivener Pjors, in "The Limitations of Mortality" (*Munae Scrivan*, pp. 40–98), argues that no other mortals have been able to achieve comparable power, and therefore the Conspirators' abilities clearly exceed the material. Consensus within the Scriveners' College and Litaria holds that this is the purposeful doing of Our Lord, who intended that the Conspirators retain enough godly might to be of use in the aftermath of the Gods' War.

8. Family Notes, various, volumes 12, 15, 24, and 37.

APPENDIX
3

Historical Record;
Arameri Family Notes volume 1,
from the collection of
Dekarta Arameri.

(Translated by Scrivener Aram Vernm, year 724 of the
Bright, may He shine upon us forever. WARNING: contains
heretical references, marked "HR"; used with permission of
the Litaria.)

You will know me as Aetr, daughter of Shahar—she who is now
dead. This is an accounting of her death, for the records and for
the easing of my heart.

We did not know there was trouble. My mother was a woman
who kept her own counsel at the best of times; this was a necessity for any priestess, most of all our brightest light. But High
Priestess Shahar—I will call her that and not Mother, for she
was more the former than the latter to me—was always strange.

The elder brothers and sisters tell me she met the Dayfather

(HR) once, as a child. She was born among the tribeless, those outcasts who pay no heed to any god or any law. Her mother took up with a man who viewed both mother and child as his property and treated them accordingly. After one torment too many Shahar fled to an old temple of the Three (HR), where she prayed for enlightenment. The Dayfather (HR) appeared to her and gave her enlightenment in the form of a knife. She used it on her stepfather while he slept, removing that darkness from her life once and for all.

I say this not to slander her memory, but to illuminate: that was the kind of light Shahar valued. Harsh, glaring, hiding nothing. I make no wonder Our Lord treasured her so, because she was much like Him—quick to decide who merited her love, and who did not (HR).

I think this is why He appeared to her again on that terrible day when everything began to weaken and die. He simply showed up in the middle of the Sunrise Greeting and gave her something sealed in a white crystal sphere. We did not know at the time that this was the last flesh of Lady Enefa (HR), now gone to twilight Herself. We knew only that the power of that crystal kept the weakening at bay, though only within the walls of our temple. Beyond it, the streets were littered with gasping people; the fields with sagging crops; the pastures with downed livestock.

We saved as many as we could. Sun's Flame, I wish it could have been more.

And we prayed. That was Shahar's command, and we were frightened enough that we obeyed even though it meant three days on our knees, weeping, begging, hoping against all hope that

Our Lord prevailed in the conflict tearing apart the world. We took it in shifts, all of us, full ordinates and acolytes and Order-Keepers and common folk. We pushed aside the exhausted bodies of our comrades when they sagged from weariness, so that we could pray in their place. In between, when we dared look outside, we saw nightmares. Giggling black things, like cats but also monstrous children, flowed through the streets a-hunting. Red columns of fire, wide as mountains, fell in the distance; we saw the entire city of Dix immolated. We saw the shining bodies of the gods' children falling from the sky, screaming and vanishing into aether before they hit the ground.

Through this all, my mother remained in her tower room, gazing unflinchingly at the nightmare sky. When I went to check on her—many of our number had begun killing themselves in despair—I found her sitting on the floor with her legs crossed, the white sphere in her lap. She was growing old; that position must have hurt her. But she was waiting, she said, and when I asked her what for, she gave me her cold, white smile.

"For the right moment to strike," she said.

I knew then that she meant to die. But what could I do? I am only a priestess, and she was my superior. Family meant nothing to her. It is the way of our order to marry and raise children in the ways of light, but my mother declared that Our Lord was the only husband she would accept. She got herself with child by some priest or another just to satisfy the elders. I and my twin brother were the result, and she never loved us. I say that without rancor; I have had thirty years to come to terms with it. But because of this, I knew my words would fall on deaf ears if I tried to talk her out of her chosen course.

So instead I closed the door and went back to my prayers. The next morning there was an awful thunderclap of sound and force that seemed likely to blow apart the very stones of the Temple of Daylight Sky. When we picked ourselves up from this, amazed to find that we were still alive, my mother was dead.

I was the one that found her. I, and the Dayfather (HR), who was there beside her body when I opened the door.

I fell to my knees, of course, and mumbled something about being honored by His presence. But in truth? My eyes were only for my mother, who lay sprawled on the floor where I had last seen her. The white sphere was shattered beside her, and in her hands was something gray and glimmering. There was sorrow in Lord Itempas's eyes when He touched my mother's face to shut her eyes. I was glad to see that sorrow, because it meant my mother had achieved her fondest wish: pleasing her lord.

"My true one," He said. "All the others have betrayed me, save you."

Only later did I learn what He meant—that Lady Enefa (HR) and Lord Nahadoth (HR) had turned on Him, along with hundreds of their immortal children. Only later did Lord Itempas bring me His war prisoners, fallen gods in invisible chains, and tell me to use them to put the world to rights. It was too much for Bentr, my brother; we found him that night in the cistern chamber, his wrists slit in a barrel of wash water. There was only me to bear witness, and later to bear the burden, and right then to weep, because even if a god did honor my mother, what good did that do? She was still dead.

And that is how the High Priestess of the Bright, Shahar Arameri, passed on.

For you, Mother. I will live on, I will do as Our Lord commands, I will remake the world. I will find some husband strong enough to help me shoulder the burden, and I will raise my children to be hard and cold and ruthless, like you. That is the legacy you wanted, isn't it? In Our Lord's name, it shall be yours.

Gods help us all.

Acknowledgments

So many people to thank, so little space.

Foremost thanks go to my father, who was my first editor and writing coach. I'm really sorry I made you read all that crap I wrote when I was fifteen, Dad. Hopefully this book will make up for it.

Also equal thanks to the writing incubators that have nurtured me over the years: the Viable Paradise workshop, the Speculative Literature Foundation, the Carl Brandon Society, Critters.org, the BRAWLers of Boston, Black Beans, The Secret Cabal, and Altered Fluid. Never thought I'd get this far, and I wouldn't have done it without all of you to kick me into action. (The bruises are fading nicely, thanks.)

Then to Lucienne Diver, the hardest-working agent in all the land. You believed in me; thanks. Also to Devi Pillai, my editor, who totally floored me with the realization that editors could be fun, funny people, eviscerating manuscripts with a wink and a smile. Thanks for that, and for picking such a great title.

And last but by no means least: thanks to my mother (hi,

Mom!), my BFFs Deirdre and Katchan, and all the members of the old TU crew. To the staff and students of the universities I've worked at over the years; day jobs really shouldn't be so much fun. Posthumous thanks to Octavia Butler, for going first and showing the rest of us how it's done. And I always give thanks to God, for instilling the love of creation in me.

I suppose I should also thank my roommate NukuNuku, who encouraged me with headbutts, swats to the face, fur in my keyboard, incessant distracting yowls, and…um…wait, why am I thanking her again? Never mind.

extras

orbit

meet the author

N. K. Jemisin

N. K. JEMISIN is a career counselor, political blogger, and would-be gourmand living in New York City. She's been writing since the age of ten, although her early works will never see the light of day. Visit nkjemisin.com.

interview

Prior to becoming a writer, what other professions did you have?

I'm a counseling psychologist and educator, specializing in career counseling of late adolescents and young adults (though I've worked with other demographics). I've worked at a number of universities as an administrator and a faculty member, and I've also done some volunteering with community service organizations and some private career coaching. It's been weird lately—a lot of my students didn't realize I was a writer, so when I ran off to write books, they were a little unhappy with me! But many of them say they're looking forward to reading the books.

When you aren't writing, what do you like to do in your spare time?

Watch cheesy movies, including anime and badly dubbed foreign films; play video games (I would give a body part to write for Squeenix or Atlus); bike and hike, though I haven't done much of the latter since moving to New York City, unless you count subway stairs; and rant against social injustice all over the blogosphere.

extras

Who/what would you consider to be your influences?

Hmm, that's a complex question. I get ideas from a lot of sources, not all of them literary. Artistically speaking I most admire Storm Constantine, Tanith Lee, Stephen King, Fumi Yoshinaga (a Japanese manga author/artist), John Coltrane (jazz musician), and the Impressionists (visual art). Spiritually—in terms of motivating me to pursue writing as a career and to improve my craft—Octavia Butler, my own personal grand-master. Intellectually—Sigmund Freud. Yeah, he was way off about a lot of stuff. But I think he got the tripartate nature of human consciousness spot-on, and I like his thoughts on dreams, too.

The Hundred Thousand Kingdoms is an amazingly original tale. How did you derive the idea for this novel?

Wow, thanks! I honestly can't say—I came up with the idea over ten years ago, probably during one of my "think about something, anything, to avoid thinking about my unfinished graduate thesis" fugues. It started as just a combination of images in my head: a child playing with planets as toys, a man with stars in his hair and the void of space in his eyes, a palace balanced atop an impossibly thin column of stone. Most of my ideas start that way, as random images that make no sense. So I start thinking up narratives that will fit them together. I was probably a comic book artist in a past life.

The creation myth of the Nightlord and Bright Itempas hearkens back to classical mythology, but depicts something wholly unique. Did you conduct a great deal of research in this area?

I did look to existing religions for guidance, since the only religion I was intimately familiar with was Christianity and I wanted to construct something with a very different—but still plausible—feel. The core of the "Earth and Sky" universe is inspired by Hinduism, some schools of which posit the existence of a Creator, a Destroyer, and a Preserver (sometimes combined into a single being, sometimes split among two or three). From there I added psychodynamic concepts, like Jung's collective unconscious; this was a concept that had fascinated me for years. What would happen if omnipotent gods were shaped and limited by this powerful, quintessentially human force? Well, first and foremost, humans would try to fit them into their understanding of the everyday world, which is divided into the day and night, with a transitional time at dawn and dusk. Of course, this made the gods inherently more complex, because there are so many other concepts that humans associate with day and night and transition—light, darkness, shades of gray; heat, cold, change; order, chaos, life. But then I considered the Christian concept of human beings having been created in God's image. Taken literally and inverted, that implies (to me) that these gods would end up being pretty darn human, once you get past the cosmic-scale power and whatnot. They love, they hate, they form relationships, they have misunderstandings. But what happens when you *do* pair cosmic power with the typical emotions—and dysfunctions—of a human family? Things just snowballed from there.

Do you have a favorite character? If so, why?

I have favorite characters of the moment. Originally Nahadoth was my favorite, just because he contained so many contradictions. He was powerful but vulnerable; incomprehensible yet very human; dark but not evil; and so on. Yeah, you can probably guess—all that stuff is pretty much catnip to me. But as I wrote the story, I fell utterly in love with Yeine, who's sort of "me" taken to an extreme—angrier, colder, more vulnerable, more impulsive. I'm nicer than she is, but sometimes I wish I wasn't. Also, Sieh ended up being a stealth favorite. I really wasn't expecting him to charm me as much as he did Yeine, but there you have it. I love that he's so ancient yet determined to attack life the way children do. I love that he slips into being an old man sometimes, and then has to get back on the wagon. Of all the characters, he's the only one I'd actually like to meet (if he were, you know, real).

Now that two of the three gods have been restored, what can we expect in your next novel?

In book two, you'll learn what becomes of Itempas after his fall from power—and what caused him to turn on his fellow gods at the start of the Gods' War. You can also expect a fuller exploration of the world of the Earth and the Sky. In *The Hundred Thousand Kingdoms* I dealt exclusively with the elite of society, and so necessarily confined the settings to places of power and privilege. In book two, I want to focus on the ordinary people of this world and show how they cope when giant trees obscure the sky and the corner grocer might be a godling in disguise. The story will focus on a young blind woman who finds a homeless man in her trash heap one morning—glowing like the rising sun. She takes him in, and this simple act of kindness lands her in the middle of a conspiracy to destroy the gods. Many of the characters from the first book will put in an appearance, but it's going to be a very different kind of story in some ways. I think it will be equally satisfying.

Finally, as a first-time author, what has been your favorite part of the publishing process?

The day my agent called to tell me the book had sold! But that's not exactly part of the publishing process, is it? Okay, the first time I met with my editor, Devi, and she gushed to me about how much she loved the book. My book! I kept trying not to erupt into embarrassing squeals and failing utterly. But I'm not done with the publishing process yet, so I can only guess at what might end up being the absolute best part of it for me: after publication, seeing readers' reactions to my work. I'm a little nervous about it, actually, but underneath the nerves? I can't wait. Speaking of which—if you're reading this, and you'd like to let me know what you think about *The Hundred Thousand Kingdoms*, go to my website at nkjemisin.com. Praise, protests, it's all grist for the mill, baby. Bring it on.

introducing

If you enjoyed
THE HUNDRED THOUSAND KINGDOMS,
look out for

THE BROKEN KINGDOMS

Book Two of the Inheritance Trilogy

by N. K. Jemisin

I am a woman plagued by gods.

Sometimes I feel as if they're everywhere: underfoot, overhead, peering around corners and lurking under bushes. They leave glowing footprints on the sidewalks of my city. (I can see that they have their own favorite paths for sightseeing.) They urinate on the white walls. They don't have to do that, urinate I mean, they just find it amusing to imitate us. I find their names written in splattery light, usually in sacred places. Occasionally they buy souvenirs from me. Not all of them realize I know what they are, but the ones who do buy from me for that precise reason.

Sometimes I love them. Sometimes they try to kill me. I even found one in my trash once. Sounds mad, doesn't it? But it's true. That's why I'm telling you this, because there are some parts that even I don't believe, looking back.

The one in the trash, then. I'll start with him.

*　　*　　*

I'd been up late one night—or morning—working on a painting, and had gone out to toss several empty cans. The muckrakers usually came with their reeking wagons at dawn, carting off the trash to sift for nightsoil and anything else of value, and I didn't want to miss them. I didn't even notice a man there because he smelled like the rest of the trash behind my building. Like something dead—which, now that I think about it, he probably was.

I tossed the cans and would have gone back inside had I not noticed an odd glimmer from the corner of one eye. I was tired enough that I should have ignored that, too. After five years in this city, I had grown inured to godling leavings. Perhaps one of them had thrown up there after a night of drinking, or spent himself in a tryst amid the thick reek. Most of them liked to do that, spend a week or so playing mortal, before settling into whatever life they've decided to lead among us. This initiation was generally messy.

So I don't know why I stopped that chilly winter morning. Some instinct told me to turn my head, and I don't know why I listened to it. But I did, and that was when I saw glory awaken in my trash pile.

At first I saw only lines of gold, blazing and bright as the sun I've never seen, limn the shape of a man. Dewdrops of glimmering silver beaded along his flesh and then ran down it in rivulets, illuminating the texture of skin in smooth relief. I saw some of those rivulets move impossibly upward, igniting the filaments of his hair, the stern, sharp lines of his face.

And as I stood there, my hands wet with paint and my door standing open behind me, forgotten, I saw this glowing man draw a deep breath—this made him shimmer even more beautifully—and open eyes whose color I would never be able to describe, even if I someday learn the words.

But as I stood there, transfixed by those eyes, I saw something else: pain. So much sorrow and grief and anger and guilt, and other emotions I cannot name because when all is said and done, my life has been relatively happy. There are some things one can understand only by experience, and there are some experiences no one wants to share.

*   *   *

Hmm. Perhaps I should tell you something about me before I go on.

I'm an artist. I make my living selling trinkets and souvenirs to out-of-towners. I also paint, though my paintings are mostly just a hobby and not meant for the eyes of others. Aside from this I'm just an ordinary woman, no one special. I see gods, but so does everyone; I told you, they're everywhere. I probably just notice them more because they're all I can see.

My parents named me Oree. Like the cry of the western weeper-bird; have you heard it? It seems to sob as it calls, *oree*, gasp, *oree*, gasp. Most Maroneh girls are named for such sorrowful things. It could be worse; the boys are named for vengeance. Depressing, isn't it? That sort of thing is why I left.

Now. Let me tell you more about the man that I found in the trash.

*   *   *

He was dead again when I got home, on the day that it all began. This was two months after I'd dug him out of my trash. His corpse was in the kitchen, at the table, where he'd slit his throat before falling forward into a pool of his own blood. I slipped on the blood coming in, which annoyed me because that meant it was all over the kitchen floor. The smell was so thick and cloying that I could not localize it; this wall or that one? The whole floor or just near the table? I was certain he dripped on the carpet, too, while I dragged him to the bathroom. He was a big man, so it took a while. I wrestled him into the tub as best I could and then filled it with cold water from the roof cistern, partly so that the blood on his clothes wouldn't set, and partly to let him know how angry I was.

I'd calmed down somewhat—cleaning the kitchen helped me vent—by the time I heard a sudden, violent slosh of water from the bathroom. He was often disoriented when he first returned to life, so I waited in the doorway until the sounds of sloshing stilled and his attention fixed on me. He had a strong personality. I could always feel the pressure of his gaze.

"It's not fair," I said, "for you to make my life harder. Do you understand?"

Silence. But he heard me.

"I've cleaned up the worst of the kitchen, but I think there might be some blood on the living room rugs. The smell's so thick that I can't find the small patches. You'll have to do those. I'll leave a bucket and brush in the kitchen."

More silence. A scintillating conversationalist, he was.

I sighed. My back hurt from scrubbing the floor. "Thanks for making dinner." I didn't mention that I hadn't eaten any. No way to tell—without tasting—if he'd gotten blood on the food, too. "I'm going to bed; it's been a long day."

A faint taste of shame wafted on the air. I felt his gaze move away and was satisfied. In the two months he'd been living with me, I'd come to know him as a man of almost compulsive integrity, predictable as the tolling of a White Hall bell. He did not like it when the scales between us were unbalanced.

I crossed the bathroom, bent over the tub, and felt for his face. I got the crown of his head at first, and marveled as always at the feel of hair textured like my own—soft-curled, dense but yielding, thick enough to lose my fingers in. The first time I'd touched him I'd fleetingly thought he was one of my people, because only Maroneh had such hair. Of course I also knew he was something else entirely, something not human, but that early surge of fellow-feeling had never quite faded. So I leaned down and kissed his brow, savoring the feel of soft, smooth heat beneath my lips. He was always hot to the touch. Assuming we could come to some agreement on the sleeping arrangements, next winter I could save a fortune on firewood.

If he was still around.

"Good night," I murmured, and then went to bed.